THE
SINGLE
NEIGHBOUR

THE SINGLE NEIGHBOUR

Senta Rich

BLOOMSBURY PUBLISHING
LONDON · OXFORD · NEW YORK · NEW DELHI · SYDNEY

BLOOMSBURY PUBLISHING
Bloomsbury Publishing Plc
50 Bedford Square, London, WC1B 3DP, UK
Bloomsbury Publishing Ireland Limited,
29 Earlsfort Terrace, Dublin 2, D02 AY28, Ireland

BLOOMSBURY, BLOOMSBURY PUBLISHING and the Diana logo
are trademarks of Bloomsbury Publishing Plc

First published in Great Britain 2025

A catalogue record for this book is available from the British Library

ISBN: HB: 978-1-5266-5064-1; TPB: 978-1-5266-8909-2;
EBOOK: 978-1-5266-5071-9; EPDF: 978-1-5266-5061-0

2 4 6 8 10 9 7 5 3 1

Typeset by Integra Software Services Pvt. Ltd.
Printed and bound in Great Britain by CPI Group (UK) Ltd, Croydon CR0 4YY

MIX
Paper | Supporting
responsible forestry
FSC
www.fsc.org   FSC® C013604

To find out more about our authors and books visit www.bloomsbury.com
and sign up for our newsletters

For product safety related questions contact productsafety@bloomsbury.com

To my mother Deike

'If we can ever cut through the fog of projections in which we live so much of our life, and look truly at another person, we can perceive an ordinary creature as magnificent.'

Robert A. Johnson

1

Him

The noise drags me slowly from a deep sleep. I'm dreaming about a big dog sniffing and scratching at the bedroom door, picking up my scent. Its shadow moves back and forth along the underside of the door, prowling, waiting.

My eyes flick open and stare at the door, which is slightly ajar. A faint orange glow from the light in the hall warms the landing. Relief floods my body as I push the dread back into the dingy cellar of my mind. Where I hope it stays.

The noise that has woken me is a gritty sound of dirty chugging. The smell of diesel fills my nostrils as the hum of a growling engine outside gets louder and more intense.

I lift my head off the pillow. It's still dark outside so I know it's the middle of the night. The bedroom window and curtains are open to allow in any passing breeze. London in May isn't normally this hot.

The cotton sheets are glued to my body from the sweat oozing from my pores. Not just from the warm air in the room, but also from the dream. I put my hand on my chest to feel my heartbeat and take a deep breath as it returns to a normal pace.

I turn my head to where Izzy is sleeping beside me, her long dark hair splayed across the pillow and her nose pointing up to the ceiling. I've always been in awe of how she can sleep on her back so peacefully, with barely a snuffle. I don't think I've ever heard her snore.

The sheet is sticky as I peel it away from my body and gently, so as not to disturb Izzy, swing my legs over the side of the bed and sit up. I pad quietly over to the window and position myself behind the bunched-up velvet curtains, my naked body safely shielded. I move my head a little to the side of the curtains and peer outside.

Parked in front of the neighbour's house to the right, under the gloom of a street lamp, is a brown lorry with 'From Home to Home Removals' painted in large letters along the side. The new neighbours must finally be moving in. My heartbeat quickens again.

The semi-detached house next door has been empty for nearly a year now, ever since Mrs Jenkins died. Izzy and I still talk about her; a sweet elderly lady who, on the surface, refused to accept any help from us but simply didn't know how to ask for it.

On a number of occasions, we had raced around to her house when we heard banging or knocking, which was her way of alerting us she was in 'a spot of bother', as she liked to call it. Sometimes she had fallen but was perfectly okay. Other times she had hurt herself and needed an ambulance, but always arrived home dismissive of any injuries, visible or not.

Her two children, Edward and Melissa, 'nasty pieces of work' Izzy calls them, didn't visit very often but organised a home help, despite the fact Mrs Jenkins didn't want strangers in her house. And her care workers changed weekly, sometimes daily, which she didn't take kindly to at all. More often than not, she refused to let them in and in extreme cases had been heard using the F-word, which really wasn't like her.

The day after Mrs Jenkins' funeral, a skip had appeared on the driveway. Edward and Melissa cleared out the house with the energy and urgency of a military-style operation. Everything was stripped out and chucked into the skip, which was full to the brim in a few hours. Izzy and I looked on from our bedroom window. Izzy pointed to bin bags squashed under an old dresser.

'Their mother's clothes – and her ashes are still warm.'

I didn't agree this was a totally heartless act – people deal with grief in all sorts of different ways – until I heard Edward talking on his phone.

I'd been on my way in to work that day as he came out of the house holding a couple of picture frames. He lobbed them into the skip, laughing, the glass shattering as the discarded family pictures lay staring up at the sky, splintered and forgotten.

'From her profile pic I thought I was meeting a young Patsy Kensit, then Pat Butcher shows up. What do you think I did? U-turn, mate. Lying slapper.'

Izzy was right. He was a nasty piece of work and so was his sister.

A week after the skip was collected, Melissa came to our front door and asked us if we wouldn't mind them cutting back our blossom tree as it was hanging over their fence.

'Your mother loved that tree,' I said, suddenly desperate to keep something of Mrs Jenkins alive.

'Well, it's kind of a hazard,' Melissa said with a little wince. 'So if you don't mind, we're getting the house ready to sell.'

'Of course,' Izzy said, smiling sweetly.

'Passive-aggressive bitch,' Izzy muttered after I shut the door.

This time I agreed.

The house was finally sold two months ago. Izzy and I have been waiting ever since to see who our new neighbours will be. It's become a regular topic of conversation and it's helped us both ignore the fact we're not having sex anymore. Not even functional sex, the kind you engage in to fulfil a physical need only, like giving your hamstrings a good stretch after a run.

It's been a relief to have something else to focus on, to distract from the glaringly obvious downward slide of our marriage. So instead, we discuss who we would like to move in next door and who we would not. We don't want a big family with young children. Too noisy. Or a couple who argue all the time. Too stressful. Or people with a dog that barks day and night.

'Or a weirdo,' Izzy said.

'What constitutes a weirdo?' I asked.

'Anyone too un-normal,' she said.

I understood what she meant. To appear even moderately acceptable in this world, you need to be a master at burying your flaws and hiding your idiosyncrasies. Some of us are better at it than others.

The truck manoeuvres out into the road and starts to beep as it reverses halfway up the driveway. The driveways to these houses are just about long enough for one car, so the truck only manages to stick its back end in, leaving the cab protruding out onto the pavement.

The engine finally cuts out and a huge exhausted sigh emits from the truck as the suspension relaxes onto the wheels, at ease. I sense it's been driving for a long time and wonder where it's come from.

The hissing dies down and the diesel fumes fade away. I look over at Izzy, pleased to see she's still sound asleep, the sheets pulled up as far as her waist. Her vest top lies loosely across her breasts and her breath is shallow.

The sound of an approaching car and loud thumping music makes me turn and squint up the road.

A bullet-shaped car glides down the street and pulls in in front of the truck. It's an orange Mini Cooper with a red racing stripe painted over the bonnet and roof. I can barely hear the engine so assume it's electric. The windows are fully down and the flaming end of a cigarette sizzles in the dark as the driver takes a last drag and drops it out of the window onto the ground.

It's debatable whether cigarette butts are litter or not as they are actually biodegradable. I desperately want to like our new neighbour so I'm willing to ignore it.

The engine switches off and so does the music. Silence descends once more. All I can hear is my own breath, slightly quickened.

The driver-side door to the Mini opens and a slight-framed figure climbs out wearing an oversized black hoodie with the hood up obscuring their face. They look mystical and phantom -like. One blink and they might disappear into the shadows, a ghostly mist, never to be seen again.

They raise their hand to the truck cab, acknowledging the driver, and walk towards the front door, pulling a set of keys from their hoodie pocket. From their small steps and hip move-ment, I can tell it's a woman.

Squinting to get a better look as she approaches the front door, I glimpse the ends of a flaxen ponytail coiled around her neck, poking out from under the hood.

It's such a warm night. I wonder why she's wearing a hoodie with the hood up. Maybe she's come from a much cooler place. Maybe she's come from the Scottish Highlands. Or Wales. Come to think of it, anywhere in the British Isles is cooler than London is at the moment.

The driver of the truck jumps out, followed by his co-driver. They meet at the back of the truck, both wearing black T-shirts with identical emblems on the left breast pocket. The uniform for the removals company. The driver wipes his brow, tired and sticky. He unlocks the roller door and both men push it up. It makes a loud clackety noise and I turn to see if it will wake Izzy but she carries on sleeping, still on her back.

I should wake her. It's all we've really talked about since the 'SOLD' sign appeared. I tell myself it's a workday tomorrow and she'd rather be sleeping. The truth is, the excitement at being the first one to see the new neighbour overrules any hovering guilt.

The two truck guys chat, mumbling. I catch the odd word: bacon, tea, kip. I know they've come a long way now.

The woman exits the house and joins the two men, her back towards me. As she talks to them, they dip their heads, listening carefully, as though under a spell. I can't hear what she's saying but a light tinkle of a whisper carries across the dead air to my straining ears, landing gently and unhindered.

The guys nod their heads, indicating they understand her instructions, and climb into the truck to start unloading. I'm pretty sure they would have saluted her or maybe even bowed had it been appropriate. This woman seems to command atten-tion and respect.

She still has her back to me, watching as the two men push a large cardboard box to the edge of the truck door. They jump down, heave the box onto a trolley, and push it towards the house. The deep breathing tells me it's heavy and I'm gripped with an urge to know what's inside.

She turns to follow them but then stops and flicks her head up, looking into the window and straight at me.

I flinch a little, leaning further away from the curtain, aware that any movement could draw attention to the fact I'm standing here watching her. I feel like a peeping Tom, or worse, especially as I'm naked, but that makes no sense as I'm the one inside. Maybe a stalker then. Or just a weirdo; a too un-normal person.

She stands, unmoving, her eyeline pointed directly at me skulking behind the curtains. Her face remains unseen, buried in the hood, but as the street light cuts across her body it illuminates the delicate curve of a soft-skinned chin.

She must have sensed someone up here, watching her. I know she can't see me in the darkened room. I'm far enough back and hidden behind the curtain, but it feels like she has X-ray vision, penetrating the thick fabric, providing her with a crystal-clear view of my exposed, naked body.

My dick twitches and I put my hand on it; a controlling, protective gesture. If watching my new neighbour arrive gives me an erection I will be more than a little worried about myself. Luckily everything stays limp enough. Not too un-normal after all.

Finally, she dips her hooded head and slips silently into the house. I let out a long breath, relieved to no longer be under scrutiny.

I creep into our matchbox-sized en suite and wonder for the millionth time why the previous owners ever bothered to squeeze this excuse of a bathroom into the bedroom, why we didn't rip it out when we moved in, and why we both insist on still using it.

While I stand at the toilet waiting to pee, I check out my backside in the small mirror behind the sink. It looks good. Still, I'm only thirty-one and, according to an article I read in a men's magazine, as long as I don't get fat, it should look like this until I'm seventy and beyond; a stubborn, tight bum to be proud of.

I sigh deeply. The thought of the energy and effort required to live to seventy exhausts me.

Sliding back under the sheet, I pull it up to my waist. A breeze enters through the window and ripples across my bare chest, cooling me down a little. I check the alarm clock on my bedside table. It's 4.30 a.m. Through the window, a blood-red tinge warms the night sky as sunrise looms.

With the image of the slight woman shrouded in black, faceless yet very much present, I turn over and close my eyes, waiting to be dragged down once again into the familiar catacombs of unwelcome dreams, a sound of rushing wind in my ears.

I pour myself a second cup of coffee and stare out of the kitchen window into our run-of-the-mill rectangular garden with a timber shed at the end, the only thing in it.

The clipped-back blossom tree behind it still looks bare and unloved on one side thanks to Edward's handiwork. There is a dug up square patch on the lawn by the new neighbour's fence where Izzy attempted to do some gardening. Although 'dug up' seems too polite. 'Torn apart by a large rabid animal' would be a better description. At least it takes your eye off the shed for a moment.

Like the master en suite, the shed is also a hangover from the previous owners when we bought the house two years ago, a modest redbrick with two bedrooms and a box room. We were only able to get the mortgage because Izzy's mum gave us the deposit as a wedding present.

Izzy didn't want to accept the money and complained that her mother was trying to buy her way into our lives. Izzy's mum was already in our lives so I didn't see what difference it made. We didn't even see her that much. I convinced her to accept it.

'We don't have to stay in the house forever. It's an investment, that's all,' I said.

I know there are things in Izzy's past, her childhood, that she's never told me about. And I've never asked. We don't

7

have to know everything about each other. I certainly don't want to share every detail from my past.

I wanted to get rid of the shed right away and lied to Izzy about how I believed sheds represented a deep-seated fear for a man of my age. A shed says you must have a toolbox and gardening equipment because very soon you will be retiring.

Izzy dismissed my objections saying I was decades from retirement and declared the shed a great storage space for outdoor cushions and the lawnmower.

Since then I have mowed the lawn once, which was a stressful and sickening experience. Not because it's hard to mow a lawn, but because the mouldy smell in the shed and the sound of the mower's engine stirred up old feelings, still lurking after all these years.

We pay a gardener now, George, to do it instead. The shed has become one of the many things we don't talk about.

Despite getting back to sleep last night, my eyelids feel heavy and my forehead aches with tiredness. I pop two slices of bread in the toaster and check the time. 7.00 a.m. There's a big delivery at the restaurant this morning and I promised Monty, the head chef, that I'd be there to check and sign for it.

I sip my coffee and keep my eyes fixed on the fence to the left of our garden, in case the new neighbour makes an appearance, although I'm not sure what form that would take. I think I'd be happy just to detect a movement or a shadow.

When I woke this morning and looked out of the bedroom window the removal truck was gone and the orange Mini was parked in the drive. A shot of excitement fizzled through me. The new neighbour has arrived and there's something about her presence that already has me enthralled. It's only a matter of time before I meet her. I'm hoping it might be this morning.

A slapping noise on wooden steps makes me turn as Izzy descends the staircase and bustles in, carrying her work satchel and a hair brush. She's wearing flat shoes and a simple cotton dress.

The flats are a new addition to her wardrobe. Up until a few months ago, unless we were heading out for a walk, she always wore one of her many pairs of high wedges, which elongate her legs and make her stand at around five foot nine. But lately she's been opting for a more practical and sedate look. She's even stopped wearing lipstick and perfume.

I still catch wafts of her elegant shower gel but I miss her musky womanly scent. Her inky black hair snakes down her back, falling in soft curls. She used to pin part of it up with loose strands hanging down framing her face, but she's stopped doing that too.

Using her fingers, she draws it into a bun at the nape of her neck. I haven't commented on any of these changes as I'm afraid of what she might say. Or rather that she won't tell me the truth because the truth would somehow reveal how she feels, or doesn't feel, about me.

My suspicions are that she's purposefully presenting her less sexy and feminine self so I won't want to pounce on her with a big erection. Not that I've ever pounced on her or anyone. If I'm right and she is avoiding sex with me, then I would have to face facts that our marriage is in serious trouble. I'm not ready to do that and so refrain from commenting.

'You look tired,' she says, as she pours coffee into her KeepCup.

She teaches A-level psychology at a sixth-form college and refuses to drink the coffee in the staffroom, and despises the staffroom in general. She says it's stuffy and cramped and that she doesn't have much in common with the other teachers, at least not since her two work buddies, both geography teachers, went travelling and have yet to return.

But lately she hasn't been complaining as much, and even mentioned a maths teacher called Polly who she said was funny.

'I was awake in the night,' I say.

Then the excitement overwhelms me.

'The new neighbour moved in,' I blurt out. 'The truck rolled up at 4 a.m.'

I fuss around getting a plate and a knife, not wanting her to see my flushed cheeks.

'She's here then,' she replies casually.

A coldness sweeps through my veins.

'How do you know it's a woman?' I say, doing my best to also remain casual.

'I met her already,' she says, like this is nothing, like she's telling me the time.

I try to swallow but there's a lump in my throat. My two slices of toast pop up, sending hot waves of sweet, cooked wheat up my nose.

'Can I have that?' Izzy says, indicating the toast. 'I've got a staff meeting at eight.'

'Sure,' I say.

She reaches around me to grab the slices and starts to butter them.

'When did you meet her?' I ask, trying to keep the tightness out of my voice.

'The other day for like two minutes. We said hi over the fence. Didn't I tell you?'

'No, you didn't,' I say, as though it's no problem, but she knows she should have told me and that it's strange that she didn't. We both know that meeting the new neighbour was always going to be a big fucking deal. I hate that she's pretending it isn't.

And now I feel robbed. I wanted to be the one who saw the woman in black first. It was my mystery experience, not Izzy's. But now there's no mystery. Izzy has already met her. My middle of the night experience seems rather pedestrian all of a sudden and I feel foolish, embarrassed, after standing behind the curtains, naked, with my dick twitching.

'What's she like?' I ask, also pretending this is a totally insignificant encounter.

'Nice. Friendly,' she says, munching on the toast.

Bland descriptions never featured in our lengthy 'who will the new neighbours be' discussions.

'Is she married? Does she have kids?'

'No, it's just her.'

It was a big enough conversation to ascertain her marital status then.

'I'll go round later, bring her a bottle of wine to say welcome to the street,' she says.

I note she doesn't say 'we' will go round later.

'I'll come with you,' I say.

'But you're working,' she says.

This is true, I am working. But I could get home before the evening shift starts.

'I'll be back for a couple of hours this afternoon. I'm trying to do more admin away from the restaurant.'

Izzy is always saying I spend too much time at the restaurant despite the fact I'm the manager and I need to be there. I have two days off a week, Monday and Tuesday, but even then I'm on call if things get busy or problems arise.

The plan is to one day have my own restaurant, then build a chain of restaurants, then an empire, of which I shall be king.

That's what I told Izzy when we still used to talk about the future. I wanted her to take me seriously, to believe in me and, back in the beginning, I allowed myself to believe the big talk too.

We don't have these conversations anymore. Our interest in the future wilted and shrivelled up along with Mrs Jenkins. And while it would seem the pressure is off to perform and prove myself, it's only temporary. I can't ignore the inevitable forever. When I'm quizzed about my plans now, mainly by Izzy's mother, I have a bog-standard answer.

'I just need to find the right premises,' I say, like it's impossible to find anywhere.

I'm aware I'm only biding my time. Eventually, it will be too obvious and undeniable that I was never going to accomplish much. When that moment comes, I'm not sure what will happen. I imagine myself imploding and disappearing in a puff of smoke, at once forgotten. Wiped from the hard drive. Deleted from the planet. If only that was an option.

I wonder what the new neighbour would think about that. Maybe she's a kindred spirit and has the same pressures to perform and be great. The idea that we might have a connection makes my brain feel supercharged.

'You're coming home this afternoon?' Izzy asks, stopping mid-munch.

'I'm trying a different routine,' I say.

She stares at me, like there's something odd on my face.

'I'll bring a bottle of wine from the restaurant,' I say.

Again she looks at me. It's not something I would normally offer to do. I sniff, appearing nonchalant. She decides not to question this either. I take this as a sign that her lack of interest in me is increasing.

She puts the lid on her KeepCup, grabs her car keys from the top of the fridge and throws her satchel bag over her shoulder. She gives me a quick kiss on the cheek, keeping both hands by her sides; God forbid she might touch me. She yells bye and the front door shudders shut behind her. I let out a long breath, only now letting my disappointment show.

Izzy's flippant casualness, and her attempts to convince me the new neighbour is no one special, has only made me more intrigued about the woman now occupying the house next door.

There's a buzzing sensation in my stomach, stirring and fizzing, whipping up, gaining momentum, making me feel more alive. Although, less dead is probably a better description.

I look out at the shed in the garden. Might it finally be of use for something?

2

Her

The car keys fall from my hand and clatter onto the driveway. Juggling my bag and KeepCup, I dump everything on the roof of my black Golf convertible. The rust bucket, as Tristan calls it. It's twenty-five years old, but exactly the model I wanted since I was a teenager.

I grew up in Mottingham in south London, a commuter suburb situated just over the brow of the hill from Chislehurst – the more leafy, upmarket place to live, where the young people drive flash cars like convertible Golfs with personalised number plates. We lived in a small terraced house on a street with kids playing on the road and wandering in and out of each other's houses. There was always something to do and somewhere to go and I loved the freedom it gave me to escape my home life. My mother hated living there. I could see from the way she peered out of the living room window at the neighbours passing by that she thought she was better than they were. She's a snob, which is one of her many traits I despise. Then she came into money herself and has become even more of a snob.

My first car was a second-hand Fiat Panda, which I bought for myself when I was eighteen with money I saved from working in restaurants and bars and babysitting. But I longed to own a convertible. So no one was more surprised than me when the Golf turned out to be a total anticlimax. After driving it for a few days, with the roof down, the novelty wore off and I realised, sadly, that cars actually mean nothing. But I kept it to prove to Tristan that I had not made a mistake in buying it.

'What's the point in having a convertible? It's not like we live in Spain, is it?'

'If you only have the roof down twice a year, it's still worth it,' I argued. But the car is a rust bucket and probably won't even be allowed on the roads soon. My carbon guilt rises every time I drive it, but I just don't have the heart to let it go.

I pick my keys up from the ground and grab my stuff from the roof. I look over into next door's driveway. The new neighbour's name is Viv. I like it. It's cute, like her Mini, which is probably electric. When Tristan said she'd arrived last night, I had a choice in that moment to either pretend I hadn't met her yet, or reveal that I had met her but hadn't told him. I was about to keep up the pretence and say nothing, but there was something about his demeanour that annoyed me, blabbing about seeing her, unable to contain himself. He was also a little smug that he thought he had seen her first. I didn't tell him the full story, of course. Yes, I had met Viv, but not as briefly as I implied.

All the curtains are drawn next door, which makes the house appear closed off and defensive. Mrs Jenkins only ever used to draw the curtains in her bedroom. I climb into the rust bucket, dump everything on the passenger seat and wedge my coffee cup behind my bag so it doesn't fall. The car's far too old to have anything as sophisticated as a cup holder. I start the engine and its familiar tired rattle fills my ears as I reverse out of the drive.

Once I hit the main road it's bumper to bumper in two-lane traffic for at least half a mile up to the lights at the five-way junction. I roll down all the windows to keep air flowing and grab my coffee cup. It's stuffy in the car and a drip of sweat slips from the base of my neck down to the middle of my back. I push myself away from the seat, hoping the sweat bobble will dry and not seep through the back of my dress. Everyone has their car windows open and music and chatter floats through the thick, hot air. Beside me, a smart-looking woman, about my age, in a white silk shirt, drives a large Mercedes. I glance at her over my coffee cup as I take a sip. She's on speaker phone, chatting loudly while applying mascara using the mirror in the sun visor. She talks with enormous confidence and authority, barking instructions about files and invoices.

They say don't compare yourself to others, but that's what people do all the time. It's how we ascertain whether we're happy or successful. The trick, of course, is to compare yourself to people you consider less happy or successful than you, but that never works because you know you're cheating. I quickly decide not to compare myself to this woman as it would not be a good way to start the day. It's not that I want to be using words like 'files' and 'invoices', but there's no denying this woman is doing life a lot better than I am. She's in charge and, unlike me, probably knows exactly what to do in difficult situations.

Finally it's my turn at the lights and I just make it through. I take a left onto a quieter residential road and weave my way through the back streets, avoiding any more heavy traffic. Tristan was put out I hadn't told him I'd met the new neighbour already. He tried to act like he was fine about it, but he wasn't. If he had met her first and not told me, I would have felt betrayed too. But he's no better than I am. He didn't wake me up last night to share the news she had arrived. And he was way too eager to meet her, offering to come home in between shifts and bring wine from work, which he never does. Did he have to be so blatantly enthusiastic about it? Has life with me become so dull that the idea of a single woman moving in next door is the only thing that gets his blood pumping?

There is a certain amount of satisfaction in having met her first. I did my best to play it down but I'm not sure it worked. We both know how invested the other was in who the new neighbour was going to be, but somewhere along the way it's become a competition with the new neighbour as the prize. I won this time, round one, you could say, by meeting her first, but I'm not proud of it. Lying to Tristan has become too easy these days. But does failing to share information qualify as bad lying? Surely it's only half bad. Still, it's not quite a white lie. All I want is to get back to a time when everything was calm and on an even keel. It takes a lot of effort to achieve that – years in fact – and I was doing so well until a few months ago. It all dates back to when Mrs Jenkins died, like her death signified the end of the allusion that I was in charge of my life. And now I can't seem to be able to get back on track, no matter how hard I try. A switch was flipped and I'm in a runaway train carriage, careening down a hill, heading for a precipice.

Every time I choose not to tell Tristan something, every time I make a wrong decision, the possibility of ever getting back to where I was slips further away. 'Must try harder' is my daily mantra at the moment. I comfort myself with the knowledge that at least I *believe* I can regain control or why would I keep trying? It could be false hope syndrome, of course – setting unrealistic goals for myself. If that's the case, I'm doomed, so I'll stick with the former reasoning that there is a way back, a way to reboot my life. I just have to hang on in there.

Tristan wasn't receptive when I kissed him goodbye, but that's normal these days too. I felt his body tense as I came close, so I kept it perfunctory. The cardboard kiss is all the intimacy we have at the moment. I do miss the days when a mere look from him said he couldn't wait to rip my knickers off and my body would throb and tingle in anticipation. But things haven't been like that for a while, and they've been even worse since Mrs Jenkins died. It's funny how her death also became the marker for no sex in our relationship. I'm not sure how he feels about it. I'm too afraid to ask as I couldn't bear to hear his response.

There was a time when Tristan noticed every tiny thing about me. He once remarked how I had clipped my hair on the right instead of the left. I was impressed. But he hasn't commented on any changes in my appearance lately, so I'm assuming he hasn't noticed, or worse, no longer cares.

The wedges were the first to go, replaced with flat shoes, or bland pumps to be precise. Then I bought a few high-necked tunic dresses. Next I faded out the make-up and, finally, started wearing my hair in a tidy bun. It all happened over a couple of months. I was relieved he didn't seem to notice at the time, as I didn't want to answer questions about the reasons for the changes, but I was also disappointed. And maybe if he had commented and asked me what was going on, I might have told him. But it's too late now. Things have gone too far. Although I knew this day would come: the day Tristan lost interest in me. It was inevitable.

I place my pass card on the machine monitor and the barrier lifts for me to drive through. I'm early enough to get one of the limited parking bays and relief immediately descends, making me calmer. The college car park only takes fifteen cars, so teachers who don't arrive in time are left scouting for spaces in local streets or paying huge rates in the public car park. For those in the western world, finding parking is a high-level stress activity and should be up there with moving house and divorce.

There are over thirty teachers in the college but it only feels crowded when we're all crammed into the stuffy, stale-smelling staffroom at once. If anyone opens a window, someone shuts it again. There are the youthful nursing course teachers, who sit by the window, talk loudly and giggle a lot. They even go on work nights out. The IT guys, who somehow took ownership of the centre of the room with its squishy sofa and coffee table, and nobody complained. The A-level teachers are by far the dullest group, situated in the darkest part of the staffroom near the loos, mostly consisting of tired ex-comprehensive school teachers who came to work in a sixth-form college to escape teaching under sixteens. I've never worked in a secondary school and, from the stories they tell me, I'm relieved I don't have to. My two friends, Sally and Mona, both geography teachers, went travelling last year and didn't come back. They stayed in Singapore, where teachers are very well paid apparently, and I've lost touch with them now. But most of my colleagues are gentle, sensitive types who probably wouldn't raise their voice if there was a fire.

Malcolm, one of the two physics teachers, talks openly about his mini nervous breakdown at the last school he worked in. He's a softly spoken man, obsessed with trams and quite vocal about it, so a clear target for rowdy teenagers. His favourite tram is in Istanbul, where he has been several times. He's planning a trip to Melbourne next and has a picture of a tram stuck to the front of his cubbyhole in the staffroom. I didn't even know Australia had trams. Anyway, it's on his bucket list, so he says.

One of the English teachers, Olly, short for Olivia, is thirty-five but seems older given the long pleated skirts and high-necked blouses she wears. She's always on the verge of smiling and apologises a lot, even if you hold a door open for her. Sorry, she says, when thanks would suffice. Still, she's very sweet and often spends her lunch break giving Malcolm pep talks about being more assertive, which Malcolm seems to appreciate. Olly also likes to bake muffins and bring them in for everyone on Monday mornings as a 'starting-the-week treat'. They are light and fluffy and sometimes still warm, which is delicious but also odd. Does she whip them out of the oven, race out of her house, rush to college in traffic, maybe breaking red lights along the way, then leg it up to the staffroom to ensure her baked goods have that just-cooked aroma and texture? It remains a mystery. She also likes to engage everyone in personality quizzes she finds online, although she says I'm not allowed to play since I'm a psychologist and therefore know how to cheat. It's not true, of course. While I have a degree in psychology, I'm far from being an expert on human behaviour. I would have no idea how to cheat but I'm happy not to take part. The other physics teacher, Tobias, was upset when he rated very low on the 'Are you a good person?' quiz, arguing that he had not understood the questions. Olly told him to relax and that it was only a bit of fun. But sometimes these things aren't fun. Sometimes the result from an inane quiz can make you worry that a) you're not a nice person, b) you're getting life wrong, c) you're destined to be miserable, or worse, d) all of the above. Hence why I'm relieved Olly has an excuse to exclude me.

There's a free car space close to the main entrance and I take it as a sign that today will be a good day. The twelve-storey college building looms overhead. It has an orange and white exterior with protruding floors sporadically placed to give a sense of design and substance. It was built circa 1970 and has continuous windows spanning left to right on each floor, which means every classroom is filled with natural light all day, no matter the weather. It's the only thing I like about the building. I switch off the engine and sit with my hands on the steering wheel, needing to feel grounded for a moment longer. My car, if nothing else, offers me a safe space. I keep my hands on the wheel, mustering the strength to go inside and get on with my day when all I want to do is swing the car around and go home.

A stream of teachers enter the building, carrying huge bulky bags, most of which are for show. There's a competitiveness in the staffroom surrounding the work bag. The bigger the bag, the busier you are and therefore the more overworked you are, so the more justification you have for complaining about being taken advantage of, as if this gives your life more meaning. I'm just as guilty of 'big bag syndrome' as anyone else. I still haven't worked out who started it, but I think it was Olly.

Malcolm passes my car, sees me and waves in through the window. I wave back. He points at his wrist, indicating I need to get a move on, and disappears through the entrance doors. I glance at the clock on my dashboard. It's five to eight. I now have five minutes to get up to the staff meeting on the fourth floor. The students don't arrive for their first class until eight-thirty and my problematic class isn't until eleven-thirty. We're starting a new module today: attachment. The stress bubbles up inside me at the thought of teaching today, a sickening churning of shame and desire.

I climb out of my car with my coffee cup in one hand and my satchel in the other. I manage to kick the door shut but have to manoeuvre my hands so I can lock it with the key. I run up the steps to the entrance, shoulder my way through the double doors into the lobby and take the stairs to the fourth floor. I'm hoping the quick burst of exercise will wake me up. Today I must behave in the appropriate manner required of a teacher and a thirty-two-year-old married woman.

My lone footsteps echo through the stairwell usually milling with noisy students and I welcome the quiet. I turn in the stairwell to take the last flight to the fourth floor when my feet slow to a stop.

There he is, leaning against the wall at the top of the stairs. Waiting for me.

3

Him

The shed door refuses to open as though it knows I'm a fraud. With my back to the new neighbour's house, I yank at the small handle again, trying not to make it shudder and expose me as the amateur shed-user that I am.

I notice the catch at the top of the door, which I'd forgotten about. I quickly unhook it and open the door, sticking my head inside. I peer at the mound of items we shoved in here the day we moved in. Cushions, bits of shelving, boxes of odds and ends. And the dreaded lawnmower, radiating a sickly and familiar odour of soggy grass and stale grease.

The air inside is thick and muggy and the added smell of wet timber and mildew makes me even more nauseous. I retract my head and take a deep breath of clean air.

The heat of the sun, high in the sky now, warms my back. I've changed into a T-shirt and shorts to look like I have 'business in the garden' but feel totally pathetic. I'm only out here, pretending to look for something in the shed that I loathe, in the hope that the new neighbour might come out to the garden and I can introduce myself.

Hi, I'm Tristan. Tris to my friends.

I cringe to myself. What a sap.

Hi, I'm Tristan. If you need anything, let me know. *Us*, know.

Again, I cringe.

A shunting, sliding noise of a curtain being opened comes from behind me, from the upstairs window next door.

I grab two faded floral cushions from inside the shed and drop them onto the grass behind me, casually glancing up.

The curtain is open and I can just make out a silhouette inside the room. It's harder to hide in the shadows in the daylight. She's standing back from the window, but it's her and she's watching me.

Heat floods my body as I turn back to take more random stuff out of the shed, doing my best to pretend I didn't hear the curtain open or see her in the bedroom.

My T-shirt is now soaked with sweat. I pull it off, roll it into a ball and throw it to one side, like I do this all the time.

I lift a box from inside the shed with the word 'books' scrawled on the top. It's heavy and my back and shoulder muscles flex as I pick it up. I put the box down on the lawn and wipe my brow, hoping to give the impression of a man well used to working the land.

A snapping sound behind me makes me look up again, blatantly this time, as it was too loud to ignore. The curtain in the window has been closed again.

I swivel around, reach into the shed and rummage in another box, desperate to find something realistic I might need. I pull out a screwdriver with a red handle. I slide it into the pocket of my shorts and pile the box of books and cushions back into the shed.

What am I doing? Trying to present myself as a person of sexual interest to the woman who's just moved in next door. And failing miserably. She must have seen right through my attempts to be physically appealing. Not that I rate myself very highly on the fanciable scale. Maybe I should have sat in an old garden chair reading a serious novel instead, or better still, not come out into the garden in the first place.

No wonder she shut the curtain. She must think I'm a sleaze now.

Then the image of her on the driveway last night drifts into my mind. Her small, delicate frame, her chin slightly raised in the direction of the bedroom window, looking at me skulking in the darkness. Naked. Exposed. Defenceless.

Blood rushes to my groin and, to avoid any embarrassing reactions to my thoughts, I put my hand on the lawnmower handle and any hardness quickly fades. Robbed of a potentially spontaneous erection in two seconds flat. That's the power it has.

I scurry into the kitchen, disgusted by my perverted behaviour. My phone on the counter beeps with a text bringing me back to reality. There are five messages, all from Monty. The first three messages are a series of question marks. The fourth says *WTF?* And the last one says: *Kill U.* He has no idea I could report him to the police for the last message.

I check the time. I'm meant to be at the restaurant now to help with the delivery. Luckily I walk to work and can be there in ten minutes. I dash upstairs to put on my suit. The thought of dealing with an angry Monty is already exhausting and gives me an ill feeling in my stomach.

Up ahead I see Monty standing on the pavement outside Lily's restaurant. His hands are on his head and his normally pale skin is bright red from sweat and stress. He's wearing a light blue Adidas tracksuit, which makes him look about fourteen. When he's all spruced up in his chef whites, he seems more his age, around thirty. His thick black glasses have slipped down his shiny nose and look like they might slide off altogether.

Monty is from Thailand and although his English is perfect, he does his best to speak it as little as possible, often using one or two words of a sentence to communicate what he wants to say, leaving you to fill in the blanks. It means people avoid starting a conversation with him, which is his intention.

I've become good at cracking the 'Monty code' and actually think it might be a more efficient way for everyone to communicate. Not only does it cut down on time, but it would make small talk a thing of the past. Conversations would be too short-lived for anyone to bother. Sun. Yes. Nice. Yes. Rain. Bad.

I used to get frustrated with Monty. He makes it so difficult for everyone else with his refusal to engage in proper conversation, but when he's on the phone, chatting away in Thai, it's hard not to question your self-worth. Why doesn't he talk to me like that, with enthusiasm and animation? Am I not good enough for him? Am I not interesting enough?

It wasn't until his sister arrived from New York en route to Dubai, smothered in designer gear and telling stories about helicopter rides and champagne parties, that I realised Monty was actually from a very wealthy family.

I was confused as to why he was working as a chef when he could probably have a string of restaurants of his own. I suspected Monty was being put through his paces and forced to pay his dues. His parents didn't want a spoilt brat for a son, although it was clearly okay for their daughter to live off the family fortunes.

I suppose the only thing worse than being entitled is being entitled and not getting what you're owed. It certainly explains why Monty is such a prick most of the time.

But he's a superb chef and, despite his questionable social skills, Lily's is lucky to have him.

When he's in a better mood, he entertains the staff with his pan-tossing and knife-throwing. He cooks with his eyes closed, not measuring or weighing anything. And when the food is ready, he yells: 'Take it hot.' One of the rare times he uses three words to communicate. The only other time he uses more words is when he's angry or has to explain the daily specials, which requires more effort than, say, 'fillet potato'.

The pavement is narrow outside the restaurant and the delivery van is parked on the double yellow lines. The driver is in the cab and talking on his phone, flicking through a paper order. Monty sees me approach and throws his hands to heaven, palms up.

'Fuck,' he shouts at me.

'Sorry I'm late,' I say. 'What's the problem? Why haven't you unloaded yet?'

'No king prawns,' he shouts, grabbing the sides of his thick straight black hair. 'Did you forget?'

He puts his face right up to mine, argumentative and threatening. I push him back gently. I've witnessed Monty's rages before and they're more akin to a child's tantrum than that of a thug about to thump you. That said, they're unsettling all the same. There's always a fear that this time he might snap.

'I'm sure we can sort it out,' I say, keeping my voice steady.

'No supermarket,' he yells, shaking his head at me, as if I've asked him to do something really painful, like put his balls in a naked flame.

I hide a smile. He has no idea how many times I've bought fish from the supermarket when the delivery comes in short or the owner, Deniz, swipes scallops from the fridge for a family barbecue and I have to replace them before Monty finds out.

'What do you take me for?' I scoff.

'We need a new supplier,' he says. 'Tell this fucking idiot to piss off.'

He waves his hand at the delivery driver, who is still on the phone, but clearly heard what Monty said and is now frowning in his side mirror. I once again note Monty's excellent command of the English language when he lets his guard down.

'Go inside and start prepping for lunch. I'll take care of this.'

'I don't want anything from this stinking van. No prawns, no sale.'

'I'll get him to go and come back with the prawns, okay? It'll be fine.'

Monty thinks about this for a moment.

'Okay,' he says.

Monty walks up to the window of the van and peers in at the delivery driver, giving him a dirty look. The driver frowns back at him like Monty's a headcase. Monty turns and marches into the restaurant, muttering something in Thai under his breath.

The driver lowers his window.

'I know the order's short, but I'm not paid to take that kind of abuse,' he says.

'Sorry. His dog just died and he's a bit emotional.'

'Oh, right,' he says, backing down.

I feel bad using a dead pet as a lie but I need to excuse Monty's outrageous behaviour before the guy drives off, never to return. The goal here is to at least get what food he has out of the van and into our kitchen.

'Can you get us the prawns in the next couple of hours?'

'Not a chance, mate,' he says.

'Okay, I'll take what you have but can you give me an empty icebox?'

He gives me a funny look.

'You'd really be helping me out.'

'Whatever,' he says, eyeing the door to the restaurant, making sure Monty isn't lurking before he gets out.

At the back of the van, the delivery guy checks his order form. The chill from the truck settles on my face and I welcome the coolness. I run my eye over the planter boxes outside the restaurant and take any dead heads off the pansies.

Deniz is particular about the planter boxes and likes them to be lush and overflowing. He says it reflects abundance. Not like the dead pansy patch in the garden at home. Izzy wanted some credit for at least trying to spruce up the garden, but I couldn't quite bring myself to praise her for what actually made the garden look even more forlorn.

Lily's is a popular French restaurant with extortionate prices and fussy service. We take your linen napkin from the table, flick it open with the tiniest wrist movement and place it onto your lap for you. And you only have to emit the slightest sigh and we're at your table ready to fulfil your every dining need. We're fully booked months ahead on weekends and we always fill the empty tables on weekday evenings and most lunchtime sittings too.

The facade is quaint and country-cottage-like, with soft white voile curtains shielding the window from the street, giving an impression of a private oasis beyond, or a vortex ready to suck you dry of all your cash. It's probably a little of both.

The Lily's sign hangs above the door, the name printed in an elegant, elaborate font with an arty graphic of a white lily sprouting out of the letter 'i'.

The delivery guy holds out the order form and I sign it. He then passes me two big boxes of iced fish to carry inside. He's going to follow me with the rest and leave it on the bar.

Once through the door into the restaurant, I'm comforted by the familiar smell that always hits me at this time of day, before the guests arrive and the kitchen gets hot and steamy. It's a subtle combination of freshly hoovered carpet, washing powder, cinnamon and fried onions and garlic. It injects me with a sense of purpose as I get into gear for the day ahead.

Being a manager doesn't come naturally to me. I find people exhausting most of the time, but I learnt at a young age how to put on a front. People only see what they want to see or what suits them to see.

It's actually been quite easy to fake it in life and I'm grateful for that. Although it's getting harder to fake it as I get older. But Lily's has become ingrained in the fabric of my existence. Every detail of the restaurant is imprinted in my memory and, sometimes when I can't sleep, I take myself on an imaginary tour.

The kitchen is located in the basement and accessed by a dusky pink carpeted staircase that descends from the centre of the restaurant. There's no dumb waiter, so we go up and down the stairs all day and night with full and empty plates. It's part of the whole Lily's experience, watching waiters emerge from the mystery kitchen underworld with plates of steaming, sumptuous food.

On the right as you enter, there are four alcoves with tables covered in linen tablecloths with silky cushioned booth seating either side. On the left, facing the alcoves, is the long bar with wine glasses hanging from above. Whoever works the bar is required to wear a dicky bow. And every glass must be polished until it sparkles and flashes in the light.

27

To the left is a small set of steps leading to the upper level of the restaurant where there are more linen-draped tables consisting of six-, four- and two-tops.

In a separate alcove halfway down the room is a coffee station and serving table with shelves. Behind the coffee station is a doorway with a staircase leading to the floor above where there are several rooms, including two customer bathrooms. It's big enough to be a spacious flat but is used as an office instead with a desk in the main room. It's where I like to spend my time in between shifts. And often on my days off, doing the books and orders.

In the desk drawer, I keep a notebook. Every Sunday night, after the staff have all left and I'm on my own, I write my three goals for the coming week. Identifying your goals regularly is supposed to motivate you to take action. And it's become an obsession. If I don't write them down, then there's no hope for me whatsoever. If I do write them down, the ever-fading light of pipe dreams just about maintains its dim glow.

My three goals are always the same because I never manage to get any of them done. 1. Organise a viewing of a restaurant/site for sale. 2. Call the bank about finance for new restaurant. 3. Eat an apple a day.

I read somewhere that eating an apple a day extends your life. I add it to my list, mostly as a filler, because apparently it's better to have three goals, not one or two. And since I'm not sure I want to extend my life, I'm not as disappointed when I don't manage to tick that box.

However, today, I feel compelled to actually achieve my goals for the week. A little stir whirls in my abdomen. Is my life really going to change? The whirling quickly becomes an unwelcome adrenaline surge; a mild panic. Do I want it to change?

Sometimes when I'm in the office looking out of the bay window, I fantasise about what life would be like if it were my flat and I lived there alone; if I could start my adult life over again, from scratch. While the hospitality industry offers opportunities and ongoing work, it was not my career of choice. Like most people with jobs they get straight out of college, I fell into it, like quicksand, right up to my neck.

And now it's my story, my trajectory. The man who worked his way up from a waiter to a restaurant business owner. That's the man Izzy thought she was marrying. Someone with a plan. Someone with prospects. Someone to be taken seriously.

Izzy and I decided to get married after a night of drinking and intense sex. Izzy had worn a pair of crotchless knickers and I had no idea I'd be so excited by them. I never saw them again though, maybe they got ripped during sex, but I'll always remember that night.

As we lay splayed and sweaty in bed together afterwards, I told her I loved her, and she had wondered if we would ever get married. In that moment, with the idea of ever losing her being too painful to bear, I said we should just do it, so we did.

If I had a second chance at a career, I'd definitely do something else. Sadly that's where the fantasy ends, as I have no idea what I would do instead.

When I force myself to look deep inside to find out what it is that's missing in my life, I just feel more empty and useless, like a plastic bag discarded in a field, going where the wind blows and settling where it drops me.

If it weren't for the wind, I might not have any life at all. This appeals to me. The idea of not having to do anything or get up in the morning for any reason fills me with a sense of relief and contentment. Do I secretly wish not to engage in life? Do I wish I wasn't here at all?

In the beginning, when Izzy and I were first together, I believed anything was possible with her by my side, which is why youth can be a dangerous stage of life. You can say whatever you want, make the boldest statements, with no fear of anyone looking for immediate results. 'I'm going to be the best in the world.' 'I'm going to be rich.' 'I'm going to own a chain of restaurants.'

Then, as the years plod on and begin to mount up behind you, these declarations come back to haunt you. Dark angels of failure, laughing and mocking, as you desperately try to forget you ever said such things. If I don't show some progress soon, the questions will stop and the disappointed looks will follow.

With Izzy, they have already started.

I trot down the dusky pink staircase to the kitchen. At the bottom of the stairs is a large canvas painting of a pink lily. I turn right, passing the wine storage alcove tucked in on the right that you have to duck your head to enter. Turning left I enter the washing-up area then through to the salad and vegetable prep section.

The sound of the Gipsy Kings blasts out, coming from the main kitchen at the back. In the six years I've worked with Monty in Lily's, the Gipsy Kings is all he listens to. He sings along in what sounds like perfect Spanish, but he's so off-key it's not even funny.

I do wonder if Monty is a gifted linguist.

I approach the kitchen and stop at the threshold. This is Monty's realm and we all know, even Deniz the owner, not to enter. No one's allowed to open a fridge or look in a cupboard.

Sometimes, when he goes home for a rest between shifts, I walk around the kitchen and do exactly that. I lifted a piece of spicy chorizo from his evening special once and ate it slowly to savour the taste – and the crime.

He didn't notice, despite his insistence that he sees and knows everything that happens in his kitchen.

Monty stands at the central hob stirring a huge pot of broth, singing his heart out. Now in his chef whites, he has an air of authority and maturity. He looks up at me and I indicate the boxes of fish I'm holding. He comes over, looks at the boxes and then at me with his eyebrows raised.

'The rest is upstairs. I'll get it now,' I say warmly, keeping him on side. 'And the delivery guy will be back in an hour with the king prawns.'

He nods once and takes the boxes from me. Not even a thank you, but that's Monty.

Thudding footsteps descend the staircase and Spencer, twenty-two years old with a mop of blonde hair, breezes in holding the rest of the fish delivery boxes, a big grin on his face.

'Morning, morning, morning.' He has the clipped accent of a posh private school boy.

He always stops for a moment after entering a room, to let the atmosphere around him settle and for anyone in the vicinity to acknowledge that Spencer has, in fact, arrived.

'Hey, Spence,' I say. 'You're on the bar today, okay?'

'Sure,' he says. 'You look knackered. Are you alright?'

'Not much sleep last night.'

'Yeah, too bloody hot,' he says.

He moves past me into Monty's kitchen, breaching the entrance threshold by a foot to stand in the sacred space. Spencer is the only one who really gets away with this.

'Monty! How are you, you sexy beast?'

Monty snatches the boxes from him, a frown on his face, but as he opens the fridge to slide the boxes in, there's a tiny twitch at the corner of his mouth. He definitely has a soft spot for Spencer and seems to enjoy being called a sexy beast.

'What lovely delight are you cooking up for the staff today? I'm ravenous,' Spencer says, rubbing his belly. 'Up all night, mate, you know what I mean?'

Spencer likes people to think he has 'a way with the ladies', his words, not mine, but I'm not sure he does at all. He had a brief relationship with one of the waitresses that didn't end well. She stormed out in the middle of a shift, labelling Spencer 'the dispenser' and leaving me in the lurch. I asked him to try and avoid getting involved with the staff in future.

'You can't get in the way of passion,' he said.

'Yes, you can,' I said. 'It's called a zip.'

But Spencer is a great asset to the restaurant. He's reliable and energetic and definitely has a way with people, a natural charm, and sometimes I wish I had a fraction of his confidence.

'Eggs salmon,' Monty tells him, which actually means scrambled eggs and smoked salmon with Monty's toasted homemade bread.

'My favourite,' says Spencer, then lowers his voice. 'Give me an extra-large portion, yeah?'

Monty nods and then shoos him out of the kitchen. 'Out, out, out.' Spencer backs away and rolls his eyes at me, like Monty is a source of exasperation for us all, but Monty's the one who just got played. Spencer got exactly what he wanted. More on his plate than everyone else.

I slope upstairs after him.

'Sainsbury's run?' Spencer says, nodding at the empty icebox lying on the sofa in one of the alcoves, knowing full well what's going on.

'Yep,' I reply.

I reach over the bar to the petty cash box, as the door flies open and Maddy bustles in, her bleached blonde bob falling into her eyes.

'Jesus fucking Christ,' she says. She's twenty-three and from Dublin. Her Irish accent is soft and lyrical to my ears, a calming wave of loveliness washing over me.

'I nearly didn't get off the bus,' she continues. 'Some woman collapsed at the back doors, the driver wasn't looking in his mirrors. I was like, stop the bus, there's someone dying here.'

'Somebody died on your bus?' says Spencer in horror. Spencer hates bad news. When a kitchen assistant had to leave because his mother had been rushed to hospital after a heart attack, his face went a ghostly shade of grey and the stem of the wine glass he was polishing broke off in his hand.

'She was grand, blood pressure thing apparently. I sat with her for five minutes. That's why I'm late.'

'Take your time. We're fully booked and first table's not here till twelve forty-five.'

'Great,' she says and bounces off downstairs to put her bag on the top shelf in the wine store.

Spencer glances after her. Maddy is a fashion student and when she's not dressed in black and white for work, she's wearing ripped-to-shreds jeans and multiple earrings. She's tall with long, slim limbs and gives off a 'look, don't touch' popstar vibe. Spencer is smitten but way out of his depth.

He asked her to go for a drink with him once – I did admire his bravery – and she enjoyed telling him never in a million years. Maddy has zero interest in him and even called him privileged to his face, which Spencer failed to see as an insult.

When he asked her out a second time, she told him not to be a letch and that letches die alone. Spencer laughed it off but, as Maddy disappeared down the stairs, his face fell and he started putting paper coasters out on the bar, which we never do, only to gather them all up again. It made me wonder if that was Spencer's greatest fear. Being alone.

Maddy always lifts the spirits of the restaurant and the customers love her. She makes a big effort to be on her best behaviour when serving, as she does like to swear a lot, although it sounds charming coming from her. You could say she swears beautifully.

'I wish I could swear like you,' I told her once.

'What do you mean?' she said. 'My language is fucking atrocious.'

'It doesn't sound so bad when you say it.'

'That's because English people treat swear words like they're special,' she said. 'They're not. They're just words. Like, you say, what the FUCK are you doing? We say, whatthefuckareyoudoing? And English people snarl a bit when they swear. Don't do that either.'

'Whatthefuckareyoudoing?' I said, remaining deadpan.

'I'm polishing the fucking cutlery,' she said.

'Good fucking job,' I said.

She laughed.

'You should give swearing etiquette lessons. You'd make millions,' I said.

'And leave all this?' she said, holding up a very shiny fork.

★

33

With a hundred pounds from the petty cash in my hand, I speed-walk to Sainsbury's, praying they have enough king prawns to fill the icebox. I'm sweltering, as the sun moves towards pole position overhead. My phone rings and I see it's Izzy.

'Hey,' I say, wondering why she's calling me. We don't normally talk during the day, at least not lately.

'Sounds like you're out and about,' she says.

I'm usually stuck in the restaurant all day and night, so I understand the surprise. I'm sometimes jealous of Izzy's more varied days, going for lunch and working from home and having weekends.

'I'm on my way to Sainsbury's. No king prawns.'

'What will happen if Monty ever finds out you do that?'

'I won't know because I will have left the country with no forwarding address.'

I hear her laugh on the end of the phone. At least we're still good on the phone, as though not having to see each other in person, disembodied, lifts the pressure off having to relate in a physical way.

'Are you still coming home this afternoon?'

After my seventies-style porn star show this morning in the garden, I'm wondering if giving the new neighbour a wide berth for now might be a better idea.

'I'll know later,' I say.

'Okay, just checking,' she says.

I hear a small crack in her voice. For a moment I think it's disappointment. But then I think maybe she's upset.

'Are you alright?' I ask.

There's a slight pause.

'Izzy?'

'I'll pick up a bottle of wine in case you don't make it,' she says in a breezy tone.

'I will try to be there,' I say.

'I think I can manage on my own,' she says, slightly sarcastic.

'I'm sure you can, since you've already met her,' I say.

'Text me when you know,' she says, a tad weary.

'Will do,' I reply, overly cheerful. She hangs up.

So much for being good on the phone.

I enter the supermarket and a blast of cool air from the air conditioning vent over the entrance ruffles my hair.

Izzy never used to be so distant. I wish I was brave enough to ask her about it. I wish she was brave enough to tell me. I wish I was brave enough to listen.

Talking about the new neighbour reignites the fizzing sensation in my stomach from this morning. And I like it.

Wandering through the fruit and veg area, I pass the wide selection of apples and stop to eye a bag of Granny Smiths. Maybe, for the first time ever, I could tick my number three goal at the end of the week.

In the fish section, I peer down at the cold, plastic-wrapped king prawns in the brightly lit fridge. There's three days left on the expiry date, not as long as I normally like. I rummage around looking for fresher ones, but there aren't any. They'll have to do. I grab all the large packets, ten in total, and feel their weight in my hands.

I hurry to the self-service checkout and scan the prawns and the apples. Why am I so excited about the new neighbour who I have barely seen once – well, twice if you include her watching me this morning? Even if she thought I was being sleazy, or worse still, perverted, she was still watching me. I decide not to question the logic of my emotions. Emotions rarely make sense, to me anyway.

'You alright, mate?' says an older man in a Sainsbury's uniform holding a cleaning cloth. I realise I've been standing here for at least a minute, lost in thought.

'Sorry, miles away,' I say.

'I thought you'd had a stroke for a second there. It happened to a friend of mine in the queue at the post office.'

'I'm fine, thanks.'

'Look after yourself,' he says and goes back to cleaning the till machines.

Look after myself. I'm not even sure what that means.

As I head for the exit, I break out one of the apples from the bag and take a bite. It's crisp and cold and fresh and I have to wipe residual juice from my lips.

There's no denying it. I definitely feel more alive today. Maybe there's hope for me yet.

4
Her

His rucksack lies at his feet and his hands are pushed into the front of his jeans. He wears black converse trainers and a black T-shirt that falls loosely around his torso. He looks down at me, standing on the bottom of the stairs. His hair is messy and unkempt, while also orderly and perfect. I should have kept walking. I'm annoyed at myself for stopping. It's time to deal with this like a responsible and respectable teacher. It's time to get back on track.

'Jude. You're in early,' I say and walk on up the stairs, but the adrenaline is bombing around my body, swamping me in fear and anticipation, sickness and longing.

He pushes his hand through his hair, not moving from where he is slumped against the wall.

'I'm waiting for you,' he says. I pause for a moment, doing my best to appear calm. 'I thought you might take the stairs, after what happened,' he says, a little sheepish.

'I can't condone any more inappropriate behaviour,' I say, fully aware that I've just implied I have condoned it in the past. If he knew me better, he'd be aware that I'm no stranger to inappropriate behaviour myself. I glance ever so briefly at his full mouth and try to ignore the sudden goosebumps prickling along my arms.

'I needed to see you. You're all I think about,' he says, bold, brazen. It strikes me again how a nineteen-year-old can be so sure about his feelings and what he wants. At his age, I was an insecure wreck. At thirty-two, I still am.

I let out a short, sharp sigh, feigning maturity. 'You have to stop this.'

He steps closer to me. A waft of his musky, fresh deodorant lingers under my nose. A familiar scent, when it so shouldn't be.

'You can't keep creeping up on me like this,' I say, sounding authoritative but I'm more panicked.

'Creeping? Thanks a lot.' He drops his eyes, stung by my words, picks up his bag and disappears down the stairwell, two steps at a time, silent as he goes.

I lean against the wall now, catching my breath. I shouldn't have engaged in conversation. I should have ignored him and kept walking. I should have told him he's nothing but a boy to me and I'm not interested and never will be. I should have told the principal about his advances from the very start. But there are so many things I should and shouldn't have done in my life, it's of no surprise that, yet again, I haven't dealt with a situation properly.

I did everything I could to stop Jude's obsession with me. I changed the way I dress and do my hair. I stopped wearing make-up and perfume. But he doesn't seem to notice any of that. I think if I shaved my head and wore a bin liner he'd still want me, which is extremely unsettling but also exhilarating. Part of me longs for the intensity of forbidden love, the hesitant touching followed by the intoxicating passion. I fantasise that Jude is my destiny and it's pointless to fight it. I know these thoughts are linked to a distinct lack of self-esteem where the attentions of a student bolster my ego. If Tristan doesn't want me anymore, at least somebody does. But none of this is bringing me any closer to completing my quest to save my soul or stop the train. I certainly wouldn't do very well on the 'Are you a good person?' quiz. Overall, I'd probably score 3 out of 10, under the heading: *Give in to the darkness, you are beyond help.*

Q. *You are a married teacher in a sixth-form college and one of your students, aged nineteen, is attracted to you and making advances. Despite your better judgement, you are attracted to them as well. What do you do?*

a) *Ignore any advances and report the situation to the principal for guidance in dealing with this delicate matter.*
b) *Resign immediately as you don't trust yourself and want to avoid any compromising situations.*
c) *Engage in some harmless flirtation – after all, it's flattering, and it's a long time since your spouse looked at you like that.*
d) *Go on a date, see what happens, but swear the student to secrecy as you don't want to lose your job or damage your reputation.*
e) *Embark on a full-blown affair. Why not? The student is of adult age – there's no crime here. And those teacher/student rules are archaic and would never stand up in court.*

Maybe I'd score 4 out of 10 if I picked option c). Still a massive failure but under the lighter heading: *Take a good long hard look at yourself.*

I stumble into one of the science labs where the staff meeting is being held, my bag slipping half off my shoulder as I blow the hair out of my eyes. I'm the last one in despite arriving early.

'Nice of you to join us, Izzy,' says Tina, the principal, eyeing me over her glasses from the front of the class. Tina is in her sixties, always in a fitted dress suit with high heels, and pearly, smooth white hair down to her shoulders. I suspect she chooses a science lab for these meetings because the teacher's desk is elevated so she gets to look down on us. She was a teacher for thirty-five years and talks to us like we're her students, which gets on everyone's nerves, but today it's totally appropriate for me. I didn't report Jude's behaviour and now I'm involved in something terribly illicit and definitely against the rules. I'm a disgrace and I don't need a quiz to tell me that.

The room is squashed full of teachers, most of whom are scrolling on their phones, already bored, and shedding any layers they're wearing as the sun beats in through the long window. Polly, one of the maths teachers, is at the back of the room marking papers and I make my way through the yawning fest of bodies to join her.

Polly only joined the college this year and she's brought a sense of fun to the staffroom with her throaty laugh and dirty jokes. She's got wild curly red hair that she keeps in check with various colourful head scarves. She's pale-skinned and very pretty with refined features. Sometimes she looks more feline than human. She's six years younger than me, outspoken and carefree, and she makes me laugh, which I so appreciate. We've had a couple of boozy nights out together – she's fond of Baby Guinness shots, Baileys with a Guinness top, and they are lethal. I ended up passed out on her couch once with missed calls from Tristan, who thought I'd been abducted. I squeeze into the chair beside her and take off my jacket; the room is stuffy already.

'What happened to you?' she says, looking me over with amusement.

'I took the stairs,' I say, tidying my hair.

'You look like you just had sex,' she says, grinning.

I manage to appear amused and surreptitiously touch my cheeks, feeling the warmth from them. Jude has this effect on me and I need to face facts that the situation is more than out of control. Tina starts to warble on about attendance records and expectations regarding grades in the upcoming summer exams. I do my best to focus on her face and what she's saying, but I can't take a word in. I'm too shaken by what happened with Jude, not only from meeting him on the stairs, but from last night.

Jude joined the intensive A-level repeat programme in September. So many students come and go through our doors that we don't have the time or energy to get to know them all personally. To be honest, I expected teaching to be more rewarding.

I do make an effort to remember names so my students feel they at least matter to me, but my job is simple: to fill the heads of whoever is in my class, for however long, with the knowledge and exam skills they need to get a good grade in A-level psychology. The interaction ends there. But I noticed and remembered Jude from day one.

He sat at the back of the class watching me as I went through the motions of teaching, which in repeat classes consists of continual testing and revision. Most of the other students paid attention and watched me too, but not like Jude. Sometimes my eyes were drawn to his at the back of the room and for a moment I would lose my train of thought. It wasn't that he had an intense or strange stare, or that he was intimidating in any way. It was that he looked at me as though he knew me and was waiting for me. I knew these responses were inappropriate and that I should have ignored him and brought the situation to Tina's attention – option a) in the quiz. But part of me was thrilled by this beautiful young man's attention, which only made me more aware of how badly I was dealing with it.

Like I do with all my students, I tried to keep Jude at arm's length, but it didn't work with him. In December, near the end of term and after a class on psychopathology, I was packing up my notes to leave for the day when he stayed back. After the room had emptied, he came up to my desk. I continued to pack my notes into my satchel, aware of a tingling sensation in my chest.

'I like your class,' he said.

'Oh, thanks,' I replied.

'There are a few things I don't understand around the memory module.' He opened his bag and took out his notepad. 'Do you have a couple of minutes?'

I hesitated. I never stayed after class to take a student through work again, but then again, no one had ever asked before.

'As long as it is only a couple of minutes,' I said, adopting Tina's schoolmistress tone. Although we're available to students after class, I instinctively knew it would be better not to be alone with Jude. He caught my eye again, this time with a little smile, and without thinking I smiled back, accidentally opening the door to boundaries being crossed.

'Couple of minutes tops,' he said.

I sat back down at my desk and he sat across from me. I stayed for almost an hour taking him over the topics he said he was having trouble with. He took new notes and double-checked his old notes but I knew he wasn't struggling with his studies. It was a ruse to spend time with me, and he knew that I knew it, but I still played along. We were supposedly discussing the constructs of memory and perception, when really he was slipping into my personal universe and I was letting him.

After that encounter, I felt awful, dirty even, for allowing this to happen. It wasn't the first time a student had had a crush on me, but they were normally juvenile and, once ignored, tended to move on to someone their own age. Jude was different. He was strong and self-assured with the maturity of a man much older. And even though I tried not to, I had fantasies about him. Me, sprawled on my back across the desk, my shirt unbuttoned, Jude's mouth on one of my nipples, his hand slipping up my skirt. It was a battle to stop these thoughts and I wondered if I was developing a sexual obsession OCD – continuous unwelcome, intrusive sexual thoughts. But these thoughts about Jude didn't distress me; in fact, I enjoyed them, so I ruled that out. Still, I needed to take control, or at least try to. So after that evening of 'extra study', I started to change my appearance in the hope of putting him off, or at least not encouraging him any further. My efforts were in vain though. Despite my attempts to appear plain and conservative, he kept waiting to speak to me after class and regarding me from the back of the room like an old lover returned from across the seas to reclaim his woman. It was both romantic and repugnant.

I wanted to tell Tristan what was happening but I didn't know how to start the conversation. Our limited level of communication since Mrs Jenkins died has mostly consisted of discussions about who the new neighbour might be. How could I suddenly blurt out that I was being harassed by a student? And that isn't even true. Jude isn't harassing me. The problem is I haven't shut him down. And I can't tell Tristan the real truth, how I have sexual thoughts about a student who's obsessed with me. It would be a betrayal, and I feel guilty about that too. So I never told him.

One evening after staying late at college, I popped to the local Waitrose to pick up dinner. It was Tristan's night off and I had promised to cook. I was wandering down the aisles trying to think of new ways to spice up a tomato pasta dish when I entered the wine section and came face to face with Jude. He was taking red wine bottles from a box and putting them onto a shelf. He looked older in his Waitrose uniform with his name badge on his shirt. He saw me first and said hi.

'Oh,' I said, trying to be casual, noticing how his long hair lapped the inside of his collar.

'I work here, nights mostly,' he said.

'That can't be easy with college on top,' I said.

'I manage,' he said, looking into my basket at the packet of pasta, a slab of parmesan cheese and jar of tomato sauce. 'Do you want a bottle of red to go with that?' he asked.

'Yes, actually,' I said.

He passed me the bottle he was holding. 'This is supposed to be good. I haven't tried it myself yet.'

'Right,' I said, acutely aware of the fact he's old enough to drink wine and is in fact an adult. For a moment option e) in the quiz seems to make the most sense. Embark on a full-blown affair.

'Cooking dinner for your husband?' he asked. He would know I'm married from the ring on my finger.

'Er, yes, I am,' I said. 'He's off work tonight, so I promised I would.'

I wondered why on earth I was offering personal information about my life.

'Lucky man,' he said, holding my gaze for a moment. I quickly put the bottle of wine in my basket and moved the packet of pasta around as though it was in danger of being crushed by the parmesan cheese.

'Enjoy your night,' he said.

'I will, thanks.'

He turned to resume shelf-stacking and I hurried to the checkout. Four beeps of the scanner and I was all done, paid, and on my way out. I stopped at the exit and flicked around. Jude was in the background, no longer in the alcohol section. He smiled at me, oozing confidence. I bolted straight through the door and out into the car park.

Later that night, after throwing dinner together in ten minutes and guzzling most of the red wine myself, I fell asleep on the sofa. Tristan woke me and ushered me upstairs. Lying in bed, my head woozy, I watched him come out of our pokey en suite, naked, and climb into bed. Why didn't I feel a fraction of the sexual attraction for him that I felt for Jude?

After bumping into him at the supermarket, I tried desperately to keep Jude at a distance and he knew it. He was frustrated and felt rejected, I could see it in his eyes and his body language, the way he stood far too still as I dashed out of the room at the end of class to avoid talking to him. I didn't trust myself around him. Thankfully, it worked, and gradually I hoped he was getting the message.

Then I met Viv. And although I didn't realise at the time, it shifted something inside me and I started to do things I wouldn't normally do. That's my excuse for yesterday anyway.

It was the end of a long day and I was packing up. Jude hadn't been in class all day and I was relieved. It had given me some time to reflect and I was ready to be harsh with him the next time I saw him. I left my classroom on the eighth floor and went to wait for the lift. The building was quiet and peaceful, devoid of the normal echoey shouts and chatter of students. In the winter months the wind charges through the stairwells causing doors to bang shut, making Malcolm jump right out of his skin. But last night, the air was so very still. I watched the light above the lift door flashing as it moved from the ground floor up. I glanced out of the window into the car park below where only a few cars were scattered now. Mine was one of them. A bird's-eye view was the best perspective of the rust bucket. The black canvas roof and the boxy front bonnet gave me a little dopamine rush and made me fall in love with it all over again. I thought about putting the roof down on the way home.

The lift doors opened and I went to enter but stopped in my tracks.

Jude was standing at the back of the lift, leaning against the wall. He was there for me, I knew he was.

'Going down?' he said.

'Er, yes,' I said, stepping into the lift and turning my back on him. I was determined to act like being in the lift with him was perfectly okay. He meant nothing to me. Just another student. I was not going to engage, and definitely not attempting the harsh chat in a lift. I pressed the ground floor button and the doors shut. The hum of the lift, which seemed noisier than usual, filled the space between us.

'Aren't you going to ask why I wasn't in today?' he said. From the volume of his voice, I knew he was still at the back of the lift. I looked up at the lift counter going down. Floor seven, floor six, painfully slow.

'Vicky in the office looks after attendance,' I said, not taking my eyes off the lift counter.

'I couldn't face seeing you,' he said.

I turned to look at him. My first mistake.

He moved closer to me. I stepped away, pressing my back against the side of the lift.

'But then I had to see you. I can't stop thinking about you,' he said, looking me right in the eye. And for the first time I saw his pain. His longing and loneliness. And I recognised it, because I felt it too.

'I have to kiss you,' he said.

'No, Jude,' I said, making no effort to push him away.

'I won't if you don't want me to,' he said, desperation in his voice.

45

And then I made my second mistake. I said nothing.

He leaned in closer, pressing his body against me. His lips brushed up against mine and my body surrendered, giving in, totally letting me down in my hour of need. Get away from him, the moral woman inside my head screamed. But all I wanted in that moment was to kiss him. To let him kiss me. To speed up the runaway train.

Ping! We arrived at the ground floor and he sprung back as the lift doors opened. Tina was outside waiting, looking down at her phone. Jude ducked past her and out through the double doors. Tina looked up and saw me – she hadn't even noticed Jude.

'Izzy? You're late tonight.'

'Marking tests,' I replied.

'Go home and put your feet up. I forgot my purse.'

I walked out of the lift as Tina got in and the doors shut.

The college was calm and peaceful again. I glanced through the double doors to make sure Jude wasn't outside waiting for me, but he was gone. My body tingled in all the wrong but right places. I was thrilled and also disgusted. What had I done?

Tina stops her warbling and dismisses us.

'Have you got any summer work lined up?' asks Polly. I shake my head. I hadn't even thought about the summer. After the exams next month, I never have to see Jude again. But rather than relief, all I feel is a sense of urgency, which couldn't be further from the right response. My new 'Are you a good person?' quiz result heading reads: *You have a borderline personality disorder. Stay away from people.*

It's now nearly lunchtime and I'm on a break but already five minutes late to class. I can't bring myself to leave the cubicle in the staff toilets. I've been sitting on the closed loo seat for the past twenty minutes, contemplating what an awful person I am and feeling sorry for myself. I take my phone from my bag and call Tristan. The moment I hear his voice I want to cry and ask him to come and collect me, take me home and make it all okay. He's on a secret supermarket run for that arsehole, Monty. Instead I keep it light, ask if he's still going to be home this afternoon. He says he's not sure, but he'll try, which probably means no. I pause for a moment, squeezing my eyes together to keep the tears from flowing. He can tell there's something wrong and asks me if I'm okay. I shake my head, no, I'm not, but I can't bring myself to say the words. Instead I carry on talking to keep my emotions in check, saying I'll pick up the wine and take it to the new neighbour on my own if he can't make it. He gets offended, I hear it in his voice. He thinks I don't want him to come. In a way I don't, but he's got to meet Viv sometime. A quick hello at the front door should suffice though. We hang up on each other, acting polite. I feel worse.

What would have happened in the lift with Jude if it hadn't reached the ground floor when it did? Would I have kissed him back, the two of us a sweaty, writhing mass in the creaky, college lift? Would I have let him pull the sides of my dress up and press the palm of his hand against the underside of my knickers? There's a throbbing between my legs. I stifle a little moan. Could I, here in the staff toilets? I raise my dress up to my thighs and move my legs apart but stop as I hear the door to the ladies bang open.

'Izzy? Are you in here?'

It's Polly.

'Er, yeah,' I shout out, standing up, pushing my dress down and flushing the loo.

'Someone from your class is asking where you are?'

'Okay,' I say.

'What's wrong? Have you got the squits?' she says then giggles. I emerge from the toilet cubicle. 'I wasn't feeling well.'

'You look alright,' she says.

'I thought I was going to throw up.'

'Maybe you're up the duff.'

'I didn't have breakfast. It can make me queasy.'

'Well, get a move on, you don't want Tina on your case. She might give you fifty lashings,' Polly says, laughing, and leaves, letting the door slam behind her. I look at myself in the mirror. I do look good, I have to admit. Full cheeks, red lips, clear skin, shiny hair. There is something different about me.

Normally, I would never have let Jude get that close to me, especially in a confined space like a lift. And I've certainly never had the urge to masturbate in a toilet cubicle before, never mind actually following through with it. Maybe the best thing I can do is stop fighting my instincts and throw myself head first over the precipice of shame and see where I end up.

5
Him

Monty is systematically picking up each individual king prawn from the icebox. Spencer and I look on as he inspects each one closely then sniffs it.

He drops the fifth one back in the box in disgust and spins to face me, his heavy frown making deep grooves in between his eyebrows.

'Supermarket,' he says, shoving the box back towards me.

'What? No, the driver brought them back in his van,' I say, acting suitably perplexed.

'I saw him with my own eyes,' says Spencer. 'And he looked worried. You must have given him a right scare, Monty. He didn't even want to come in. He said he had to nick this order from another restaurant. I mean, he hardly stopped off at Tesco on the way, did he?'

Monty grunts and nods his head, agreeing with Spencer, who is very convincing. The more Spencer talks, the more believable he sounds. But being an expert liar can make you forget what it's like to tell the truth. It can make you superficial and, worse than that, it can make you forget who you are. I should know.

'What made you say that?' I say to Monty, genuinely curious. He's never once copped all the other times I've bought fish or meat from Sainsbury's.

'Plastic,' he says, peering at me, suspicious.

Monty's nose never ceases to amaze me. It's because the prawns weren't as fresh as I would have liked. They'd been sitting in the plastic wrapping for a few days and he could smell it.

He once smelled pork on a waiter, a schoolboy who only worked on Saturdays, and forced him to empty his apron pockets. Sure enough, he had a half-eaten wild boar sausage wrapped in a napkin, part of the special for the day. He had 'stolen' it from the kitchen when Monty was on a break. He mumbled an excuse about it going spare, but Monty never has spare food.

I don't think I've ever seen Monty as angry as I did in that moment. He scrunched both hands into fists and held his breath, on the verge of exploding.

Thankfully I was there or we might have been sued for abusive and threatening behaviour. I swept the boy out of the kitchen and up the stairs just as the banging and clanging and Monty's perfect English diatribe erupted.

Hands shaking, the boy said it might be better if he looked for another restaurant job and I agreed. I suggested he try the steak house up the road.

'I owe you one,' I say to Spencer back up at the bar.

'What do you think he would do if he found out the truth?'

'Tear me limb from limb.'

'He wouldn't,' says Spencer. 'He's a big teddy bear, really.'

'No, Spencer, he really isn't,' I assure him. 'And don't ever think that.'

Spencer swallows, unnerved. 'He's not really a nutter, is he?'

'Everyone's a nutter if you push the right button. Monty's button is supermarket food or anything to do with food.'

Spencer nods, grabs a cloth and starts polishing glasses from the washer. I wonder what Spencer's button is. My gut tells me it's death and his fear of it.

My button is everything that happened to me pre-2007. The day I arrived at university was the beginning of my new existence. The new Tristan.

Growing up, one of my neighbours had an older sister who went to university in Manchester and never came back. Not even for a short visit. It was the talk of the cul-de-sac.

All I remember was being relieved there was a way out, that I could leave and never return. It was the moment I decided university would be my escape plan as well. Not only from my adoptive parents, Martha and Bradley, but from the person I had become.

It became a do-or-die situation as I had no Plan B. The fear of being stuck living with Martha and Bradley for any longer than was absolutely necessary propelled me to study hard. And it worked.

They came to the train station to see me off. Although it was more about appearances with them. Waiting on the platform, Bradley's hand twitched impatiently by his side as he rolled forward and backwards on the balls of his feet. Martha was completely over the top, blowing me kisses through the window (as if we ever had that kind of relationship). I waved back as the train pulled out of the station.

Little did they know I had no intention of ever returning.

I applied to halls of residence late and had to sleep on a camp bed on the floor in the hall's bar with fifty other students waiting, like vultures, for the statistical percentage of first years to drop out and vacate their rooms so we could move in, the polyester pillow still warm.

The university had three halls of residence, housing over a thousand students, and this particular hall consisted of four blocks. It was rumoured that the plan for the building was based on the same plan as a local prison. Each floor in each block had eight rooms, and each corridor had shared shower and bathroom facilities and a communal kitchen. Corridors were gender specific, starting with boys on the ground floor.

In the main block, there was a large, light-filled refectory serving breakfast and dinner with a traditional roast on Sundays. Other students complained about the quality of the food, turning their noses up, leaving full plates of food untouched. I always finished every morsel.

Finally, after two weeks on a camp bed, on a grey, rainy Sunday afternoon, I moved into C-block. I shuffled into the lobby, soaked to my skin from the deluge outside, to find it quiet, almost deserted.

A guy appeared from the ground floor corridor heading upstairs. He stopped when he saw me standing in the entrance, wiping the rain from my eyes, a large, sopping wet holdall and rolled-up bedding in a bin liner at my feet.

'Want a hand?' he said, indicating my bags.

'Sure, if you don't mind. Third floor though.'

'Me too,' he said, throwing my holdall over his back and heading for the stairwell. I quickly picked up the bin bag and followed.

'I'm Will,' he said, craning his neck to look back at me.

'Tristan,' I said, traipsing up the stairs behind him.

'You know these halls were built using plans from a local prison.'

'I heard,' I said.

We shuffled down an empty, windowless corridor to my room. The air in the hallway was stale and damp with a hint of incense and cigarette smoke.

I unlocked the door and pushed it open. Will walked in ahead of me and dropped my wet bag on the floor.

The room was relatively spacious with a timber desk and a bookshelf beside the window. The branches from a huge oak tree outside scraped against the glass in the wind like skeleton hands waving hello. There was a metal-framed bed with a sheet, duvet and pillow laid out, all pale green, provided by the halls, and a small sink behind the door with a small light above a mirror.

A built-in wardrobe stood at the end of the bed. Apart from the regulation bed covers, everything else was an orangey brown colour. The desk, the lino floor, the thin curtains, the wardrobe, the door. The tree outside. Even me when I looked in the mirror, as the orangey glow gave my face a strange tinge.

And I loved it. It was my room and I was free; free to be who I wanted to be.

'It's grim at first, but you get used to it,' said Will. I pulled a face, pretending to agree the room was on the dire side. I thanked him for carrying my bag.

'I'm at the end of the corridor on the right,' he said and swaggered out.

I unpacked my things, not that I had much. A few books, toiletries in a Tesco carrier bag, some writing pads and pens and a selection of T-shirts, hoodies and jeans.

I had saved for two years so I would be able to buy myself some decent clothes. Martha always insisted on buying me clothes online and then expected me to wear them whether they fit properly or not.

But I had never complained, about anything. I didn't want to rock the boat.

That evening, Will stopped by my room to invite me to the student union bar. It was 'two pound a pint' on a Sunday night. He had another guy with him, Pete, who waltzed into my room, uninvited, looking around.

He told me how the guy in the room before me had said he hated the hall food and got his parents to pick him up and take him home when really he'd just been homesick. Pete shook his head, indicating this was a pathetic reason.

I wasn't sure if it was pathetic or not. I couldn't ever have imagined being homesick.

'Have you unpacked then?' Pete asked, frowning.

I was suddenly embarrassed. I wasn't sure if I had too much stuff or not enough. By the curious look on Pete's face, it was obviously not enough.

'I need to get some posters or something for these walls,' I said quickly, so they wouldn't think I was as bland as my lack of belongings might suggest. Or that I was okay with bare walls, which I was.

'Cover as much of the brown as you can,' Pete said, then gave me a big smile. 'It's the only way to survive.' I liked him straight away.

'I've got a spare poster you can have,' said Will. 'It's of Stewie from *Family Guy*. My sister gave it to me.'

'I'll take it,' I said, laughing.

They were both architecture students. Will from London. Pete from Nottingham. I told them I was from Dorset, which was the only truthful thing I told anyone about my past from that day on.

Even Izzy.

My mother died when I was six. She dropped dead on the spot while hanging the washing out in the garden. She was thirty-three. My father couldn't cope with me on his own as I was, in his words, a bit of a tearaway, so he handed me over to social services for 'some breathing space' to get his life in order.

But he never came back to claim me and never visited.

I found out much later, when I had left college, that he had developed a drink problem, a problem I think he had before my mother died, and was living in sheltered accommodation. I tried to find him, but each time I located the hostel or bedsit he was apparently staying in, he'd moved on. I gave up.

I should have felt relief that I had been saved from him and a life of poverty and neglect, but I didn't. Not a day goes by I don't wish he had kept me, no matter what the circumstances. I had to accept he was a weak, spineless man, limbless like a worm, where the only option he had was to go to ground.

When I imagine where he is now, I see a dingy bedsit with newspaper spread over the floor. The air is rancid, and lying in the shabby sheets on the bed is my father, cocooned in his own waste, barely able to wriggle. It's a grotesque thought that makes my chest tighten as the fear of becoming him takes a grip. I might be spineless too. I'm certainly not showing strong signs of being anything else right now.

Martha and Bradley were my foster parents first before they adopted me. And they were perfectly fine and up to the job. They were solid and dependable; exactly what an abandoned child needs. She was always there for me with a nutritious snack when I came back from school. And he would bring me every Saturday morning, without fail, to kick a football around in the local park for exactly thirty minutes.

To anyone looking in, it was an idyllic family setting and I was, of course, fortunate to have landed on my feet.

I played the happily adopted child well. I kept up in school and had excellent manners, and said things like 'yay' and 'wow' in the moments I knew required that kind of response – for example, when Martha said I could have ice cream after dinner.

But I resented them and their magnolia-coloured house. It had a strange smell that never went away and that I never got used to – a mixture of musty clothes and wet gravel.

I made the necessary effort though. From the minute I arrived, aged six, I sucked it up, pretending to be a happy, contented child, even training myself to laugh convincingly at Bradley's bad jokes, puns mainly.

The way I saw it, I had no choice but to play along with the charade. Instinct told me I needed to keep Martha and Bradley on my side, as they were my only hope. The social worker who had dropped me off at the house that day had been very specific with his instructions.

'Be a good boy, okay? You want this to work out.'

From his serious tone, I knew that the alternative, whatever it was, was not going to be pretty.

During the first few weeks living with them, I didn't speak at all. I was scared to open my mouth in case I said the wrong thing, or worse still, burst out crying and wasn't then able to stop. I believed that either outcome would not have boded well for me. My mother had just died, I was beginning to understand that my father wasn't coming back, and there I was in a strange home being offered chocolate chip cookies, which I later discovered was a rare treat.

The dry biscuits cut my throat as I tried to swallow and smile at the same time.

It became a matter of survival, and as soon as Martha and Bradley broached the subject of calling them mum and dad, I agreed with fake enthusiasm. And when they announced they were going to adopt me, I said my biggest 'yay' yet.

I told myself they were only words and didn't mean they were actually my mum and dad.

In many ways they really did do their best. My school uniform was laid out for me every day and my packed lunch ready on the kitchen counter.

I was allowed to watch half an hour of television a day and we always had dinner together. They would ask me how school had been, and I would say it was great regardless of whether it was or not. Then they would generally discuss things that had to be done around the house and in the garden. Bradley better fix that shelf in the garage but he needed a special kind of screwdriver. What colour should they paint the downstairs bathroom? Should they get the carpets steam-cleaned again?

Bradley had converted the garage into what he called a man's cave, but it was nothing of the sort. It had what can only be described as unidentifiable crap overflowing on the shelves and floor. Old paint pots, oil cans, numerous broken bicycle pumps and big rusty screws. There were two old bicycle frames and boxes stacked on top of boxes, rotting in the damp.

He also had a shed at the back of the garden stuffed full of even more crap as well as the lawnmower, which he liked to get out on a Sunday afternoon just to make sure the neighbours could hear him mowing the lawn.

In the middle of the garage was a trestle table with plastic chairs that wobbled when you sat on them because the concrete floor was uneven. Bradley had the neighbours over for poker nights occasionally. Maybe twice a year.

He would have liked to have more 'nights with the lads' as he called them, but he didn't like paying for the refreshments. I heard him speaking to Martha about it.

'A few beers and snacks set me back thirty quid,' he moaned.

'It's not worth it, Bradley,' Martha replied in her whiny voice.

The funny smell in the house was strongest in the garage and the kitchen, which is why I began to suspect the origin of the unsavoury aroma came from Bradley himself.

One evening he fell asleep on the sofa and I snuck up and put my nose to his bare forearm sticking out of his rolled-up shirt sleeve. I took a big sniff and the stench made me retch.

Bradley worked in finance, but he never talked about it. He left every morning at eight, wearing a dark blue suit, and arrived home every evening at six-thirty, not a second later. And it never changed. He never had a day off, not even if he was sick.

Martha tried to be affectionate towards me, giving me short sharp squeezes with her spindly arms every now and then, but I couldn't stand her touching me.

It wasn't her fault, of course. The problem was I could still remember my mother. Her fresh, smiling face with glistening blue eyes and wild, golden hair, her warm arms wrapped around me, pulling me into her, part of her being, two souls in one.

I didn't have any photographs of my mother, only images I could muster from memory. And the more time passed, the more perfect the image of her became. She was a goddess rising from the ocean, carried by dolphins.

On one of Bradley's 'lads' nights', I crept into the kitchen to listen at the door to the garage. I was ten years old and curious what Bradley was doing with his friends. Were they smoking and drinking? I wondered if I'd be able to get my hands on some of the alcohol to see what it tasted like.

I could hear them talking and one of the men was telling a story about how his wife was volunteering at a homeless shelter. The man was proud of his wife's charitable nature and boasted how she was always thinking of others.

'I know what you mean,' Bradley said. 'It's like me and Martha. We wanted to give some of those kids, all on their tod, a second chance in life, so we took Tristan in and we're bringing him up like he's our own.'

'And he's lucky,' chimed in another voice.

'Taking in a child like that. Not everyone's that generous,' said another.

'It's not about being generous,' said Bradley, his voice a tad smug. 'It was just something we felt we had to do, we didn't even think about it. Just signed up and took the first child that came along.'

'That boy's a credit to you, Bradley.'

'People like you should get an award for what you do.'

'I don't need an award,' said Bradley, but his tone implied he'd be happy to receive one. 'To know we gave a child in need a good home is all we care about.'

I backed quietly away and went straight to my room, lay on my bed and gazed up at the florescent stickers of the moon which Martha had stuck to the ceiling. Despite Bradley's shameless bragging, I knew I should be grateful to them, but the trade-off was imbalanced. While they had given me a roof over my head, fed me and kept me safe, I had added far more meaning to their life than they had to mine.

I was a badge of honour; a way to garner respect and admiration from their friends and neighbours. I gave them something to feel worthy about. In return, I lost a sense of who I was. With all the pretending and the lying, my true self had disappeared, down a drain and into the sewers. Where it remained. Sloshing about until the day I left.

Even when I got to college and settled into halls, I couldn't quite drag myself up from the murky depths.

That was until I met Izzy.

Not that I bared my soul to her, far from it. But the feverish passion I felt for her unleashed the part of me that was desperate for love and real affection. The part of me that longed to be touched, and by someone I wanted to be touched by.

But in the last two years I have been slowly sliding down that drain again, hopelessly trying to wedge myself in the pipe to stop from plunging into the dark well below, though my hands and feet keep slipping.

Then, in the dead of night, I laid eyes on the woman in black and somehow she summoned me back to the land of the living.

6

Her

I met Viv two weeks ago. It was a muggy Saturday afternoon and, to distract myself from thoughts of Jude, not to mention the obvious problems in my marriage, I went supermarket shopping. I pushed the trolley aimlessly up and down the aisles, randomly picking up items, peering at packets then putting them back. Did we need frozen oven chips? What about gluten-free jam tarts? I wandered into the gardening section surrounded by joyful, hopeful plants in brown plastic pots, little orphans waiting to be selected and given a home. When we first bought the house, I'd had plans to create a vibrant, flourishing garden, but since Tristan refused to mow the lawn or even look at the shed, I had lost interest too.

I was about to ditch my trolley and scurry out of the supermarket when some cheerful pansies caught my eye. Some were yellow and mahogany, others white and lavender. They were bright and beautiful and screaming 'pick me' to every passing shopper. I grabbed a tray and put it into my trolley. An elderly man, perusing the other pots, gave me a knowing nod. I told myself it was a gardener's nod – from one green-fingered soul to another.

Once home, I put the pansies outside by the back door, proud of my impulse purchase. I was excited to wake up in the morning and see them waving at me through the kitchen window. Maybe it would reignite Tristan's desire to have a garden, and a wife, worth spending time with. Maybe gardening would make me less of an un-normal person. I said I didn't want our new neighbour to be a weirdo when I was really talking about myself.

I don't want to be a weirdo and I worry that I am. Gardening definitely qualifies as normal behaviour. Serial killers should garden. People would trust them more and suspect them less.

For my new and only flower bed, I chose a section of grass halfway up the garden next to Mrs Jenkins' fence. As the trowel penetrated the lawn and hard ground beneath, I was exhilarated by the sense of control it gave me, something I had not had a lot of lately. I dug away, on my knees, covered in dirt, shovelling soil and muck out of the patch. I paused for a moment, wondering if tight against the fence was the right place for the pansies. I looked up into the sky trying to ascertain the position of the sun. Would they get enough light? Tough, I thought. The hole was pretty much dug now and would look awful if I left it. The pansies would just have to do their best to survive, like the rest of us.

Midway through scooping the earth back into the flower bed around the newly planted pansies, I heard a familiar squeak followed by a creaking sound. I stopped and wiped my hair from my eyes, leaving a smudge of earth across my forehead that I tried to remove with the back of my wrist but knew I had probably only added to the problem. The familiar sound was the noise of Mrs Jenkins' back door opening. Either it was a burglar or the new neighbour had arrived.

Bent forward on my hands and knees, taking care not to flatten my pansies, I squinted through a narrow slit in the fence. The shadow of a person moved across the garden, swishing in and out of my restricted view. I switched to another slit, trying to see who it was, but the image was fragmented and unclear. I couldn't tell if the person was male or female, young or old. The sound of footsteps on the narrow stone path that snakes up the centre of the garden told me they were moving down the garden to the end.

I leaned even further into the fence, my nose squished against the timber. My right eye shut and my left eye pushed so close to the fence it was in danger of getting a splinter. Then the fence shuddered and shook and I shot backwards onto my bum, nearly taking the heads off the pansies. I landed in the most unflattering way, my legs crooked and sprawling in the air, the slope in the garden making it hard for me to sit up immediately. Through the hazy sun, I saw a woman's pretty face surrounded by a halo of soft blonde hair peering down at me. There were stars in my eyes, either from the blood rushing too quickly to my head or from sparkles in her hair.

'Hey,' she said. 'Were you spying on me?'

'Yes,' I replied. 'I totally was. Sorry. Are you the new neighbour?'

I managed to heave myself onto my elbows, hoping I looked less ridiculous propped up, as though I had planned to lie in my garden like this.

'I suppose I am,' she said. 'Do you need some help?'

'I'm fine,' I said, scrambling to my feet. I wondered how she was managing to look over the fence at me. She must be very agile and light to climb up on the other side, I thought. She glanced down at the butchered hole in the ground barely holding my flowers upright.

'I like your pansies,' she said.

'Thanks. It's kind of an experiment. I'm not really a big gardener.'

She tilted her head slightly. With her long slender green eyes, she looked like a lizard princess inspecting me.

'I'm Viv,' she said.

She slipped her arm over the fence and held her hand out to me. I wiped my muddy hands on my jeans and stepped forward, standing either side of my pansies, and shook her hand. Her hand was hot and strong, which surprised me as I half expected it to vanish into thin air, along with the rest of her.

'I'm Izzy,' I said. 'Welcome to the street.'

'Do you want to try my homemade elderberry wine?' she asked.

'Er, sure,' I said.

'Come through,' she said, waving for me to follow her over the fence.

'I'll walk around the front,' I called to her, hoping she wasn't expecting me to climb over.

A splintering noise made me step back as two lower panels in the fence swung into my garden creating a flap. Viv stuck her head through, looking up at me.

'Secret door,' she said with a big grin. 'We'll need one if we're going to be friends.'

I stared at her, unsure what to think. Had she broken my fence? Or was it her fence?

'It's not broken, just loose,' she said, reading my mind.

What the hell, I thought, and got down on my knees and crawled through to the other side. I stood up and tried to dust myself down.

'Sorry, I'm a bit mucky.'

'Best way to be,' she said. 'Natural and fresh.' She reached forward and gently wiped the smudge of dirt from my forehead.

'Thanks,' I said, feeling awkward to be touched by someone I'd only just met.

She was wearing short red wellies and denim dungarees with a bright pink vest underneath, and was holding a garden hose in her right hand. The dungaree and vest straps had fallen off her right shoulder and I noticed how her skin was sallow and creamy. She wasn't wearing a bra, but her breasts were pert and round, standing up unaided as if by magic. Her hair was wilder and longer than I had first perceived, flowing over her shoulders and down her back.

She dumped the hose on the ground and I followed her through the back door and into the kitchen, which was completely unchanged since Mrs Jenkins had lived there. The same old rickety country-style cupboards, the stained and peeling linoleum breakfast bar. The only new addition was a small wooden dining table with a chipped veneer top and four timber chairs with worn and shredded fabric-covered seats, literally on their last legs. I was surprised this was her furniture. Had she found it in a skip? Maybe it was temporary until her actual furniture arrived.

There were three unpacked boxes and a tarnished stainless steel kettle sitting on Mrs Jenkins' old gas hob.

Viv bustled around, looking in the boxes.

'I have glasses somewhere.'

I was tongue-tied. I couldn't say 'I like what you've done with the place', as she clearly hadn't done anything. And I couldn't say 'so what are your plans for the place', in case she didn't have any and liked it the way it was.

'I'm only here for the day. I'm not officially moving in for another couple of weeks.'

That explained it and I was relieved there was no call for me to comment at all. I sat down on one of the chairs and my bottom sank into the middle of the worn cushioned seat reminding me of sitting on a toilet. I wondered how many other bums had sat there before me in order to cause such sagginess.

'Here we are,' she said brightly and pulled out two dusty goblets from a box. She blew into each of them, clearing out any cobwebs, and put them on the countertop, which also needed a good old scrub. She then lifted an even dustier wine bottle from a shopping bag on the floor, which was filled with a cloudy liquid I could only describe as rust-coloured. I eyed the bottle, fearful of putting the murky solution anywhere near my lips.

'I've been trying to make my own elderberry wine for ages but keep messing it up. This is the first year it's actually drinkable.'

Using a corkscrew she pulled the cork out of the top of the bottle. It slopped more than popped though, which made me even more suspicious. She poured the wine into the glasses, nearly filling them to the top. I half expected it to bubble and emit vapour. It didn't look drinkable at all, but I know nothing about homemade wine and thought this might be what it was supposed to look like. Also, my need for Viv to like me meant I wasn't going to refuse or question the offering.

'Last year my bottles exploded because the fermentation hadn't finished. And the year before, a spider got into the batch, which was another disaster.'

She passed me a glass and picked up hers.

'To new neighbours,' she said and took a gulp.

'Cheers,' I said and took a tentative sip that made me wince and my eyes water. It wasn't just the sourness of the vinegar taste, there was something pungent about it too.

'Pretty horrible, isn't it?' she said, holding her glass up and looking at it with disgust.

'I wouldn't know,' I said. 'I'm not sure how it should taste.'

She swooped my glass away from under my nose and dumped both glasses in the sink.

'I don't want to poison you on our first date,' she said playfully. 'Maybe wine-making isn't for me, but I like trying new things, don't you?'

'Who doesn't?' I said, wracking my brain for something new I had tried recently. Did gardening count? Or encouraging a student to fall in love with me? But I didn't think that was the type of activity Viv was referring to. In fact, it would have been better if I hadn't been able to think of anything at all.

She reached down and took a bottle of Bacardi from the same bag the wine was in.

'This'll clean our palates,' she said, grabbing two more goblets from the box on the counter and blowing them free of dust. I wondered where she'd been storing her boxes or, if she hadn't been storing them, where on earth she had been living before this.

She sloshed two rather large measures into the glasses and left the bottle open on the side. She downed half of hers and took a deep breath, rolling her neck a little. I took a sip. It was four in the afternoon and I didn't want to get tipsy and let my guard down. My instincts told me that Viv was one of those people who liked to get you to 'open up'. Then I'd have to tell Tristan where I had been, drinking in the afternoon with the new neighbour, and I didn't want him to know about her, not yet anyway. I wasn't sure why.

'Is it just you moving in?' I asked.

'Just me,' she said. 'Relationships don't really suit me.'

'I don't think they suit a lot of people,' I found myself saying, looking down at my wedding ring finger. I'd taken my ring off to plant the pansies, so there was no reason for her to assume I was married. I wondered if I was being a people pleaser, or if I really believed what I had said. Did I want Viv to think I was one of those people not suited to relationships?

'What do you do?' I asked her.

'I'm an artist,' she said. 'Sculpture mainly.'

'Really,' I said, genuinely impressed.

'Let me guess what you do,' she said, flicking her eyes over me. I fiddled with my hair, suddenly self-conscious.

'I would say you do a job that requires self-control.'

'What does that mean?'

'That you have to be on your best behaviour,' she said.

Her accuracy sent a chill through me.

'Oh, I know, are you a police woman?'

I stared at her, frowning in surprise. She giggled.

'Obviously not. Go on then, tell me.'

'I'm a teacher in a sixth-form college. A-level psychology.'

'Teacher is kind of the same as a police woman,' she said. 'You have to be well behaved all the time, don't you? No swearing at the students, and make sure you don't accidentally offend someone, especially these days.'

'I suppose. I don't really think about it,' I said, feigning nonchalance as Jude's face came to mind.

'I couldn't do it,' she said. 'I'd get fired on the first day for being inappropriate.' She laughed, but it was all getting too close to the truth for me.

'I'm sure you've got plenty to be getting on with,' I said, removing my bum from the sunken seat, half expecting it to make a suction sound as it released my cheeks from its grasp. I didn't want to outstay my welcome. I also didn't want to be analysed anymore in case I started revealing things about myself that I would then regret. In that moment, I had felt very alone, aware that I had no one to confide in about Jude, no one who would understand anyway. I've barely seen Sophie, my best friend from school, since she got married, moved to France and had kids. She's too far removed from my life now to understand it. I know what she'd say though: 'You always have so much more fun than me.' I would roll my eyes. Then she'd say: 'But seriously, fucking stop it or you'll end up with nothing.' My inner Sophie is my voice of reason; the normal voice that struggles to restrain my increasingly erratic behaviour.

'Wait,' Viv said. 'I have something you might like.'

She slipped into the adjoining dining room and I heard a ripping and rustling sound. I stood in the kitchen, not sure what to do with my hands. I had an urge to look in the shopping bag and rifle through her unpacked boxes. Instead, I squeezed my hands into the back pockets of my jeans and tried to adopt a casual waiting stance.

'Here it is,' she called out from the other room.

I felt pressured about what she was going to give me. What if it was a painting or sculpture, created by her, that I didn't like? She would expect to see it up on my kitchen wall or on the mantlepiece in my living room when she popped over to borrow a cup of sugar.

She appeared at the kitchen door holding a bulging cloth bag with the handles tied tightly at the top. She crinkled her green eyes as she held it out to me. At least it wasn't a painting or a sculpture. Maybe it was a wall hanging. That would be a bit too hippy for me and Tristan.

'Don't look now. Wait until you get home.'

Relief flooded through me. Any awkward moment had been averted and I'd have time to work out a way to store the item without hurting her feelings.

'Thank you, that's so kind,' I said, taking the bag.

'If you don't like it, bring it back,' she said, touching me on the arm. But I knew I wouldn't do that. Whatever was in the bag I was going to have to keep. It would be rude not to.

Viv came out into the garden with me and held the bag as I crawled back through the fence. She appeared once again at the top of the fence, as if a gust of wind or a cloud had lifted her up there, and passed the cloth bag down to me. It wasn't particularly heavy or light, so impossible to make any guesses regarding the contents, but she handled it gently suggesting it was fragile.

'Do you live on your own too?' she asked. Something told me she knew the answer to that question already, the same way I knew the answer when I asked her. I still hesitated though.

'No, with my husband. It's just the two of us.'

'Oh, you didn't mention him,' she said, a twinkle in her eye.

'Didn't I? Thanks for this,' I said, referring to the bag, ignoring her curiosity.

'See you in a couple of weeks,' she said, and was gone.

Her back door made a crunching sound as it shut and silence fell once more upon the garden and the house. I asked myself again why I hadn't mentioned Tristan. Was it because I didn't want her to become more interested in him than me, or was it that I wanted her to believe I was a free spirit, like her, not tied down to anything or anyone? Either way, whatever the reason, I clearly cared what Viv thought of me.

I walked back into my own kitchen running my tongue over my teeth, the foul taste from the elderberry wine still lingering in my mouth. I put the cloth bag on the clean, polished dining table we'd bought in IKEA, still with zero scratches or stains. I sat down on one of the four wooden chairs, also still in mint condition, and stared at the bag. I wiggled my bum around and decided that Viv's old sunken chair was actually far more comfortable than this unforgiving sturdy one. Maybe we need to be nicer to our backsides, ensure we always have a soft landing.

The bag slumped in the middle of the table, misshapen, although I wasn't sure what shape it was meant to be. Whatever it was, it was going to say a lot about Viv's first impression of me. I pulled it towards me, slowly untied the handles and let the bag flop open. Inside was a silky mound of shimmering fabric. I put my hand in to feel the material, which was smooth and soft. Maybe a shawl or a dress. If it was a clothing garment, I knew immediately it wasn't something I would ever have the confidence to wear. I lifted it out, letting it unravel slowly, standing to allow the full length to unfold. Finally it slithered out of the bag completely and I held it up in front of me.

It was a long, slinky, delicate taupe-coloured cape with a hood and silver fastener at the top. The light through the window caressed the material, rippling across it, creating gentle waves in the fabric. It took my breath away. I wasn't sure when someone would wear something as elegant as this. Maybe on stage in a period drama. I ran the length of it over my bare arm, mesmerised by how the material swirled together so effortlessly, forming a snake-like shape and then fanning out again, wavering in the late afternoon sun.

My wardrobe is packed full of clothes I never wear, and Tristan's is only ever half full. I contemplated moving some things from my wardrobe into his, but I didn't want to have to answer questions about it. We still haven't put a wardrobe in the spare room and the box room still has unpacked boxes in it. I had to find a home for the cape and the only option was to edit my wardrobe and make space for it. I freed up three hangers to give the cape the room it needed to avoid being crushed and wrinkled. I selected a shirt, a blazer (which I had actually never worn) and two pairs of jeans I'd kept from when I was nineteen. I folded them carefully, put them into a bin liner and dumped them in the boot of my car, getting rid of the evidence.

Running back up to the bedroom, I stood in front of my open wardrobe, staring at the cape, biting the nail on my little finger. There was plenty of time to try it on before Tristan arrived home. I stripped down to my underwear and threw my garden clothes in a pile in the corner of the room. I slipped the cape from its hanger and swept it over my shoulders, allowing it to settle around my body, falling midway down my calves. The silky sensation caressed my skin, brushing up against my legs and sliding across my back. I turned to look at my reflection in the full-length mirror on the inside of the wardrobe door, my underwear partly visible in the gap running down the middle. Rising up onto my tiptoes, my calf muscles tensed, giving more shape to my legs. I turned for a side view, watching the material slink and flow down my lower back and over my bum, and realised how much I had missed being womanly and sexy. I had been hiding away, afraid of the effect my exposed femininity might have, the power it could unleash within me and the consequences that could follow. I felt bold and brave, channelling an ultimate feminine being who didn't care about the destruction she caused in her wake. 'Fuck everyone else,' she calls into the forest. 'All that matters is the pursuit of my own pleasure.' I imagined her voice to have a slight reverb.

Carefully, as though handling an explosive device, I removed the cape and hung it back in the wardrobe. I planned on telling Tristan all about Viv and the elderberry wine and cape as soon as he arrived home. Maybe even about Jude. But when he walked through the door that night and sloped upstairs for a shower saying he needed to wash the smell of Monty's lobster special out of his hair, I decided some things are on a need-to-know basis. And you don't have to tell your spouse everything; in fact, you should definitely keep some things to yourself.

This morning, I told Tristan that I had only met Viv briefly, which made it almost acceptable that I hadn't told him about meeting her at all. But to have been inside her house, and drunk her homemade wine and accepted an extravagant gift and not told him about it, well, that was a whole other level of deception. There was no choice but to add this secret to the others. At least I wasn't as ashamed of this one.

7
Him

The lunchtime shift has gone smoothly and Monty only had to shout 'take it hot' three times, which we're all pleased about.

Maddy flops back on the sofa seats in one of the alcoves, exhausted. Spencer is washing crystal brandy glasses behind the bar.

'I'm getting old,' Maddy moans.

'That's why you need to grab life's opportunities while you can, like having a drink with me later,' Spencer says in a jovial manner.

I'm surprised at how he continues to be a glutton for punishment. Either that or he's so arrogant he can't accept that Maddy simply isn't interested. My feeling is it's the former.

Maddy leans up on her elbows and narrows her eyes, looking forward to cutting him down to size then wiping the floor with him. I focus on cashing up the till.

'You know what your problem is?' she says to him.

'I'm irresistible?'

'You see, I don't know if that's a line or you actually believe it.'

'What does it matter, if it's true?' he says.

'It matters because if it's a line, you're just a creep. But if you really think it's true, which it isn't, then you are genuinely a sad fucker destined to die alone.'

It's not the first time Maddy's pressed Spencer's 'death button', but she's never been quite this antagonistic before.

Spencer tries to laugh it off. 'Ooh, is it that time of the month?'

I cringe for him. He's so inappropriate sometimes, you wonder if he grew up in another universe. And he's no match for Maddy. She will win.

Maddy doesn't move from her position, lounging on the sofa. She ignores his comment. Nice power move, I think.

'You're kind of doomed, whichever one it is. And once your baby boy looks fade, and they will, and your girth expands, all sooner than you expect, and you can't pull the girls anymore – bang, that's when the loneliness will hit you, deep in your flabby gut.'

Spencer turns to me and scoffs, like he hasn't a clue what she's talking about and expects me to be just as confused.

'You're mad,' he says to her, shaking his head.

It's a terrible comeback and I almost step in to save him as Maddy eyes him with interest, shifting swiftly from grazing leopard ripping into the carcass of a gazelle to circling vulture waiting to feed on the rotting bones.

'What is it you fear the most, the silence or the truth you're nobody special?' she carries on, relentless, not that he's even listening to her anymore.

Spencer folds his cloth for polishing glasses and leaves it on the bar top.

'I'll be back at six to set up for tonight,' he says to me, grabbing his wallet and keys from the whiskey shelf.

'Is that it?' she says, goading him.

Spencer ignores her and heads for the door, walking past her long protruding legs.

'Are you fucking serious?' she says, amused. 'Did I get the dispenser to shut up?'

Spencer stops and turns to her, suddenly unafraid of her sharp tongue.

'I thought you were a nice person, that's all,' he says and walks out, the door swinging shut behind him.

I hide a smile, impressed by Spencer's accidentally cutting remark. The beauty of it was it came from the heart and that's always hard to compete with.

'Did you hear that?' Maddy says, as though Spencer's the one who was harsh.

I keep my head down and carry on cashing up.

'I think he got the message this time,' I say.

'He's a fucking idiot,' she blurts out and, huffing and puffing, takes the stairs down to the wine store to get her bag. She's not happy about Spencer saying she isn't a nice person. Looks like Maddy has her buttons too.

I check the time. If I leave soon, I can be home at four and then back to work for six. If Izzy's not there, I'll drop in on the new neighbour and welcome her myself.

Izzy's rust bucket isn't in the drive, so she's not home yet. I glance over at the new neighbour's house. All the curtains are open and there's a green plant on one of the window ledges.

I scramble for my front door key, in a rush now to get in and clean up before going next door to introduce myself.

As I enter the house, I'm struck by the golden afternoon light streaming in from the kitchen windows, filling the hallway. The house feels brighter and warmer than usual, although I'm never normally home at this time. I put the bottle of wine on the hall table and take the stairs two at a time to the bathroom upstairs.

Splashing water on my face, I go over what I'm going to say to the new neighbour. Shall I go with a casual approach?

Hey, I heard we had a new neighbour. This is just to say welcome.

I imagine swinging the bottle between my fingers and cringe. Spencer could get away with that, but not me. I could try a more helpful tone.

If you need anything, just ask. I believe you met my wife, Izzy?

I believe you met my wife? Who am I, lord of the manor?

Just be yourself, that's what people always say, but it's not that easy for some of us. I envy people who really know who they are.

I wasn't even myself with Izzy when I first met her. But I was so in love, which was a confusing amalgam of intense pleasure and pain. Barely able to concentrate if she wasn't within five feet of me and struggling to keep my hands off her when she was. It didn't matter who I was or wasn't. Being with Izzy changed me into somebody else; a person I much preferred. I was funny, for one thing. And sexy. And smart with potential, all because I was with her. I don't feel the same way anymore and it makes me sick to even think about it.

I brush my teeth with Izzy's whitening toothpaste and slap a smidgen of aftershave on my face. Just enough to create a faint aroma. But I forgot how strong it is and even the tiniest amount fills the bathroom. I quickly rinse it off. I only bother with it for special occasions, not that we've had many of those lately.

Hopefully Izzy won't be home too soon and won't venture up here straight away and smell it. Even if she does, I doubt she'll ask me about it.

My work shirt still looks presentable and the top button is undone. I have a slightly hairy chest, so I'm pleased to see a few strands poking over the top.

I charge back downstairs, two steps at a time again, and pick up the bottle of red I took from work, all paid for and recorded in the till. It's a nice Crozes-Hermitage. If the new neighbour asks about it, I'll say it's medium-bodied with a hint of cherries and peppery spice.

Although I'm not sure 'body', 'cherries' and 'spice' are the right words to be using around this woman, especially after my wannabe-stripper performance in the garden earlier.

I do up my top button. Better to look serious and proper. My phone beeps with a message. It's from Maddy. *Whats Spencers problem. Oversensitive or what.*

He can handle it, I message back.

I wait for a moment. She doesn't reply. I don't want to tell her not to worry about it, as she was actually quite horrible to him – he's the easy target here, not Maddy. And I don't want to agree with her either, because even if Spencer is oversensitive, his reaction was still warranted. But I do believe he can handle it.

I take one last look at myself in the small round mirror in the hall, happy enough with how I look. Smart, relaxed, friendly, that's the vibe I'm going for.

There's still no sign of Izzy. It's nearly four-thirty, which means she'll be home soon. I want to do this without her, the same way she did it without me. I feel totally justified.

Standing at the new neighbour's front door, bottle of wine in hand, I press the familiar doorbell. The buzzing sound makes me think of Mrs Jenkins and how her mere presence had somehow kept me and Izzy close and together.

Waiting for the door to open, I begin to panic. What if she invites me inside?

I loosen my collar. I'll say I have to get back to work, which is true. It's also my excuse for Izzy as to why I couldn't wait for her.

I'll say I manage a restaurant and mention which one it is, in case she wants to come in sometime for a meal. No, too smarmy. I'll leave out the bit about which restaurant and coming in.

Keep it short and sweet. In and out. Minimal words. Smile, but not too much. If she mentions the shed this morning, I'll shrug, like it's nothing. Yeah, I was looking for something. No big deal.

Get a grip, she's not going to mention the shed.

'Hello,' comes a voice from above.

I step back from the front door and look up at the window. It's her.

She's wearing a bathrobe with the hood up. Like last night, the hood is large and floppy and covers half her face. Also the sun is reflecting off the window, making it hard for me to see her properly.

'Hi, I'm Tristan from next door. Your neighbour. I was just bringing you this,' I bluster, holding up the bottle of wine. 'To say welcome and all that.'

'Oh, that's really kind.' Her voice is silky and distant.

'I'll leave it on the doorstep. Sorry to have bothered you.'

'You haven't bothered me,' she says.

'It's red. French,' I say, getting flustered. 'From the restaurant I run, manage.'

Stop talking and don't mention cherries or spice.

'Sorry, I'm not used to talking to strangers in a window,' I shout up.

'Who says we're strangers?' she murmurs, looking down at me. I squint with the sun in my eyes, wishing I could see her more clearly.

'We're neighbours now, aren't we?' she says.

'Right, well, if you need anything, just ask.'

'Why don't you bring the wine back later, Tristan?' she says.

She pronounces my name Tris-tan. Like it's two words. I like it.

'Later?' I say, a lump in my throat.

'I'm having a housewarming party. I'd love you and Izzy to come.'

'Party. Right. Cool.' Don't say 'cool', never say 'cool'. 'Sounds great. I might not be there till late as I'm working.'

'At your restaurant, yes.'

I never said it was my restaurant, but who am I to correct her.

'I'll tell Izzy. I'll take this with me then.' I hold the bottle up again, like it's a trophy.

'We'll have a drink together later,' she says.

I raise my hand, a gentleman's gesture for 'see you then' and walk back down the drive. Only when I reach the bottom of the drive do I hear the window shut.

I come back into the house, close the door behind me, taking a moment to recalibrate. In retrospect that seemed to go rather well. I look at myself in the mirror again. I'm a little flushed, not because I'm thinking about having sex with the new neighbour, but because it matters to me what this woman thinks of me.

Although, if I'm honest, I'm also thinking about having sex with her.

I allow myself to fantasise how that would play out. Me, naked, lying on my back, ready, waiting. Her, lowering slowly from above in a cloud of silver mist, wearing a barely-there lace nightdress with a hood hanging over her eyes. A gentle breeze lifts her nightdress above her waist, as she comes to sit perfectly astride my quivering torso, 'Bohemian Rhapsody' blasting in the background.

The sound of Izzy's rust bucket rattling onto the driveway breaks my reverie. I open the door as she switches off the engine and waves at me through the windscreen. I wave back. Not a gentleman's gesture this time, more of a boyish hello.

'You made it home,' she says, entering the hallway and dropping her bag on the floor. She sees the wine on the side. 'Well done for getting wine. I forgot.' She's being warm and friendly. I feel guilty about my epic fantasy about the new neighbour.

'I've already been round with the wine. I have to get back to the restaurant.'

She pauses for a moment. I'm not sure if she's annoyed or not.

'I only spoke to her through the upstairs window. She said to bring it back later. She's having a housewarming party and we're invited.'

'Ooh, a party,' she says, her warm demeanour a tad false now.

'I'll try to get off work for ten-thirty. We can go over when I get back, if you want.'

'I'll probably head over earlier than that.'

'No problem,' I say, casual. She gives me a smile.

'What's her name again?' I ask, as though off the cuff. She never told me her name this morning and I never asked.

'Viv,' she says.

Viv. I like that too.

8

Her

My finger hovers over Jude's name in the register on the iPad. I have to leave it blank. No green tick for 'in attendance'. After our run-in on the stairs this morning, I'm not surprised he's absent from class again. Maybe that's it now. He's finally given up. An uncomfortable squeezing in my chest makes me breathless for a moment. I don't want to be the reason he drops out of college or messes up his exams.

'You alright, miss?' Students are allowed and encouraged to call teachers by their first names but some of them can't shake the habit of saying 'miss' and 'sir'. They can find it hard to adapt to the more hands-off approach in a college, where it's up to them to turn up to class. If they miss more than three classes and they don't have a doctor's note, they're out, simple as that. I glance up, distracted, to see all twenty-five pairs of eyes blinking at me. I've been leaning on the desk with my head dipped, which isn't the best look for anyone, let alone your teacher. I tell them I'm fine and get busy taking my laptop and folder from my work bag. I drag myself through the lesson, making a conscious effort not to allow my voice to become monotone.

'Studies have shown that the level of sensitivity a mother shows to her baby is key to the types of attachment we make later in life.'

'So it's all my mum's fault then,' calls out a girl from the back row, causing the room to break into titters of laughter.

'Pretty much,' I say, pleased to have any student engage. It shows they're listening at least. It's a good place to end the class, even if it is ten minutes early. I give them their revision for the weekend and flop in my chair as the last student files out. The quiet brings instant relief and my body feels heavy, as though sickening for something. The door swings open again, hope rising in the back of my throat. It's Polly and, although I'm relieved, part of me is disappointed it's not Jude. She wants me to come for a drink after work. The two physics teachers, Malcolm and Tobias, are going to the Tavern so we'll go to the Tiger's Head, which according to her has the best beer garden in a twenty-mile radius. I wouldn't have minded having a drink with Malcolm and Tobias but Polly has a thing about hanging out with physics teachers.

'They're even more boring than maths teachers,' she said, when I asked her about it. I pointed out that she's a maths teacher and she's not boring but she said that's because she doesn't hang out with maths or physics teachers. Then she added chemistry teachers to the boring list as well but said biology teachers were okay.

I check my phone. Tristan hasn't messaged to say he'll be home so I'm assuming he's stuck at work as usual. I tell Polly I'll come for one but that I'm driving. She says it's no problem and that she's quite happy to drink my daily alcohol units on top of her own. I wonder what Polly would think if I told her about Jude. Would she find it funny and tell me to have sex with him? No one's ever going to say that, I tell myself harshly.

The Tiger's Head was once a charming, traditional pub with rickety, high stools lining the bar and a sticky patterned carpet that smelled of stale beer. Then the owner succumbed to social pressure, gave the place a full makeover, and now it looks like any other generic pub in England. But the staff are friendly and Polly's right, it does have the loveliest beer garden, with a green lawn surrounded by timber fencing covered in ivy and colourful climbers. Picnic tables line the sides with large purple parasols floating above each one. Later, when the sun goes down, the fairy lights along the top of the fence will twinkle and the night lights buried in the planter boxes will make the ivy glow.

Polly and I take a seat halfway down the garden beside a flourishing passion plant. Polly has stuck to her word and is having a double vodka and tonic to make up for my alcohol-free beer. It's three-thirty on a Friday afternoon but, to a lot of teachers, it's Friday night as soon as the last bell goes. If we go home first with plans to venture out later, there's a huge chance we'll fall asleep in front of the telly and miss the night altogether. Polly takes a big swig of her drink and savours the moment as it slips down her throat and into her stomach. She lets out a big sigh. I wish I wasn't driving. There's nothing I'd rather do right now than deaden my emotions with a double vodka. The beer garden is still pretty empty, with a few leftover customers from lunchtime occupying other tables before the evening crowd arrives.

'So, what's up?' Polly says to me.

I frown at her, acting perplexed.

'Is that your "I don't know what you're talking about" face?'

Heat rushes to my cheeks. I hope I'm not blushing.

'If you don't want to tell me, that's fine,' she says, grinning.

Either she has an impressive sixth sense or I'm far too easy to read. I wonder again if I should tell her about Jude. I could casually mention how a student in one of my classes has a crush on me and I'm not sure how to handle it. But what's the point in watering it down? If I'm looking for reassurance that I've handled the situation well, I'm not going to get that from anyone, not if I include every detail. Even if Polly said it was okay, she wouldn't mean it. She glances over my shoulder towards the door to the beer garden.

'That's all we need,' she says. I follow her gaze as three young guys swoop in under a parasol, plonking their drinks down and slipping their long legs under the table. I vaguely recognise them as students. One is tall and well built with long hair. He spots Polly and gives her a cheeky grin.

'Alright, Polly,' he says.

'Hello, Alex,' she replies, in her most teacherly voice.

'Can I get you girls a drink there?' he says, brazen as anything.

'No, thank you,' says Polly, turning her attention back to me. I hear smirking behind us as the other lads give Alex a ribbing for crashing and burning.

'Little fuckers,' Polly mutters to me.

'Does that happen a lot? Students flirting with you,' I ask, hoping suddenly that I'm not the only one with this issue.

'Alex is just a chancer.' She lowers her voice and leans closer to me. 'That said, you can't ignore the fact he's good-looking with chunky biceps. You've got to have your wits about you.'

'What do you mean?' I say. 'You fancy him?'

'Of course I don't fancy him, but put me in a dark night-club with too many of these,' she says, rattling the ice in her glass, 'and a fruity eighteen-year-old tells me he's twenty-six, I'm quite likely to believe him, bring him home and shag his brains out.'

I throw her a mock judgemental look and Polly roars laughing. She has a deep guttural, naughty laugh and it makes me laugh too.

'At least eighteen's an adult,' I say.

She shakes her head. 'I have a rule. No one younger than me, so no one under twenty-five. You see, anyone under twenty-one is just gross, and anywhere in between is too risky. I mean, it could be okay but it could be gross, so I don't go there.'

'Good rule,' I say, trying not to overdo the approving tone in my voice. 'So Alex doesn't have a crush on you then?' I ask.

'Put it this way: if I had him in a room on his own, he'd be whimpering at the door to get away, shaking in his little white trainers.' Polly roars laughing again.

That's the difference between Alex and Jude. Jude wouldn't be shaking or trying to get away from me. He wouldn't be afraid. He'd be pressed up against me and I'd probably go for it this time. Who cares about consequences? 'All that matters is the pursuit of my own pleasure,' cries my inner feminine spirit. I take a huge gulp of my zero beer, wishing again it was a double vodka.

'Jude,' exclaims one of the guys behind us. I nearly choke on my drink but don't turn around.

'You all alright for pints, boys?' It's Jude's voice. I stay focused on Polly, who is talking about a jacket she's seen on sale. The other lads say they're fine. I wait for a second and hear the door to the beer garden swing shut. I glance around. He's gone.

'I have to go,' I say to Polly, downing the rest of my beer. 'I forgot I promised Tristan I'd be home after work.' This is partly true. And if Tristan does come home early and I'm not there, he might go round to see Viv without me.

There's a heaviness in my heart, a dread that things between me and Tristan might be more than a little rocky.

'You're white as a sheet. Are you sure you're alright?' Polly asks.

'Yeah, just dying for a proper drink,' I say. 'Me and Tristan are saying hi to our new neighbour. They moved in last night.'

'New neighbour?' she says with a dirty grin. 'Male or female?'

'Female, young, pretty and single,' I say, filling her in quickly.

'Disaster for you then,' she says.

'I met her already. She's lovely.'

'She might be befriending the lady of the house so she can sneak in there and steal your husband.'

I shake my head fondly, like I find Polly amusing. I have accepted the fact Tristan will find Viv attractive, why wouldn't he? She's a perfectly formed, naturally beautiful, sexy woman, right on his doorstep. And he's already stirred up by her arrival, having seen her arrive in the dead of night, while I was left sleeping. But I hadn't thought about Viv finding Tristan attractive. A pulsing, nagging sensation ignites in the pit of my stomach, a smouldering jumble of fear and jealousy, neither emotion offering any reassurance or clarity. What right do I have to be jealous when I've been in compromising situations with one of my students?

'Will you be okay?' I say, apologetic for leaving so soon.

'I'm meeting friends here in a bit.' She gets on her phone. Polly has no qualms at all about hanging out by herself. I head quickly into the pub and slip down the side corridor towards the front exit. I keep my eyes forward, not looking left into the main bar. The exit is up ahead. I'm about to push through the door when Jude appears holding a pint and packet of crisps. He looks older than his nineteen years, the same way he did in his Waitrose uniform.

'Oh, hi. I'm just leaving,' I say.

He glances left and right to see if anyone can see or hear us. I know I should keep walking or at least step through the door to show intention to go, but my feet refuse to move. Is this it? Am I finally going to kiss him, right here, in a public place? And where will it lead? A quick fuck in the toilets? Is that really what I want?

'I'm sorry, for everything,' he says, looking me straight in the eye. His stillness and confidence make me uneasy. 'I'll back off,' he says. 'The last thing I want is to make you feel uncomfortable or creeped out.'

'Thank you,' I reply, adopting Polly's teacherly tone.

He gives me a sad smile and goes out to the garden. I step out of the pub and hurry back towards the college car park. My head hangs as I watch the pavement disappear under my feet with every step. Jude's apparent maturity only serves to highlight how I'm the one with a pathetic crush on him, not the other way around. What I said to him in the stairwell had the impact I intended, but now I'm the one who feels dumped. I'm the one who feels stupid, while he's out enjoying himself with his friends.

Apart from the rust bucket, the college car park is empty. I climb into my car and put my hands on the steering wheel to anchor myself. I read way too much into Jude's feelings for me. I believed there was a deep, almost mystical, fatalistic connection between us, when really it was a cheeky crush of a student on his teacher. He pushed the boundaries and I had been pathetic enough to let him, convinced the strength of his feelings for me meant the rules did not apply. If I had not been so easy to flatter, so insecure in myself, I would have dealt with the situation in the proper way and never have allowed him to kiss me in the lift.

Now I'm gripped by an urgency to fix things with Tristan. Make him feel loved again, the way I did when we first met. He'd had a lost look on his face sitting at a table with Will and Pete in the student union bar. I'd met Will and Pete in freshers' week but Tristan was new. I caught his eye, immediately holding his attention and, in that instant, something had woken up inside me; a familiar sensation, an emotion I'd long forgotten, lying dormant in the deepest, most locked-away part of myself. I couldn't identify it straight away, but when Tristan placed his hand on the small of my back later that evening at the bar, I knew what it was.

Connection.

Somewhere along the way we've lost that and I can't work out where or when it happened. I've tried retracing our steps, but there's no single moment or event that signifies a change. It's a black mould that starts behind a kitchen cupboard and slowly, unseen at first, spreads up the wall, seeping in behind the plaster where it continues to fester. You don't see it coming but once it takes root, it's impossible to remove. My eyes well with tears and I blink them away, refusing to feel sorry for myself. I only have myself to blame for everything. After all, I'm the one with the faulty genes; the one most likely to fuck things up.

The rust bucket shudders to a halt on the driveway and I see Tristan standing at the front door. I've never been more pleased to see him. I give him a wave. He waves back. I need to apologise for not sharing the fact that I met Viv two weeks ago, but for now all I want to do is hold him, smell him, rip his shirt off, run my hands over his body. I don't even want to take my clothes off. I'll just pull my dress up and we can have sex on the hall floor.

I stroll up to him and he stands aside to allow me to enter. I see a bottle of red wine on the hall table as I drop my bag on the floor.

'You bought wine,' I say. We can drink it instead. I'm sure Tristan won't mind being late in to work if he's getting laid – it's been at least six months since we last had sex.

'I went round with it already. I have to get back to the restaurant,' he says, jangling his keys in his pocket. An icy chill settles around my shoulders. He didn't wait for me. 'She's having a housewarming party and said to bring it back later.'

'A party?' I say, trying to sound nonchalant, but I can see he's flustered and excited. Thrilled, even. He's trying to hide it but he's so transparent, and my desire to pounce on him vanishes in an instant. He says he'll get off early and expects me to wait for him so we can go together. I say I'll probably drop around before that.

I've already made up my mind to get wasted. Anything to escape these incessant feelings of inadequacy.

He gives me a kiss on the cheek and I detect a waft of his aftershave. It's subtle but it's there. Not only did he put it on to meet the new neighbour, but he went to the trouble of trying to disguise it. At the door he turns to me and, as though it's a casual afterthought, asks what the new neighbour's name is. I tell him it's Viv. He pauses for a second, just long enough for me to see the spark in his eye, then he says bye and shuts the door behind him.

I pick up the wine and check the label. It's at least a thirty-pound bottle. He was definitely aiming to impress. If I'd questioned him about that, he would have reminded me it's a joint present, which it would have been if we'd brought it around to the house together. I take the bottle to the kitchen, grab a corkscrew from the drawer and proceed to open it. I like Viv and she deserves a nice bottle of wine, but I deserve it more.

I take a huge swig straight from the bottle. Fuck. This.

9
Him

I pull two dead heads off the pansies outside the restaurant, about to enter, when my phone beeps with a message. It's from Deniz, the owner. He wants a table tonight for him and his wife, table one, the first booth as you enter. I let out a sigh. He knows how busy we are on Fridays and Saturdays and that we'll be fully booked.

I wonder if he's doing it to test me or to flex his boss muscle, but Deniz isn't like that. He's just chancing his arm and won't mind if it's not possible. Still, the impetus is on me to make it happen.

The minute I step foot in the restaurant, the creamy aroma of Monty's beef bourguignon wafts up the stairs and into my nostrils. My stomach juices bubble and churn, notifying me of how ravenous I am.

I'm half an hour late for the beginning of set-up, not that I always have to be on time, but I prefer to be. Spencer is already behind the bar sliding the wine glasses into the overhead rack. He looks tired around the eyes but the minute he sees me, he grins.

'And where have you been?' He says it like I've been up to something slutty.

'I had to pop home. Everything alright?'

'Yeah, except Monty's being funny.'

The hairs on the back of my neck shoot up.

'What do you mean, funny? Bad-mood or telling-jokes funny?'

'Hard to say.'

The mild panic begins to spread through my body making me weary. I simply don't have the heart or the energy to deal with Monty tonight.

'When I asked him what the staff meal was, he said beans on toast and started laughing,' says Spencer.

'Monty laughed?'

'Do you think he might be losing it?'

'I'm sure it's fine. I'll talk to him.'

Spencer goes back to hanging the glasses and I turn the iPad at the end of the bar to face me so I can check the bookings. We're jam-packed but I can move a couple from table one upstairs to a two-top that I'll swipe from a larger table. I'll put a chair at either end to make up the numbers.

We start the table layouts generously and then reduce space if we have to, keeping an ear out for signs of rumblings when the guests arrive. If need be, we quickly furnish any potentially disgruntled tables with free glasses of prosecco, which normally does the trick. Once people are drinking they tend to be happy enough.

I message Deniz back: *No problem. See you later.*

'Where's Maddy?' I ask, turning to Spencer. He sniffs, his cheery disposition vanishing. He flicks his head towards the upper section of the restaurant.

'Laying tables,' he says.

It's clear he hasn't forgiven her for her unkind comments earlier. I was hoping Maddy would have apologised by now, but she obviously hasn't.

I put off checking on Monty and find Maddy on the upper level setting a table for ten due in at seven-thirty. She's wearing a black and white headband with her fringe almost falling in her eyes. I say hi and tell her we need to take one of the two-tops from the ten-top and put a chair at either end instead.

'Spencer's not talking to me,' she says, matter-of-factly.

'Right,' I say, preferring not to get involved.

'He's such a wuss. It's not like I meant what I said, is it? It was work banter. We all do it.'

'Have you told him you didn't mean it?' I say.

'For fuck's sake. I shouldn't have to.'

She's scrambling not to take responsibility for her harsh words. If she was joking, then this is all Spencer's problem and nothing to do with her.

'It's between you and Spencer,' I say.

'You're a great help,' she says and struts off to finish laying the cutlery on the table.

I take the staircase down to the kitchen. The bright lights, sounds of clanging pots and smells of sweet and savoury aromas awaken all my senses at once, flooding my brain with the adrenaline I need to get through the shift. And the party later.

The thought of meeting Viv in the flesh conjures up my fantasy again – her delicate frame lowering towards me as her lace night-dress rises. A rush of pleasure charges through me. In a few hours I'm going to find out what it feels like to be in her presence.

Bill, our weekend washer-upper, is scrubbing pots left over from lunchtime. He's sixty-five years old and a retired social worker. He has a good pension, so he told me, but prefers to keep working and active. 'I want a job with no hassle and no responsibility,' he explained at the interview. I gave him the job on the spot and he's the best washer-upper we've ever had and is gradually becoming a more permanent fixture, working week days too. He's also a level head in the kitchen. Not much gets him rattled.

I say hi to him as I pass by the washing-up area. He nods hello back and then quickly pulls a mock panic face, pointing towards the kitchen. Something is definitely wrong with Monty. I give Bill the thumbs up, like I've got this.

I walk on past the salad and prep area, where the assistant chef, Sita, slices peppers at lightning speed. She's thirty-five, married with three kids and has the poise of a ballet dancer. She also has a huge tattoo of a tiger on her arm, which wards off any first impressions that she might be fragile. I pause for a second to say hi. She looks at me with a grim look, nodding towards the main kitchen. I give her a thumbs up too, but I'm not feeling confident at all, just slightly nauseous.

Not daring to breach the threshold even an inch, I proceed with caution into the kitchen. Monty is singing along to the Gipsy Kings as he slices up some fish fillets.

'Hey, Monty,' I say, holding my hand up to say hello, but it looks more like I'm saluting him. He glances at me then goes back to his fish-cutting.

'All okay? Have you got everything you need?'

He stops singing and leans on his chopping board. The Gipsy Kings carry on in the background but, without Monty accompanying them, it sounds like they're one man down.

Knowing full well this is the calm before the storm, I say nothing, staying by the entrance, waiting patiently for him to explode. If he starts throwing pots, at least I can duck behind the wall. He's never aimed a flying pot at anyone on purpose, but when he's in a blind rage, he doesn't much care where they land.

He raises his head and stares at me, his eyes blinking behind his heavy-framed glasses.

'I thought we were friends,' he says, in a tight voice.

He's speaking in full sentences, so he's more angry than he looks. And 'friends' is a bit of a push. 'Colleagues' would probably suffice.

My heart sinks. What if this is about the Sainsbury's run today? Did someone he know see me buying the prawns? Did he find the receipt, which I'm sure I put in the secret petty cash box? Or did Spencer tell him, by accident of course?

Our first customers are due in twenty minutes and I need to know Monty isn't about to have a meltdown. I decide to come clean and am about to say, 'So, about the prawns,' when he holds the knife up, weighty in his hand, and points it at me.

'You're looking for a new chef,' he says, almost spitting the words at me, barely able to say them, the pain too much for him.

I have no idea what he's talking about and tell him that.

'I saw the advert. On the internet,' he yells at me, jabbing the knife in my direction. Then he does the strangest thing and starts referring to himself in the third person.

'People come to Lily's for Monty's food because Monty is one of the best chefs in London. That's why you can't get a table at Lily's, because of Monty,' he shouts, pointing the knife at himself now, which unsettles me more, as the end of the knife is far closer to his torso than it was to mine.

I quickly get on my phone, looking for this advert.

'I swear, we are not looking for a new chef. And we're not allowed to just fire you, okay? Employment law.'

'You want to fire me?' he screams, banging his knife on the chopping board.

'I didn't say that.' I manage to keep my voice steady and start referring to him in the third person too in an attempt to keep him calm. 'Why would we want to replace Monty? He's the best chef we've ever had,' I say.

Monty snorts, pacing up and down behind the countertop, knife still in his hand.

I find the advert online and read it out: 'Top head chef required for busy south London restaurant. At least five years' experience.'

'And the phone number?' he says, shaking the knife at me. I see it's the number of the office upstairs.

'I really don't know what this is about. Maybe it's a typo,' I say, searching for a sensible explanation.

'Do you think I'm thick in the head?' he yells.

I nearly tell him that I do. To even think we would replace him is madness. It's a moment of realisation for me; Monty is as insecure as the rest of us, probably more so.

'Let me find out what's going on, okay?'

'You have five minutes,' he growls.

And I know he means it. I don't even ask what he will do in five minutes if I can't adequately explain the advert. I don't want him to feel he has to follow through on a threat, so the less he commits to now the better. And I'm not going to tell him Deniz is coming for dinner in case he makes a scene in the restaurant.

I rush back upstairs, passing Sita who now has earphones in and is bobbing her head as she shreds cabbage with her hands. I pass Bill who looks at me wide-eyed, which isn't very encouraging. I give him a reassuring smile and run up the stairs to the bar, as two more evening staff arrive. Nicole and Adrian, both A-level students at a local school. They're good workers and always bring a freshness to the weekend shifts. They say smiley hellos to everyone and bounce down the stairs to put their jackets in the wine alcove.

At the bar, Spencer puts clean wine glasses on a tray for Maddy. Maddy doesn't take her eyes off Spencer, waiting for him to crack or break. But Spencer, quite skilfully, avoids eye contact. This could quite possibly be the biggest blanking in history. Maddy's tapping foot tells me that, for once, Spencer holds the power. Sadly, he doesn't know it.

'Monty thinks we've advertised for a new chef to replace him.'

'What?' Spencer says.

'He said, Monty thinks we've advertised for a new chef to replace him,' Maddy says in a humorous drawl, trying to get a reaction from Spencer, who continues to ignore her and stays focused on me.

I explain about the ad online.

'Maybe Deniz is opening another restaurant,' Spencer says.

'Maybe,' I say, hoping he's right.

'Deniz will be needing waiters and barmen too,' he says, totally implying he'd like to move jobs. Maddy, unable to hide her annoyance, grabs the tray of glasses and marches up the small set of steps to the upper level as Nicole and Adrian bound upstairs, tying their aprons and sticking pens behind their ears.

'You're not going to leave, are you?' I say to Spencer.

'I can't work with Maddy. She's evil.'

I hear my phone beep with a message and take it out of my pocket.

'She told me she didn't mean what she said. That it was work banter.'

The message is from Izzy: *Bring more wine. We should arrive with a bottle each x*

'She said that?' Spencer asks, surprised.

'Yes, so please, no more talk about finding another job.'

Spencer shrugs, humming now as he wipes down the bar. I send Izzy a thumbs-up emoji. I'm not sure I like the way I'm becoming a thumbs-up guy.

'Tristan with a T,' booms a big voice.

Deniz is standing at the door. He has a jolly smile on his face and his arms outstretched ready for a man hug. He reminds me, as he often does, of a laughing Buddha. He's early and I'm worried about Monty but quickly plaster on a smile.

He calls me Tristan with a T because for the first month I worked for him he called me Christian. I didn't correct him straight away and then it became too difficult and awkward to point it out, so I let it go. When it came to my first pay cheque, the accountant corrected him. He still thinks it's hilarious and I like that we have this private joke. It bonded us early, which makes me feel more secure in my job.

Deniz is six-foot-five with a large, stocky frame and thick black hair. The man, in a word, is formidable. But what I like most about Deniz is that he leaves me alone to run the restaurant my way with little interference. He owns a number of other bars and restaurants, so he has enough to keep him busy. He says Lily's is his favourite and I believe him.

Deniz grabs me and hugs me, accidentally shoving my head into his armpit, which thankfully smells of expensive aftershave. His wife, Gina, totters in to join him. She's mid-thirties, fifteen years younger than Deniz, and squeezed into a short, satin red dress with stiletto heels.

'Put the man down,' she says, shaking her head at us, as though she's driven demented by her husband's antics on a daily basis.

Deniz releases me and Spencer comes out from behind the bar to take Gina's jacket. Gina gives Spencer a demure look, wrinkling her nose.

'Hello, Spencer, darling,' she purrs. But Spencer has the nous not to flirt with the boss's wife.

'Nice to see you, Mrs Demirci.'

'I managed to move some bookings around and have table one for you,' I say, a hint of pride in my voice as I usher them to the first alcove. I want Deniz to know there were logistics involved in accommodating him at such short notice.

He pats me on the back and squeezes my shoulders. It strikes me how physical he is and how unphysical I am.

Gina slides into one side of the booth and Deniz climbs into the other, knocking the table and making everything shake momentarily. Spencer suggests a bottle of Deniz's favourite wine, the Fleurie. Deniz grins and tells Spencer he's golden.

'And a voddie and T for you, Mrs Demirci,' Spencer says to Gina.

'You know me too well,' she says, giving him a wink.

Spencer heads for the stairs to get the wine. Gina gets up and goes to the ladies and I ask Deniz about the advert and explain how Monty thinks he's being replaced. Deniz chuckles.

'I'm opening a new restaurant in that old hardware shop on Widmore Road,' he says. 'I've only just got the lease but I want a chef on board early. Don't tell the missus. I'm calling it Gina's, so it's a big surprise.'

Relief floods through me. Monty can't argue with that. Although this news is a reminder of how I'm not lifting a finger to improve my own life. I wasn't even aware the old hardware shop was up for lease. This is the sort of thing I'm supposed to know and act upon, number one on my weekly list of goals. At least I can tick number three today as I did actually eat an apple.

Deniz suggests we have fun with Monty and wind him up some more. I allude to how that might not be the best idea. Maddy comes to the table to say hi to Deniz.

'And how's my best waitress?' he says to her.

She beams at him and stays for a chat. I slip away as though all is calm and then charge down the stairs to the kitchen. It's been more than five minutes. I pass Spencer on his way up with the wine.

'It's too quiet down there,' he says.

'I'm on it,' I say, speeding past him.

I stride past Bill who's having a cup of tea before the mayhem starts, and Sita, still with her earphones in, whisking a large bowl of creamy dressing, and head straight into Monty's sacred space, breaching the threshold by at least three inches.

All the hob rings are off. There are no bubbling pots. The oven is cold and the counters are clear. Monty leans against the wall at the back of the kitchen inspecting his fingernails. I am powerless before him. All I can do is grovel.

'I've spoken to Deniz. The ad is for a chef for a new restaurant he's opening. It has nothing to do with Lily's.'

Monty looks at me, tight-lipped. He folds his arms.

'He's not looking to replace you,' I continue. 'He would never do that.'

He glares at me.

'Have I ever lied to you?' I say.

His eyes narrow. I worry I've gone too far and that he does secretly know about all the supermarket food I've palmed off on him over the years.

He unfolds his arms and moves his neck from side to side. Either he's getting ready to walk out, pulling pots and pans down behind him in his wake, or he's finally relaxing.

'No, you have never lied to me,' he says, holding his head high.

I swallow, keeping my face still, praying he doesn't see the guilt in my eyes.

'There you are then,' I say. 'Now, are you cooking tonight or am I sending everyone home?'

'Go, go, go,' he shouts at me, grabbing his chef hat and firing up the hob. He's back to three-word sentences so he's definitely feeling better. I'm about to give him a thumbs up but stop myself then dash upstairs.

This is not the evening I had planned. Nothing today is happening the way I expected. Things are changing and the thought that my life might not stay the same fills me with a mixture of dread and desire and I'm not sure which is which.

The last of the customers trail out the door shouting promises to be back soon and blowing us all kisses. It's only eleven but I'm eager to get going. I hope the party isn't over before I get there.

I wanted to get off by ten-thirty but with Deniz's surprise visit, Monty's meltdown and Spencer and Maddy not talking, I was forced to stay. Again, not what I was expecting.

Maddy divvies out the tips into individual piles. Adrian and Nicole grab theirs and bustle out, announcing they're going clubbing. I feel the urge to say I'm going out as well, wanting them to know that I have a life outside the restaurant too, but I don't. Nobody will care what I'm doing.

Bill emerges from downstairs, picks up his tips and heads out the door: 'Toodle-oo, everyone.'

Monty went home after the last main course was served. He didn't even tell me he was going. He let Sita finish up. When I asked her if she minded, she said she didn't at all and that working with a chef like Monty was a dream come true. I wondered what other warped dreams she had.

I quickly cash up the till as Maddy brings the last of the dirty glasses from the upstairs area to the bar to be washed.

'Leave those till tomorrow,' she says to Spencer, trying again to break the impasse between them, but Spencer ignores her, putting the glasses into the glasswasher.

'How long are you going to keep this up?' she snaps at him. Spencer carries on loading the glasswasher.

'You're such a child,' she says and walks off in a huff.

'Can you lock up?' I ask Spencer.

'Sure,' he says.

I pass him the keys and grab my wallet and house keys from behind the bar.

'I'm impressed with your staying power, by the way,' I say.

'Staying power has never been an issue for me,' he replies with a cheeky grin.

Outside on the pavement, I take a deep breath. The cool air feels fresh and green. I sniff the sleeve of my shirt checking if I smell of onions and garlic.

My hand goes to my hair. I haven't even checked my appearance. I could run into the house first and have a quick wash before the party, but what if Izzy's already been and is home now? It would be strange to go without her and so late as well. I bend down to check my hair and teeth in the wing mirror of a parked car on the road. I'm relieved to see I'm still presentable. Anyway, arriving late to a party can make you appear cool and interesting.

I head off down the street, past a large crowd of punters outside the Fox and Hounds pub beside the pond. I need to arrange a work night out. Maybe after a Saturday night shift I could bring everyone clubbing. I'm sure Deniz would let me treat the staff. I wouldn't normally have the energy to even think about something like that, but at the moment I'm buzzing. I imagine myself walking into the new neighbour's house, party in full swing, with a smart bottle of red in my hand.

Then I remember Izzy's message. I'm supposed to bring an extra bottle of wine. I turn around and dash back to the restaurant.

Pushing the door open, I expect to see Spencer behind the bar where I left him a few minutes ago. But he's not there. Maddy's nowhere to be seen either.

I hear noises coming from downstairs. I go to the top of the pink staircase to venture down to the wine alcove but stop in my tracks. Maddy, skirt pulled up around her hips and Spencer, trousers around his ankles, are going at it hard, pushed up against the large painting of the lily. I turn away quickly and hurry back out onto the street, abandoning Izzy's extra-bottle-of-wine idea.

Leaning against the restaurant window for a moment, I take a deep breath. Maddy must have finally apologised and one thing led to another. She must have also fancied Spencer from day one.

More importantly, it's been a long time since I've fucked like that.

Izzy and I were once caught on a fire escape staircase in the fancy hotel of our graduation ball. Her ball gown was up by her ears and, like Spencer, my suit trousers were bunched around my ankles. We were interrupted by a deadpan security guard who didn't say a word, just flicked his head for us to move it. We'd set the alarm off when we opened the door.

We had to travel back down in the lift with him. I suppose he wanted to make sure we didn't jump off at another floor and try it again.

Although it was an excruciating lift journey, we harboured little shame over the incident. For years we giggled about it, until one day we stopped talking about it altogether. Like we forgot it had ever happened.

A sadness sweeps over me. If we don't remember the fun stuff, what hope do we have?

Time check. Eleven-thirty. The party might well be over by now, or at least at a scraggly end.

I don't care. I'm still going.

10

Her

The half-empty bottle of red wine accompanies me upstairs as a symbol of my defiance and ability to take charge of my life, although it's just the drink talking. I know it, and the wine knows it. It's a symbiotic relationship. The wine gives me false confidence and I allow it to alter my perceptions. I take another swig from the bottle and swing open my wardrobe door. Tonight I am going to wear something feminine and sexy. I am going to pin my hair up with some loose strands falling over my cheeks and I will put on lipstick. I am back. No more hiding in the shadows, not that it did me any good. In fact, all it really accomplished was to push Tristan further away. I take another gulp of wine. Anything to keep the pain mounting inside me at bay. I stoop down to put the wine bottle on the floor and wobble as I stand up again, blood and alcohol rushing to my head. It hits the spot and a feeling of contentment washes through me. Wine should be available on the NHS. I have a lot of good ideas when I'm tipsy.

I flick my right leg – the flat shoe flies off my foot and lands on the bed. I do the same with the left foot. I pull my tunic dress up over my head and drop it on the floor. I run my eyes over my reflection in the mirror. My lacy bra gives me just enough cleavage to get noticed and my high-legged knickers accentuate the curve of my upper thighs, but my legs look short. Rummaging in the bottom of my wardrobe, I find a pair of platform wedges with silky straps. My bare feet slip into them with ease and I tie the straps lightly around my ankles. The straps aren't actually needed, they're just for show, like so many parts of my life. I stand slowly so as not to fall and check myself in the mirror again. The six-inch platforms add half a foot to my height, making me just over five foot ten. Turning around I look over my shoulder to scrutinise my bum, squinting, unsure what to make of it. I decide that it's still there, which has to be good news. I reach down to grab the wine bottle but forget how much taller I am now and nearly topple forward. I manage to steady myself by leaning on the wardrobe door, which creaks under the strain.

My hand moves along the dresses and tops and jackets hanging in my wardrobe until it falls on the slinky cape Viv gave me. I wonder if I should wear it tonight. It would look stunning over a mini-dress with my platform wedges. It would certainly be a dramatic entrance. I run the material through my fingers. Am I feeling brave enough to wear an item of clothing that says 'I am woman, bow before me'? No, tonight is not the right time, although I doubt there will ever be a right time. My hand wanders back over the hangers and stops at a black wraparound dress. I wore it to a psychology seminar a couple of years ago and got chatted up by a marriage guidance counsellor with a dazzling smile. I told her I was straight and married and she said what a shame and I agreed.

The wraparound dress fits snuggly around my body, falling to just above the knee, cupping my breasts in a crossover style to give the illusion of extra fullness. I shake my hair loose from the tight bun at the back of my neck and am surprised by how long it has grown as it spills over my shoulders, free from confinement. I strut out of the bedroom, into the bathroom and yank open the cupboard below the sink where my make-up bag has been hidden away. I place it in the sink and pull the zip, watching the tiny teeth part as the bag opens to reveal the shiny, glittering array of compacts, casings and colourful eye shadows with various pencils, sticks and mascaras swimming among them. I had forgotten how well stocked it was.

I start with eyes, smoky. Then my lips, a dab of pale pink gloss followed by a dusting of rosy pink blusher. My hair comes next.

Using my hands to sweep it up into a messy, loose bun, sections fall through my fingers and land gently around my face. Lastly, one small spray of my favourite perfume, just enough to settle in my hair and on my shoulders. I breathe in the musky aroma and an image of Jude floats into my mind, here in this bathroom, my dress hitched up and his head between my legs. I squeeze my eyes together willing the image away. I try to picture Tristan instead, but all I feel is sad.

I check my teeth in the mirror; the wine has stained them red. I brush them with my whitening toothpaste and stand back to review my appearance again. Considering I'm semi-inebriated now, I am pleased with how I look. Then I frown at myself. Do I look okay? Is it too much? I see my mother's face, bland, unemotional. She never commented on anything I did or the clothes I wore, except for one time when I was going to my first school disco, but that didn't mean she wasn't always judging me.

The wine bottle is now three-quarters gone. I message Tristan to bring another, saying we both need to arrive with one. He replies with a thumbs up, which just makes me sad again, desperate even. Tears are building behind my eyes. It's the drink. Swilling wine on an empty stomach is never a good idea. Suddenly I don't want to go to the party, not on my own anyway, not without Tristan. But I also don't want to go with him and watch him drool over Viv, which he's bound to do as she's beautiful and charming and wild and free and creative and independent, the list goes on. I don't feel like I'm any of those things.

The sound of a smooth electric guitar drifts into the bathroom, distracting me from my lack of self-esteem. I leave the bathroom and go to our guest bedroom, which looks out over the back garden. It's stuffy in here and feels empty, despite most of the space being taken up by the double bed from our old flat. We always said we'd put a futon in here so we could use the room as a study. Never happened.

I peer out of the window into Viv's garden next door, following the sound of the music. There is bunting on both sides of the fence, and candles and lanterns are dotted around. Bob Marley's sweet subtle tones make me sway from side to side. Leaning on the window sill, I wonder if the problem is that I can't be loved. Tristan thought he could love me, but actually he can't. Not even Jude hung around. I'm not feeling sorry for myself, just looking for a rational explanation. The world is full of the haves and have-nots, maybe the same goes for love. Some have less in their life than others.

A few people spill out into Viv's garden, laughing and talking. They're certainly animated and loud. One of the men in the group is smoking in that nervous way people do when they first get to a party. Dragging on the cigarette, gathering all the bravado they can from the rolled-up nicotine to bolster their confidence, and then blowing it out of the side of their mouth in anticipation of making a good impression. I don't smoke, but I'm just as insecure. We all have our ways of dealing with a party situation, especially the kind where you don't know anyone. Well, I don't need Tristan to come to this party with me. I can manage it alone and Viv's practically my new best friend after all. I smile at myself, forever grateful to wine for giving me the boost I need to behave like the woman I'm not.

The last time I walked up Viv's driveway I was sober and Mrs Jenkins still lived here. She'd be delighted to know some-one like Viv has moved in and is having a party. Mrs Jenkins told me her two regrets in life were that she hadn't been to enough parties and she'd never smoked weed. I floated the idea to Tristan about smoking a joint with her and he agreed it would be a nice thing to do, but she died before we had a chance to follow through.

The front door is open but not enough to see into the house properly. Underneath the summer beats is an increasing hum of jumbled voices. A woman roars with laughter from somewhere deep within the house. I steady myself, push the door open and step into the dim hallway that appears at first to be moving. I wonder if I'm actually too drunk to be here, but then my eyes adjust to the light. Hanging from the upper and lower ceilings are huge swathes of creamy white sheets, rippling in the mild breeze. Every wall is covered, including the kitchen and living room doors. I glance up the stairs, looking for another door, a sense of a house, but all the walls on the landing are covered too. I have come as far as I can. There is no way forward. I'm about to turn and leave when a blonde head appears through the hanging fabric where the kitchen door should be. It's Viv, head tilted, her green eyes glimmering.

'You made it,' she says. 'Come in, get a drink.'

I follow her through the gap in the sheets and emerge into the kitchen where everything is also covered in giant, flowing pieces of creamy fabric, falling over the cupboards and appliances, hiding them away like embarrassing family members. The old kitchen table is nowhere to be seen and the sunken chairs have been pushed to one side with small cushions placed on the seats, probably to avoid anyone's bum cheeks getting stuck in them.

The counter has been wrapped in a metallic silver cover with bottles of wine and spirits and mixers scattered about on top. A long tower of stacked paper cups balances precariously at one end and on the floor are two large buckets full of beers on ice. Several groups of people stand around in the garden. The woman with the big laugh throws her head back and laughs again, like one of those happy people in Coke adverts. I spot the man I saw from our box room window, still smoking nervously, nodding vigorously at something another man is saying. The crowd in the kitchen is slightly more sedate. People stand in threes and twos having what appear to be interesting conversations. I hear the odd word or phrase: creche fees, TikTok, ice baths, A.I. One group gathers around the silver-covered counter topping up their drinks. Others lean against the side with the hidden appliances. The house looks completely different to how it did before when I had my backside wedged in a spindly chair, drinking vile elderberry wine.

Viv puts a paper cup in my hand, filled with clear liquid and an ice cube bobbing about in it. I take a sniff. Gin and tonic, not my favourite, but I've had more than enough wine.

'Love your dress,' Viv says, running her eyes over me.

'I like yours too,' I say.

She's wrapped in a continuous piece of silky material snaking around her body and waist, sweeping across her chest and then around her back and up to her neck where it rests on one shoulder, draping down her arm. The rest of the fabric falls around her legs and trails along the floor behind her. It's like a very elegant, designer toga and not something I could pull off. Her blonde hair is piled high on her head with strings of pearly beads twisting through her hairline. She is shimmery and dazzling. She eyes me from under her lashes and smiles. Again she reminds me of a princess, not of lizards this time, but of a magical underworld. I take a quick sip of my drink and look around the room. The gin hits my stomach, firing up my insides.

'Everybody, this is Izzy, my neighbour.' Everyone in the kitchen looks up and says hello. I smile, doing my best to appear sober. Viv grabs my arm and marches me out to the garden where the air is fresh and the lingering cigarette smoke feels familiar and comforting. Outside the back door, on a white stone plinth, is a shiny, black sculpture of a serpent, its head poised to strike.

'One of yours?' I ask.

'Part of my serpent collection,' she says. She calls back to the house for someone to turn the music up. It's a well-known eighties track but I can't remember the name. Lots of bass. She dances on the spot in front of me, slow, soulful.

'I like what you did with the house,' I say.

'Gives it an arty feel, don't you think?'

'Definitely,' I reply, looking over her shoulder at our dreary-looking house next door. The white paint on the upper window sills is peeling and the dark brown render is fading in parts. Are Tristan and I fading as well, slipping away from each other?

'I hope Tristan can make it too,' she says.

'He had to work.'

'At his restaurant, yes, he was telling me.'

He told her it was his restaurant. His need to impress her turns my stomach, but watching Viv moving around to the music in her golden aura, I understand why. I want to impress her too. I knock back the rest of my gin and tonic.

'By the way, I didn't tell Tristan about us drinking wine together or about you giving me the cape.'

She tilts her head again, like I'm an object of interest or – if she *were* a lizard princess – a source of food.

'Am I your dirty little secret?' she says.

'One of them,' I reply.

'Don't worry, you can trust me,' she says, putting a slight emphasis on the 's' in the word 'trust'. I'm not sure whether she's joking or not, or if she's actually talking in a lizard-like way, or if I imagined it. Either way, I'm not sure I do trust her but that doesn't mean I don't want to be her friend. In my drunken haze, the idea of having a girlfriend right next door, someone to talk to, makes me want to cry with relief. She puts her hand down the front of her dress and pulls out a thin, perfectly rolled joint. 'Fancy a smoke?' she says.

I really shouldn't after all the wine and gin, but I don't want to be unsociable.

'Sure,' I say.

She takes my hand and leads me to the bottom of the garden where there are two striped deckchairs facing each other. She lowers herself into one with grace and aplomb. I, on the other hand, lurch too far to one side, narrowly miss the seat and only just recover my position before Viv has to get up and save me.

'I'm okay,' I blurt out as I settle back into the chair. I hate deckchairs. Getting in and out of them requires practice, at least three goes, especially after one gin and tonic and a bottle of wine. I attempt to sit up normally but I'm too far back so awkwardly slide myself down and forward. Viv giggles, watching me. I giggle too, as it is all rather ridiculous. She lights the end of the joint and takes a big long drag and passes it to me.

'I'm dying to see you in that cape,' she says. 'I was hoping you'd wear it.'

'It's stunning,' I say. 'The most beautiful thing in my wardrobe.'

I take a deep drag of the joint, hold the smoke in my lungs for a moment before coughing and spluttering as I exhale. I apologise and say it's been years since I smoked. Then a calmness descends upon me as my brain switches to 'don't give a fuck' mode. Viv takes another drag and points her face to the sky to exhale.

'All the more reason to wear it.'

'I don't know whether I have the right personality for it. It's intimidating,' I say, being totally honest.

'What's the right personality?' she asks.

'Ballsy,' I say.

She passes me the joint again and I blink before reaching out to take it, seeing double. I am so wasted now, but at the same time perfectly content in my stupor. Nothing matters anymore. Not Tristan, not Jude, not my mother, not my past, not Mindy my dog. I exhale, feeling freed and free.

'You're definitely ballsy,' she says.

'Nope, I'm really not.'

'What are you then?' she asks, moving to the end of her deck-chair so she can lean closer towards me.

'I'm a mediocre teacher and a bit of a crap wife. I'm no good in the garden or the kitchen, unless heating food counts. And I lead nineteen-year-old boys on so they try to kiss me in lifts.'

Viv pushes my hair back off my face. 'You are very beautiful,' she says. 'I'm not surprised teenage boys have crushes on you.'

'It wasn't a crush,' I tell her. 'Jude was different.'

'Is this another one of your dirty secrets?'

'Actually, it's my only other one. I only have two.'

'Two's acceptable,' she says.

She jumps up and grabs my hands to pull me to standing. It takes quite a bit of effort to get me out of the stupid chair.

'It's my favourite song,' she says, dragging me to the middle of the garden. Viv closes her eyes and sways to the music. A few of the other guests join in too, surrounding Viv, the nervous smoker and laughing woman among them. I manage to shuffle my feet and bob my head, which is quite a feat considering my present condition. Viv moves her arms around in front of her like she's casting a spell on me, her flashing green eyes fixing on mine, which I'm sure are half closed. The nervous smoker cuts in front of me, doing a funny robot dance that makes everyone clap and cheer. I step back to make room for him, and the next thing I know I'm staring up at the darkening night sky, my head spinning at frightening speed. The nervous smoker's face appears above me, frowning. He asks me if I'm okay. I squint up at him, his facial features swirling before me, then roll over and vomit, rather loudly, as the entire contents of my stomach empties out onto the flower bed I now realise I'm lying in.

'Give her some space,' I hear Viv say. I try to raise my arm.

'I'm fine,' I manage to croak before everything goes black.

11

Him

A hip-hop track drifts over the roof of the new neighbour's house, which is full of light and the sound of voices.

Our house is in darkness. Izzy must still be at the party. Normally the hall light is on if one of us is home, and that at least gives some sense of life inside. It's a shell, I think; empty even when occupied.

The party's still in at least partial swing. I'm surprised by the level of relief I feel; the fear of missing out was more intense than I realised. I should know better than to allow myself to have high expectations.

My motto in life tends to be *keep expectations low and you won't be disappointed*. But I've clearly set myself up for disappointment and it's too late now. The damage is done. I am expecting something awesome and life-changing to come out of meeting Viv tonight, although I'm not sure what exactly.

The front door is ajar but I still knock before entering. Stepping into the hall, the sounds of revelry are more robust now and coming from the back garden.

There is a small orange light on the hall table but the rest of the space and walls upstairs are draped with white sheets. It gives the house a clubby, 'city pad' vibe as opposed to the underwhelming, small semi-detached house that it is.

There is a slit in the sheets at the end of the hall, which leads to the kitchen and garden. I approach with caution, peering through the gap. Candles and fairy lights glimmer in the garden where most, if not all, the guests are gathered.

I can estimate, from the volume of the voices, that there are about twenty people outside. I've become an expert in judging noise levels from working in a busy restaurant. I know what fifty people sound like compared to ten and whether they're raucous or not.

One of the people outside must be Izzy. I squint into the distance, trying to distinguish Izzy's body shape from the others. I can't see her and now I'm wondering if turning up late is more awkward than cool. I'm also empty-handed. Hopefully Viv brought wine with her.

'Hello, Tris-tan.'

Her soft, tantalising, slightly teasing tone makes me freeze. She's standing behind me. I slowly turn to face her, breaking into a warm smile.

'Hi,' I reply. My voice makes a gurgling sound as the word gets stuck in the back of my throat.

Her oval green eyes blink at me, alert and interested. Her slender shoulders are bare and her creamy skin and delicate features are luminous in the low light. Her dress, a satin mist of gossamer fabric, wraps around her frame, and strands of her flaxen hair escape from the bun on her head, flowing over her shoulders and down her back.

She smiles at me and a burst of heat rushes to my head. I expected her to be beautiful and intriguing but not so mesmerising and enchanting.

My throat has gone dry again. I try to swallow to moisten things up before attempting to speak again.

'Glad you could make it,' she says.

'Sorry I'm so late. I got tied up at work.'

'Let me get you a drink,' she says, gliding past me. A waft of her perfume drifts up my nostrils, warm and sweaty, an animalistic musky scent.

I follow her into the kitchen which is all white and silver. There is a couple kissing in the corner. The man holds a lit cigarette in one hand. They're not even that engaged in what they're doing, too drunk to really care.

The rest of the guests are in the garden and the music is at a medium level. I'm assuming it was louder earlier. The smell of old, sticky beer rises from the floor where someone must have spilled a drink. I glance into the garden again but I can't see Izzy.

Viv pours a large shot of gin into a plastic cup and splashes some flat tonic on top. She says she's out of ice and I say no problem, taking the drink and downing half of it in one go.

'Izzy's upstairs,' she says casually. 'Sleeping it off.'

'Excuse me?' I say, wondering if I heard her correctly.

'She was drinking on an empty stomach and got sick.'

'Oh, I'll take her home. Is she okay?' I ask, instantly snapping out of my Viv fascination. Izzy is sick. She needs me to do the right thing.

'Leave her. She's fast asleep in my bed,' Viv says, waving away my worries.

'I don't think she'd want me to do that,' I say. And I don't want to do that either. The thought of sleeping alone in our bed while she's next door in Viv's makes me very unsettled.

'Come and see for yourself,' she says, drifting back out of the kitchen. I take another gulp of my gin and follow her into the hall, averting my eyes from her undulating hips as she mounts the stairs to the landing.

She pushes open the door to the bedroom and leans against it so I have to squeeze in beside her to see inside. There is a small globe light on the floor emitting a subtle glow. Izzy lies on her back in the massive bed surrounded by silky pink sheets and pillows. She lets out little puffs as she exhales, fast asleep.

'Sorry,' I whisper to Viv. 'She doesn't normally get drunk and pass out at parties.'

'I'm sad to hear that,' she replies, not bothering to keep her voice down. 'Izzy deserves to be naughty sometimes, don't you think?'

I look down at Viv, now only a few inches away from me. She gazes up at me, her head barely reaching my chest.

'Don't you like to let loose sometimes?' She lifts her hands, slipping her fingers into her hairline, gathering loose strands and pushing them behind her ears. She raises her chin and I'm completely distracted.

'Of course, I mean, I'm just, well, you know, I think Izzy will be mortified if I don't take her home.'

'Take her home, but have your drink first,' she says.

I show her my cup is empty, smiling.

'Or at least another one before rushing off,' she says.

All I can do is nod.

In the kitchen, she pours me another gigantic gin with a droplet of tonic. The couple have now stopped kissing. The guy smokes a cigarette while she munches through a packet of crisps, cheese and onion flavour. I doubt there'll be much kissing after that.

Viv leads me into the garden and past the other guests, saying hello to everyone, introducing me as Tris-tan from next door, and then down to the bottom of the garden where there are two deckchairs.

I lower myself carefully into one of them, bending deep at my knees first to make sure I get the position right. Viv settles into the chair across from me. She puts her hands up over her head in a relaxing position, but as her arms move, the top of her dress falls a little, exposing the upper curve of her breasts.

I look away. We both know she saw me at the shed this morning, strutting my substandard stuff like a prize turkey. I don't want her to think I'm a letch.

'Tell me about your restaurant,' she says. 'Is it fancy?'

'Yes, very,' I say. 'But I'm the manager, not the owner.'

She pulls her arms down from above her head and leans forward, settling her hands in her lap.

'You made me think you were the owner,' she says, eyeing me with slight amusement.

'Actually, you made that assumption.'

'Next you'll be telling me you're not the manager but the person who washes up.'

'Sometimes I wish I was. It's a lot less hassle.'

She leans further forward, an indication that I have her undivided attention.

I proceed to tell her all about Monty and his moods and the supermarket food and the Gipsy Kings. As I tell her stories, she says things like, 'no, really' and 'that's hilarious'. She's totally enthralled by my anecdotes and laughs in all the right places.

I begin to wonder if I'm funny enough to be a stand-up comedian. Maybe I have enough material about working with Monty to get me started. I hide a smile, aware my ego is running wild, but being in Viv's presence makes me believe I could achieve anything and it's a feeling that leaves me breathless.

When I run out of stories about Monty, I tell her about Spencer and Maddy's spat that went nuclear. I love that she finds me interesting.

There is a lull in the conversation but I'm comfortable with it. I've done a lot of talking. It's her turn now.

'What were you doing in your shed this morning?' she asks softly.

Blood races to my cheeks and I'm hoping she can't see my reddening face in the dark.

'I saw you from the window upstairs,' she says.

It's an intense moment, at least it feels like that. I manage to feign loosely recalling the shed incident.

'This morning? Oh, yeah, I was looking for a screwdriver. Are you saying you were watching me?'

Knocking it back into her court is a good strategy and makes me sound very normal and her slightly not. It's about survival. I need to come out of this well.

'It's empowering to watch someone when they don't know you're watching them, don't you think?' she says, her voice almost a purr.

'I wouldn't know, you'd have to ask a stalker,' I say, keeping it light.

She smiles and pushes both her knuckles up against my knees, as though locking me in place.

'When I arrived last night, it felt like someone was watching me from the window upstairs in your house.'

'Really?' I say, as the pressure of her knuckles sends a throbbing pulse up my legs straight to my groin, where things start to stir.

'I liked it,' she says, looking right at me.

The stirring below increases, growing. I swallow. She liked it. It's a moment of truth. Do I continue to deny it and risk making her feel silly, or do I own up and reveal my perverted behaviour. Maybe it's not perverted if she liked it. I realise there's no way out of this.

'The sound of the truck woke me up and then I looked out of the window,' I say.

'And then continued looking,' she says, teasing me.

'I wasn't officially "watching you". I was more being nosy.'

'Hiding in the shadows,' she says, placing her palms on my knees now and slowly splaying her fingers. Her fingers are just above my knees but it feels like they're only an inch from my crotch. I jump to my feet, appalled and terrified I'm going to lose control.

'I should probably take Izzy home. Thanks for having us and welcome again to the street.'

Viv gets up too. 'I'm pleased we're neighbours,' she says.

I smile and hurry off, trying to ignore the stiffness in the front of my trousers. Taking the stairs two at a time, I burst into the bedroom to get Izzy.

The pink sheets are ruffled. But the bed is empty.

12

Her

My eyes snap open and I stare at the ceiling. My heart is pounding. I'm in a state of panic although I'm not sure what about. My head, heavy as lead, forces me to stay lying flat on my back. I move my eyes to the right and see a window with the curtains half drawn and notice a warm orange glow inside the room. I wriggle my fingers and feel the silkiness of the sheets beneath my body. There's a pain in my throat, a burning sensation. I manage to roll over onto my side. I cough and splutter, forcing my rib cage to heave. I look down as a droplet of saliva escapes the corner of my mouth and silently plops onto the mottled grey carpet. With great effort, I lift my head and gaze around the room. A light hum of voices talking over the throb of background music brings me to my senses. I'm still at the party. I must be in Viv's bed. Images of the flower bed and vomit come flooding back to me. I groan. I lay my head back on the pillow waiting for my heart to slow. Something woke me with a start. I trawl back through my memory. It was a dream, a nightmare, where a decrepit old crone was trying to strangle me. My hand shoots to my neck, making sure everything's as it should be.

I sit up relieved to be awake, although my head is splitting with pain. I should be embarrassed by my behaviour, falling over and being sick, and normally I would be, but I'm not. Maybe I've lost whatever morsel of self-respect I've been clinging on to, or maybe I'm still stoned. Then I remember sitting on the deckchairs with Viv. Me telling her about Jude. Her telling me I'm beautiful and the rush of joy I felt.

Getting out of bed is easier than I thought it would be. Standing up, my dress falls back into place and I don't feel as dizzy or drunk anymore. Even the headache eases. In fact, I'm quite steady and together. My strappy shoes and bag have been neatly placed beneath the window. I pick them up and decide to slip out the front door and go home. I can apologise to Viv tomorrow. I take my phone out of my bag. No messages. The time reads 00.10. Tristan must be home by now. He can't be at the party or he would have known what had happened to me and taken me home. I walk out onto the landing but I'm dying for a wee and doubt my bladder will hold until I get home. I use the bathroom quickly, the chatter and music from the party louder in here, coming from the back garden. I wander into the back bedroom, curious as to where Viv is and what she's doing. It looks out over the garden and also part of ours. Our shed sits at the end of our garden, passive and inactive; a symbol of suburban life, Tristan says. Seeing it from up here, I realise he's right. It's everything that's wrong with our marriage. It's so much easier to blame a shed.

I peer down into Viv's garden where people still stand around drinking. It's completely dark now and the fairy lights and candles along the edges of the garden twinkle invitingly. Overexcited pop music pumps from the speaker. It's too much for my ears and I start to feel ill again. I'm definitely partied out. I'm about to leave when my eyes are drawn to the bottom of the garden where two people sit in the deckchairs. The end of the garden is not as well lit as the front, so it takes a moment to see that it's Viv, sitting on the left. I recognise her silky dress and feminine frame. She is leaning forward and has her hands on the knees of the man sitting in the chair across from her. He is laughing at something she just said. She is laughing too now. He looks towards the house for a moment and I see it's Tristan. Instinctively I step back from the window, not wanting him to see me. He says something else to Viv and she tilts her head at him, giving him her full attention. My chest tightens, promising to suffocate me if I don't breathe normally. I wonder if it's an asthma attack, but it's not. It's jealousy and it's raging inside me. Cut my skin and my blood would run green. I stumble onto the landing, down the stairs and out the front door, leaving it open.

Pushing my own front door open, I slam it shut behind me and make a beeline for the stairs, dashing up just fast enough for my swimming head to cope with, and into the bathroom to stick my head down the loo. Maybe something else caused me to vomit. Maybe it was one of Olly's leftover raspberry muffins that I picked at this afternoon. It did taste a bit funny. I splash water on my face, manage to run my toothbrush over my teeth again and crawl into bed, too fatigued and sickly to take my dress off. Lying flat on my back, on top of the covers, I stare at the paper lampshade hanging from the ceiling. Another temporary fixture that we never replaced. It has a small tear on one side where I tried to hoosh a fly out of the room. Maybe everything about me and Tristan was only ever going to be temporary. A house made of straw.

I close my eyes and images of Jude drift into my mind. It's comforting to think about him. I take myself back through the day, seeing Jude on the stairs, going for a drink with Polly, speaking to Jude in the pub. He comes closer to kiss me but then he's Viv and she's holding my face in both hands. She goes to kiss me thinking I'm Tristan. I squeeze my eyes tighter shut, allowing myself to sink down to where unsavoury memories lurk, waiting for the opportunity to invade my mind.

I once peed on my mum's boss's expensive oriental rug. I was nine years old and while I had no idea why I did it at the time, the haunting feelings of shame have lingered. I was simply too old for my behaviour to be considered unintentional. And it wasn't.

I did it because of my dog; a white Labrador I called Mindy. I didn't know what to call her at first but I saw the name in a book at school and decided it suited her. I was eight years old when my mother brought her home as a puppy. My mother never wanted a dog, despite me begging for one. I had given up asking when Mrs Hartman, who lived across the street, got a Jack Russell puppy. Mrs Hartman's house was bigger than ours and she had a husband and three children. She was an elegant woman, always smiling and unruffled. And her children were sporty and forever arriving home with trophies. The addition of a cute puppy was more than my mother could bear. She would scowl out of our living room window watching Mrs Hartman's children scamper up and down the street playing and laughing with the little dog, or eye Mrs Hartman with contempt as she carried it under her arm. She never said anything, but she didn't have to. The hunched shoulders and tightly closed lips were enough to tell me she had a problem. Mrs Hartman made her feel inadequate.

It would have been easier for my mother if Mrs Hartman had flaunted a fancy new car rather than a puppy. At least she could have dismissed this as materialism. But a puppy was in a whole other sphere of competition. A puppy said super woman. A puppy said good parent. A puppy said perfection.

I liked Mrs Hartman. She was always nice to me and had kind eyes that crinkled at the corners when she smiled. 'Anyone can get a stupid puppy,' snapped my mother one night over dinner. We hadn't even been talking about Mrs Hartman or the dog. Two days later my mother arrived home with a cardboard box and called me into the living room. 'Here you are. You got what you wanted,' she said. I opened the box. Inside was a shivering, white fluffy snowball with two big eyes blinking up at me. She thumped her tail on the bottom of the box but the vibration made her topple over. I reached in and picked her up with both hands, holding her up to my face. She flattened her ears and starting wriggling with excitement, licking me all over.

'Don't let it do that,' said my mother. 'It cleans its bum with that tongue.' But I didn't care. When I told her I was calling her Mindy, my mother shrugged. 'I don't care what you call it as long as you walk it and pick up the poo.'

From the moment I held Mindy in my hands, my life changed. I had something to live for, which meant I must have felt I had nothing to live for before. Mindy slept on my bed, even though she wasn't allowed to. And every day she sat at the living room window, her wet nose pressed against the glass, waiting for me to come home from school. I began to be first out of the school gates instead of the last and my mother knew why. 'All this charging about. The dog isn't going anywhere,' she would say. But when I saw Mindy at the living room window, and her ears pricked up with delight at the sight of me, my heart would swell, about to burst out of my chest. The minute I was in the front door she threw herself at me and I would fall to my knees to hug her and play with her. Sometimes the feeling in my chest was so intense that it hurt and I would hold Mindy close, over-whelmed by how much love there was inside me.

My mother had no interest in Mindy. I thought she'd love her once she got to know her, but she didn't, which I found confusing. How could she not adore Mindy the way I did? Mindy was nothing but an inconvenience to my mother. She was always just 'the dog'. And she yelled at Mindy when she did something wrong, like chewed one of her favourite Chelsea boots or the corner of our sofa. Although Mindy did have an amazing capacity to eat the most unusual things and once consumed half a roll of toilet paper.

I reassured myself that Mindy's position in the house was safe because she was an important status symbol. Mindy was a big two fingers to Mrs Hartman, only she didn't know it. In fact, Mrs Hartman clearly didn't spend much time thinking about my mother at all. My guess was, Mrs Hartman had tried to be neighbourly and my mother had made zero effort in return. But I got on well with Mrs Hartman and her children and they all adored Mindy and invited me to the park with them to walk the dogs. Mindy would bound through the grass and trees, chasing scents but never straying far from me. She always came when I called her and didn't like it if she couldn't see me. Mrs Hartman explained how this was called pack mentality and how dogs can get stressed when they can't see their owner. And I had felt proud to be referred to as Mindy's owner. Mindy was mine. She belonged to me and I would have killed for her. In the end, the best I could do was take a pee on a rug.

It was a Thursday afternoon and I could see my mother standing at the school gates waiting for me. She was a personal assistant to a property developer called Clive. She worked three half days and two full days a week. On the two full days she would pick me up from school and bring me back to the office where I was expected to sit in silence on the stiff leather sofa and wait for her to finish her day. But once I had Mindy, I resented having to do this even more than usual because I knew Mindy was at home, waiting for me, waiting for her pack to return. Thursdays were one of my mother's half days, so I could rush straight home and take Mindy for a walk with Mrs Hartman and her children, as they often went to the park after school.

But that afternoon there was something odd about my mother. It was a warm summer's day but her arms were crossed tightly across her body and she was hunched over, as though walking against a biting wind. As I got closer I could see her face was drawn and pale and the corners of her mouth were drooped. She saw me approaching and started walking down the hill ahead of me and I followed. I knew something was wrong but I didn't think for one minute it had anything to do with me, or Mindy. At the bottom of the hill, before the high street began, she pulled me aside outside the local library.

'Something's happened,' she said.

A feeling of dread began to build in the pit of my stomach.

'The postman rang the bell, she was barking, and when I opened the door, she just ran out.'

'Who? Mindy?'

'Yes, who else would it be?' she said. I noticed she was wringing her hands now.

'Did you go after her? Is she alright?'

'She raced off up the road, there was nothing I could do.'

'You're supposed to lock her in a room when you open the door. You know she'll run off. She runs off to find me.'

'I thought she was in the living room, but she was in the kitchen.'

It wasn't a good enough excuse and she knew it.

'Where is she now? Is she lost?' I said, tears welling in my eyes, terrified for Mindy being alone and frightened somewhere.

'I thought she'd come back by herself. Then I got a call from the police.' She folded her arms around her torso even tighter, unable to look at me. 'She got hit by a car on the dual carriageway. I'm sorry.'

I stared at her, wide-eyed, waiting for her to tell me Mindy was okay. She gave me a grim look. 'Her back legs were crushed, she couldn't stand up.'

'Where is she now?' I said, my voice shrill and panicked. Mindy would feel abandoned if I wasn't there.

'The vet said we should put her down. She's gone.'

'Gone?'

'She's dead.'

Suddenly I was dropping, plummeting like a runaway lift, sinking into the concrete pavement below and beyond, down down down. My head was fuzzy and heavy and I was cold all over, unable to process the information. Mindy was dead. My mother could have been saying bananas were red for all the sense it was making to me. I couldn't take it in.

'I want to see her,' I managed to say.

'Didn't you hear what I said?' There was mild panic in her voice. She wanted this to be over and done with quickly.

'I want to see my dog,' I said again.

She brought me to the vet's clinic where I sat on a hard plastic chair, shivering while my mother had a quiet word with the receptionist. There was a cat in a carrier beside me, blinking out through the mesh, and an Alsatian across the room with a white plastic collar around his neck, his long tongue panting, dripping saliva onto the floor. I felt like a patient too, a wounded animal in need of medical attention to stop the pain.

A woman in a blue smock and trousers came through the 'no entry' door and knelt in front of me. 'Hi, Izzy. I'm Laura,' she said in a gentle voice. I looked into her eyes, which were moist with empathy. She knew what I was going through. She understood. 'Would you like to see Mindy?' I nodded. She took me by the hand and led me down a corridor. I glanced back and saw my mother's face at the window in the door, watching me go. The corridor had shiny brick walls painted blue, but the smell of disinfectant mingled with air freshener wasn't quite enough to eradicate the lingering odour of cat wee. She brought me through another door and into a large bright room with stainless steel counters and units.

Laura let go of my hand and opened the door to one of the freezer units. It made a slight suction noise as cold vapour escaped from inside. She kept her back to me, but I could see there were a number of large bags inside tied at the front with tags on them. She slid one of the bags out from a shelf, shut the door and brought it over to the shiny countertop. She opened the top of the bag.

She beckoned me over. 'Here she is, love.' But my feet wouldn't move. I was stuck, not just to the spot, but in space and time. How could Mindy be lying silently in a bag that had just been taken out of a freezer?

Laura put an arm around me and steered me to the countertop. She squeezed my shoulders tight, letting me know she was there for me. I looked down at Mindy, lying on her side, her eyes shut and her tongue poking out from the side of her mouth. She was too still. I put my hand out to touch her. She was so very cold. And she hated to be cold, always sneaking under the duvet with me at night until she got too hot and then had to lie flat out on my bedroom floor to cool down. Her fur wasn't frozen completely, but crisp to touch like frosty grass. Her facial expression was one of forced sleep, like she was pretending to be asleep because her life depended on it.

'I bet she was an amazing friend to you,' Laura said.

'The best,' I whispered. And in that moment I knew there would never be another friend like her, dog or human. I started to cry, not hysterically, even though I felt like howling my head off. My chest was too tight with pain for such an outpouring, as though it would implode and crush my insides if I let it out. Of course, the pain had always been there, dormant, lying in wait. I had lived with the fear of losing Mindy since the very first day she arrived. I was her owner. She was my pack. I placed my hands on her body and put my forehead to her face. 'Goodbye,' I whispered.

When we got home I went straight to bed, the pain in my chest still too much to bear. Every time I thought about Mindy or felt the emptiness in the room without her, the pressure shot to my head and tears would stream from the corner of my eyes. My mother kept coming in and out, checking on me. At first she was sympathetic, offering me hot chocolate and biscuits, which I declined. I didn't go to school the following day and she didn't question it. But when I refused to get up on Monday, she huffed and puffed because she had to stay home too. I heard her on the phone to her boss, Clive. 'Yeah, my tonsils are still like golf balls but I'm sure I'll be alright tomorrow.' I wondered why she didn't tell him the truth. Surely dead family pet was far more of a valid excuse.

Later that day I managed to get myself out of bed and even had a couple of bites of a cheese sandwich at the kitchen table. My mother was pleased and thought this meant I was over it. She attempted to share some soundbites that she honestly believed were wise words. 'Best to put it behind you now.' 'Mustn't dwell on the past.' But everything she said only made me feel more desperate and lonely.

'I wish I could have said goodbye properly,' I said. I was upset and missing my dog but my mother took it as a personal attack and started banging pots around as she washed up.

'What was I supposed to do? Take you out of school and bring you to the vet?'

I hadn't considered that as a possibility until then.

'I told the vet you'd be too upset and better to get it over and done with,' she said.

'What?' I said, confused, my mind racing. She chucked the washing brush in the sink and pulled her rubber gloves off finger by finger.

'I did what was best for you.'

She marched out of the kitchen into the living room and put the telly on. Not only had my mother let Mindy run out of the house, and not only had she not gone after her, but she hadn't taken me out of school to say goodbye before she died even though that had clearly been an option. My mother didn't have a clue what was good for me. I willed myself not to cry, swallowed my grief, buried my anger and went back to bed. I dragged myself into school the following day and didn't tell anyone about Mindy. If I'd even mentioned her name I would have broken down. In an attempt to get on with things, I told myself that what had happened to Mindy was a terrible accident. But the resentment and the fury simmered away, buried but not forgotten, waiting to rear its head.

It was raining that fateful day when my mother picked me up from school to head back to Clive's office. Her hair was glossy and just-washed and she was wearing a black dress suit with shoulder pads and big collars. I thought she looked like Cruella de Vil. She had the radio on in the car as usual, to fill the silence. I sat in the back, staring out of the window. I caught her glancing at me in the rearview mirror. I normally talked, despite the radio being on too loud, but since Mindy died, I had stopped talking altogether. To her anyway.

At the office I slumped on the sofa with my hands in my tracksuit bottom pockets. I knew the drill: sit down, shut up, don't move. My mother went back to her desk and carried on typing and answering the phone. The office was a large shiny white warehouse with a double-height space over half of the building where the reception area and my mother's desk were located. The polished floors glistened and a stainless steel staircase rose from the middle of the main space up to Clive's open-plan office, which spanned the upper level. I had never been upstairs or seen Clive's office and, until that day, I had had no desire to either. Clive paid no attention to me and I had zero interest in him, but I did wonder if his feet smelled as he didn't wear socks with his smart suede loafers. And for someone so rich, I thought it was strange his suit trousers didn't quite reach his ankles. He had waxy hair and a long face, like a horse, and always looked serious and morose. My mother worshipped him. Yes, Clive, no, Clive, can I get your nosebag for you, Clive. She also acted differently at work and used her work voice, which went up at the end of her sentences. This was also how Clive talked so she was actually mimicking him and, while this hadn't really bothered me before, I began to hate her for it. She cared more about what Clive thought of her than she did about how I was feeling. Or about holding Mindy by the collar when the postman rang the doorbell, or pulling me out of fucking school to say goodbye to my dying dog.

She held up some letters to me indicating she was going to the postbox and that I should continue to keep still and quiet. I looked at her without turning my head or moving my body. She rushed out, eager to make the last collection on time. I imagined myself sinking into the sofa, as though I was part of the leather. I turned my head, feeling camouflaged, watching Clive as he trotted down the stairs, stepping sideways as he went, so he could get down faster. He called out for my mother: 'Jo? Jo?' He didn't bother to ask me where she was, or even look at me. I was invisible.

He entered the kitchen and I heard him put the kettle on, clicking his fingers and humming to himself. Then something came over me, an urge, a compulsion. I got up from the sofa and walked towards the staircase. I stopped at the bottom and looked up to Clive's office. I had no idea what I was doing or intending to do, but I could still hear him singing in the kitchen. I lowered my head and walked as softly as I could up the stairs, curious now to see what his special office looked like. Would everything be gold and covered in diamonds? Would he have a throne for a chair? I paused at the top of the staircase and peered around. The open space stretched towards a huge window at the back of the building where a curved mahogany desk was positioned. And he did have a very high-backed chair. The count in his counting house. I padded over to the desk and saw that the desk and chair were on a large, thick rug. The rug had an intricate coloured pattern weaving through it and was soft yet sturdy underfoot. Even I knew, at that young age, that it was special and more than likely expensive.

And that's when I did it. I pulled down my tracksuit bottoms along with my knickers and carefully positioned myself in front of the desk and over the central part of the rug. Then I let loose, ejecting the contents from my bladder, letting it gush and splash onto the rug, becoming a duller more muted sound as the rug absorbed what it could. I hadn't realised how badly I'd needed to go to the toilet, so I must have peed for a good ten to twelve seconds. The area of the rug I was peeing on was quickly saturated, making the excess wee trickle over the edge of the rug and onto the floor. I finally finished, gave myself a little wiggle to expel any last drips, pulled up my knickers and tracksuit bottoms, being careful to take wide steps to avoid the enormous puddle I had created. I stood back and viewed the sodden dripping rug, still not comprehending what I had done.

'What's going on?' came Clive's sharp voice.

He was standing at the top of the staircase with a cup of coffee in one hand and a biscuit in another. It struck me how Clive, and my mother, in all the years I had been sitting quietly on that sofa, had never offered me a biscuit.

'Nothing,' I said.

'You're not allowed up here. Go back downstairs.'

I walked towards the top of the stairs, as my mother came up. Her eyes widened on seeing me.

'Jesus,' she gasped. 'What are you doing up there?'

I ignored her and continued walking down the stairs and back to the sofa. I had just returned to my slumped position when Clive's voice rang out through the office.

'Holy fucking Christ. She pissed on my oriental rug.'

This was followed by a harrowing scream, which belonged to my mother. I felt surprisingly calm and, for the first time since Mindy died, a smile appeared on my lips.

My mother, red-faced and sweating, frogmarched me out of the office and manhandled me into the back of the car. She climbed into the front, hands gripping the steering wheel.

'Why?' she asked, turning to look at me, but I stared out of the window. I wanted to say 'because I hate you', but that wasn't quite right. I had wanted to hurt her and embarrass her in front of Clive the horse. I wanted her to be mortified and maybe lose her job. I wanted Clive to look at her like she was a disgusting person because her daughter was disgusting.

The following day she took me to the doctor, worried I had a behavioural issue, and he recommended I see a child psychologist, which my mother arranged. The psychologist was a lovely, kind German woman called Anna. She asked me why I thought I was there in her office. I told her I had peed on my mum's boss's oriental rug, in his office. She put her hand to her mouth and I could see she was trying not to laugh. I was surprised by her reaction and aware she probably shouldn't have reacted like that. Then she apologised, but admitted that it did sound kind of funny. Then I smiled and she smiled and then we laughed about it. She wanted all the details. What did the rug look like? How big was it? What happened afterwards? What did Clive say? I told her about his holy fucking Christ comment and my mother's piercing scream and we giggled some more. Then, casually, she asked me why I had done it and I said because my mother killed my dog. Her face fell. No more laughing. 'You lost your dog?' she said. 'That's terrible. I'm so sorry. That must have been awful.' Then out of nowhere I started sobbing, so much so I couldn't catch my breath. Anna sat beside me, rubbing my back, letting me cry until I couldn't cry anymore and my sobbing reduced to short sharp breaths. I said I was sorry for crying. Anna said you should never apologise for crying. She wanted to know all about Mindy and what my life had been like with her and asked me why I thought my mother had killed her. I told her the story and said I hated my mother for not letting me see Mindy before she died. Anna said that was a horrible thing to happen. She also said that sometimes people make bad judgement calls, not because they want to be nasty or hurt people, but because human beings get it wrong sometimes.

When the session was over, I left the room and my mother went in to speak to Anna. My mother was in there for about twenty minutes. A boy about my age and his father were sitting across from me in the waiting room. The father kept checking his watch and glancing at me, as though it was my fault they had to wait. Finally, my mother came out of the room, looking rather red-faced again. We didn't speak on the way home, and once home I went to my room. When she called me for dinner, I went to the kitchen to get my bowl of pasta to take to my room to eat, as had been our arrangement since the peeing-on-the-rug incident, but this time she asked me to stay and sit down. I really didn't want to.

'I have something to say,' she said.

I was exhausted after all the crying with Anna and the talking about Mindy and I had no interest in anything my mother had to say.

'Please,' she said quietly. She'd never used that tone before and rarely that word, so I sat down. She took a deep breath, biting her lip, but didn't say anything, so I started eating my pasta. Then she leaned across the table and put her hand on my hand and I stopped eating.

'Sorry,' she said.

'Okay,' I replied. 'Can I go to my room now?'

'I'm sorry about what happened with Mindy. I should have held her collar when the postman came to the door and I should have gone after her when she ran away, and I should have taken you out of school so you could see her before she died.'

It was the first time she had ever apologised to me, for anything. It was also the first time she had used Mindy's name. I eyed her lips, which were pushed together, and glanced at her hands, now rolled into fists, pulling the skin tightly across the knuckles. There was nothing relaxed about her. Even her hair looked tense. She was saying what she thought she should say and probably what Anna had told her to say. My mother had no problem saying it, she wanted to do the right thing, but she was just going through the motions. She didn't really feel responsible or sorry, not because she was a nasty person but because she didn't have the capacity. My mother had no real love in her, not for Mindy, and not for me. That was the day I realised there was something wrong with my mother and began to worry that there might be something wrong with me too.

'Sorry about Clive's rug,' I said.

My eyes open and wince shut again in the extreme brightness, but not before getting a glimpse of my surroundings. At least I'm in my own bed this time. Feelings of inadequacy, guilt, fear and disgust charge through me as I struggle to identify the cause. Then, in one giant gushing wave, I see everything. A snapshot of the entire previous day and night. I bat most of the unwelcome emotions away, demoting them to hangover anxiety, not to be taken seriously, but the simmering inadequacy remains, virulent and insistent. The image of Viv with her hands on Tristan's knees and him, laughing, keeps appearing in my mind. Maybe it was nothing; just part of a story she was telling him that required her to put her hands on his knees by way of illustration. Or maybe they were flirting. Why shouldn't Tristan laugh and be touched by Viv? It's more of a betrayal to Tristan that I haven't told him about Jude. Unable to face myself, let alone the day, I pull the sheet up over my head. The door squeaks as it opens and I feel a weight on the bed. It's Tristan, sitting beside me.

'How are you feeling?' he asks, a hint of kind humour in his voice.

'I'm a disgrace,' I mumble through the sheet.

'Sorry I wasn't there when you got sick. I got stuck at work. Monty nearly walked out.'

'Bloody fucking Monty,' I say, pulling the sheet down so I can see him.

'Actually, I think that's his full name,' he says with a grin.

I smile back. Tristan is funny. I must have forgotten. He's already dressed and showered and smells nice. He's glowing, which is not a word I would normally use to describe a man.

'Did you enjoy the party?' I ask, casual.

'I had one drink then came to bring you home but you'd already left.'

One drink. Unlikely.

'Did you get a chance to talk to Viv?' Again, I keep it casual.

'Briefly,' he says, not faltering. My husband is a good liar. This is new. This is something I didn't know.

'She's very beautiful,' I say.

He sniffs, like he hasn't heard me, and gets up.

'I have to get to work. Will you be okay? I brought you a bucket.'

I look over the side of the bed and see the dark blue bucket from the garden with a cobweb hanging off the handle. The plastic smell from it makes me queasy.

'Thanks,' I say. 'That makes me feel so much better about myself.'

He gives me another grin, ruffles my hair so it falls into my eyes, and leaves, shouting goodbye as he heads down the stairs.

So it's come to this. Ruffling my hair like a child.

I must have fallen asleep again because when I wake the sun has moved on and is no longer shining directly in my eyes through the window. I heave myself out of bed, throw on a pair of loose running shorts and a black T-shirt of Tristan's with a Batman logo on it. It swamps me, which is exactly how I want to feel today, covered up and hidden away. I plod down the stairs to the kitchen, tugging the T-shirt further down over my body. The cooker clock says 12.18. There's still coffee in the pot. I pour the dregs into a mug and stick it in the microwave to blast it and then drop two slices of bread into the toaster. My bag is on a kitchen chair. I take my phone out and see a message from Tristan asking if I'm okay, and a message from Polly: *Weird night.*

Call me, followed by a horror face emoji. I pull out a chair to sit down, ignoring the fact the microwave is beeping and my toast has popped up. I reply to Polly's message: *Me too. Chat later.* Then I message Tristan: *Yes, I'm alive.*

I take my coffee from the microwave, but it's too hot to drink straight away so I butter my toast and gaze out of the window. My eyes are drawn to the ever-static shed at the back of the garden. It makes my heart heavy just to look at it.

A smattering of colour catches my eye. The once dry, unsightly patch of dirt by the fence with my shrivelled dead pansies is now full of new fresh, perky, vibrant ones. Forgetting about the shed of doom, I amble out to the garden to take a closer look. Maybe Tristan did it, but he hates the garden. In fact, the patch, along with the shed, has become another item on our list of things we no longer talk about. Viv's head appears over the fence. Again, it seems odd that she can climb up with such ease. She must be very flexible as well as agile.

'Morning,' she says, peering down at me with her head tilted.

'Hey,' I say. 'Sorry about last night.'

'Whenever I see you, you're lying on your back,' she says, with a little laugh. I nod in response. It's true, I've fallen over twice now in Viv's presence.

'Do you like it?' she says, indicating the pansies.

'You did it?' I say.

'It didn't take long. Anyway, I owe *you* an apology.'

You do, I think, for flirting with my husband while I was passed out cold in your bed. Actually, 'flirting' is too passive a word. 'Connecting' is more accurate and damning. But I can't only blame Viv. Tristan was in the garden of his own volition, sitting rather well in a deckchair, paying Viv the kind of attention he used to pay me. But I've had moments with Jude, so we're as bad as each other. And my desire to have a friend is just about trumping the jealousy.

'I'm the one who puked in your bushes and had to be put to bed,' I say. Although, maybe she's apologising for putting her hands on Tristan's knees.

'I'm the one who gave you gin and weed.'

'Yes, it's all your fault,' I say with a feeble grin.

'What are you doing right now?'

'Mostly feeling sorry for myself.'

'Fancy doing something fun?' she asks, with a mischievous look.

I smile at her. You bet I do.

13

Him

Izzy's key is still in the front door when I get back to the house. I put it on the side table in the hall where she normally leaves it. I won't tell her she left it in the door as she'll be mortified enough after throwing up and passing out at the new neighbour's housewarming party.

I find her in the bedroom, lying on top of the bed covers fast asleep, still in her dress, one shoe on. I go downstairs, grab the bucket from outside the back door, fill a pint glass with water and bring them both upstairs to her. I gently take off her other shoe and roll her into bed, pulling the sheet up to her waist.

Stripping down to my boxers, I squeeze into the en suite to wash my face, thinking about Viv with her hands on my knees. The energy between us was intense. I would never be unfaithful to Izzy, but there's something magnetic about Viv that pulls me to her. Blood rushes to my groin and suddenly I'm hard as a rock. Fuck.

I quietly shut the bathroom door and, with one hand on the wall, begin to relieve myself conjuring images of Viv on the driveway the night she arrived. As she looks up at me watching her from the window, her face buried in the black hoodie, she moves her hand down the front of her jeans, staring right at me. Shit. It's all over rather quickly.

I slip into bed beside Izzy and try to concentrate on anything but Viv.

Finally, thoughts of the garden shed send me off to sleep.

★

The dream of the prowling, sniffing dog outside the bedroom door wakes me with a start again. I'm unsettled and confused for a moment, but there's no denying the flutter of excitement in my chest.

The image of Viv on her driveway looking up at me is front and centre in my mind. I quickly dismiss it and jump out of bed. I have to get to work. I can't spend my morning masturbating in the bathroom.

I glance over at Izzy and wonder if she might be up for having sex, which is totally ridiculous and selfish of me. Her mouth is wide open and her hair is stuck to the side of her face as she sleeps off her night from hell. Instead, I wrap a towel around my waist, go to the main bathroom and step into a cold shower.

Cold showers are supposed to be good for your immune system and some say they prolong your life, so I don't take them too often for fear I might live to be ninety. They're also excellent for getting rid of inconvenient erections.

I say goodbye to Izzy who has woken up and is mortified about passing out at the party. I do my best to lighten the mood, ruffle her hair and go.

The front door shuts and I stop for a moment. I've never ruffled Izzy's hair before – well, not seriously anyway. It definitely came from a place of affection, but of what kind? The kind you show to a pet? I decide not to think about it.

Apart from Viv putting her hands on my knees for a few seconds, I have nothing to feel guilty about. I'm allowed to have sexual thoughts about another woman as long as I don't follow through. I'm allowed to masturbate to whatever thoughts and fantasies I want. It's my own private business. Same goes for Izzy.

But Izzy and I have drifted so far apart recently we can barely see each other on the horizon. I feel it every day and even more now that Viv has arrived. Viv has brought a new energy into our lives, like a mini volcano rumbling next door, the potential to explode simmering under the surface.

Should we be afraid? When a volcano erupts, it annihilates everything in its path, burning and melting what was once alive and breathing.

One thing I'm certain of, as much as I might want things to stay the same, they never do. Sometimes I initiate change myself, like getting away from Bradley and Martha. Other times change has been forced upon me. Unavoidable, uncontrollable and unforgettable – an emotional tsunami. Most of the time I drift. A plastic bag in the wind.

But I am not afraid, not this time.

Being in Viv's presence last night reignited every cell in my body, putting me on full charge, if only for an hour. And I can feel the results today. My walk is that bit faster as my heart insists I keep up with its new pace, and I'm pretty sure my shoulders are slightly further back than they normally are. I'm also breathing more deeply, even though the air is sticky and warm.

I'm fifteen minutes early to work and the front door is already open. I smell onions and garlic cooking the minute I enter, so I know Monty is here, and I hear the hum of a vacuum cleaner coming from the upper level. Lucia, our cleaner, rigorously hoovers the carpet. I shout hi to her and she looks up and waves. She has earphones in and I wonder what she listens to. Is it the radio or true crime podcasts? Whatever it is, she's always completely engrossed.

I take the stairs two at a time down to the kitchen, passing the spot Spencer and Maddy were going at it hammer and tongs last night and wander through to the kitchen, relieved and pleased to hear the Gipsy Kings.

I never get tired of listening to the Gipsy Kings. In fact, I find them reassuring. As long as I hear them, I know it will be a good day.

On closer examination, it means Monty rules the restaurant and the staff with his moods. Gipsy Kings equals good mood. Good mood equals good day. Everyone happy. But if Monty is in a bad mood – or worse, if the Gipsy Kings aren't playing – we know there's a serious problem.

Monty's power over the psychological wellbeing of everyone who works in Lily's is quite extraordinary, and for the first time in all the years I've worked with Monty, I'm a tad resentful. I've always felt proud and relieved that I have the ability to contain the beast, but now I'm asking myself, at what cost? These feelings dissipate quickly as the sound of the Gipsy Kings gets louder. I probably shouldn't take myself too seriously at the moment, as I'm definitely on a new-neighbour high of some kind.

I hover at the entrance to the kitchen, careful not to breach the threshold. I say hi to Monty, who has his back to me as he washes asparagus in a giant colander at the sink. He flicks around and nods at me, barely looking up. I take a step back. There's something different about him.

At first, I can't put my finger on it, then I realise he's not wearing his glasses and he looks strange – younger, even. His eyes appear swollen around the edges with slight bags underneath.

'What?' he says, annoyed. I realise I'm staring at him.

'Sorry,' I say. 'You look different without your glasses on.'

He shrugs like it's no big deal. But it is. I've never seen him without his glasses, not even for a second.

'Are you wearing lenses?' I say, wishing I could drop it, but I'm so intrigued by seeing Monty's actual face. It's as though his soul is on show.

He doesn't answer me. I'm about to say 'it suits you', but stop myself.

'Soup and bread,' he says to me. He's talking about the staff meal. Staff lunch meals are always lighter than the evening meal.

'Lovely,' I say. I stay hovering, wanting to look at him one more time without his glasses on.

He looks up. 'What?' he says again, even more annoyed. I hold up my hands to indicate nothing and back out of the kitchen. I head up to the restaurant, meeting Spencer on his way in. We have a quick chat about the bookings today, which include two tables of eight. I tell him Monty is wearing contact lenses.

'No glasses?' says Spencer in amazement. 'I have to see this.'

He goes to take the stairs to the kitchen but I stop him.

'Don't make it obvious.'

We quickly discuss why now, why today; has he always had lenses and never worn them to work, or is this his first time? Which leads to more questions about whether or not Monty has a social life. We've never heard him talk about going out and we've never seen him go anywhere.

We conclude that Monty is an enigma. Spencer decides to have a gawk at Monty later, when it's more natural to be in the kitchen.

Maddy bustles in, fresh-faced and smiling. She barely looks at Spencer and focuses on me. Spencer slips in behind the bar and busies himself with folding the glass cloth. She asks me how I am but doesn't hang around to hear my answer and disappears down the stairs to put her bag in the wine store. I glance at Spencer, who distracts himself with the bookings page on the iPad.

Maddy comes back up the stairs, tying her apron. I tell her we need to set two eight-tops upstairs and she goes to do it.

Spencer calls out after her: 'I'll bring the wine glasses.'

'Cheers,' she yells back.

'We're talking now,' he says to me.

'Pleased to hear it,' I say.

Spencer nods over my shoulder and I turn to see a tall young woman with a cropped haircut. She looks to be early twenties and is wearing a long summer dress with thin straps and white trainers, a woven basket satchel across her body. Her short hair is tucked behind her ears and her dark brown eyes dart around the restaurant, self-conscious. I wonder if she's walked into the wrong place. Maybe she's looking for the clothes boutique next door.

'Can I help you?'

'Is Monty here?' she says in almost a whisper.

'Sure, come in and take a seat,' I say, indicating table one. 'I'll get him for you.'

I give Spencer a curious look and head down the stairs to the kitchen.

'There's a woman upstairs to see you,' I say to Monty, trying to sound casual.

Monty's eyes widen, in either surprise or delight, it's hard to tell. I see now that his eyes are actually a green-brown and I decide I quite like him without his glasses.

He starts pacing the kitchen, running his hands through his hair, looking at the clock on the wall, and I realise his response is not one of delight or surprise, but panic. He mutters that the woman is early.

'You're expecting her then?'

'Later,' says Monty, not quite upset enough yet to give me full sentences.

'Shall I ask her to come back this afternoon?' I say, quite enjoying watching Monty out of his comfort zone.

'No,' he blusters and quickly smooths his hair, checking his appearance in the reflection of the oven door. He grabs a piece of kitchen roll and rubs his teeth with it, although I'm not sure what that will achieve. Monty has white teeth anyway.

He takes a deep breath and looks at me, eyebrows raised. He's asking for my opinion on his appearance.

'You look great,' I say, hiding my amusement. Monty nods and ploughs on past me up to the restaurant. I follow, determined not to miss this.

In the restaurant, Monty – acting the gentleman – gently ushers the woman outside the restaurant.

Spencer has gone from the bar. I hear Maddy's infectious laugh coming from the upper level. I go up the steps and find Spencer leaning against a table and Maddy standing in between his legs, his hands resting on her hips.

They jump apart and Spencer knocks a glass over on the table.

'We need to get set up, guys,' I say.

Spencer, tray in hand, swishes past me and back down to the bar. Maddy looks at me, sheepish.

'We kind of made up.'

'I can see that.'

138

'It's not what you think.'

'I'm not thinking anything,' I say.

'We understand each other,' she says.

From one shag at the bottom of the stairs? I want to say, but don't. Even me and Izzy after thirteen years don't really understand each other.

'I know we were at each other's throats yesterday, but it was all part of it, you know?' she says.

At the bar, Spencer whistles to himself as he stocks up the fridge with mixers.

'So all is forgotten?' I ask him.

'Pretty much,' he says to me, trying to be nonchalant.

'I don't want to lose Maddy, okay?'

'Relax,' he says. 'It's all cool.'

But Maddy is not cool. Maddy is a serious individual who won't take kindly to being dispensed with. Although it's not fair to judge Spencer on the basis of one previous break-up.

At the window I part the voile slightly to see onto the street. Monty is outside with the girl. He talks quietly to her, stroking the palm of her hand with his forefinger.

In all the time I've worked with Monty, he has never worn contact lenses and never had a girlfriend – that I've known about anyway. Does this delicate young woman know all the facets to Monty's complex personality? Of course she doesn't, not yet anyway. Monty is putting his best foot forward and don't we all in the beginning.

Spencer comes up behind me to see outside too.

'Monty has a girlfriend then,' he says. 'I thought he was gay.'

That explains why Spencer is so confident around Monty. He probably assumed Monty fancied him. He probably assumes everyone fancies him.

'It explains the contact lenses,' I say.

I add 'vain' and 'ability to show kindness' to the already long list of character traits I have stored in my brain for Monty.

Monty comes back inside and Spencer and I quickly disperse. Spencer grabs the ice buckets and plummets down the stairs. I flick around on the iPad, pretending to be engrossed in table plans. Monty pauses in front of me, his arms folded. I look up.

'I need an advance on my wages this month,' he says in perfect English.

'Right,' I say, hiding my surprise. Monty never asks for money up front. In fact, he never talks about money. 'How much?' I ask.

'All of it,' he says.

'I'll check with Deniz but I'm sure it'll be fine.'

He nods at me and goes downstairs. I peer out of the voile again but the waif-like girl has gone. I wonder if Monty's in some kind of trouble.

By the time the two tables of eight are seated, watered and wined, everyone's in full work mode. The two A-level students, Nicole and Adrian, think nothing of going up and down the stairs with plates and cutlery for four hours flat. I admire them for their energy and demeanour, always pleasant, never complaining. They don't even wince when Monty shouts 'take it hot' in their face. They just take it hot.

I pass Monty the order for the first table of eight. He glances at the chit and then shakes his head in disgust. I know it's because someone ordered the fillet steak special to be cooked well done. I say nothing as he huffs and puffs and flings open the fridge door. The resentment stirs in my gut again. I push it away, unwilling to add any stress to the work environment. Monty's always like this. There's no point having an issue with it now.

Maddy comes downstairs carrying dirty plates and shoves them on the counter for Bill to wash up. Bill asks her if she's alright.

'Racist arseholes on table six,' she says. There's a fighting spirit in her tone that worries me. She tells me they were taking the piss out of her Irish accent, saying 'thirty-three and a third' like 'dirty tree and a turd'. I say I'll take care of it but she refuses to let me step in.

'I can handle it,' she says and flounces back upstairs. Bill shrugs at me, impressed by Maddy's confidence.

I decide to keep an eye on table six, four guys in their thirties, already on to their third bottle of Fleurie, a heavy enough wine for lunchtime, plus the pre-drinks at the bar. Maddy waltzes straight back up to the table, putting on her strongest Irish accent.

'Is there anything else I can get for you there, fellas?' she says, itching for a reaction.

'Is there any chance,' says one of the men with a pudgy face, putting on a terrible Irish accent, 'that you're a secret member of the IRA.'

'Take no notice of him,' says another of the men. 'He thinks he's funny.'

'And he really isn't, is he?' Maddy says.

'Dirty tree and a turd,' says the pudgy-faced man, grinning at his friends.

Spencer is at the table beside them serving bar drinks. He glances over. I step up to the table.

'Would you like to see the dessert menu?' I ask them.

'What do you think?' the man asks Maddy. 'Shall I have the raspberry "bomb"?'

Maddy leans over, in full breach of his personal space.

'I think that's the perfect dessert for an English twat.'

The pudgy-faced man, no longer laughing, pushes her away from him. It's an instinctive reaction, but Maddy makes a big thing of it.

'Don't put your hands on me.'

Spencer comes flying over, tray under his arm, ready to defend Maddy.

'Everyone calm down, please,' I say.

'Apart from this stupid prick, everything's fine,' says Maddy.

'Who do you think you are, talking to me like that?' he says, getting unsteadily to his feet, cheeks flushed.

I step between Maddy and the pudgy-faced man, placing my hand on his chest.

There haven't been many situations like this to deal with at Lily's. Monty's mostly the biggest challenge. Of course, people can have too much to drink and need to be put in a taxi home, but generally our customers are well-behaved, genteel folk.

We've had a few couples row at a table in hushed whispers and call the bill early, sometimes one storms out, leaving the other to deal with the sympathetic looks from other customers.

We had a break-up once where a man told his girlfriend it was over and he didn't love her anymore. It seemed to come out of the blue, as the actual words, heard clearly by one of our waiters, were delivered at the end of the meal over empty coffee cups. Why would anyone choose a restaurant to break up with someone, and at the end of the meal?

It must have been spontaneous. He walked out and left the woman at the table in total disarray. She tried to pay the bill several times, even though her now ex-boyfriend had paid on his way out and we had told her that.

What had caused the man to suddenly end things? Was it an act of cruelty? Or had the woman revealed something about herself that switched the light off for him? It made me wonder if falling out of love can be as instantaneous as falling in love.

I keep the pressure on the pudgy-faced man's chest, despite the sweat oozing through his shirt onto my hand. I'm aware of Maddy behind me, giving him death stares.

The best way to deal with this is to get him and his friends quietly and peacefully out of the restaurant with as little disruption to other tables as possible. But the mild resentment over Monty from earlier has been reawakened, free from the box I thought I had locked it in, threatening to make an appearance.

The pudgy-faced man's eyes narrow as his lips morph into a sneer. He's just a bog-standard thug throwing his weight around. Alcohol is no excuse. I'm sure he has his reasons for being a dickhead, but he's still a dickhead.

'I'm going to have to ask you to leave,' I say, sticking to the quiet-and-peaceful plan.

'What about her, calling me a twat?'

'I'm afraid I agree with her.' I indicate he follow the rest of his lunch party down the stairs to the lower restaurant. One of his friends, clearly embarrassed, tells him to come on and says they'll settle up the bill.

But the pudgy-faced man is not moving.

'Listen to your mate,' I say.

'Or what?' he says, lifting his chin, indicating he's ready for a fight.

I lean into his ear. 'Thing is, you were right about her Irish connections.'

I give him a tight smile, almost apologetic.

He's not sure if I'm joking or threatening him, but either option doesn't really fit the vibe of being gobby in a restaurant. And the alcohol is making him question his better judgement. After a moment, he pushes me aside and makes for the stairs, deciding it's time to bail.

'The food in here is shite anyway,' he says loudly, so everyone can hear.

I stay close behind him as he lurches from side to side, making his way past the bar to the exit.

Monty and Bill's heads poke out from the top of the stairs from the kitchen. Monty is frowning, after hearing the comment about his food. Spencer and Maddy follow too.

The man reaches the door. His friends are waiting outside. I secretly will him to keep walking, knowing he'll probably have an urge, a compulsion, driven by pride, to turn around and have the last word.

He pauses at the door. He turns to look at me, weighing up if he wants to go nuclear on this.

'Wanker,' he says and pushes through the door onto the street.

I'm surprisingly calm and, if I'm honest, rather pleased with myself. I played the tiniest bit dirty, which I would never normally do.

'You okay?' says Maddy, coming up to me. 'I'm sorry for winding him up.'

'He was a prick,' I say.

'He most certainly was,' says Spencer.

Maddy slips her arm around Spencer's waist and gives him a squeeze.

'Get back to work, you two,' I say, wondering if they are in fact the real deal. Or will one of them, one day, see something in the other they don't like and just call it a day, with no warning. Maybe after a meal in a restaurant.

My phone beeps with a message. It's from Izzy. There are also five missed calls from her. The message says: *Call me. In A&E with Viv.*

14

Her

Viv chatters away as we hurtle along a country lane in her bright orange Mini. There's something unnerving about electric cars. It's the absence of noise when you accelerate, not like the gas-guzzling rust bucket. I grip the side of my seat with my left hand so she can't see how terrified I am by her driving. We approach a right-hand bend showing black chevrons indicating a sharp turn. Before I can shout, she slams on the brakes and my whole body lurches to the left as she takes the bend at forty miles an hour. She drags on a cigarette, blowing the smoke out of her half-open window, but I'm starting to feel carsick. We're heading to Shoreham, a quaint old English village that I've been to once before with Tristan for lunch, although it's a distant memory. Viv turns to me, taking her eyes off the road.

'What do you think?' she asks me. I don't know what she's talking about. I've been so concerned with holding on for dear life, I haven't heard a word she's said.

'Sorry, about what?' I say, keeping my grip on the seat and staring ahead in case she fails to notice an upcoming hazard like another car on the road. She turns to face the front and puts her foot down as the road ahead becomes clear for about a mile.

'About the lady who lived in the house before me,' she says. 'I found a box of her stuff in one of the wardrobes, crockery and candlesticks. Shall I call her family?'

'They'll only throw it in a skip. Keep it or give it to charity,' I say.

'You liked her, didn't you?' she says.

'We both did,' I say, remembering how Mrs Jenkins used to wave at me from her living room window in the morning.

Finally, Viv slows down as we drive into the village. The huge 'reduce your speed' sign probably did the trick. We weave our way through the narrow roads, passing country cottages covered in flowering climbers with colourful, overflowing window boxes, across a little bridge with a meandering river running beneath. Up ahead is an old wooden entrance to some church grounds. In the distance a medieval spire rises from among lush green conifers. We park right outside the entrance, where a sign reads: *Blessed are the dead which die in the Lord*. It doesn't mean much to me, which probably means I will go to hell, if there is such a place, and especially after all the carry-on with Jude. Not to mention the constant lying, which is a first-degree sin.

We climb out of the car and the warm breeze brushes against my bare arms. I glance at myself in the reflection of the window as I shut the door. I got dressed in a hurry and it shows. I'm wearing an old vest top which has lost its elasticity and a pair of shorts that are a tad too short. I shunt them down an inch or two to avoid my bum cheeks hanging out. Viv is wearing a tissue-thin white cotton dress with almost invisible straps. She has a silky slip on underneath shielding her underwear. Her wild hair is clipped up but most of it is flowing over her shoulders and down her back. I'm not particularly tall and Viv is around the same height as me, five foot four, but I feel large and cumbersome around her.

Across the street from where we are parked is a pub called Ye Olde George Inn nestled among the cottages. It has a tiled roof and black picnic benches with parasols outside. Viv takes my hand and leads me down the narrow road, past the pub and back towards the bridge, swinging my arm as we go. She tells me the plan is to walk along the river then have a late lunch in the George. She pulls two bottles of water from her floppy bag and passes one to me.

'To keep the hangover at bay,' she says.

Grateful for the fluids, I guzzle half the bottle and then wish I hadn't as it sloshes about in my stomach making me queasy.

We reach the bridge and I follow her down the footpath that winds alongside the river. The path is clogged with families and buggies and dogs but Viv is undeterred and hurries me past the other walkers until we're out in front, streaming ahead, leaving the chaos behind. The footpath soon becomes a green woodland path lined with long grass and yellow and white daisies. We're still hugging the water's edge as we walk, the low grassy banks and gentle babbling of the river creating a tranquil and calm effect. Through the trees I can see fields and hills stretching into the distance.

A sense of peace descends, a feeling that everything will be alright. A Golden Labrador breaks through the trees and bounds towards us, ears flat, tail wagging. Viv and I fall to our knees, scratching his ears and ruffling his fur. I'm reminded of Tristan ruffling my hair. The Labrador sits beside us, panting, enjoying the affection. The owner, a woman in her sixties in hiking boots with a walking pole, breezes up to us, fresh-faced. We tell her how lovely her dog is and she smiles with pride. She carries on walking back the way we came and the dog quickly follows at her heel. Viv carries on along the river but I'm transfixed for a moment, watching the dog run after his owner, his pack. A pang of sadness hits me, making me momentarily cold. I push thoughts of Mindy away, alone and afraid that day without me. I've never told Tristan the full story, only that I had a dog that died when I was young. I know it's unusual, weird even, to still be emotionally raw over something that happened so long ago, so I keep it to myself. And the peeing-on-the-rug incident is not something I'm eager to share with anyone either.

Viv shouts for me to catch up and I turn and hurry along, following her as we stray off the path and ramble into the high grasses and wild flowers. We continue on under low-hanging trees and through clusters of midges until the grasses recede and we emerge from the undergrowth into a clearing where there's a bend in the river. The bank that leads down to the water's edge is speckled with more wild daisies and buttercups. Viv stops and takes a deep breath, throwing her arms out.

'Ready?' she says and whips her dress and silk slip up, pulling them over her head with ease. She unclips her bra and kicks off her trainers. She flicks her knicker elastic with her thumb and grins at me.

'Best not go all out. It's a family place.'

She runs down the riverbank, her hair trailing behind her, her perfect curves and soft skin shimmering in the sunlight, and plunges into the river, releasing a deep breath as the cool water hits her warm limbs. I glance around. The coast is clear so I slip out of my trainers, take off my vest and shimmy out of my shorts. I unclip my bra and drop it onto the pile of clothes. The breeze swirls around my cleavage, giving me a feeling of freedom and abandon. I race down the bank and wade into the water to join Viv. She giggles and splashes me and I let myself sink beneath the surface, fully submerged where all is quiet. I come up for air, sweeping the wet hair off my face, and push backwards so I'm lying face up looking at the blue sky. Viv appears beside me, also on her back.

'It's beautiful here,' I say.

'You're beautiful,' she says to me. She takes my hand and we lay there, two half-naked figures floating in a river, contented, safe.

A child screeches nearby and we lower our legs and sink into the water up to our necks, shielding our nakedness for reasons of decency but also shyness, on my part anyway. A group of children scamper down the bank to the water's edge where they stop and eye us curiously.

'Is it cold in there?' one of them asks.

'Freezing,' says Viv.

'Mum, can we go swimming?' shouts another child at the top of her lungs.

'Keep walking, everyone,' calls a woman from the woodland path. She's too far away to see us. The kids, although disappointed, run back to join their mother. Viv and I look at each other and let out a relieved sigh.

'I'm really pleased you moved in next door,' I say.

'It's like we've known each other forever,' she says.

I agree and venture it's called fast friends. She says it's more like fast soulmates. I feel a stab of guilt over Tristan. He's my soulmate. At least he was. Then I remember Tristan with Viv's hands on his knees and the guilt vanishes.

We climb up the bank and jump around trying to air-dry, holding our breasts to stop them bobbing about. The sound of more approaching voices makes us dress in haste. We lie back on the grass, which is slightly crisp to touch. If the hot weather keeps up, it'll be yellow and straw-like in no time.

'Do you think it's climate change, this weather?' asks Viv.

'Yes,' I say. 'Mankind is doomed.'

'So it doesn't really matter what we do then?' says Viv, rolling onto her side and propping her head up with her hand, her skin already turning a light beige from the sun.

'Well, don't stop recycling,' I say. 'You never know.'

'I'd like to paint you,' she says.

'And Tristan? Would you like to paint him?' I want to know who she likes best.

'Oh, yes, him too,' she says. 'Or maybe do a sculpture of you and a painting of him, oil on canvas.'

Viv has no shame and I like that about her. She leans in, her face close to mine. Her lips look soft and full. Then she kisses me gently on the lips.

I don't move. I've never kissed a woman before – well, except Amanda Stokes in primary school and that was only because we were playing a game. I'm also not sure if this is a 'girls that are friends' kiss. Is it supposed to be funny or sexual? My crotch throbs slightly, but that could be from the thrill of it.

It's different to kissing Tristan. Men are a different species, I suppose. She smiles down at me, reaches out and arranges my wet hair around my face on the grass. Her touch is delicate and sends tingles through my skull.

'I could paint you, just like this. A modern Aphrodite in all her glory.'

'Wasn't Aphrodite the goddess of love and beauty? Because I think that's a bit of a stretch.'

Viv throws her head back and laughs, allowing me to see right into her mouth. I'm surprised to see she has a few fillings in her back molars.

'Aphrodite is also the ultimate symbol of femininity,' says Viv, lying back.

'Hmm, again, a bit of a stretch,' I say.

'You're funny,' she says.

As funny as Tristan? I want to ask. I roll onto my side, facing her. Her eyes are closed, her face in the sunshine. I reach for my phone, feeling bad that Tristan's working while I'm out frolicking with the new neighbour, who he clearly has a crush on. And now she's kissed me and I don't know where that leaves things. Letting her kiss me is definitely worse than him letting Viv put her hands on his knees.

There's no message from him, which must mean he's still at the restaurant. He probably thinks I'm still at home sleeping off my hangover. I see the message from Polly again, about her weird night. Maybe if I'd stayed at the pub I might have kissed Jude. But a kiss with Jude would have led quickly to the point of no return. Viv kissing me seems far less risky.

We walk back along the river and through the trees, chatting as we go. Viv tells me about her last art exhibition and how one person bought four pieces, all from her serpent collection. She said the buyer also wanted the sculpture she has in her garden, but she kept it for herself. She slips her arm through mine as we walk.

We grab a table outside the George and order two lemonades and two baskets of wild haddock and chips. Viv asks for extra tartar sauce. My hangover has completely gone now and I wolf down my entire basket of food in about three minutes flat. I watch Viv across the table as she talks then laughs out loud at a random notion she's had. I laugh too, so as not to miss my cue. I'm not really listening to what she's saying as I'm too mesmerised by her. If anyone's a modern-day Aphrodite, she is. How can anyone resist her?

We drive back in silence. The sun, fresh air and greasy food has slowed our systems down, making us dreamy and weary. And Viv isn't driving like a maniac now and seems to be in no particular hurry. As we get nearer home, she reaches over and pushes a strand of my hair behind my ear.

'What are you doing now?' she asks.

'Nothing,' I say, hoping to keep hanging out with her. She suggests we stop and get some wine and then order pizza. I say that sounds great.

We pull into the Waitrose car park near my work. I point out my college building in the distance, jutting up into the sky.

'Do you like your job?' she asks.

'It's very rewarding,' I say.

'Liar,' she says, grinning at me.

'It is,' I insist. 'Nothing makes me more happy than when a student does well,' I say, knowing I sound insincere. I do care about my students, but it's up to them how well they do in their exams.

'It's alright if you don't like your job.'

'Why? You like your job.'

'Sometimes I don't. It's hard making a living from art.'

'Okay, fine, I don't like my job. It's boring, teaching the same syllabus day in, day out, year after year, but it pays the mortgage.'

'Is that what they'll put on your grave? She paid the mortgage?'

It's better than 'she led students on and lied to her husband'. Or is it? Actually, anything is better than 'she paid the mortgage'.

'I don't care what they put on my grave,' I say, trying to sound cool.

The doors slide open and the air conditioning blasts us from above. In the bright overhead supermarket lights, Viv looks even more golden and tanned, her cheeks pink. She walks in the direction of the alcohol section and it's only now it occurs to me that Jude might be here. This is his Waitrose. I slow down, contemplating going back to the car. Viv turns and flicks her head, encouraging me to keep up.

'I'll get some snacks,' I say. She seems to accept this and pushes through the barriers to where the wine and beer is on display. Keeping my head down, I hurry along to the snacks aisle and grab popcorn and a large packet of salt and vinegar crisps.

'Izzy?'

It's Jude, of course, standing behind me in his uniform. He's holding a box of Ryvita packets, which he is stacking on the other side of the aisle, where there is a large trolley full of other boxes and products. I'm immediately self-conscious, as I always am around him.

'I wasn't sure it was you,' he says, his cheeks flushed. He swallows and puts the box down. I've thrown him off. Then I remember I'm wearing a skimpy vest and very short shorts and my hair is down and wildly curly after getting wet and drying naturally.

'I've been in the countryside for the day,' I explain, hugging the popcorn and crisp packets tight to my chest.

'Listen, what I said yesterday at the pub,' he says in a low voice.

'Let's forget everything, okay?' I say, interrupting him. 'You've got exams coming up.'

He looks at me, lost, hungry. I should have waited in the car. His eyes sweep over my legs and then my face and hair.

'You look incredible,' he says. My heart rate jumps, making me giddy, and I'm relieved when Viv comes swanning up to us with a bottle of red wine and a carton of pineapple juice.

'We can make piña coladas with the rest of my Bacardi,' she says, holding up the pineapple juice. I attempt to usher her away, saying a quick goodbye to Jude. But Viv's already eyeing Jude with interest.

'Who's this?' she asks.

'Jude,' he says. 'One of Izzy's students.'

'You all done?' I say to Viv, indicating the wine and juice, trying again to whisk her away.

'I'm Viv,' she says, staying focused on Jude. 'So what's Izzy like as a teacher? Is she any good?'

'Don't be asking him stuff like that,' I say. 'Don't answer that,' I say to Jude.

'She's pretty good,' says Jude, grinning. Viv looks from me to Jude and then back to me again. Please don't let her think she's putting two and two together because she'd be right.

'We have to go,' I say to Jude and reach to take the wine and juice from Viv. 'Let me get this.' But Viv holds on to it.

'Don't be silly, it's my shout. And we won't drink all the Bacardi by ourselves.' I glare at her, willing her not to invite Jude to join us, my hand still on the carton of juice, trying to get it off her. 'Leave it,' she says kindly, tugging it away from me. But she pulls too hard and loses her balance. The carton falls from our hands and explodes on the floor, spilling everywhere. I reach out to grab her but instead she steps back and slips on the spilt juice. She flies up in the air and lands awkwardly on her side with her left leg twisted underneath her, the bottle of wine miraculously still in her hand.

'Shit,' I shout, going to her. Jude follows.

Viv leans up on her elbows, wincing in agony. 'My leg doesn't feel right.' Jude and I look at her leg. From the knee down, her leg is pointing in the wrong direction. Viv grips my arm tight then passes out.

By the time the ambulance arrives, she's regained consciousness and howls in pain as they lift her onto the stretcher. I say I'll follow in her car. Jude says he'll follow later but I tell him there's no need. He reaches out to take my hand and I let him hold it for a second before disengaging myself.

'Thanks for your help,' I say.

'Take my number,' he says. 'In case you need anything.'

'Really, you've done enough,' I say. The last thing I need is sex texts with Jude.

At the hospital, they let me through to see Viv, who is in an examination bay. They gave her pain relief in the ambulance but she's still whimpering in agony and holding her fist to her forehead.

'They're sending me for an X-ray. Do you think I'll need surgery?' she asks, biting her lip. Judging by the twisted shape of her lower leg, I'd say that's inevitable.

'Let's wait and see,' I reply.

Two porters arrive and wheel her down to X-ray. I try to call Tristan, but there's no answer. I try him again and again, suddenly needing to speak to him, to know he's there.

What if I no longer had Tristan to call? I'm gripped by an intense loneliness and sit down on the hard plastic chair in the now empty cubicle. It's an all-too-familiar feeling and, if I'm honest, I've had it my whole life. Even when Mindy was alive, it was lurking in the undergrowth of my mind somewhere. I try to ignore it, push it away. Most of the time this works, but it's lingering now. I don't have anyone else except Tristan. I call Tristan again; still no answer. I send him a message.

There's a swishing noise as a cleaner comes by with her mop and bucket on wheels. She is wearing white overalls and blue gloves. She gives me a sympathetic look, one that says you'll get through this. She must see a lot of worried faces working in an A&E department. But the smell of detergent and the echoing trundle of trolleys and monitors awakens my senses and brings on a new feeling. One of hope.

Tristan and I ended up in A&E when we were first together. My housemate, Sheila, had had too much to drink and was having her stomach pumped. Sheila was wild and unrestrained, a loose cannon who thought nothing of downing a bottle of vodka by way of a funnel. If I had been at the party, I would have stopped her, but I wasn't. She'd gate-crashed a sports society house party, believing she'd find a fit, energetic rugby player up for a night of passion. Instead she nearly killed herself.

She'd managed to get home in a taxi but the driver had to ring on the door to ask for the fare to be paid. It was a hostage situation: pay the money and I'll hand over your comatose friend. Tristan was with me thankfully and, between the two of us, we got her into the house and onto the sofa. Her face had a strange sheen to it and her skin was cold to touch. I put a blanket over her, tucking her in, but Tristan was worried. I was sure she'd sleep it off as she normally did, but when her lips started to go blue, Tristan called an ambulance. When it arrived, we couldn't answer the paramedics' questions about what she had ingested, but we knew it was likely to only be alcohol. Tristan and I followed the ambulance in a taxi and sat in the waiting room for news. And that's when it happened. Tristan reached over and took hold of my hand. It was an attempt to comfort me, but also himself. But more than that, it gave me a sense of being connected and together, and something unknown stirred inside me.

Our relationship since meeting in the student union bar was still relatively casual, mostly meeting up at the weekends. We'd either end up back at his flat or at my house for drunken sex. There was no denying we liked each other and there was an inexplicable bond between us; something that attracted us to each other that first night. Whatever it was, it had kept us together for nearly a year, no questions asked, no analysis of why or where we were going. But that night in the hospital, when he took my hand, my feelings for him shifted.

I stared down at his hand holding mine and then looked up at him, seated beside me. He had an anxious expression on his face and his eyes were glued to the doors leading to the emergency department. Suddenly, I admired everything about him: the way his eyebrows drooped at the corners, and his nose, which, while larger than an average nose, was exactly the right size for his face. His cheekbones, high and defined, lifted every part of his face when he smiled. His mouth was full and I loved the way his two front teeth were slightly crooked, with one sitting slightly over the other. He hadn't shaved that day and had a five o'clock shadow. I glanced down at his legs, which were long and strong. He sensed my eyes on him and I quickly returned to staring at his hand in mine. I wanted to keep it there forever. Then, out of nowhere, I admitted to myself that I loved him. It came as a welcome revelation. Until that moment I had been secretly worried I was like my mother – unable to express real emotion, let alone show love towards another person.

I picked up his hand and kissed it briefly. A compulsion more than just an expression of affection. From that day on, Tristan had the power in our relationship, only he didn't know it.

Sheila's parents had arrived in a flurry, still in pyjamas, jackets half hanging off them. I tried to imagine how my mother would react if it had been me in the hospital. Not only would she take the time to get dressed properly, possibly shower first, but she'd probably arrive wearing lipstick, having applied it en route.

Now, sitting in the hospital alone, I miss Tristan so much my whole body aches. Somewhere along the way I've lost him. My phone beeps with a message. It's Tristan and he's in the waiting room. I rush out and see him standing at the desk in his suit, having come straight from work, his hair floppy, falling over his ears. He needs a trip to the barbers, but he does look handsome. He sees me and I immediately slow down, not wanting to appear panicked. After all, I'm not actually worried about Viv. I want to throw my arms around his neck and feel his arms around me, but I don't, not sure how my affections would be received and terrified I'd create an awkward moment, one that might lead to the kind of 'chat' I've been avoiding. He puts a hand on my arm and looks at me, full of concern.

'What happened? Is Viv okay?'

Not am I okay, but is Viv okay. He's right to ask about her first, she is the one who's hurt, but it sits uneasily with me.

'She slipped in the supermarket and broke her leg. She'll need surgery.'

I see him looking at my curly hair. 'We went for a dip in the river in Shoreham. My hair got wet,' I explain.

'Shoreham?'

'It was Viv's idea.'

'Did you have lunch?'

Why does he want to know if we had lunch?

'Just pub grub.'

He nods, like this is acceptable, but my heart sinks – he's jealous I got to spend the day with Viv, not that Viv got to spend the day with me.

'Are you okay?' he asks me, finally.

I'm about to say that no, maybe I'm not okay, when a nurse comes to the door and calls my name. They've taken Viv into theatre and it could be a while. I rub my eyes with tiredness, exhausted from the events of the day, and last night.

'Go home,' Tristan says. 'I'll wait.'

Like I'm going to let that happen.

'I should be here when she wakes up,' I say, purposefully making it sound like I'm more important to Viv than he is, which I believe I am. We are fast friends, fast soulmates. Part of me wants to tell him that we kissed. Part of me wants to tell him all about Jude as well. But that could signify an immediate end to everything here and now, in the A&E waiting room and, despite my jealousy over his jealousy, I'm not ready to do that.

A gentle prodding on my arm stirs me from a restless sleep.

'Izzy?' Tristan's voice drifts into my consciousness.

I open my eyes, immediately dazzled by the bright strip lights in the hospital. I've been sleeping with my head on his shoulder. I don't remember putting it there or even falling asleep.

'Viv's out of surgery. We can see her.'

I sit up, fully awake now. I glance out of the window. It's dark now.

'Shouldn't you be at the restaurant?' I say.

'Spencer and Maddy have it under control.'

We take the lift to the ward where Viv has been placed. Standing in the lift with Tristan, I think about the lust I felt for Jude only a few days ago. I eye Tristan, trying to muster the passion I once felt for him, but he's only interested in the lift counter going up. We get out on the fourth floor and amble along the ward past the beds, looking for Viv. Then we see her at the end of the long room, lying flat on her back, her leg in a cast on a pillow.

'Jesus,' Tristan says quietly.

'Be positive,' I mumble back and lead the way up to her bed. She is awake, but still groggy. Her hair is flattened against her head and seems darker than its usual pale blonde, but her green eyes are just as sparkly and piercing.

'Hey,' I say.

'Izzy,' she murmurs, grateful to see me, and takes my hand.

'Hi, Viv,' says Tristan, coming in beside me.

'You came too,' she says, smiling up at him.

'How are you feeling?' he asks.

'Better since they pumped me full of morphine,' she says. She is very relaxed and has a dreamy look about her. Tristan glances down at me holding Viv's hand, taking note.

The doctor appears as if from nowhere, like he stepped off a cosmic conveyor belt. He asks Viv a few questions. He has a large head that seems too big for his shoulders. He's charming and calming. I'm curious, as I always am with doctors, if this is their real personality. Are they like this all the time or when they get home does the mask slip? Do they slag off their patients and colleagues to their spouses? Are they mean to their kids?

The doctor asks if we're Viv's family and we tell him we're just the neighbours.

'Is there a family member you can call, or a friend?' he asks Viv. 'You're going to need help when you're discharged.'

'God, no,' she says, waving away his concerns. 'I don't need people fussing over me. I can look after myself.'

'You need to rest the leg, only a little weight-bearing, for at least four weeks.'

'We can help,' says Tristan, piping up. I was thinking the same thing and I'm annoyed now he said it first. The doctor agrees this is a better option.

'That's nice of you,' says Viv, putting her hand on her heart, clearly in morphine wonderland. I'm not sure she'll want to accept our kind offer when the drugs wear off. If she doesn't want a friend to care for her, I doubt she'll want us to do it.

'She can stay with us in our house until she's properly up and about again,' I say, going one step further than Tristan. If he's happy to look after her, let's do it under our roof. And the thought of him slipping off next door to 'attend to the new neighbour' isn't very appealing.

Viv drifts off to sleep and I think how peaceful she looks. I glance at Tristan, who is also looking at her. He has a funny expression on his face but I can't work out what it means. It's either awe or concern. It doesn't matter which it is, they're both annoying.

We exit the hospital together. I have the keys to Viv's car and suggest I drive it back to the house. It feels odd, the two of us sitting in Viv's cool orange Mini, me in the driver's seat, Tristan where I was sitting only hours earlier. He runs his hands over the smooth leather dashboard.

'It's slicker than I thought it would be,' he says. I don't respond. I don't know what he wants me to say. Yes, it is. No, it isn't. Yes, it's better than the rust bucket.

'Are you alright?' he says. I hear the frown in his voice.

'I feel bad for Viv,' I say, like her pain is my pain. 'She's going to find it hard to be laid up, not able to work.'

'Do you think the bed in the spare room will be comfortable enough for her?' he says.

'Of course it is,' I say, trying to keep the mounting irritation out of my voice. I mean, what kind of question is that? Does he want to buy new bedroom furniture now? Is he finally going to redecorate the spare room just for Viv?

'It's about time we got a new bed for that room,' he adds, casually, looking out of the window.

Oh, it's so touching, really it is, the trouble and expense he's prepared to go to for Viv to be comfortable. I slam on the brakes, coming to a red light, jolting Tristan out of his seat so he bumps his head on the roof of the car.

'Oops, sorry,' I say.

15

Him

Izzy emerges through the double doors to meet me in the waiting room. I'm taken aback by her long legs falling out of a pair of skimpy shorts and the loose vest top over a lacy bra. Her hair is incredibly curly, resting on her shoulders. Given the recent changes in the way she dresses and presents herself, I do my best not to appear too surprised. She immediately reminds me of the Izzy I first met: unpredictable, untamed, exciting.

She comes straight up to me, her forehead wrinkled in concern and stress. I want to hug her and tell her it's okay but doubt she wants me to do that. Instead I ask how Viv is.

She tells me Viv fell in a supermarket, broke her leg and probably needs surgery. I watch as she pushes her wavy hair from her face. She seems self-conscious and explains she was in Shoreham with Viv and that they went swimming in the river.

I'm more than a little confused. When I left for work this morning, Izzy was lying in bed nursing a hellish hangover, riddled with shame. She says they had lunch in a pub. I have a vague memory of Izzy and I going for a walk in Shoreham and having a pub lunch too once.

'It was Viv's idea,' she says, as though this shuts down any further need for explanation. I ask her how she is – it must have been stressful rushing Viv to hospital – when a nurse appears at the door to tell us they're taking Viv into theatre.

Izzy rubs her eyes, clearly exhausted. I suggest she goes home and rests and that I'll wait. But she insists on staying, saying Viv will want her to be there when she wakes up. I stifle a smile.

We've barely known Viv twenty-four hours and here we are in A&E behaving as if she's a cherished family member. In fairness to both of us, Izzy and I have been thinking about who the new neighbour would be for more than six months now, or maybe, unconsciously, since Mrs Jenkins died. And Izzy did meet Viv a few weeks ago, although I'm pretty sure now the encounter entailed more than a wave over the garden fence like she implied. I wonder what else she isn't telling me.

As much as I avoid asking questions about us, right now I have a yearning to know the truth about everything. Why did she stop wearing make-up? Why doesn't she want to have sex with me anymore? Why didn't she tell me about meeting Viv? Why is she keeping things from me? Instead I offer to get her a coffee.

When I arrive back, she's asleep with her head propped up in her hand. I put the coffee down, sit beside her and gently manoeuvre her around so her head can rest on my shoulder.

I sip the scalding, weak coffee from the plastic cup and check my phone. No panic calls from work, which is a relief.

My mind wanders to the supermarket where Viv broke her leg. What was Izzy doing in a supermarket with Viv anyway? What were they buying? I'm not jealous, just intrigued. So intrigued I forget how hot the coffee is and burn my tongue.

A cleaner mops the floor around me and I get chatting to her. She says it'll be much busier later, around midnight. 'Fights, accidents, overdoses, stomach pumps.' She could easily have been reading from a shopping list.

I really need to go to the toilet but I don't want to disturb Izzy. I'm pleased she's asleep. It's a good way to avoid inevitable conversations that might claw their way to the surface if we were just sitting here, side by side, waiting, with nothing to distract us. We might be forced to rip the plaster off.

I'm not ready to do that. I'm not sure I ever will be.

Outside it's finally dark. It must be getting on for nine o'clock. I've always been good at reading the time by sunrise and sunset.

As a child I was obsessed with how few daylight hours there are in the winter months. I used to wake early and sit on my bed looking out at the black sky, willing the sun to rise, waiting for light to hit my part of the world so the feelings of hopelessness would dissipate and leave me ready to face the day with a fake smile.

My arm is now completely numb from the weight of Izzy's head on my shoulder. The same nurse from before comes over to us. Viv is out of surgery and we can see her now. I gently shake Izzy, making sure her head doesn't slip off my shoulder.

Her eyes shoot open and she sits bolt upright, disorientated for a moment. Her cheeks are flushed after her snooze but she's also glowing from catching the sun today.

We take the lift to the ward in silence. I put it down to the fact Izzy is still half asleep and probably not in the chattiest of moods. She glances at me and I instinctively look away, fixing my eyes on the lift counter. I'm sure she has questions for me too, probably starting with why I insisted on staying at the hospital as well.

We get off at the fourth floor and I let Izzy lead the way. I'd rather proceed with caution. I'm not sure how I'll feel when I see Viv. Will I feel the same as I did the night before – aroused, intrigued, in awe? Maybe it was all in my head.

I follow Izzy through the ward, two steps behind, checking every bed, when Izzy stops in her tracks. At the end of the ward, in the last bed on the right, is Viv. Her blonde hair, a messy halo of gold, gilds her pillow, and her left leg, in a full cast, lies on top of another pillow.

'Shit,' I say.

'Don't be negative,' says Izzy and marches up to Viv's bedside.

I follow, appearing beside Izzy, attempting to be casual.

Izzy holds Viv's hand and I ask how she's feeling. She gives me a warm smile, focusing her crystal green eyes on me, and says how nice it is to see me.

She looks vulnerable. Not frail or weak, just fragile, and I have an urge to sweep her up into my arms and carry her away with me, although I have no idea where I would take her. Another idea, another dream with no plan.

The doctor arrives. He's about forty years old with sandy-coloured hair and perfect teeth. He gives us a wide, confident smile, which puts us all at ease. I'm drawn to how clean and shiny his nails are.

His main concern is Viv's aftercare and I'm sure they need to free up the bed. Viv says she doesn't want a fuss or to call anyone to help so I blurt out that we'll look after her, referring to myself and Izzy. I speak before I've actually considered it, but Izzy doesn't seem phased by my suggestion. Izzy suggests Viv can stay with us, in our house, until she's up on her feet.

Izzy thought I was offering to go in and out of Viv's house to care for her, but I wasn't. I'd also meant for Viv to move in with us but say nothing. Viv seems open to the idea.

The doctor is pleased with the arrangement. They're keeping her in for a couple of nights and, all going well, she can go home on Monday.

Izzy and I barely exchange glances, both unsure what the other thinks about Viv coming to live with us for a while.

For me it's quite simple. I can't wait.

Izzy drives Viv's Mini back to the house. I like being in Viv's car. It smells of her musky scent. I make a comment about the interior leather finish, just to make conversation. Izzy stares ahead, either distracted or purposefully not listening to me. I'm not sure which I prefer.

I ask her if she's okay and she says she's worried about Viv not being able to work. I imagine Viv lying on the bed in our spare room and ponder aloud if Viv will be comfortable enough staying with us. Izzy says she will.

I suggest we get a new bed for the spare room. We've always said we would and, with someone coming to stay now, it seems like the perfect time. Then Izzy slams on the brakes to stop at a red light. I bounce in my seat and hit the side of my head on the window.

She apologises and carries on driving. She definitely seems distracted. Maybe she's not happy with Viv coming to stay with us after all. It is a big undertaking considering we barely know her.

The tingling feeling floods my nervous system again and this time it's a familiar sensation. I had the same experience on the train when I waved goodbye to Martha and Bradley and headed off to college to start my new life, although I didn't know what that new life was going to be yet.

When Viv arrived next door, I felt a shift inside me, like everything was starting to change or move, although I wasn't sure in which direction.

I may have only just met her, but she feels familiar to me, as though I've known her my whole life. It's how I felt about Izzy too. When we first met, anyway.

During our wedding ceremony in the registry office, as we said our vows, I had to muster every ounce of self-control not to start blubbing. The fact that Izzy, this amazing woman standing beside me, loved me enough to be my wife, to promise to love and cherish me in sickness and in health, was overwhelming.

I thought nothing of making my promises to her; of course I would love her forever.

Our wedding was small. Six guests in total. I pushed for the smallest wedding possible so it didn't seem strange that my adopted parents weren't attending, which could lead to questions about why I never saw them. I had given Izzy various stories about them moving to Dubai and then to New Zealand, which I'd really warmed to as it's the farthest country from England.

For the first few years, after leaving home, I sent Christmas cards to Martha and Bradley but then stopped that too. I considered it a weaning-off period. My biggest fear was that they'd come looking for me or turn up unannounced, 'popping in for a visit', but they never did. And I doubted, by the time I got married, that they ever would now.

It was easy to cut ties because I didn't need anything from them. I got full student loans and worked in bars, so didn't require financial support. Not that they ever offered. In fact, Bradley had done everything he could to steer clear of the subject.

When Martha asked me where I'd be living at university, Bradley quickly shut her down. 'Don't be asking him personal questions,' he said. 'I'm sure the lad has it all worked out.'

You see, Martha and Bradley were happy to pay the extra living costs incurred by having a child, like food, board and clothes, but shelling out for higher education was not in their remit. And I was pleased it wasn't or they probably would have tried harder to stay in touch.

I had Bradley pegged from the start. If spending thirty pounds on refreshments to host his friends for a poker night sent him into a state of anxiety, the idea of his adopted son needing thousands of pounds for university would have triggered a total breakdown.

He was never going to give me a penny and I knew that, but I also knew he wouldn't be able to live with the embarrassment of his 'loving son' never visiting. I'm sure he invented a cover story for the neighbours as to why I never darkened the cul-de-sac again, something that cast him in a good light.

Izzy's mum, Jo, came to the wedding, wearing a yellow dress and yellow hat. Izzy said she looked like an ice cream cone and was trying to upstage her. But there was no fear of anyone upstaging Izzy that day. She wore a simple silk dress that shimmered around her elegant frame. She looked like a goddess. And I felt like the chosen one who had slayed the dragon and won the fair maiden's hand.

We had lunch in a local fish restaurant. It was low-key and understated, which was what we both wanted. Izzy's friend, Sophie, who lives in France, came with her husband, François. And Will and Pete came too. Pete brought his girlfriend, who we'd never met and was painfully shy and hardly spoke.

Jo asked me across the table over lunch where my parents were, and said that she had been hoping to finally meet them. I said they were in New Zealand and that it was too far to travel, what with Martha's blood pressure issue. She eyed me with curiosity and I ignored her.

I hadn't been rumbled in seven years, I wasn't about to let nosey Jo drag the truth out of me now, at my wedding.

At the beginning of our relationship, when Izzy asked me about Martha and Bradley, I said they were nice and had looked after me well, but other than that I had nothing in common with them. She said I was lucky I didn't have to see them, alluding to how she wished it was the same with her mother.

Jo had too much to drink during the lunch and while we were all having coffee, she pulled herself to her feet to make a speech, one hand on the table to support her lurching body. Jo is a woman of few words so this was out of character. She talked about struggling as a single parent, raising a child and working full-time, then moved on to how it had all paid off and she was now able to gift us enough money for the deposit for a house.

She whipped out a cheque and paraded it around the table for all to see. It was embarrassing for everyone and even though people didn't want to look at the amount, they didn't have much choice.

It was a cheque for fifty thousand pounds. My jaw hit the floor, as did everyone else's except Izzy's. She grabbed the cheque and shoved it back in her mother's bag, telling her it was not the right time or place for gifts.

I said a huge thank you and told her she was too generous. Whatever Izzy's issues were with her mother, it was still a wonderful present. Jo basked in my praise, as Izzy downed an entire glass of wine.

The day after the wedding, we flew to Paris for our three-day honeymoon. The first day was a write-off due to our monumental hangovers. Lunch had spilled over into a pub and on to a nightclub with Will, Sophie, François, Pete and Pete's quiet girlfriend. We'd been knocking back tequilas at three in the morning and Izzy had to throw up on the plane.

When we finally ventured out into the glittering city of love for a slap-up meal in a fancy restaurant, I broached the subject of the cheque.

'We're not taking it,' Izzy said to me over the flickering candle on our table. 'She's trying to buy her way into my good books.'

'Why is she in your bad books?' I asked. 'Apart from being a snob, she's not that awful.'

'Clive, her boss and now fuck buddy, gave her some shares in his company and she made a ton of cash from it. That's not "making an investment".'

'It's still a lot of money,' I said. 'We could buy a house.'

'Plenty of people rent; in fact, most people do,' she said.

'Okay, if that's what you want. But tell me what she's done or did to make you hate her so much.'

'I don't hate her,' she said, waving me away. 'If we accept the money and buy a house, she'll think she has a right to come over whenever she wants.'

'It'll probably be a couple of weekends a year. I can live with that.'

Izzy took a gulp of her wine, clearly not savouring the taste of the thirty-euro bottle.

'Fine, we'll take the money,' she said.

This was even more confusing. Rather than explain her feelings of resentment, she gave in.

That night back at the hotel, while I was brushing my teeth wearing only my underwear, Izzy moved in behind me and slipped her hands down the front of my boxers. We never made it to the bedroom.

That's how it was with us back then: spontaneous, urgent, intense. Every cell in my body belonged to her. Maybe over the years, as my cells naturally died and stopped regenerating, my love for Izzy diminished along with them. Tiny, minuscule lights going out one by one.

It's hard to know when everything started to wither and wilt. My feeling is it began the day we moved into the house. It came with too much baggage. The money from Izzy's mother that left a sour taste in Izzy's mouth. The problematic shed that caused a row. And the realisation that life was draining away. I had yet to make a success of my life, not that I had a plan on how to achieve that. I read somewhere that action follows thought, but it really doesn't.

Slowly, gradually, my belief in Izzy, in our us-ness, began to fade. I knew, in time, all that would be left would be a sense of nothingness.

I could see it coming. I could sense it. I felt powerless to stop it.

16

Her

College is less chaotic than usual. It's the last week of classes – revision only – and you're doing well if a third of your students show up. I'm pleased to see my class is half full, which is a decent turnout this close to exams. I scan the tired, angst-ridden faces in front of me and relax. No Jude at least. I pop by Polly's class but it's empty. I check with Vicky in the office and she tells me Polly called in sick. I send her a message, checking she's okay, but she doesn't get back to me. She lives nearby and I decide to go and see her during my break in case she needs anything. I could also do with a chat. Maybe I'll confide in her about everything that's been going on. Jude, Viv, Tristan. My dirty secrets. Viv is due home from hospital this afternoon and Tristan will be there to welcome her. I wish it could have been me, but it would have been too strange to take the morning off work when Tristan can easily do it. He did his best to hide his excitement about Viv's imminent arrival, but I heard him humming in the shower and he took longer than usual to get dressed, probably deciding what to wear. God, he is so transparent.

Yesterday I waited until he went to work before I went over to Viv's house to get her clothes for hospital and for when she stays with us. She had given me a list of what to pack, including art materials. Tristan hung around until the last minute to leave, hoping to come next door with me but I managed to stall until he left. His fascination with Viv continues to sicken me. The more I observe it, the more disconnected I feel from him. But I hold the power. I'm Viv's female friend and that trumps husband of female friend. If this is a competition, I'm streets ahead already, simply because of my gender.

I was surprised to find Viv's house in total chaos and almost wished Tristan had been with me. Apart from the hanging sheets, which had been taken down and dumped in a pile in the empty living room, she hadn't lifted a finger to tidy up after the party. There were cans and ashtrays strewn all over the house. The kitchen floor was sticky to walk on and the whole house smelled like the Tiger's Head before its makeover. The serpent sculpture outside was totally out of place among the mess and debris in the garden. I cleared up the empty cans and crisp packets, but it was going to take hours and a total blitz to get it properly clean.

Entering her bedroom was like walking into a yet-to-be-organised jumble sale. Clothes sticking out of boxes and drawers. The wardrobe doors were open only because you couldn't close them due to piles of clothes bulging out from the bottom. Nothing was hanging up, because she had no hangers. I didn't remember it looking this bad on the night of the party. She must have woken up the morning after, attempted to unpack and lost interest after five seconds. Then decided to buy pansies to plant in my garden and spend the day with me instead.

I managed to find clothes that sort of resembled the items on her list. There was no way I could find exactly what she wanted. I would have been there all day. When I got to the hospital, I found the doctor with the oversized head sitting on the chair beside the bed.

'Dr Bergen was telling me how lucky I am. It could have been a lot worse,' she said, giving him her pussycat smile. Dr Bergen quickly stood up, smoothing the front of his suit, flattered by Viv's attentions. And why wouldn't he be? He's only human.

'Are you chatting up the doctors now,' I said to her after he left.

'I was being friendly,' she said with a cheeky smile.

It should have been obvious from my very first meeting with Viv that she doesn't follow social norms or rules. She doesn't care about order and prefers chaos. She does whatever she wants when she wants, and when you add it all up, coupled with her underworld, lizard-princess charm, she is, in essence, a whole lot of trouble. And it's too late to back out now. Tristan and I have welcomed her into our home and our lives. The runaway train just shifted up a gear.

Polly's flat is above the Boots on the high street, so it's not far to walk. It's even more humid and sticky today. There might be a storm coming or at least a smattering of rain to wash down the dusty streets. Everyone I pass appears weary and parched. My big work bag feels heavier than normal and sweat trickles down my cleavage. I should have left my bag in the car, but I've been devoid of sensible thinking for weeks now. There's a Spar shop on the way and I stop to buy a packet of custard creams, anticipating a good old chinwag with Polly, as long as she's not too sick. My inner Sophie, voice of reason, isn't getting through to me at the moment. Either I'm choosing not to listen or it's getting drowned out by my insistent thoughts about Viv and Tristan and Jude. The mood I'm in at the moment, I might even tell Polly about the carpet-peeing incident and I've never told anybody about that.

My bravery dissipates the minute I'm standing at Polly's front door. I'll probably wimp out and resort to talking about superficial and banal rubbish. The intercom bell is silent when I press it. The few times I've been here, I've been with Polly so I'm not sure if it's broken or not. I step back and look up at the open window, the light grey curtain static in the heat. I press the intercom button again and Polly's voice floats through the little box.

'Hello?'

'Polly, it's Izzy. Are you okay? Vicky said you're sick.'

'Oh, hi. Come up,' she says.

A buzzing noise tells me to push the door and I enter the small hallway with the steep, narrow staircase leading up to Polly's front door. I take the stairs slowly, plodding almost, weary from the heat. The door flies open and Polly appears in a golden light wearing a T-shirt and shorts that are more like hot pants. Her hair is tied in a long, loose ponytail and she smiles at me, fresh, bright and definitely not sick. She throws her arms around me, pleased to see me, and my bravery returns. Polly is certainly someone I can trust.

'I brought custard creams,' I say, handing them to her.

'Old lady biscuits. Love it,' she says.

'I take it you're feeling okay then,' I say, looking around at her messy flat with clothes hanging over the back of chairs and the sofa. Although compared to Viv's house, it's immaculate.

'I couldn't face work today. Two very late nights in a row and a hangover this morning that I thought was going to kill me.'

She goes to the kitchen area and puts on the kettle. It's a neat, bright, open-plan flat with a large bay window allowing plenty of light in. I take a seat on the sofa, facing the TV. The sofa is soft and comfy and I find myself relaxing. I notice an Xbox and two controllers on the floor in front of the television.

'You've got an Xbox?' I ask, surprised. I don't remember her having an Xbox before. I wonder if we might play a game.

'It's not mine,' she says.

She comes to the sofa and leans over the back to talk to me, lowering her voice.

'I've had a guest,' she says, nodding to the closed bedroom door. 'He's in the shower.'

'What? You should have said,' I say, getting up, mortified for gate-crashing her party. Our big chat, if it was in fact going to happen, can wait.

'Don't leave,' she says. 'I'm kind of hoping he'll go, to be honest. He's been hanging around all weekend, brought his bloody Xbox over. I'm worried he thinks he's moving in.' But I don't want to stay. Any desire I had to spill my guts to Polly has evaporated.

'Something happened on Friday night,' she says, putting her hand on my arm and pulling me back down onto the sofa. 'Don't judge me,' she says.

'It's your business who you see,' I say, trying to get up again. 'I'll see you in college tomorrow.' But her hand stays firmly on my arm.

'After you left the pub on Friday, Malcolm and Tobias turned up so I stayed and had a couple more drinks with them. Then I kissed someone.'

'Shit, it's not Malcolm, is it?' I say, quickly realising it can't be Malcolm as he was in the staffroom this morning.

'God, no, but that would be easier. It was a student,' she says, blushing now.

I stare at her, a chill running through me as I wrack my brains for the right response. 'What about your age limit rules?' I say.

'I was pissed,' she says. 'I took leave of my senses, or they took leave of me.'

She puts her forehead in her hands. 'Everyone else had left and it was just me and him at the bottom of the beer garden. He was telling me this story about his manager at work or something and it was really funny. Then before I know it, I'm snogging his face off.'

Where's your self-control, woman? I think, judging her, feeling the urge to put my hands on my hips, but it's only because I'm envious.

After all these weeks beating myself up about my indecent behaviour with Jude, Polly kisses a student, brings him home and has sex with him all weekend. Compared to her, I'm almost a model teacher. I've been way too hard on myself.

'I wasn't planning it. He came back here to call a taxi and things got out of hand. Shit, do you think I'll get fired?'

She looks at me, worried now.

'How old is he? Alex, right? He must be eighteen.'

'Alex?' she says.

'The cheeky lad who offered to buy us a drink?' I check the bedroom door, really hoping I can be gone before he comes out.

'It wasn't him,' she says, appalled.

'You said you kissed a student,' I say, confused now.

'I did, but not Alex.'

A cloud of dread swoops in around me, wrapping me up, tightening my rib cage. Before she even says his name, I know it's him.

'His name's Jude. He's in your class, I think. Repeat psychology.'

I frown, feigning confusion over who Jude is, then pretend to have a vague idea of who she's talking about. I yank my arm away from her hand and stand up, heading for the door. I'm not even trying to be subtle about leaving. I'm running now.

'He's nineteen,' Polly says, following me. 'It's not against the law.'

'It's none of my business, really,' I blurt out. 'But he's one of my students and this will be awkward,' I say, which is true.

'He's actually really mature. And there's only a couple of weeks left of term.' I can't believe she thinks it's okay. 'If he wasn't a student at the college, no one would care,' she says.

'Sure, if you say so,' I reply, fingers on the door handle, ready to bolt.

The door to the bedroom swings open and Jude appears in a pair of shorts, bare chest, rubbing his hair dry with a pink towel.

'Jude, you know Izzy,' Polly says.

Jude peers out from under the towel. I throw my eyes to the floor, not wanting to look at him. The truth is, I'm trying to arrange my face so I don't look judgemental or jealous. I want to maintain a neutral expression, mildly friendly, possibly disinterested.

'Yeah, hi, Izzy,' he says, bouncing on the sofa, both arms along the back of it, the pink towel around his shoulders.

He bounces onto the sofa, both arms along the back of it, the pink towel around his shoulders.

'Sorry I wasn't in class today,' he says. 'I got waylaid.' He leans forward, grabbing Polly and pulling her down onto his lap. Polly, embarrassed in front of me, flails around trying to get up.

'Stop it,' she says, giggling despite herself. Jude plants a big kiss on her lips and then lets her get up. Polly gives me a look, half startled, half thrilled.

'I have to get back,' I say, managing to keep it together, though I'm pretty sure if I don't leave soon, I will projectile vomit all over him.

'Don't rush off on my account,' Jude says, eyeing me with mischief. What is he playing at? Flirting with me in Polly's flat where he's been hanging out all weekend? He continues to stare at me, that same stare he used to give me from the back of the classroom. 'Oh, yeah,' he says, now remembering about Viv and the accident. He's about to ask me how she is, but I don't give him a chance.

'I really have to go,' I say quickly and duck out of the door, down the stairs and onto the street, speed-walking back to college. When I saw Jude at the supermarket on Saturday, he'd already been with Polly, but still made it clear he'd drop everything if he could join me and Viv for a drink. I have never felt more pathetic and undeserving than I do right now, and that's saying something.

I limp my way through the afternoon class to break and brave the staffroom. I'm expecting it to be quiet and it is. The nursing staff have all packed up and left for the summer, which makes it feel even more deserted and devoid of life. By the end of the day, the college building is airless and stifling and I can't concentrate, unable to stop thinking about Jude and Polly, so I give the four students in my last class a pep talk about their exams and send them home early.

The rust bucket is one of three cars left in the car park. I climb in and put my hands on the steering wheel to rest for a moment. My limbs are weighed down, my arms too heavy to even put the key in the ignition. A creeping darkness begins to swell in the cavity in my chest and I can't place the source. One minute it's emanating from my solar plexus, then my gut, then my brain. All at once everything inside me contracts, pushing tears from my eyes. I quickly blink them away, burying the urge to cry in the back of my throat.

I'm an idiot. A fool. I believed Jude was in love with me and there was a special, karmic bond between us, which made it

acceptable that I hadn't reported it or dealt with it properly.
I convinced myself that our relationship didn't fall into the
ordinary, run-of-the-mill 'student crush on teacher' category. I
fought the attraction I had for him, when really I was secretly
hoping, waiting, for the day I gave in to it.

There was no special connection with Jude. He's just a
charmer, a chancer, maybe a sex pest. To think I nearly mastur-
bated in a toilet over him. Bile slips up my throat. I swallow and
manage to slot the key into the ignition. I'm nothing more than
a desperate, confused woman in her thirties, whose marriage is
slowly disintegrating, and who was easily flattered and aroused
by the attentions of a handsome young man. All it took were a
few lingering looks from the back of the classroom and I was
eating out of his hand. Dressing down and not wearing make-up
had all been part of the game. The more I tried to push him
away, the more I was responding to him, the more he desired
me. And I knew it.

I try again to locate the origin of the spidery inky mass
spreading through my body. It's mostly coming from my gut,
but that's just the surface. It goes deeper, layer after layer, to
every cell and fibre of my being. Is it guilt, from engaging
in an affair of the heart with a student behind Tristan's back?
No, it's deeper than that, and now the twisting, gnawing sensation becomes familiar. I've experienced this before – a thick tar
bubbling up from the hidden recesses of my mind and body,
back to haunt me.

It's my shame. Shame from today, from the past, from places I
can't even remember, lurking beneath, waiting for an opportunity to stick its head above the parapet and murmur, you can't
hide. It's from failing Tristan; for being more interested in and
excited by a nineteen-year-old student than I am by him. It's
from kissing the new neighbour. It's from peeing on Clive's rug,
and from having a mother like mine, who lacked the capacity to
love me and caused the death of my dog. This sticky tar feasts on

my shame, increasing and multiplying, a virus on the rampage, mutating in order to survive.

My phone beeps with a message from Tristan: *The patient has landed x*

Viv's in our house. The thought relaxes me and the murky hot tar recedes a little. For some reason, I need Viv.

17
Him

The taxi van pulls up at the end of our drive and I go out to meet it. I'm wearing a fresh, casual shirt over jeans. The last three times Viv's seen me, I've been wearing a suit, and I'm including the time I talked to her at the window. This is a more natural version of myself.

The driver climbs out. 'Special delivery,' he says to me, sliding open the back door. We did offer to collect Viv from the hospital but she insisted on sorting out her own transport. She's also only agreed to stay for as long as absolutely necessary.

Two crutches appear first from the back door and I rush forward to assist. Viv looks out at me from inside the taxi.

'I'm not sure how I'm going to do this,' she says, her leg sticking out in front of her in a full cast. She gives me a slightly embarrassed smile.

'My advice is, go for it, see what happens,' I say with a grin.

'Great, thanks,' she says, smiling back, but more at ease. She pushes herself forward and grips the edge of the car door frame. I hold out the crutch for her good side first, which she takes, but she's not agile enough on her crutches yet for the required ergonomics to heave herself into an upright position.

'You'll have to step up there, mate,' the taxi driver says to me. 'Pardon the pun, love,' he says to Viv. Relieved the taxi driver has forced my hand, I quickly slide my arm around her waist and lift her gently out of the car so she's standing on one leg, doing my best to focus on the task at hand rather than the closeness of her body to mine.

'Good man,' the taxi driver says, grabbing Viv's bag from inside and putting it over my shoulder for me. He slides the door shut, climbs back into the taxi and pulls away, giving a toot as he goes. We both watch him drive off, as though he's abandoned us.

'I hope you don't regret this,' Viv says, looking up at me, her face leaning against my shoulder.

'Not at all. What are neighbours for?'

'I'm not sure I'd do it for you.'

'Now you tell me,' I say.

She laughs, which again makes me wonder if I'm funny enough to do stand-up. I help her to the front door and it's only now I wonder how on earth we're going to navigate the stairs. Should we have put her in the living room on the sofa bed instead? No, that would have been too weird for everyone. Once inside the hallway, we both eye the staircase like it's Mount Everest.

'Last chance to pull out,' she says. 'Seriously, I can stay in my own house.'

'I'll carry you up. It's only a few stairs,' I say.

She allows me to sweep her up, her arm around my neck, my arm under her knees, holding her bad leg straight. She feels light and delicate, as though she might float away were she not weighed down by the leg cast. I carry her up the stairs, proud of the ease with which I do this, and into the spare room where I carefully place her down on the bed.

'Thank you, Tristan,' she murmurs. My ego is going mad. Flex your biceps, it roars. Of course, I don't.

I prop her leg up with a pillow, put her crutches by her side and retreat to the door. I'm not sure what to do. Should I offer her something to eat or a cup of tea? Maybe she wants to sleep. Izzy and I have done our best to make the spare room inviting. There are crisp clean sheets on the bed and I brought a painting in from the hallway to hang on the wall, a picture of a bluebell wood that we picked up at a car boot sale. Izzy put my R2-D2 speaker by the bed – my Secret Santa present from Spencer last Christmas. He definitely went over budget. It's hard to know if he was being lazy or generous.

The only other person who's ever stayed in this room is Izzy's mother, Jo, who always complains how sleeping on the bed is akin to sleeping on a bag of tinned cans. That suits Izzy just fine. The less Jo visits, the better.

'I'm really grateful to you and Izzy,' Viv says. 'It's only for a while, until I've got the hang of those,' she says, indicating the crutches.

I wave away her thanks.

'Actually, do you mind passing them over to me again? I'd like to go to the bathroom,' she says.

I pass the crutches to her, almost tempted to throw them up in the air and catch them. She hops up on one leg and wobbles as she balances herself.

'Maybe today's not the day to be trying too much,' I say.

'What am I supposed to do, pee in a bucket?' she says.

I put my arm around her waist for the second time. 'Tomorrow you can try on your own,' I say.

We make it across to the bathroom and I leave her to it. I offer to make some tea and a sandwich and she says that would be lovely.

I bounce down the stairs, whistling to myself. I quickly construct a cheese and tomato sandwich and pop a peppermint tea bag into a cup of hot water. By the time I get back upstairs, she is still in the bathroom. I call out to her, asking if she's okay.

'I'm afraid I'm not,' she calls back. I open the door to the bathroom and poke my head in. She is sitting in the bath with her broken leg in the air.

'I lost my balance,' she says, her voice low. 'I'm more useless than I realised.' A tear trickles down her cheek and all I want to do is protect her.

'The first day on crutches is always the hardest,' I say. Then I swoop in, hooking my arms under her and lift her up. I'm not quite sure how I manage to do it at such an odd angle, but I do. She puts both her arms around my neck this time, her head close to my chin as I carry her out of the bathroom and back across to the bedroom.

Feeling more gallant and knight-like now, I gently lay her back on the bed. She keeps her arms around my neck for a moment, then says 'thank you' again before releasing me.

'I don't think I've ever been carried so much in one day,' she says.

'First time for everything,' I say, grabbing the plate with the sandwich and putting it beside her on the bed. I tell her Izzy will be home soon, to put her at ease. Viv clearly needs a woman around to help her wash and dress.

She pats the side of the bed, inviting me to sit down. I perch on the end instead, wanting to behave properly and respectfully.

'Did Izzy tell you we went skinny-dipping in Shoreham?'

'No, only that you went swimming,' I say, imagining Viv rising from the water, glistening, dripping, flowers nestling in her flaxen hair, which barely covers her naked torso. Suddenly I'm very hot. I need to get out of this room. I know if I stay I'll say something stupid, or worse, do something humiliating. Don't forget the 'sad man' shed incident.

I make excuses about needing to be at work, which is true, so not actually an excuse. It's my day off but Deniz is on holiday in Mauritius. I know this because Gina told me. Deniz always makes it sound like he's doing something extremely low-key for his holiday, like camping in Wales, and he never returns with a sun tan, which must be near impossible to achieve given his sallow skin. And I can't leave Spencer and Maddy on their own, especially with Monty the way he is at the moment.

I shout goodbye again, charge down the stairs and out the front door. It's only now the guilt sneaks up on me. I imagined Viv naked in the river in Shoreham. I didn't imagine Izzy.

Maybe that's okay. I don't have to attribute meaning to every thought I have; my inner and outer worlds are not connected and don't need to be. But if that's true, why does it feel like my fantasies of Viv are endangering my very existence? Suffocated by my own imagination.

I start my walk to work and send Izzy a message that Viv has arrived.

This mystery woman, who came under darkness, who I watched from behind a curtain, naked, and who watched me, is now in our house and I'm no longer sure if it's a good idea. We didn't think it through – at least, I didn't.

The door to Lily's is propped open by a folded piece of card wedged under the door. Having the door open creates a cross breeze through the restaurant, but Deniz insists on the door being shut at all times. He says everything gets covered in dust from the high street and that bits of rubbish get blown inside. It's also too noisy and so not in keeping with the whole hidden–oasis vibe. When customers enter, calmness and serenity are supposed to immediately descend.

I agree with Deniz on all fronts so kick the piece of card away from the door, lean over the bar and pop it in the bin.

Spencer bounds up the stairs carrying cellophane-wrapped table linen to set up the tables for evening service.

'Alright, Tristan,' he says. 'How's Izzy's mate doing?'

'She's our new neighbour actually.' So my friend too. 'She had surgery but she's on the mend now.'

Spencer pulls a face at the word 'surgery'.

'She'll be staying with us for a while, just till she's up and about,' I say.

Spencer raises his eyebrows so they're nearly in the centre of his forehead. I'm not normally this open about my private life (which amounts to anything outside of the restaurant) but I'm curious what an outsider thinks of the situation.

'Staying with you?' he says. 'How long have you known her?'

'Few days,' I say.

'That's weird, isn't it? Having a stranger in your house.'

'She didn't have anyone else to call.'

'Is she pretty? Is that your angle?' he says, grinning, as Maddy comes flying down the steps from the upper area and joins us at the bar.

Spencer fills her in on my situation, leaning close to her over the bar.

'You need to talk to Monty,' she says with an ominous nod.

'Why?' I say, panicked that Monty's having another meltdown.

'He's always looking for recipes for disaster.' They both laugh.

'Hi, Monty,' I say to Monty, who is now standing behind them.

Maddy thinks I'm joking and gets a fright when she turns and sees him. She ducks down the stairs mumbling something about napkins and Spencer inspects a clean glass, promptly dipping it in hot soapy water.

Monty flicks his head at me, indicating he wants to talk in private. I come out from behind the bar, immediately weary, unsure I have the energy to deal with Monty today. I'm beginning to realise what an enormous drain he is on everyone.

Up until recently, I told myself he added character and authenticity to Lily's as the moody but brilliant chef, but there are other talented chefs in London. Deniz's advert for his new restaurant might unearth more than one.

It would be easy enough to get rid of Monty. One wrong move on my part and he'll leave, never to return. It could be the best thing for Lily's, and for me.

Monty ushers me to the window to ensure no one can hear him.

'What's the problem?' I say, feeling a little kamikaze, like I want this to be it, the day Monty walks.

'My advance?' he says, fixing his bulbous eyes on me.

Shit, I forgot about Monty's request for an advance on his wages.

'Sorry, I'll message Deniz now,' I say. Even though I know Deniz will be totally fine with it, I decide not to make it easy for him.

'You didn't ask?' he says, his forehead collapsing into a fierce frown.

'I just said I'll do it now,' I say, taking out my phone.

Monty starts pacing. There's not much room in front of the window so he only takes two steps right before he takes two steps left. Squint and he could be dancing.

'I asked you to do one thing for me,' he whispers.

He's speaking in complete sentences. This could get nasty.

'There's no guarantee he'll agree to it,' I say, riling him on purpose.

He puts his face closer to mine.

'You said it would be fine.'

'And it probably will be.'

I'm playing with him now. It's payback for all the moody tantrums over the years, all the times he upset the staff or yelled too loudly or threatened to leave in the middle of service.

'Probably isn't good enough,' he says, spitting as he talks.

'If you're in trouble,' I begin to say, wondering if getting the advance could be a life-or-death situation.

'I'm not in trouble. I need to pay for something.'

I give him a doubtful look, indicating I'm not sure that's a good enough reason, prodding the bear some more.

I have no idea why I'm winding him up – I wouldn't dream of it normally – keep Monty sweet, keep Monty happy, is the general rule. But I'm angry with him. Not for asking for an advance, which he is more than entitled to, but there's something about his tone tonight that's particularly grating. Actually, Monty's tone is always like this. It's me that's different, not him.

'I'll call Deniz myself,' he says, waving me away.

'Go ahead,' I say.

Have I finally had enough of Monty? It's taken six years, but tonight might be the night. I'll reach the point of no return in a minute and he could very well walk and I'll have to turn our customers away. I'll say we have a gas leak and give them a voucher for a free bottle of wine when they rebook. I can handle this.

'I'll tell Deniz you can't do your job. How you mess up the orders and give away free stuff,' he says, attempting to blackmail me.

What a shit. I don't do either of those things but I don't want any doubt placed in Deniz's mind about my honesty and loyalty.

'You think Deniz will fire me?' I say, ready to take him on.

'Anyone can be a manager,' he hisses.

'That might be true, but nobody likes you, Monty. You're a rude pain in the arse who makes everyone's life a misery. But I'm nice and I keep this place running like clockwork. Deniz needs me more than he needs you, but sure, call him. Here, use my phone. Let's see who he believes.'

I hold out my phone for him to take.

He ignores the phone and lowers his head, his fists tightening into balls.

I see Spencer move towards me, afraid, protective. In the corner of my eye, I see Maddy at the bar too now.

'What are you saying?' Monty says, his voice low.

'I'm saying, I'm sick of you.'

'You're sick of me?' he says, his voice rising.

'I've had enough. We all have. So you can either behave yourself and get on with tonight's service while I call Deniz about your advance … or you can fuck off.'

I pull the door open for him to leave. Part of me wants him to walk. Part of me wishes I had kept my mouth shut.

His face is red now from the pressure building in his head as the blood pumps to his brain, overloading his system. He's about to blow.

He looks from me to the door, trying to process the situation. It occurs to me it's unlikely anyone has ever spoken to him like this before. He has no frame of reference. He's never played out the 'what if my tantrum doesn't work?' scenario because it's never failed him.

Silence follows. Nobody moves, nobody breathes. We are in uncharted waters.

Will Monty stick to his guns and walk out, which is what I'm expecting? Maybe he'll smash the place up and we'll have to call the police.

I glance at Spencer again and see he's now standing in front of the expensive brandy bottles, shielding them. Maddy has her phone in her hand, finger hovering.

We're always worried Monty might flip and I'm no longer willing to pander to his moods. Spencer and Maddy are afraid of him and that's my fault. I've allowed Monty to control us all with his bullying tactics.

'I'm not putting up with it anymore. It's too hard, for everyone,' I say, still holding the door open, indicating he's free to go.

Then the strangest thing happens. Monty's shoulders drop and his bottom lip begins to quiver.

'Nobody likes me? Is that true?' he says.

'You're not very nice to people, so what do you expect?'

'I cook staff meals. Good ones. And you,' he says, pointing at a startled Spencer, 'always gets more than anyone else.'

Spencer coughs, clearing his throat. 'And I appreciate that,' he says.

'But you don't like me?'

'Of course, I *like* you,' says Spencer, not wanting to be in anyone's bad books. Maddy frowns at Spencer, not impressed with his sucking up at such a crucial time. But I'm grateful to Spencer. It's exactly the right thing to say at this moment.

'And you?' he says to Maddy.

'Most of the time you ignore us and when you're not ignoring us, you're yelling at us,' she says.

He squeezes the bridge of his nose with his thumb and forefinger as if trying to release the tension in his head. I wonder if it's possible to give yourself a brain haemorrhage. He takes a huge inhale through his nose then lowers his head and disappears down the pink staircase to the kitchen, hardly making a sound as he goes.

Spencer looks at me wide-eyed.

'Maybe he's gone to get a knife,' Maddy whispers.

189

'Stay here,' I say to them, forceful. I'm not normally forceful.

I follow Monty downstairs, past Bill who is scrubbing a giant pot at the sink and doesn't see me. Past Sita bobbing her head, earphones in, balling melons. And straight into the kitchen, breaching the threshold by about two feet. The rules no longer apply and I've nothing to lose.

Monty washes his hands in the small sink at the back of the kitchen. He dries his hands on a paper towel and then uses the corner of the towel to dab his eyes. I'm unsure if I'm annoyed or amused by his 'poor me' act. I never had Monty down as a martyr.

He leans on the counter for a moment.

'I'm getting married,' he says. 'That's why I need the advance. For a ring.'

His voice is calm and measured, but he's still talking in full sentences, so we're not in the clear yet.

'The girl from yesterday?' I ask, mirroring his calmness, trying to hide my utter surprise.

He nods. 'Flora.'

'Flora, right,' I say.

This is a lot to digest. First of all, someone wants to marry Monty, which is astonishing in itself. Second of all, why aren't his wealthy parents paying for it, or at least contributing? Maybe he is actually a family outcast.

'I didn't even know you had a girlfriend.'

'She works in Sainsbury's. I met her there.'

'You shop in Sainsbury's, the one down the road?' I say, trying to keep the surprise out of my voice. I'm more alarmed at hearing this than I am shocked by the news he's getting married given how much Monty despises big supermarkets. He believes they destroy food.

'Dry foods only, nothing fresh,' he says, defensive.

The mild panic makes me undo my shirt collar. I didn't recognise his fiancée from Sainsbury's, but then I'm always in such a rush when I'm in there so never pay attention to the staff and generally use the self-service checkout. What if Flora's seen me buying plastic-wrapped king prawns or scallops or fillet steaks? What if Monty knows?

'Congratulations,' I say in a bright voice. 'I'll talk to Deniz and arrange your advance.' I turn to leave the kitchen, in need of a stiff drink.

'One more thing,' Monty says. I turn back, forcing a smile, fearing this is it, this is the moment he tells me he knows I've been lying to him about the Sainsbury's runs.

'You're invited,' he says. 'To the wedding.'

It's too late to stop my jaw from dropping. His cheeks flush, embarrassed by my reaction. He quickly puts Gipsy Kings on, singing along, opens a fridge and slides out a tray of fillet medallions.

If Monty's inviting me to his wedding, close friends and family must be thin on the ground. His tears were real. This job is all he's got and to hear that nobody likes him must have cut deep.

'Monty?' I say, wanting to take back my harsh words.

'Go, go, go,' he says, flapping both arms at me, reverting to three-word sentences again.

My instincts tell me my relationship with Monty has now changed, although I'm not sure if it's for the better or not, or who benefits, me or him.

I slope back upstairs to Spencer and Maddy, who are still looking worried.

'Business as usual,' I say.

Maddy and Spencer let out a big sigh and dash up the short stairs to finish prepping the tables. I slip in behind the bar to call Deniz and arrange Monty's advance.

While I felt ten feet tall going head to head with Monty – and it was long overdue – any feelings of triumph or pride have vanished. Monty needs Lily's. Despite the bling sister who visited him once and the supposedly chatty calls home to Thailand, me and Deniz and the staff in Lily's might be all he has. And now Flora.

Spencer sweeps in behind the bar to grab wine glasses. He says well done to me, and thinks I'm a nutter for taking Monty on, but also a genius. I tell him Monty's getting married to the girl who was here before.

'Is she pregnant?' he asks, as though this is a totally acceptable conclusion.

I tell him I have no idea of the situation and that it's no one's business.

'Come on, we've never seen her before, then Monty rocks up wearing contact lenses and suddenly he's getting hitched. That's well fishy.'

But Spencer's comments say more about him than they do about Monty. Spencer's view of marriage is that it's a trap and you would only do it if you were tricked or coerced into it.

I remember how radiant Izzy was on our wedding day and how lucky and in love I felt. I yearn to feel like that about her again, but when I try, all I can muster is an image of Viv, her face in shadow, lowering from the ceiling in a lace negligée.

I grab my phone to call Deniz, aware that Monty's request is urgent, when a faint, unpleasant aroma hits my nostrils. I assume it's coming from outside, maybe an issue with the drains. I glance up, distracted by a rotund man with grey thinning hair standing before me, rolling forward and back on the balls of his feet.

My eyes widen in horror. It's too late to pretend I feel any other way.

18

Her

'Viv?' I call out as I enter the house and shut the door behind me.

'Helloooo,' she calls from upstairs. A rather joyful hello that might suggest she's still on morphine.

'Be up in a sec,' I shout back and walk through to the kitchen to get myself a glass of red wine. The hot tar might have simmered down but I still need to deaden the lingering pain. I'll bring the half-full bottle and an extra glass upstairs in case Viv wants a drink too. I'll tell Viv about Polly and Jude. It could also be the right time to ask her if she's interested in Tristan. If she says she is, maybe I can share him with her like in a ménage à trois from a film noir, which never ends well but everyone has fun while it lasts. The thought brings the bubbling tar to the surface again. I'm definitely not the 'sharing my husband' kind of woman. I wonder if he's the 'sharing my wife' kind of man.

Viv is sitting in bed watching something on her iPad. There is a half-eaten sandwich on a plate on the chest of drawers and the dregs of a herbal tea in a cup. The sandwich has the crusts cut off. I know Tristan did that. He's done that for me before when I've been sick. The room is not how I expected it to be with Viv in residence. She's taken everything out of the holdall I packed for her and dispersed it around the room. How did a pair of socks end up in the corner? Her idea of unpacking must be to throw everything over your shoulder and see where it lands. The bed covers are ruffled and scrunched up at the end as though kicked away in frustration. Couldn't she have just sat on top of the duvet? She does have a broken leg so I can't expect the room to feel like a Buddhist temple, especially after seeing the lack of order and tidiness in her own house.

She shuts down her iPad and focuses all her attention on me. She tells me how Tristan was an angel when she arrived and that I'm lucky to have a husband like that. Is that why you had your hands on his knees? I want to say, but don't. When Viv looks at me like this, with such intensity and interest, it's as if the sun is shining only on me, transmitting warmth and lightness, forcing the black tar to recede even further. I don't want to ruin this moment with awkward questions or accusations, and I'm the one she kissed, after all – as far as I know anyway. I pour a large glass of wine for myself and then hover the bottle over the second glass, glancing at Viv.

'I can't,' she says, shaking a bottle of painkillers at me. I clink my glass against the pills and take a huge gulp, eager to get the wine into my system fast.

'How was work?' she asks. 'Lots of sweaty students drooling over you?'

'Not today,' I say, flopping back, glass still in hand, lying next to her on the bed, allowing the tension to seep out of me. She leans over and places her hand lightly on the top of my head, soothing me. I welcome her touch.

'Polly, one of the maths teachers, had sex with Jude, the student you met in the supermarket,' I say, raising my head for another mouthful of wine.

'Really?' she says. 'I could have sworn he fancied you.'

'I think he fancies everyone,' I say. 'He stayed at her flat all weekend. I mean, she's a teacher in the college. She could lose her job.'

'He looked of age to me.'

'He is, but it's still frowned upon.'

'I love it when things are frowned upon,' she says, grinning down at me.

'What's the worst thing you've ever done?' I ask.

'Define "worst",' she says.

'The thing you're most ashamed of,' I say.

'I don't do shame,' she says. 'It's a waste of time.'

'Okay, what about the most badass thing you've ever done that you don't feel shame about?'

'Define "badass",' she says. I lean up on my elbows and peer at her. I'm not sure if she's just avoiding the question.

'You know what I mean,' I say.

'I did a bungee jump once. Is that what you mean?'

'Sure, that's badass,' I say, giving up. Either she's a master at evasiveness or she genuinely doesn't understand the question. As the wine slips into my bloodstream, I decide I don't care.

'Are you okay? Can I get you anything?' I ask.

'I have everything I need,' she replies.

I drain my glass and shunt around so I can put my head on her lap. 'I'm pleased you're here,' I say.

'I think it's time,' she says, gently pushing my hair behind my ears.

'Time for what?' I ask, wondering if she's going to kiss me again and how I would feel about it.

'Time for the cape,' she says.

19
Him

'Hello, Tristan,' he says, going red in the face, probably because of my stricken reaction to his sudden appearance.

'Bradley,' I manage to say.

'Have you got a minute?' he asks, as though I see him all the time.

I usher him to the upper part of the restaurant, as far away as possible from any arriving customers, to the very back where a two-top is wedged in against the wall. It's the worst table in the restaurant and can easily be forgotten about, although we've never had any complaints. Spencer calls it desert island, which might appeal to some.

Maddy and Spencer give me a questioning look as I show Bradley up the stairs. I'll tell them he's an accountant if they ask me about it later.

Bradley sits sideways at the table. His portly girth won't allow him to slot properly into the snug space. He has a tatty backpack, which he tries to lean against the leg of his chair, but it falls over, lying flat on the ground, spineless.

I sit square on, hands on the table, doing my best to look like I'm totally fine with seeing him out of the blue after thirteen years, ready to answer any questions about how I lost contact. *Life ran away with me and, when you and Martha didn't get in touch, I thought it was the same for you.* He can't argue with that and it's an adequate enough cover story for both of us. We can all emerge smelling of roses. If only Bradley did.

'You're a difficult man to find,' he says. 'Needle in a haystack,' he adds with a grin, still believing that smiling after you say something indicates it's amusing even though it isn't. I reciprocate the smile, not wanting this to be any more awkward than it is already.

'Would you like a coffee or something to eat?' I ask.

'No, you're alright, thanks,' he says.

He shifts in his seat, clearly finding this as excruciating as I do. I want to ask him how he found me, but I don't see what difference it makes. They could have found me years ago if they'd wanted to, although I'm grateful they didn't.

I do the maths and guess he's around sixty-five years old, but he easily looks ten years older than that.

'How are you?' I ask, wondering when he's going to tell me what the hell he's doing here. Maybe he needs money. I'd be happy to give him some. I could spare a few grand.

'I realise it must be a bit of a surprise, my turning up out of the blue. A blast from the past,' he says, venturing another smile which he quickly abandons this time.

My mind jumps to worst-case scenario: now they've found me, will this be the first of many unsolicited visits? I decide there's not much I can do about it. I still owe them for taking care of me.

'Yes, it is a bit of a surprise, I won't lie.'

'Anyway, I don't want to keep you as I'm sure you're busy,' he says. 'The thing is, Martha died a few days ago.'

This takes a second to land and I'm not sure how to respond. I'm aware I'm not really feeling anything.

He glances around. 'Nice place you've got here. Is it yours?'

'No, I'm the manager,' I say.

'She really loved you,' he says.

I stare at him, trying to muster sympathy, but his comment has annoyed me. Martha didn't love me, not really – neither of them did – and I didn't love them.

'I wanted to look you up sooner, you know, but she insisted it was up to you. She didn't want to push it.'

'Life gets in the way and we all get busy,' I say, playing the get-out-of-jail-free card for both of us.

'Exactly,' he says, warming immediately to my theme.

'I'm sorry for your loss,' I say, emphasising the word 'your'. While this must be heart-breaking for Bradley, it isn't for me and it would be disingenuous to pretend otherwise. I didn't even grieve when my own mother died. Shock led to panic led to desperation, which is where I stayed until the day I left.

'I'm having her cremated,' he says. 'Then I'm going to scatter her ashes in the garden at home.'

He says 'garden' like it's luscious and well cared for, when I know it's probably still the same old square of bare, patchy grass with the rickety shed containing the overflow of crap from the garage, as well as the lawnmower.

The shed was visible from my bedroom window and every day I looked out at the soggy boxes and old appliances squashed up against the window, inmates, desperate to escape the suffocatingly small space.

'That's a nice idea,' I manage to say.

'It'll be a small service,' he says.

Of course it will. Bradley won't want to shell out on a decent reception.

He pauses, waiting for me to speak, maybe to express an interest in attending the funeral.

'I'll do my best to be there,' I say, my mind on the hunt for a good excuse not to go.

'Right,' he says brightly and picks up his floppy, tatty backpack and unzips it. 'Martha asked me to make sure you got this. Her dying wish, if you like,' he says.

I push myself back from the table, feeling increasingly uncomfortable. Whatever it is he's about to give me, I don't want it.

He takes a large scrapbook from the bag and pushes it across the table to me. It has bits of paper hanging out of it and looks old and loose and on the verge of falling apart. On the front of the scrapbook it says: *Tristan*, with a love heart above the 'i' replacing the dot.

I'm beginning to feel nauseous now. I don't want a scrapbook from Martha, a reminder of the fake me living my fake life.

'Open it,' he says, eager to see my reaction.

'I don't want it, if that's alright. I hope you don't mind.'

'Really?' he says, leaning back in his chair, which gives a strained creak. 'Don't you want to see pictures of your mother?'

I want to say Martha wasn't my mother, so no, I don't want to see the pictures. Instead, I gently slide the scrapbook back towards him, hoping he gets the message, no offence taken, no questions asked.

'I'm not talking about Martha,' he says. 'I'm talking about your birth mother.'

I eye the scrapbook, my mouth suddenly dry.

I pull it back towards me and slowly open it to the first page, where there is a black and white photograph of a new-born baby. Beneath it is my date of birth.

I turn to the next page and the next, seeing pictures of the same baby only bigger. On page four, I freeze. There's a rushing sound in my ears as everything around me falls into the background, small and distant except for the large colour picture of my mother standing in a doorway, smiling at the camera, me sitting on her hip. The caption below reads: *Age 2 1/2*. I trail my finger over the picture, remembering her face.

With no photos of my mother, my only recollection of her has been reliant on snippets of memories and a lot of imagination.

In this picture she's smiling but looks tired around the eyes. Her hair isn't golden like I thought it was, but light brown. Her smile cuts through me, stirring the feelings of loss, buried deep in my gut. I had forgotten how her teeth were crooked at the front, like mine. I remember her soft laugh. I can hear it in my head. And the way she smelled. Fresh and sweet.

Without any pictures for reference, I had begun to question if she was even real. Had she existed in the way I remembered her, or was she a fantasy I conjured up in my mind? But now, with these pictures in front of me, it's evidence that she was real. Evidence that she loved me and I loved her.

'She was an attractive woman,' says Bradley, trying to be chatty but only managing to sound inappropriate.

I keep turning the pages. Me, my mother and my father on a beach, all in woolly hats. The caption reads: *Ireland (age 4)*. I didn't even know I'd been to Ireland. I glance at the picture of my father. He's attempting to smile but I don't really recognise him and only feel sadness.

Bradley warbles on in the background about how it was my mother's scrapbook and that the social worker had dropped it to the house two weeks after I arrived to live with them, but because I wasn't really settled yet he thought it would be better to wait before giving it to me.

'When you started calling us Mum and Dad, I thought it would only confuse you.'

I continue to turn the pages of the scrapbook, my hands trembling. All those years and they had pictures of my mother, my father, my real life, stashed away, probably in the shed of horror.

A picture of me standing over a wrapped gift with a big bow on it, beaming so hard you can barely see my eyes. The caption reads: *Christmas Day (age 4)*.

'I'm sorry if it was wrong to keep it from you,' says Bradley with a nervous laugh. 'Martha wanted to give it to you, but I was worried it'd do more harm than good.'

Another picture, this time of me wearing blue wellies, holding a fishing net. The caption reads: *Lake District (age 6)*. The year my mother died and my life stopped. The year I ceased to exist.

A surge of emotion bulldozes my system. I'm six years old again and I'm terrified, too afraid to speak because if I open my mouth I'll start crying and won't ever be able to stop.

I hear Bradley zip up his backpack. 'I won't keep you, job done and all that,' he says. I'm aware of him standing but I can't bring myself to look away from the pictures. He clears his throat, awkward, waiting for some normal social pleasantry, but I can't muster a word.

The front door to the restaurant makes a distant click as it shuts behind him. I turn the pages again and find myself staring at a strip of passport-sized photographs of me and my mother. We are laughing together and in one of the photos she has her hand over my eyes as a joke. The caption reads: *My boy (age 6)*.

Maddy's white DM shoes with the multi-coloured stars appear on the carpet beside me. She asks me if I'm alright but her voice sounds miles away. All I can hear is my heart beating, churning, suffering. She puts an arm around me, rubbing my shoulders, trying to bring me back to the land of the living.

A glass of whiskey appears in front of me. 'Get that down you, mate.' It's Spencer's voice. I look up at him, barely able to focus. I take a large gulp of whiskey.

'Who the fuck was that guy? The ghost of Christmas past?' he says. He's not teasing. He's deadly serious.

'Something like that,' I manage to say. The whiskey works, immediately dulling my emotions.

'Is he okay?' A sharp voice behind me makes me turn. It's Monty. Behind him is Bill, his apron all wet from washing up.

'Anything I can do?' says Bill.

'I'm okay,' I say, forcing my well-practised fake smile but, given everyone's concerned faces, I'm assuming I don't look the best.

Monty comes up and peers at me closely. It's very unsettling, especially as we're all still getting used to him not wearing glasses, but at least it shakes me out of my trance.

'I'll make you some chicken soup,' he says and heads back to the kitchen.

'Am I hearing things or was that Monty being nice?' says Bill.

'I can hear *you*, Bill,' shouts Monty from halfway down the stairs.

'I thought I was too old for people to surprise me anymore,' says Bill, chuckling to himself as he goes back to the kitchen.

Spencer sits across from me. Maddy still has her warm hand on my shoulder.

'What's with the scrapbook?' asks Spencer.

'It's a family album,' I say. 'That man was Bradley. He and his wife, Martha, adopted me when I was a kid. He came to give me this,' I say, indicating the scrapbook, 'and to tell me Martha died.'

'Shit, sorry,' says Spencer, getting to his feet and loosening his dicky bow. 'I'll go and cover the door, yeah? Take your time.' Spencer scoots off, not wanting to hear anything more about somebody dying.

'I'm so sorry,' says Maddy. 'Do you want me to call Izzy?'

Izzy, I think. Do I want Maddy to call Izzy?

'I'll go home early, it's fine,' I say.

Maddy gives me another squeeze. 'Not before Monty's chicken soup. What did you say to him, by the way? He's like a different person.'

If only I could be a different person.

20

Her

Standing in front of the mirror in my wardrobe, in just my underwear, I caress the sensual, silk fabric of the cape still on the hanger.

'What am I supposed to wear underneath it?' I shout to Viv through the door.

'Anything,' she calls back. 'Don't think about it.'

I slip the cape off the hanger, hold it up over my head and let it fall, sliding my arms easily into the gaping sleeves. It settles on my body, smoothing every contour, making me feel desired and desirable. I pose in the mirror, turning sideways, up on my tiptoes to make my bum look more pert.

'What's taking so long?' Viv shouts across the hall.

'Coming,' I call back, ruffling my hair and crossing the cape across my body to cover my underwear. Then, out of nowhere, my mother's voice enters my head.

Is that what you're wearing? she says.

I was thirteen years old and getting ready to go to my first school disco. Sophie and I had made friends with a group of girls at school – Alison, Sonja and Lisa. Sophie had insisted that we needed to 'branch out' and extend our friend group or risk slipping into obscurity; those were her exact words. And we hadn't been to a disco yet so it was definitely about time. We decided the best way to weasel our way in with the trendy girls was to take up smoking. It seemed to be the one thing they all had in common and the one thing that would make Sophie and

I eligible new friends, and it worked. We had to practise first, smoking out of my bedroom window at home, so we could puff on a ciggie like a pro. When my mother caught me smoking, she simply said 'not in the house'. No lectures about how it was bad for my health or threats of punishment if she caught me smoking again. She also didn't mind how late I stayed out at night and was often in bed when I got home. The relaxed attitude to smoking was another wake-up call. She didn't care about anyone or anything, which only intensified the shame I felt over Mindy. My mother couldn't be trusted with an animal, let alone a child.

As far as my school friends knew, my mother was as strict and concerned as their parents about smoking. 'My mum'll kill me,' I'd say, rolling my eyes and sucking on mints. The girls would nod, feeling my pain as they took deeper drags on their cigarettes. But when Sophie witnessed my mother's lack of interest first-hand, she thought it was cool. 'You're lucky your mum's so laidback,' she said to me. Sophie's parents insisted on strict curfews and if she was even a minute late she was grounded for a week. But she was the lucky one.

On the days my mother was working, I would bring the girls back to my house after school to drink tea and smoke copious amounts of cigarettes out of my bedroom window. We used to talk about the boys we fancied and how far we'd go with them. Alison said Matthew Trainer in our year had touched her down there in the school toilets. She said it had felt weird and we all screamed and buried our faces in my duvet. And now the school disco was looming and we were obsessed with what we were going to wear, who we were going to kiss and who we would let touch us down there. I was secretly not going to let any of the boys touch me anywhere, but I might kiss one of them. Sophie confided in me that one hand down her bra for five seconds was as far as she was willing to go.

The excitement about the disco was so intense it kept me awake at night. The build-up was unbearable and, for the first time since Mindy died, I didn't feel as painfully sad going to bed.

One thing my mother was good at was giving me money. Not because she wanted me to be happy or because she was particularly generous, as she would like to believe, but because she wanted me to have what everyone else had. Her snobbery made her terrified of being looked down upon. And I used this to my advantage. If I needed new clothes, or extra cash for cigarettes, I would casually drop into conversation how someone else's mother had implied we weren't as wealthy as they were. So when I wanted a new dress and shoes for the disco, I mentioned, in passing, how Alison's mother had asked me if I'd like to borrow a dress as Alison had a lot of clothes she never wore. Well, my mother couldn't get her purse out fast enough and shoved a hundred pounds into my hand. 'You tell Alison's mother you've got plenty of dresses,' she said.

Sophie and I marched into Topshop with the other girls, on a buying mission, and spent an entire afternoon trying on every dress, skirt and outrageously skimpy top we could get our hands on. Alison and Sonja settled on low-cut, stretchy styles that barely covered their bum cheeks. Their parents would never approve. The plan was to change in the woods near the school before the disco. Lisa was naturally more conservative but only because she didn't have a very positive body image. She was always saying her belly was flabby, when it wasn't. She opted for a white dress that came above the knee. Sophie went for an office look with a top and a pencil skirt. She said she wanted to be taken seriously. I chose a black sleeveless dress that hugged my body. It was short, but it didn't ride up. I also bought a pair of platform boots to go with it. The girls were jealous, as they would never be allowed to wear boots like that. I lied that my mother was going to be out the night of the disco and that I had great hiding places. They thought I was so lucky to be left alone at home.

When the day finally arrived, my whole body was charged with adrenaline in anticipation for the night ahead. We were meeting in the woods behind the bus stop so Alison and Sonja could change. I didn't hide what I was wearing from my mother. If she didn't care about my dog, or me smoking, or how late I stayed out, it was unlikely she was going to be concerned by my fashion choices. I backcombed my hair a bit, like Alison had shown me, and put the dress and boots on and admired myself in the mirror. Standing on my own, without the other girls flapping around me in the changing room, distracting me, I was able to take a proper look at myself. My hair was thick and full with a wispy bit hanging across my eyes. I had eyeliner on my inner lids making my eyes stand out, and pink gloss on my lips that made my whole face glisten and shine. The dress slipped neatly into every curve of my body and over my breasts, which were finally starting to fill a bra. I stuck my chest out, creating a deeper curve in my lower back. The platform boots made me taller and my legs appear longer. I put my hands on my hips, my chin slightly raised. It was the first time I had felt like a woman as opposed to a girl and I was filled with confidence – until my mother wandered into my room looking for the remote control for the telly. It was never in my room. It was always down the side of the sofa, so I knew it was a ruse to have a look at me.

'Is that what you're wearing?' she said with a frown.

'I didn't ask for your opinion,' I said, defensive but proud of my grown-up response. When you have an immature parent, it makes you more adult, not the other way around.

She ran her eyes over me and shrugged.

'You look like a prostitute and your legs are too chunky for boots like that.'

I carried on fussing around with my hair, as though I didn't care what she thought, but inside I was dying. She'd never had an opinion about anything I did, so it was totally unexpected and I wasn't prepared. I suddenly felt silly and awkward in what I was wearing.

'What do you know?' I said, wishing I had something more profound and hurtful to throw back at her.

'I'm trying to stop you embarrassing yourself,' she said.

'In that case, you can stop worrying,' I snarled. 'There's only one thing that embarrasses me and that's you.'

And that's when it happened. She slapped me across the face. At first I didn't know what to do or say. I stood there holding my cheek. She looked appalled, shocked by what she had done.

She had never hit me before. She had killed my dog and allowed me to smoke and wander the streets at night, but she had never laid a finger on me. And she never did again.

'I was only trying to help. You didn't have to be rude,' she said. I readjusted my dress in the mirror, feigning confidence, grabbed my small, glitzy clutch bag that cost all of three pounds fifty and strutted out of the house, rather loudly due to the platform boots. At the disco, I danced and chatted with my friends, and sipped vodka from a bottle stashed in Evan Thomas's jacket. But all the while, I was cringing inside, my mother's words infecting my mind, attacking what little self-esteem I had. The lip gloss now felt sticky and gloopy on my lips and when I caught a glimpse of my reflection in a window I thought I looked more like a witch than a prostitute. But I didn't think my legs were too chunky for the boots. My mother was the one with chunky legs. They were nearly the same width from her thighs to her ankles; still, I always thought she looked elegant in the dress suits she wore to work. At the time I was still scrambling to find an identity of my own and too young to understand that my mother was simply envious of my youth. She would rather have left me teetering on the edge of obscurity, as Sophie would say, than help me become a confident woman.

She nearly destroyed me the night of my first disco but, thanks to Gary Bennett, I survived. He was a good foot shorter than I was, even without the platform boots, and wanted to get with me. I wasn't sure how that was going to work given the height difference, but he had the ingenious idea of standing on a toilet seat so he could kiss me, which is exactly what we did. Gary said I was pretty and that he'd always fancied me. Gary saved me that night.

My mother and I never talked about the slap, the same way we never discussed Mindy or peeing on Clive's carpet. She was terrified of stirring up old feelings and looking like a bad person and that suited me fine. And she never commented again on what I wore, but I just assumed she thought I looked awful all the time. It's hard to know what was worse – the criticism or the silence. She still managed to slip in the odd put-down, but they were so subtle that it could take me a couple of days sometimes to realise she had been having a dig. By then it would be too late to say anything. The opportunity to strike back was lost.

When I was sixteen she had a boyfriend she brought home and who stayed the night. She'd had other casual boyfriends, but I never met them and they never came to the house. This guy was called Ravinda and the whole thing lasted six weeks. He was a nurse at the local hospital and really smart. He knew more about the Second World War than my history teacher did.

In week one, he laughed and talked a lot, telling stories and jokes, and even cooked for us with fresh ingredients. My mother didn't like all the spices he used, but I loved and I enjoyed having him around. He lifted the mood and my mother was on her best behaviour, being sweet and attentive, which I found amusing. Ravinda, none the wiser, had no reason to believe this wasn't my mother's true self. Around week three, the arguing started. I wasn't sure what the problem was exactly, but my mother's voice had reverted to its normal deadpan, unemotional tone. 'I'm not some desperate woman who needs a man in her life,' I heard her say.

By week five, Ravinda had lost his spark. He was broken. Worn down. Maybe even having an existential crisis. I passed him on the way into our house one afternoon. He had just arrived and was in his nurse's uniform. I asked him how he was, pleased to see him. 'I think it's going to rain, judging by the grey clouds,' he said. I wanted to commiserate with him and say my mother had nearly broken me too. He was on his way out of our lives and I felt guilty that I hadn't warned him, even put a note in his jacket: *Get out while you still have your dignity.*

By week six, he'd stopped visiting altogether and my mother had adopted a snotty expression, a defence mechanism, that implied this was exactly the outcome she wanted. A few weeks later, she found a T-shirt belonging to him crumpled under her bed. It had a yellow smiley face on it with the words *don't worry be happy.* I was having breakfast when she held it up to me, between her thumb and forefinger. 'Look at this rubbish,' she said and threw it in the bin. I carried on eating my cereal. Then she said, 'It's tricky having a boyfriend with your teenage daughter around.' I stopped eating and looked at her as she picked up her car keys and left for work. It was later that day, while I was half asleep in geography class, it dawned on me how her comment was her way of blaming me for the fact it didn't work out with Ravinda – further evidence that my mother possessed no self-knowledge and took absolutely no responsibility for anything she did or said. I tried to retrieve Ravinda's T-shirt from the bin later that night, but she'd already emptied the remains of her chicken noodle soup on top of it.

As always, I excused her behaviour, like I did on the night of the disco and after Mindy died, convincing myself she had no awareness or control over her emotions, so could not really be held accountable for the hurtful things she said and did. The truth is, I didn't want my mother to be too horrifying, weird or strange, afraid of how that would reflect upon me. As long as I believed she had no choice, my fear turned to pity, which made her easier to tolerate. But the fear was always there. Was I damaged too? Was I incapable of normal emotions? I had loved Mindy with all my heart, but maybe dogs didn't count. Ravinda had told me that Hitler had a dog.

By the time I was seventeen, we had learnt to keep communications to a superficial level only, never mentioning past events, some of which were too challenging and terrifying for her to face. I was convinced if I did confront her, her head would literally implode in front of me. Instead, we developed a workable way of relating and behaving towards each other: she acted like everything was totally fine between us and I let her. Sadly, any relationship with my mother was better than none. Just because I resented and disliked her, didn't mean I didn't need her.

I chose to study psychology because when I mentioned it in passing to her as an option, she went a newspaper shade of grey. So I stuck to it. It was a stealth punishment that I couldn't resist. She never asked me about my studies, but sometimes, when I was home for the holidays, and she did or said something unkind or inappropriate, I'd pull a mildly contemplative expression implying I had the ability to analyse her, to see right through her cold exterior to the truth about the damaged person inside. She'd stay out of my way for a couple of days, too afraid of what my diagnosis of her behaviour was, too afraid to ever look at herself and take responsibility.

Her fear and avoidance was her saving grace as it conjured some semblance of compassion within me. It's the reason I never cut her off completely. And as much as she behaves like she calls the shots in our relationship, we both know I do now.

I poke my head around Viv's door, nervous to reveal myself in the sacred cape.

'Let's see it then,' she says.

'I look a bit slutty.'

'Even better.'

I step into the room, still on my tiptoes, and do a twirl, the satin material shimmering around me. I giggle as I turn this way and that, modelling the cape for Viv.

Viv says nothing. I stop twirling.

'What?' I say, self-conscious, pulling the cape around me.

'It was made for you,' she says, wistful. 'How do you feel in it?'

'Bold and naughty,' I say, bolstered by her approval. 'And very feminine.'

Viv grabs her phone and plays a track through the R2-D2 speaker. 'Let's Groove' by Earth, Wind & Fire blasts into the room. Viv bobs her head to the music.

I sway in my bare feet as Viv whacks up the volume, singing along. For a moment, it looks like she might get up off the bed and attempt to dance, and her broken leg is definitely moving more than it should be. Then I'm dancing, the cape swinging around me, underwear and body on show. I jump up on the bed, turning around, allowing the cape to wrap around me, wiggling my bum at Viv. She whoops and moves her upper body around to the music.

I jump around to face her, but it's an ambitious move and I lose my balance, falling over her, hands either side of her body so as not to squash her. Viv squeals, laughing. I manoeuvre myself so I'm lying on my back beside her, the cape splayed out beneath me. We carry on dancing with our arms. I roll onto my side and prop my head up with my hand, aware how my hips curve. I'm all woman. She turns her head to face me. I look at her lips, thinking about kissing her again, curious to know what it would be like this time. Heat rises from my feet, charging up my body. The song comes to an end.

'Izzy?' she says quietly.

'Yes,' I reply, ready to take a huge leap into the unknown, if that's what needs to happen. It's partly the wine talking, but mostly I want to be desired.

A loud bang from downstairs makes us jump. It was the front door shutting.

'Hello?' I call out.

'Hi,' Tristan calls from downstairs.

'Shit,' I say, pulling the cape around me. 'He's never home this early.'

'What's the panic?' says Viv.

'Keep him talking,' I say, running out of the room to change. As Tristan's footsteps come up the stairs, slightly heavier than usual, I'm already in our bedroom changing at lightning speed. I hear him go into Viv's room. Light, indiscernible chatter follows. The cape slips neatly back onto the hanger, which in turn slides back into the wardrobe, hidden away again. I pull on a pair of jeans and an oversized shirt and check myself in the mirror. I look flushed, there's no denying it, but there's nothing wrong with that and Tristan won't notice anyway.

I wander back into Viv's room like all is normal. Tristan leans against the window sill, his arms crossed and head tilted as he listens to Viv, who is joking about the very active day she's had. He says hi. I say hi back, but there's something different about him. He gives me a quick once-over glance. I push my hair behind my ears, self-conscious again. He stands up from the window and announces he's hungry and heads for the door.

'Can I talk to you?' he says on his way out.

'Sure,' I say, as though this is totally normal when it so isn't. We never encourage 'talk', at least not lately.

I look at Viv and blow out a long breath – that was close.

'Why don't you want him to see you in the cape?' she whispers.

'It's a can-of-worms situation,' I say, And I still haven't told him Viv gave me a present, let alone what it is.

'He'd love it,' she says, yawning.

Viv snuggles into bed. She says the painkillers make her sleepy and asks me to turn the light off as I go. I grab the wine glasses – one used, one clean – and the bottle of wine and leave Viv to rest. I take it slow down the stairs, preparing myself for whatever it is Tristan wants to talk about. In the kitchen, Tristan stares out of the window into the garden. So much for being hungry.

'What's up?' I say, keeping it casual, but I'm thrown by his mood. I'm not sure if he's annoyed or sad or stressed. He's just so very still.

He turns to me. 'I have to ask you something,' he says.

Oh, God.

21

Him

The soup is thick and creamy and spicy with tender pieces of chicken floating under the surface. The hot liquid slips down my throat and into my stomach, its warmth radiating to parts of my body I didn't even know were cold. It confirms my believe that Monty is a culinary wizard.

The whiskey and soup calm my emotions after Bradley's unexpected visit. Receiving confirmation that my mother's love for me had been real and not a figment of my imagination, and hearing that Martha had died, was a perfect storm. A death and a rebirth.

Another mouthful of magical soup tricks my senses into believing all is well and I slowly turn the pages of the scrapbook again, wanting to imprint every detail into my memory. Just because the scrapbook is in my possession now doesn't mean it won't get lost or destroyed one day. You can't rely on anything or anyone to be around forever.

I reach the end. On the last page, instead of photographs, there are two paintings by me as a child.

One is of a lion. I know this because it says *Lion by Tristan* at the top in an adult's handwriting. But it doesn't look like a lion, more like a Jack Russell with long spindly legs. The other is of our house, again a title given to the painting. It's a wonky square with four windows drawn into the corners, and a tree in the garden with another square underneath it, a picnic blanket perhaps.

A memory springs from the depths of a forgotten time of sitting with my mother on a chequered blanket underneath a tree. I am peaceful for a moment. Maybe more peaceful than I have ever been. I look at the empty soup bowl and wonder if Monty did actually lace it with something.

The bottom drawer in the office desk is stiff to pull open, as it hardly ever gets used, and there's nothing much in it apart from some old order books. I go to put the scrapbook in it when another strip of passport photographs fall out.

It's of me and Martha. I'm about seven years old in the pictures but I have no recollection of ever being in a photo booth with her. Although I don't remember being in one with my mother either.

In the photos, Martha has her face pushed up against mine, smiling excitedly at the camera, while I stare ahead, looking past the lens, blank, expressionless.

In an instant, the comforting effects of the soup and whiskey are annihilated by the horrifying reality of what my life was like. In the same way that I hadn't seen pictures of my life before my mother died, I also hadn't seen pictures of my life after, not including the forced school and birthday photographs that Martha framed and scattered around the house. I never looked at them.

But this strip of pictures, in my hand, shows the emptiness behind my eyes. Martha must have seen the strip of photographs in the scrapbook of me with my real mother and wanted to emulate it.

Martha's smile tells me she really wanted it to work out with us. She wanted her love to be received and then reciprocated. But I never accepted her love so she was doomed from the start. We both were.

Another memory blasts into my consciousness of a hot day in our local park. I was ten years old or thereabouts. Martha had laid out a blanket on the grass beside the railings of the playground and had a picnic for us. I don't remember what she brought in the way of food, but she must have pushed the boat out and spent extra money on snacks. The chances are she never told Bradley.

Some kids from my class were in the playground already and I rushed off to play with them, relieved I had a good reason to get away from Martha. I pretended Martha wasn't there.

Even when she leaned on the fence and called to me, trying to coax me to take a break with her and have a drink and a snack on the blanket, I carried on playing, pretending I couldn't hear her.

One of the other boys was called away by his mum for refreshments on the other side of the playground. He invited me to come with him and I willingly accepted. I sat on his mother's blanket and ate his mother's snacks and drank his mother's orange cordial.

I could see Martha through the fence on the other side of the playground, sitting on her blanket on her own. I didn't feel a thing.

Poor Martha. Another foster child might have loved her back, might have needed her, or at least allowed her to love them. If she had given me the scrapbook from the start, maybe things would have been different. We'll never know now.

'Monty wants to know how the soup was,' Maddy says, coming into the room.

I shove the pictures of me and Martha into the back page of the scrapbook and slide it into the bottom drawer.

'Incredible,' I say.

'He gave it to us for the staff meal, big servings as well. And he smiled, at least we think he did. Bill's calling you the Monty-whisperer.'

I'm dubious as to whether this is good news or not. I don't want Monty to be different – maybe less of a prick, but other than that, I like him the way he is. Has Martha's death and the arrival of the scrapbook started a chain reaction? Does everything *have* to change now?

'He's still playing the Gipsy Kings,' Maddy says, 'so maybe the new Monty is only visiting for a while.' But I'm pretty sure the new Monty is here to stay. I released him into the wild, albeit by accident, and now we'll have to see how it pans out.

I leave Maddy and Spencer in charge for the rest of the evening service and take the long way home through the back streets. The sun rests low in the sky but it'll be another hour until it sets, so I know it's around eight o'clock. I meander along the roads glancing in at the front windows of houses. People watching television, a family around a dining table, a man sitting in front of his laptop with an expression on his face that implies he's saving the world.

What would the front window view have been into my home with my mother and father? My father asleep on the sofa, which I have memories of, and makes sense now that I know he had a serious drink problem. Present but entirely absent.

You might have seen my mother making animals out of play-dough with me. Or me at five years old eating spaghetti with a huge oversized napkin stuck in the neckline of my T-shirt.

And what about through the front window of Martha and Bradley's house twenty-five years ago? A sullen child, sitting with his back way too straight and his hands neatly in his lap as a plate of sausages and mash is placed in front of him. Martha's treat on a Friday. 'It's my favourite dinner,' I would say, even though it wasn't.

I lied about everything. It was easier that way.

Our house looms at the end of the road. Izzy should be home by now, looking after Viv. The house seems well lit for once, compared to Viv's next door, which appears dull and unlived in, like it did after Mrs Jenkins died.

Thoughts of Viv drift into my mind, but she's not in the lacy bodice with the hood up this time, or emerging naked from a river. She's flopped in the bath where she fell earlier, vulnerable, helpless. All I feel is sympathy towards her.

I'm relieved to have moved on from what can only be described as a boyish obsession. Izzy is just as obsessed with Viv though, spending the day with her, skinny-dipping and holding her hand in the hospital.

Even before Mrs Jenkins died, Izzy had been slipping away from me. If I was to pinpoint the exact moment when the bond between us broke, it was during one of the nights we took her mum, Jo, for a trimonthly dinner. It's two years ago now, but the memory of that evening shines forever brightly.

Izzy insists on at least three-month interludes between seeing her mother and always books a mid-range restaurant, mostly Italian. This isn't because she's tight, far from it, but because when the bill comes, we always end up paying. They do this little dance where Jo makes an obligatory reach for her bag, taking time to fish around for her purse, as Izzy slaps her credit card on the table.

'It's on us, Mum,' she says.

'Oh, thank you,' Jo replies, as though surprised.

Izzy resents the sense of entitlement her mother has. When I tried to ask Izzy about it, she shut me down. 'It's only a dinner and it's not like we can't afford it,' she said. So I stopped mentioning it.

Izzy's insistence on paying every time is directly related to Jo's wedding gift; the deposit for the house. Izzy feels indebted to her and it wasn't until that night that I witnessed for the first time how Jo expects to be fussed over; she expects payback.

As the waiter slopped white wine into her glass, there was a smug expression on her face. Sitting across the table from her, watching her taste the wine, I realised Izzy had been right about Jo's plan to carve herself a place in Izzy's life where she could be centre of attention.

For the first time I wished we hadn't taken the money. Of course, Izzy doesn't have to put up with it. If she cut Jo out of her life, Jo couldn't ask for the money back. The problem is Jo has a hold over Izzy, and that evening I saw the toxic nature of their relationship.

It was also the night I realised I'd lost Izzy.

We were waiting for our desserts. Jo likes to have three courses plus coffee, and a brandy. We also cover her taxi fare home. She laid her eyes on me, running her forefinger around the rim of her glass, playful, verging on flirtatious.

'So, Tristan, what's new with you?'

'Not much,' I said.

'Something must be going on. I mean, what about this plan for your own restaurant? Anything happening there?'

I was about to offer my standard excuse about needing an investor, which I've given Jo on numerous occasions, when Izzy jumped in to defend me.

'Leave him alone. He is perfectly fine the way he is.'

A mild discomfort swept through me as Izzy drained the rest of her wine and emptied the last of the bottle into her glass. *I'm perfectly fine the way I am?*

'That's still the plan,' I said, sounding confident. 'I just need an investor.'

'I could talk to Clive, if you want. He likes to get involved in start-ups.'

'Mum? Tristan has to find a premises first and do a business plan,' Izzy said, snapping at her. 'You can't invest in nothing.'

I tried my best to hide my surprise. Izzy seemed to know a lot about what I needed to do to get a restaurant of my own and was fully aware I had made zero effort so far. How long had she been thinking like this? How long had her faith in me been lost?

'I'm looking at a place next week,' I said, lying to salvage a scrap of self-respect. Jo nodded, satisfied. Then Izzy did something that confirmed my suspicions.

She patted my arm. A 'don't worry about it' pat. A 'you did your best' and 'it's okay to be a failure' pat.

In a split second, from one single hand gesture, the invisible, fragile ribbon connecting us was severed, two frayed ends left blowing in the wind. She no longer believed in my potential. She had given up on me.

Later that evening, at home on our own, she ranted about her mother's audacity and rudeness, which she always does after having dinner with her. I waited for her to ask about the premises I said I was viewing and why I hadn't told her about it. She never did.

She knew I was lying. Or worse, she didn't believe it would lead anywhere.

And the first of the light bulbs went out. I wish I'd tried harder to keep it on.

Music comes from inside the house. A funky disco beat. I put my key in the door and enter slowly. It's coming from Viv's room.

I shut the door behind me and take the stairs two at a time. At the top, I pause, light on my feet, hearing Izzy and Viv giggle and whoop.

The door is ajar and I see shadows moving across the wall and a silky material swooshing around, in and out of sight. They haven't heard me come in. I'm about to stride into the room or at least call out hello when curiosity gets the better of me.

Instead of making my presence known, I slide up to the crack in the door and peer in, fully aware I'm once again in peeping Tom mode.

Izzy is dancing on the bed, her long wavy hair trailing down her back, moving as freely as her arms.

She's wearing a shimmering cape with a hood and nothing else except her underwear. As she dances, the light, silky cape travels over her body, slipping over her bra and swishing around her thighs and knickers. She's on fire, oozing confidence, laughing, having fun. She flicks her hair and looks over her shoulder at Viv.

She loses her balance and falls on all fours with her hands either side of Viv. Viv squeals in delight, her arms still moving to the music, her broken leg propped on a pillow. Izzy rolls onto her back and lies beside Viv, her chest rising and falling as she catches her breath, the cape spread out beneath her. She moves her hands up and down her body to the music.

I can't take my eyes off her.

She turns onto her side to face Viv, propping her head up with her hand. The cape has fallen to one side, revealing the gentle arc of her hip. She's talking to Viv, but I can't hear what she's saying. Viv eyes her, sultry, seductive. My whole body tightens as the jealous boy inside me comes storming to the surface, guns blazing. *Don't look at my wife like that*, he roars. I clench my fists, suppressing the Neanderthal urge to claim my wife and beat off all competitors, not only for her affection but for her attention. I want her only focused on me.

The track is coming to an end and I snap out of my jealous fog. I don't want them to think I witnessed any of this or that I was spying on them, which I was. I also don't want to embarrass Izzy and walk in on her private moment. I'm sad that it's private. 'Private' meaning 'does not concern Tristan'.

I carefully descend the stairs, open the front door and bang it shut.

'Hello?' I call out.

There's a pause.

'Hi,' Izzy replies, calling back down to me, a forced natural-ness in her tone.

Overhead, I hear footsteps running from Viv's room to our bedroom. I stomp up the stairs, making sure they know exactly where I am, knock on Viv's door and enter.

Viv is lying on the bed, as she was moments before. She has slightly flushed cheeks. I know Izzy is in our bedroom, probably changing out of the mystery cape. I lean against the window sill and ask Viv how the rest of her day was. She jokes about how she did a 10k run.

Izzy breezes into the room wearing jeans and a white shirt with her hair tied back. She says hi and pushes loose strands of hair behind her ears, something she does when she feels awkward. I maintain a calm and casual demeanour but my heart plummets, settling somewhere in my intestines.

Izzy doesn't want me anymore and it's my fault. She doesn't believe in me anymore and that's my fault too. After avoiding this conversation for months, I now want to have it. I have to know if there's any point going on or if this is it.

I say I'm going to get something to eat and ask Izzy if I can talk to her. She swallows before answering. It's enough of a hesitation to tell me she's unnerved by the request. She knows as well as I do that this could be the moment of truth between us, or at least the start of the downward spiral we've been trying to ignore.

It's gloomy in the kitchen so I flick on the undercounter lighting, which throws a comforting, warm glow over the glossy white kitchen cupboards.

I peer out into the garden, pondering what I'm going to say to Izzy and how I'm going to word it. Will I ask her how she feels about us first, or is that a cop-out? It's definitely a cop-out. I need to lead this. I owe her that much.

The shed lingers at the bottom of the garden in the shadows, a persistent pest. Normally, even thinking about the shed conjures feelings of anxiety, but tonight, I have no reaction to it. Tonight, it's just a place to store tools and unused home furnishings. Am I actually over the shed?

'Hey,' Izzy says, coming into the kitchen.

In the soft lighting, with her hair falling around her face, she looks even more beautiful. And I'm ashamed.

All this time I thought she'd lost faith in me, when it was me who never had any faith in myself to start with.

I have not done one thing to pursue my so-called ambition of owning my own restaurant, or any other ambition for that matter. I can't even manage to eat an apple a day.

If Izzy doesn't want to stay with me, I'll let her go. I will give her whatever she wants. Maybe I can live in the office above the restaurant.

'I need to ask you something,' I say.

She swallows again and forces a smile. She knows there's a big question coming and she's dreading it as much as I am.

What if she says yes to ending things, or what if she says yes because she thinks it's what I want? I could open with 'I still love you'. Maybe lose the word 'still'.

'What is it?' she says, leaning on the counter with both hands, bracing herself for the inevitable conversation and revelations. I take a deep breath.

'I want to know … if you'll come to Monty's wedding with me?' I say, completely bottling it last minute, not prepared to end it, now or maybe ever.

22

Her

A repetitive thumping sound penetrates my subconscious but not quite enough to wake me fully from my deep sleep. The dull banging comes again, up through the floor, through my pillow and into my head. This time I open my eyes and wince with annoyance. The persistent and familiar thudding is coming from Viv's room as she bangs her crutch on the bedroom floor three times, no more, no less. I reach for my phone and check the time. 9.05 a.m. Not much of a lie-in for my first day home for the summer. I lift the thin sheet off my body and drag myself out of bed. She must think I'm downstairs and probably wants a second cup of tea. Tristan would have already brought her breakfast before leaving for work early, again. If it's not a delivery, it's paperwork or issues with organising Monty's wedding. The reception is now being held at Lily's and you'd think it was a royal wedding the way Tristan's running around. He's asked me twice already what I'm going to wear. 'A dress,' I said, as though it's obvious, which it is. He nodded like this was an intriguing choice. I expected him to spend more time at home, with Viv being our house guest, but he's here even less.

Maybe if she alternated the one, two, three rhythm, the thumping might not be so irritating, like a one, two, one, two. Or a one, miss a beat, two, three. Anything to break the monotony. Viv has been staying in our house for nearly two weeks and I can't pretend it's working out well. I've already cleaned up the party mess in her house and run a mop over the kitchen floor in anticipation of her moving home.

It was Tristan's suggestion to bang the crutch on the floor as the best way for Viv to communicate with us. I backed him up but she didn't like the idea.

'Can't I just send a text?' she said. We convinced her it was far more practical to thump the floor than send a text. But it's grating on my nerves. Intermittent banging, dripping noises and loud music are all forms of torture.

There's no denying Tristan and I have become Viv's lackeys. If I'm not trudging up and down the stairs with cups of tea and snacks (she eats little and often, like a nibbling hamster), I'm folding clothes and cleaning up after her. For the past two days, she's been sketching portraits of random people in an A3 drawing pad, images plucked from her imagination or memory. She says she's decided to focus on the human rather than the reptile.

I pull on one of Tristan's shirts and slope across the hall to her room. I have to step over her clothes to enter properly. Her bed is covered in pencil drawings of faces and her breakfast tray has been pushed to the end of the bed, the cup and plate about to topple off, and there is a toast crust on the floor. I live in hope that she's summoned me to pick up the crust. It's not that I mind the mess – it's hard for her to dress and tidy up with a broken leg – it's her lack of awareness of it that I find hard to accept. Can't she see the place is a tip? Doesn't it bother her? I pick up a T-shirt and pair of silk trousers from the floor and fold them, but it doesn't seem to register. She's clearly preoccupied with something far more interesting than housework.

She sits pillar-straight in the bed, pulling her hair into a high ponytail. As she smooths it back, I see the beginning of dark roots at the edge of her scalp. I thought she was a natural blonde, which was stupid of me, as only a child could naturally have hair that colour. On closer inspection, her roots are speckled with greys. She must be one of those people who goes grey early. My friend Sophie started going grey at sixteen.

'I didn't wake you, did I?' she says. She doesn't wait for me to answer. 'Only I need another sketch book and some HB pencils. I'm getting close to something,' she says, sounding frantic. She's been wearing the same vest and pair of pyjama shorts for the past three days, not that I'm keeping track. I tell her I'm going shopping later and can get her art supplies then. She asks when I'm going exactly, giving me an intense look. I tell her I'll get ready and go now and she relaxes. I put the folded clothes on the chest of drawers and pat them, trying to convey the message: folded clothes, good. Unfolded clothes on the floor, bad. I pick up the crust of bread and the tray and several other dirty mugs. I glance in the small wastepaper basket, half full of pencil shavings with more littering the carpet around it.

'Izzy?' she says as I'm leaving. 'You know the first thing I want to do when I'm back on my feet properly?' I'm tempted to make a joke about using a vacuum cleaner. 'A day trip to Shoreham,' she says. 'With Tristan as well this time.'

'That would be fun,' I say, worried my words sound hollow, but she smiles, pleased with my response. I imagine Viv stripping down in front of Tristan and frolicking in the river with him. Maybe she *is* angling for a ménage à trois. While I'm grateful to Viv for coming into our lives – she's been the perfect distraction for me and Tristan, taking the pressure off having to talk about all the items on our 'please ignore' list – I have to draw the line at a threesome. Tristan and I are far more comfortable with our heads in the sand, hoping that something or someone else will magically sort out the carnage that surrounds us. Or, better still, that everything stays exactly as it is, no one asking questions, least of all us, and we carry on going through the motions, avoiding the loss we would have to endure otherwise, of each other, of our life together, of the belief that we were doing okay.

But surely we deserve a second chance of some sort. The big question is, are Tristan and I equipped to navigate our way out of the wilderness we now find ourselves in?

Q. You and your spouse have stopped communicating, no longer have sex, are both attracted to other people, and hiding secrets from one another. With trying to save your marriage in mind, what do you do?

a) *Become obsessed with your new neighbour and invite her to stay with you in your house when she breaks her leg, hoping her presence will give you both what you feel is lacking in your lives.*

b) *Agree to an open relationship and see what happens. It will either make your relationship stronger or destroy what little you had left to work on.*

c) *Separate for six months with no contact, freeing each other to see other people, then meet up again to see if there's anything worth salvaging. You'll either fall in love all over again or feel sick with sadness that the meaningless sex and affairs of the past six months have left you incapable of real emotion.*

d) *Get couples counselling to gain insight and understanding into how you lost your way and how best to move forward together (without revealing your innermost secrets. Not everything needs to be shared).*

e) *Ignore the problems in your marriage and carry on as you are until something happens or doesn't happen, and by that time you'll probably be too old and too tired to act upon it. Sure, most marriages are like this anyway and it's very costly to get divorced.*

f) *Tell your spouse the truth about your shame, guilt and insecurities. The worst that can happen is they pack their bags and leave, disgusted and shocked by your revelations. The best that can happen is they accept you for who you are.*

We're currently embedded in option a), which offers a very low score of 2 out of 10 with the headline: *Time to call it. Neither of you were marriage material in the first place.* But if I had to choose now, I'd probably pick option e) which has a rock-bottom score of 1 out of 10 with the headline: *You are a lost cause and don't deserve to be married.*

I don't think either of us would ever pick option b) or c). Still, the runaway train has reached the precipice and is teetering on the edge, waiting for the final push.

If Tristan and I had been solid to begin with, I wouldn't have been flattered and aroused by the attentions of a student and we certainly wouldn't have found ourselves in this situation with Viv. I would not have got painfully drunk and gone to her housewarming party alone, or headed out for the day with her to Shoreham. Instead, we would have behaved like new neighbours normally do – friendly yet distant until relations and boundaries are properly established. Always proceed carefully with strangers, even when they're on your doorstep. Especially when they're on your doorstep.

The stationery shop is on the high street near my college and across the road from Boots and Polly's flat. The window to her flat is open and I'm curious to know if, two weeks later, Jude is still there, playing on his Xbox. 'You dodged a bullet,' I tell myself, trying to ignore the pangs of regret and humiliation. Jude and I were not the Romeo and Juliet of the modern world, kept apart by red tape and marriage. It was all in my head and I would do anything in this moment to feel just a little bit better about myself.

The cash till is by the window and the server, a woman in her sixties, flaps her linen shirt collar, sweltering as the sun beats in through the glass. I pay for two A3 sketch pads and let my eyes wander to Polly's front door across the street, scanning the pavement in case I see her or Jude. I could message her and say I'm outside if she fancies a coffee. Although, if she is still seeing him, having to endure listening to her ramble on in detail about the hot sex she's been having might not be the best thing for me right now. I'm about to leave the shop when the door to Polly's flat opens and she walks out with Jude in tow. I quickly become interested in the greeting cards by the door, rotating the stand too fast for the person browsing on the other side. Peeking up over the top of the card stand, I watch them walk off up the street, his hand on the top of her buttock. He nuzzles into her neck and Polly leans into him. I can't take my eyes off them and end up with the side of my face pressed up against the shop window watching them disappear down the road. Jude is the last thing I need or want, but he made me believe I was someone else for a while. He made me believe I was a desirable, sensual, beautiful, strong, out-of-reach woman. I was a goddess. The ultimate symbol of femininity. But I'm nothing of the sort.

The shroud of loneliness returns, settling ever so gently on my shoulders again as though I won't notice it's there. Outside the shop, with the A3 sketch pads in my hand, the jostling shoppers and stifling fumes from an idling double-decker bus make the heat more intense. Keeping my head down, I bolt back to the rust bucket, parked in the college car park. College isn't officially closed for another few weeks but the building looks abandoned and hollow without the usual hum of students and activity. I was praying for the summer term to finish, to escape my working life and the temptations of Jude but, now that it has, I miss Olly and Tobias and Malcolm. I even miss Tina. Tina is the much-needed older woman in my life, another Mrs Jenkins, and I'm rudderless without them all.

The rust bucket's engine rattles as it springs to life. I can't face going home yet. Viv is in no mood to focus on me or listen to my problems – all she wants to do is sketch and thump her crutch on the floor. I take a right turn instead of left and head for Lily's restaurant. It's only 10.30 a.m. so I'm hoping Tristan and I can have coffee together. I haven't been into Lily's in over a year despite Tristan saying I should pop in – although he hasn't said that lately.

I pull into the Queen's Head pub car park across the road from Lily's. Lily's facade is white and welcoming, with perky, blooming pansies in the planter boxes outside. For someone who appears to despise gardening, Tristan manages to take perfect care of those flowers. Butterflies in my stomach swirl with apprehension about how Tristan will react when I show up. Should I message him first? That might be too formal and I don't want to make a big deal out of it. I'm dropping by because I am literally in the area.

The restaurant is cool as I enter and the door bumps softly shut behind me. Spencer comes running up the stairs with ice buckets and stops when he sees me. It takes a moment to recognise me.

'Izzy?' he says.

'Hi, Spencer,' I reply. 'How are you?'

He gives me a warm hug and an obligatory kiss on the cheek, saying it's been too long and how lovely it is to see me. A warm aroma of garlic potatoes and lamb stew wafts up the stairs and my stomach clinches, grumbling with hunger. I didn't have breakfast. Maddy comes tearing down from upstairs, talking at the top of her voice.

'There's no coffee cups. What's Bill up to?' she says, as an older man with a gentle face emerges from downstairs carrying a tray of clean coffee cups.

'What's that, Madeleine, my darling?' he says with a smile. I assume this is Bill. Maddy apologises and bows to him as he walks by, taking the cups up to the coffee station.

'That's more like it,' Bill says.

'Look who's here,' Spencer says to Maddy. Maddy comes over and embraces me.

'Great to see you,' she says in her soft Irish accent. I always wondered if Tristan was in love with Maddy. His eyes often glaze over when he talks about her, but I think, I hope, it's more of a little sister vibe. Not that Tristan and I know what it's like to have siblings. Although I've always imagined it would be amazing and wonderful and wish I had a truckload of brothers and sisters. Spencer and Maddy look at me, expectant. They're wondering what the hell I'm doing here.

'Is Tristan around?' I ask. Maybe he's on a Sainsbury's run. They both look confused.

'He's not here today,' Spencer says.

'He was in briefly this morning, but he was on the nine-thirty train,' Maddy says.

Tristan's on a train. I have no idea where he's going, but I can't let on to Spencer and Maddy.

'Oh, I thought he was on the lunchtime one. No worries.'

'The funeral's at three. He said he didn't want to risk being late. It's two changes to Dorchester,' says Maddy.

'Yeah, such a pain,' I say, managing to keep my voice steady.

'Did you know her?' asks Maddy.

'Not very well,' I say, searching my brain for some clue or hint as to who the fuck has died. 'What was her surname again? I want to send flowers, that's why I popped in. I was at the florist's and whoosh, it went right out of my head.'

'Isn't it Woods, the same as Tristan's?' Maddy says, giving me a strange look. Oh God, it must be his adopted mother, Martha. Woods is Tristan's original family name. I don't know what his adopted name was.

'His adopted name was different. Don't worry, I'll call him.'

'Are you okay? Do you want a coffee?' asks Maddy. I assure them both I'm fine and that I need to arrange sending the flowers. I duck out of the restaurant and take refuge in my car.

Tristan's adopted mother died and he's gone to the funeral. A simple sentence so speckled with lies it's hard to choose which one is the biggest. Is it the fact that he didn't tell me she'd died? Or that he's gone to a funeral without mentioning it to me or asking me to come with him? Or is it that he told me his adopted parents moved to bloody New Zealand when all this time they've been living in Dorchester? I know he hasn't seen them in years and didn't want to. He never said why and he didn't have to. I never questioned it because it's his business. The same way my relationship with my mother is my business. We've never forced each other to explain our pasts. We both preferred it that way.

It takes me a while to construct a text to Tristan. I can't pretend I don't know about his adopted mother because Maddy and Spencer will tell him I came into the restaurant. But I don't want to give the impression I'm hurt by the lies because I'm actually not. There are many sentences pertaining to my life that are speckled with the same amount of lies, if not more.

- One of my students had a crush on me and I fell for him, that's why I've been dressing down.
- My mother killed my dog and I've never forgiven her, which is one of the reasons I loathe her so much.
- When I was ten, I peed on Clive's oriental rug and had to see a therapist because I was deemed to have psychological problems.
- I saw Viv put her hands on your knees at the party and I know you liked it, that's why I've been competing with you for Viv's attention.
- I kissed Viv and thought about doing it again.
- My mother is damaged, which means I am too probably, you just don't realise it yet (or maybe you do, which means it's your lie too).

I send the text: *I know you're going to Martha's funeral. I'm sorry. I hope it goes okay x* By the time I get home, he still hasn't responded. I pull into the drive and stop the car abruptly. A teenage boy, no more than sixteen, is sitting on the front doorstep, elbows on his knees, chin in his hands. He stands up when he sees me. He's wearing baggy jeans and an oversized hoodie, a bulging backpack over his shoulder.

'Can I help you?' I ask, getting out of the car, slightly on guard.

'I'm looking for Vivienne Parsons. Is she here?' he says. I don't even know Viv's surname. Parsons sounds like the last thing it would be.

The boy has a soft voice and his hands are clenched with nerves. I glance up at my bedroom window and see Viv's face peering out from behind the curtain. She shakes her head slowly and backs away out of sight.

'She lives next door,' I say, not wanting to lie, which is ridiculous since I lie to my husband all the time.

'One of the neighbours said she's staying with you because she broke her leg,' he says with a shaky voice. He seems lost, in all senses of the word. 'I'm Jordan Parsons. I'm her son.'

23

Him

Eat and run. A phrase with three interpretations. Eat a meal and rush off, which is deemed rude. Two, have a meal in a restaurant and scarper without paying. Or it can refer to being efficient. Today I plan to invent a new version of this phrase: funeral and run. Or pay your respects and slip out the back before anyone sees you.

The imposing arches of the crematorium nearly make me turn around and scurry back to the train station. The design is supposed to instil a feeling of peace and timelessness – at least that's my assumption. It doesn't work for me. Instead it fills me with dread and I imagine my back shoved against my bedroom door, trying to keep the bloodthirsty dog with the big fangs from forcing its way in. If he does get in, he'll rip my throat out.

On the train I received a text from Izzy. She knows I've come to Martha's funeral. She must have called the restaurant, which she rarely does these days. It's going to be tough to explain why I didn't tell her about Martha or today, but that would have required starting from the beginning and I'm not even sure where the beginning is or how far back in time I would need to go.

The biggest lie I've ever told her is that Martha and Bradley live in New Zealand. Although I'm not sure it's the worst lie. Scale and morality aren't necessarily linked. I will fall on my sword. In fact, falling on an actual sword might be a better solution.

I've been at home less over the past two weeks and, given that Viv is staying with us, I would have thought I'd be trying to spend more time in the house. But it hasn't worked out like that.

On Viv's first morning, I brought her breakfast, and when I entered the room, the window was shut and the room was stuffy. Viv pulled herself up in bed, yawning, some crusty sleep in the corner of her eye.

I asked her how she was feeling and she said she was sore but definitely better and thanked me for bringing her breakfast.

She pushed her hair behind her shoulders, twisting it so it stayed back, and blinked a few times, waking up properly. It was hard to equate this woman sitting in bed in our spare room, wiping crusty bits from her eyes, about to eat buttered toast, to the mystery woman who had arrived under darkness and watched me watching her from behind the curtain.

The sexual energy and excitement her very presence awakened and stirred within me only makes me feel more empty and sad now. That woman doesn't exist. The woman munching toast, spilling crumbs all over the covers, is not the same one. I miss her though. For a moment I felt truly alive again and filled with hope. I ate an apple because of her.

All is not lost though, or at least it wasn't until now. Seeing Izzy dancing in the cape, her confidence and femininity, her sense of fun and exuberance, made me realise how much I've removed myself from her. The woman I adored and married, the woman who saved me, the woman who gave me hope in myself and my future, has become a speck on the horizon. Just about visible but barely in my universe, and I'm doubtful I'm in hers. I don't know how to make things right or if the gaping hole between us is even repairable. She doesn't look at me the same way she used to and hasn't for a long time. She no longer has faith in me and how can you patch that? Faith is a one-time thing. Once it's gone, it's gone.

I decided not to reply to Izzy's message yet. I need to think about what I'm going to say.

I haven't been in a crematorium before, not that I remember anyway, but the cushioned chairs are a warning I might be sitting for a while. I slip in along the back of the room with several empty rows in front of me so I can easily leave at the end, hopefully unnoticed. The bulk of attendees are seated in the front rows, maybe thirty people.

Bradley is dressed in a dark blue suit that looks very much like one of the suits he used to wear to work, and faces the room as he tips back and forward on the balls of his feet.

I keep my eyeline low and imagine myself blending into the background. I would rather Bradley didn't see me but he immediately does and gives me a wave. A subtle nod of his head would have sufficed. Quite a few people turn to see who he's waving at. I pretend to tie my shoelace.

'It's Tristan, everyone,' he says loudly, ensuring my attempts to hide are in vain. I hear murmurs and shuffling and sniffing. This must be what it's like to be famous, to cause a stir when you enter a public place and have nowhere to hide, trapped and cornered.

'Tristan? My oh my, look at you,' says a woman with a black shawl around her broad shoulders. I don't recognise her, but assume she's one of Bradley and Martha's neighbours.

'You remember Eric,' she says, pulling a young man from behind her, about seventeen years old. 'He would have been a bubba when you went off to university, and then to Brussels and then the United Nations in New York. Where are you now?'

So that was Bradley's cover story. I was a big, global success, far too busy to visit.

Eric peers at me, trying to focus. I say hi to him. He smiles at me, but it's more than a friendly hello. It's a 'I'm having a good time' smile. Eric is high and his mother doesn't realise.

'I'm in London now,' I say to the woman.

'Isn't that wonderful,' she says. 'You meant the world to Martha.'

I muster a smile as they return to their seats at the front.

Bradley says a few words during the service about Martha's big heart. He mentions my name, saying that when they adopted me, it was the happiest day of her life and how all she'd ever wanted was to be a mother. Everyone turns to look at me again, probably to see if I'm crying. I stare ahead, ignoring them all, invaded by the memory of that day. It was not the happiest day of my life.

Then a realisation grips me, an overwhelming, intense pang of guilt. Martha must have been devastated when I never came back to visit or kept in touch.

She would have had to accept that there was no bond between us. Maybe she worked out I had faked it all. That all the 'yays' 'thank yous' and 'awesomes' were just for show. She must have felt so empty and alone, rejected and unloved, abandoned and isolated. Which is how I felt when my mother died.

I found my mother face down in the garden. It's a blur of a memory and not one I allow myself to revisit. But sitting here at Martha's funeral, sharing Martha's pain, it's impossible not to remember what little fragments still exist.

My mother was hanging out the washing and I was sitting at the kitchen table. I'm not sure what I was doing but I was calling her and calling her. 'Mum-meee, Mum-mee.' I ran out into the garden and saw her lying on the grass under the washing line. There was a white sheet half hung up with one corner flapping in the wind. I thought she was playing so I jumped on her, hugging her body. 'Mum-mee, Mum-mee.'

Then people were standing over her and I was being carried back to the house, but I didn't want to go inside, I wanted to stay until she woke up. Then nothing. No memories until the social worker in the car.

I wrack my brain trying to remember what happened before that. Did I go to her funeral? Where did I stay that night? All I remember is how I felt. Stripped of all essence. Stumbling, with nothing to hold on to, lost in a dark fog.

That day, a clamp was placed around my heart, put there to stem the pain and stop it bleeding out. It was an emergency measure, as I knew I would not have been able to cope with the horror of the situation. And then, as though in a dream, Martha and Bradley were peering down at me, offering me a biscuit.

The problem is, I never took the clamp off.

Everyone sits down as the minister says a few words but I stay standing, frozen in my realisation that Martha's pain is my pain. Martha was me. I was Martha. We had both been fucked over. Left for dead, trying to survive.

I shuffle along to the end of the aisle and duck out of the double doors, panicked, looking for a place to hide. I bolt down a corridor hoping for it to lead me somewhere, anywhere. I find the men's room and enter. It smells strongly of bleach and faintly of urine. At least it's empty.

I fall into a cubicle and shut the door behind me, slamming it by accident, making the flimsy walls shake. I lean against the back of the door, taking deep breaths. I'm not sure what's wrong with me or what's happening. My gut begins to heave and I bend over, resting my hands on my knees, taking the weight of my torso before I collapse. Something wants to leave my body, pushing its way up my throat, ready to be expelled into the world, but it's too big and gets stuck, a ball the size of a fist. I'm sure I'll suffocate.

It's been suppressed for too long. Twenty-five years. Stuck in a box, the lid too heavy to lift, but all the time growing in size and power.

The pain is intense, too much to bear, and I'm afraid of letting it out, but the urge is so strong that if I don't give in, I'm convinced my chest will burst open and my heart will stop.

A slow moan, starting in the depths of my stomach, reaches my throat that tightens as I try to squeeze it back down. But it's too powerful. Then it's here and my mouth is open but no sound comes. I am bent over so far now my head nearly touches the floor. I'm about to run out of air.

I take a huge gasp and let out a strange, eerie sound, like the muffled cry of a wounded animal. Again, I gasp for air and again I heave and moan, until the tears come, spilling down my face. A wordless wailing for the mother I lost and the foster mother who had no child.

24

Her

Q. *Your new neighbour is staying with you while she recovers from an accident. Her estranged teenage son turns up on your doorstep but she doesn't want to see him. What do you do?*

a) *Respect your new neighbour's wishes and lie to the boy, saying their mother is at a hospital appointment, and to come back another day. It is actually rude to show up unannounced.*

b) *Tell the boy the truth: their mother is here but doesn't want to see them. There's not enough honesty in the world as it is. Don't add to the web of deceit.*

c) *Welcome the boy into the house, despite your new neighbour's wishes not to see him, and let them get on with it. It's not your job to lie.*

d) *Bring the boy to his mother's house to wait there instead – at least it gets him off your doorstep. Then hope your new neighbour comes to her senses and sees him. Sometimes people need a little push in the right direction.*

The score headings for this quiz are mostly short and sweet. *a) You are weak, b) You need an empathy check, c) Hurray! You are a grown-up, d) Well done. The situation is now worse.* I went for option d) because all of the above required too much decision-making over something I know nothing about. I have no idea about Viv's family history. I'm shocked to discover she has a teenage son. She must have been a teenager herself when she had him. But I'm more shocked that she's rejected him. Although it makes sense.

She's proud to say she's a free spirit and that relationships don't suit her. She likes to live her life on her own terms. An artist who pleases herself. Where would she find the time to raise a child? Even I know it entails school runs, shopping and cooking.

Immediately after showing Jordan into Viv's house, I wonder if I've made the right decision. Jordan is now under Viv's roof and Viv will have to face him, especially if she wants him to go home, wherever home is. Judging by his bulging backpack, I'm assuming he isn't planning on returning anywhere soon.

'She didn't really get a chance to unpack before the accident,' I say, attempting to explain away the chaos and disarray in the house.

'It's alright,' he says, shrugging.

I leave him sitting in one of the saggy-bottomed chairs. He doesn't look any happier to be in Viv's house, only more shrunken and worried. I tell him Viv will be back soon and that he can join us for dinner later. He nods, not that he seems pleased. I couldn't send him away. Even if I had wanted to, I would not have physically been able to say the words or shut a door in his face. There is one thing I know, without a doubt: if I had a child – which I'm not planning on doing – I would never abandon or reject them. I would never leave them home alone and I would care if they started smoking or staying out late at night. And I would do my best to be kind no matter what. That still doesn't mean I'm qualified to be a parent. With all the best intentions in the world, I'm sure I'd fail on even the simplest things.

'I let him in to your house,' I say, putting the drawing pads and new pencils on the bed among the many sketches and pencil shavings covering the duvet and the carpet. Viv's face is deathly pale. She is standing on her crutches, gripping the hand rests.

'He's in my house?' she says, not quite processing the information.

'I didn't know what else to do,' I say, aware there were three other options to choose from.

'What's he doing here? Did he tell you what he wants – I mean, he must have said something?' she asks, clearly beginning to panic.

'All he said is he wants to see you. And he's got quite a big backpack with him.'

'Oh, God, oh, God,' she says, rooting around in a plastic bag and pulling out an unopened packet of cigarettes. 'You don't mind, do you? I'll open the window.'

'Sure,' I say, opening the window for her. She rips open the packet and quickly lights a cigarette, taking a deep, nervous drag. She rests her hand on the open window as she blows the smoke outside, half of which filters back into the room anyway.

'He can't stay,' she says. 'He lives miles away from here with his grandmother. And I don't know him and haven't seen him for years. And he doesn't know me. The whole thing's ridiculous.' The strain on her face is ageing her by the second.

'You don't know why he's here yet. Maybe he's passing through and wants to say hi,' I say when all I really want to do is scream at her: *He's your fucking son, what is your problem?*

'But why now?' she says. 'Why today, why here?' She's clearly stalling and I realise, with great sadness for Jordan, that she doesn't want to see him. She takes a sharp, double inhale on her cigarette as though trying to incinerate herself. Then we both hear it. The familiar squeak followed by a creaking noise: the sound of Viv's back door opening. Viv quickly retracts her hand from the window and drops the cigarette in a cup with cold tea in the bottom.

'That's him,' she mouths at me, pointing to her garden next door in panic.

It's strange to see her so discombobulated. I thought she was the woman least likely to be rattled by anything. In the event of a three-minute warning of a nuclear attack, Viv would shrug her shoulders, c'est la vie, and open a bottle of Bacardi. How wrong I was.

She moves to the edge of the window and I join her as we peer out, watching Jordan amble up the garden to the two deckchairs under the blossom tree. He hovers for a moment, then slowly begins his descent to a seated position, his back to the house. He's quite a heavy boy, tall, well built and chunky. As his bum hits the chair and he leans back, the fabric tears and his backside pokes through the gap.

'He's broken my deckchair,' Viv whispers to me.

'Looks like it,' I reply.

We continue to observe him. He doesn't seem worried about the fabric splitting or maybe he hasn't noticed or assumed it was like that before. His head dips forward and then a flurry of smoke rises and surrounds his head.

'He's smoking,' Viv says.

'Yes, he is,' I reply.

'He does have a lovely-shaped cranium,' she says, slightly wistful.

Her curiosity is almost childlike, like she's observing a wild animal in its natural habitat. She's in awe of this boy, this child she gave birth to yet has no connection to. And there's nothing like a bit of perspective to review your own life. Even my own mother, with her very questionable parenting skills, if you could call them skills at all, was there for me in her own dysfunctional way. She made me packed lunches, picked me up from school and cooked me dinner. She even got me a dog, not that that ended well. Suddenly I'm appreciative of her efforts, no matter how small.

'I said he could join us for dinner,' I say, still watching Jordan, smoking, with half his backside hanging out of the deckchair.

Viv runs her hands through her hair, mumbling to herself. She starts to rifle through her clothes, picking up items from the floor.

'Fuck, fuck, fuck,' she says. 'I've got nothing to wear? I mean, what should I wear?'

'Borrow something of mine.'

'Yes, yes, maybe a dress with a suit jacket or something,' she says.

She's actually not making sense now. The previous Viv, the wily, entrancing, intoxicating lizard princess who moved in next

244

door and stirred things up between me and Tristan, has absolutely left the building. The woman in front of me, pulling her hair out over what to wear to have dinner with the teenage son she doesn't know, is an utter mess. What will Jordan think of his mother? What is he expecting from her? Will he be disappointed or simply happy to finally see her again?

I'm sure she has her reasons for not raising her son herself, but to have a 'no contact' policy, that's the part I find hard to understand. What's the point in being unconventional and free-spirited if you can't take some responsibility for the harder things in life? If my mother was immature as a parent, Viv is a toddler.

When I return to Viv's house, Jordan is now sitting on the back doorstep. He jumps up when he sees me and quickly stubs out his cigarette, embarrassed to have been caught smoking.

'Don't mind me,' I say. 'Smoke if you want to, but it is really bad for you.'

'Yeah, I know,' he says, putting his hands in the front of his baggy jeans.

'Viv's back now, if you want to come over.'

He stares at me, shoulders hunched up by his ears.

'Does she want to see me?' he says.

'Of course,' I say. 'She can't come to you because her leg's in a cast.' He seems to take this onboard but is clearly hesitating.

'I haven't seen her since I was six,' he says, biting the inside of his cheek. 'I've tried to call and message and stuff. This is the first time I've found out where she lives.' I feel a tightness in my chest as my heart crumples for him.

'I'm sorry.' It's all I can muster.

'I don't want to push myself on her, you know, if she doesn't want to see me.'

'But she does. It's a shock for her, that's all.'

'Nah, this was a bad idea. I should go,' he says, totally losing any of the courage it took to come here in the first place. He grabs his backpack, throwing it over his shoulder.

'Please, stay for something to eat. See your mum. She's totally fine with it.'

'Fine?' he mumbles, repeating after me. We both know 'fine' doesn't convey eagerness or qualify as a warm invitation. I could insist that she's excited to see him, but I don't want to lie. I'm also not sure how Viv is going to behave. I don't think she's sure either.

'I shouldn't have come,' he says and heads past me to the door.

'Jordan,' I say, following him. He stops at the door. 'You've got this far, don't leave now.'

'I know the score,' he says. 'Thanks for trying.'

He trundles out of the house, backpack weighing down his shoulders. I race after him, calling his name again until he stops.

'You ever need anything, you know where I am. I'm Izzy.' He gives me a sad smile and walks on. He's never coming back.

Viv sits up in bed, sketch pad resting on a book, smudging pencil strokes across a page. The crutches are upright against the wall.

'He's gone,' I tell her.

'I know,' she says, concentrating hard on moving her hand over and back as she draws. 'I saw him leave.'

'It was his decision. I invited him over and said you wanted to see him.'

'He changed his mind, obviously,' she says, but there's relief in her voice. I'm itching to yell at her again. *Aren't you even the least bit concerned? Don't you want to know your own son?*

'I know what you're thinking,' she says. 'But he's better off without me.'

In the kitchen, I slop olive oil over six chicken thighs in a dish, enough to feed Jordan if he had stayed, and Tristan, although Tristan won't be home for dinner. He'll probably head back to the restaurant after the funeral. Tristan still hasn't replied to my text. I send another one: *Hope the funeral wasn't too bad. Bit of a situation here with Viv but all sorted. Tell you when I see you. x* I delete the last two sentences and press send.

I hear a phone beep behind me and turn to see Tristan, his hair dishevelled and his suit jacket creased.

'Hi,' he says.

'Hey,' I reply, still holding my phone.

'The front door's wide open,' he says.

25

Him

The train back from Dorchester isn't busy at all and I sleep most of the way home. Even my legs are hollow with exhaustion. And despite the mugginess, I'm cold, bunched up against the side of the seat with my head against the window.

Izzy's text hangs heavy on my phone. Anytime I go to reply, my words seem insincere, or offhand, verging on rude. I decide there is no way to reply in a text, or in general. What am I supposed to say? *Thanks. Sorry I didn't tell you.* Or *No big deal. Explain later.* But I don't want to explain later. Dread seeps into my bones, telling me this is not going to be one of those conversations that gets pushed aside and filed under 'not important' with all the other ignored debris from our lives.

I close my eyes and hope the train never stops.

By the time it rolls into the station, my head is fuzzy and my eyes are sore, like I've just swam fifty lengths of a pool with no goggles. I call Spencer to check in on the restaurant. Everything's running smoothly and Monty is still on his best behaviour, so I tell him I'll go straight home and won't be in this evening. Spencer says Izzy came to the restaurant this morning. I pretend that I spoke to her. But hearing Izzy came to the restaurant is promising. I wish I'd been there.

The walk home from the station is a good thirty minutes, but I'm up for it. Anything to restore my body with energy (and to put off facing Izzy a while longer).

As I turn onto our street, I see the front door to our house is wide open. I quicken my pace, glancing over at Viv's house as

I head up the drive. Light frames the edges of the living room curtains. I enter our hallway and see Izzy ahead in the kitchen on her phone as my phone beeps with a text. She looks up, surprised to see me, or maybe startled.

'Hi,' she says.

'The front door's open,' I say.

'Is it?' Izzy says, alarmed.

She walks past me into the hallway and shouts up the stairs to Viv. There's no answer. Izzy runs upstairs as I close the front door. She comes back down again, looking grim.

'She's left,' she says.

'I saw a light on next door,' I say.

'She scarpered,' she says, disappointed.

'Are you okay?' I put my hand on her arm, wondering if she had a row with Viv.

'Not really,' she says.

'Let's get a drink,' I say, opening the front door again. 'I know I could do with one.'

She nods and follows me out of the door, pulling it shut behind us.

'I was making chicken for dinner.'

'I'm not that hungry,' I say.

'Me neither,' she says.

We stroll up the road together. The sun sinks behind the houses, casting an amber glow across the inky blue sky, and the air is fresher than it's been in weeks. Izzy takes a deep breath. I ask her what happened with Viv and she tells me about Viv's teenage son.

'I probably shouldn't be as upset as I am, but it was the saddest thing,' she says.

'Viv isn't who we thought she was,' I say.

'Who did you think she was?' she asks.

'Somebody else,' I say, which is honestly my best answer.

'I just wanted a friend,' she says.

Hearing her say that, realising how I might not even be a friend to Izzy anymore, it strikes me how lonely we both are.

We duck into the Imperial Arms, about a ten-minute walk from our house. It's been well over eighteen months since we've been here and the bar staff are different. In fact, it's been ages since Izzy and I have been anywhere together.

The pub is cosy and old, having kept all its historic charm and quaintness, and the familiarity puts me at ease. Izzy seems more relaxed too as she slips into a cushioned seat in a small bay window. I order two pints of Guinness, which the young girl serving pours quickly, like lager. Maddy says the English ruin Guinness and that it should always be poured in two stages to let it settle.

I bring the pints to the table and Izzy says thanks.

'How was the funeral?' she asks. There's no loaded intonation in her voice or anything to suggest she's annoyed I didn't tell her.

'Sorry I didn't get back to your text. I didn't know what to say.'

'Don't worry about it,' she says.

We sit in silence for a moment, both taking large gulps of our pints.

'You don't have to talk about it if you don't want to,' she says.

I want to tell her everything, I really do, but it's like there's a band around my chest tightening slowly, not allowing me to breathe, let alone get the words out.

'There's not much to talk about, really,' I manage to say. 'We weren't close.'

'It was nice of you to go then,' she says, taking another swig of her Guinness, leaving a creamy foam on her top lip that she first attempts to lick away, then wipes the residual with the back of her hand.

'Why didn't Viv want to see her son?' I ask, feeling it's the right time to change the subject, or rather, deflect, but it's as though Izzy hasn't heard me.

'Why did you tell me they lived in New Zealand?' she blurts out. 'I mean, it's pretty basic information and it's not like I'm

251

going to care where they live. I just don't understand why you couldn't tell me. What difference does it make to anything?'

And there it is. Laid out in front of me. Nowhere to run. No story to hide behind. I'm going to have to be honest. Tell her how I reinvented myself when I left for university and how I never wanted to see Martha and Bradley again as it would only remind me of the pain of my childhood, which was so unbearable at times I thought about killing myself.

Then a switch flips in my brain and it's super Tristan to the rescue. This guy wears sharp suits and has swagger and charm and confidence. He's the grown-up version of me as a child when I was living with Martha and Bradley. He's smart and resourceful and knows exactly how to handle situations such as these. He leans into my ear. I've got this, he says.

'They did live in New Zealand. They moved back last year. Didn't I tell you?'

Izzy sits very still, studying me. 'No, you didn't,' she says.

'Sorry. To be honest, I felt bad I hadn't been to visit them. It's years since I've even talked to them and, like I said, we don't keep in touch.'

'I thought Martha couldn't travel because of her blood pressure.'

Good good. Bring on the cross-examination.

'Not for short visits, no. But Bradley said she missed England so they came back.'

'What did she die of?'

I realise I have no idea. I never asked.

'Brain haemorrhage.'

'That's awful. Why didn't you tell me about the funeral?'

'I only just found out about it myself and I was going to tell you later. I didn't want you to feel like you had to come. Actually, it was a nice service and I saw some of the neighbours from when I was growing up and I had a drink with Bradley afterwards. He said sorry he couldn't make it to the wedding.'

'Right, so am I going to meet Bradley now?'

'He's moving back to New Zealand pretty soon but he wants us to visit.'

The lies tumble out of my mouth like cannon balls leaving crater-sized holes in the pub floor. I take another swig of my pint and some of the beer gets caught in the back of my throat. I cough into my hand, managing to make it look like I'm just clearing my throat.

'We should start planning then,' Izzy says.

I frown, unsure what she's talking about.

'Our trip to New Zealand,' she says firmly.

'Absolutely,' I say, still channelling super Tristan, who has no doubt in his mind whatsoever that a trip to New Zealand can be put on the long finger indefinitely.

Izzy smiles at me, an indication she believes me, and I instantly return to not-so-super Tristan as the reality of my blatant, cowardly lies hits me hard. I have just pushed Izzy even further away, maybe to the point of no return.

But some lies are too big and too dense to ever come clean about.

'I'm sorry I wasn't there when Viv's son showed up,' I say.

'You were at a funeral,' Izzy says, full of understanding, which only makes me feel worse.

We sit in silence, finishing our pints. Anyone looking in the window might think we were two strangers sharing the same table.

26

Her

I'm lying in bed, staring at the familiar ripped paper lampshade hanging from the bedroom ceiling. I wonder what woke me this time and assume it must be Viv's thumping crutch again. But then I remember she's left. I stretch my arm out to Tristan's empty side of the bed. He's so quiet when he leaves in the morning. Either he's naturally gifted at stealth movements or he makes an extra special effort not to wake me in order to avoid conversation. The way I'm feeling at the moment, I decide it's definitely the second option.

Last night, when Tristan arrived home, I nearly burst into tears and threw myself into his arms, like a child needing comfort and reassurance that they're not alone, that Jordan isn't alone. I didn't, of course. The front door had been left wide open, which was a much-needed distraction for both of us. Viv had snuck out without telling me. This is probably what Viv does when life gets a bit difficult or challenging. She bolts, leaving the stable door open. I expected so much more from her. Maybe 'free spirit' is simply code for 'selfish' and you can't be both a parent and a free spirit. They are mutually exclusive. Being a parent requires sacrifice, even for someone as woeful at parenting as my mother. I'm aware I'm being judgemental and I really don't know why I'm so cross with Viv.

Tristan suggested we go to the pub when he saw I was upset. I was so surprised by this, as we haven't been out as a couple for a while, that I said yes and walked straight out of the door, leaving my dish of chicken thighs on the kitchen counter. Tristan's face was drawn, suggesting exhaustion. It was strange to stroll along the pavement side by side, as we hadn't done that in a long time either. And I'd missed it – the connection, the sense of togetherness. The tears threatened to make an appearance again but I pushed them away. I was still emotional over Viv's treatment of Jordan, at least that's what I told myself. I gave Tristan a facts-only version of what happened. 'Poor kid,' he said. He then said Viv wasn't who we thought she was. I clarified that I had only wanted a friend, the subtext being that he might have wanted more. But it didn't seem to register, which made me wonder if I'd been wrong about Tristan's feelings for Viv.

We automatically gravitated to the Imperial Arms. It's closest to our house but it was also once our favourite pub for a Sunday afternoon. They used to have a billiards table in the back room and the two of us would play for hours. Once inside, Tristan slipped into old patterns and ordered two pints of Guinness without asking me what I would like first. I didn't mention it, as I would have probably had a Guinness anyway. Then Tristan said nothing. I gave it a minute or so to see if he would bring up Martha's funeral and all that it implied, but he didn't. Did he really think it could simply be added to our 'not to be discussed' list? There was always going to be a tipping point and this was it. Plus, the list was full and in danger of becoming a spreadsheet.

I was more than aware that the outcome from pushing the issue could signify no coming back. No restoring of the equilibrium I was trying so hard to achieve. It was terrifying to plough on ahead anyway, but the events of the day were making me reckless.

'How was the funeral?' I blurted out, struggling to keep the frustration out of my voice. He should have been the one instigating this conversation, offering an explanation. It was his elephant in the room. He said he was sorry he hadn't replied to my texts. I told him he didn't have to talk about it if he didn't want to, code for 'this is a safe space for you to tell me everything'. But he took me at my word and changed the subject, asking about Viv's son again. But I couldn't let it go, as much as I wanted to. Not this time.

'Why did you tell me your adopted parents lived in New Zealand when they don't?'

He stared at me, frozen to the spot, not expecting me to be so in his face. I kept my tone soft and kind, reassuring him that it made no difference to me where they lived. I just wanted to know why he felt he couldn't tell me the truth. He nodded his head and moved his pint from one coaster on the table to another. This is it, I thought. He's going to explain himself. Then he started talking, rather fast.

His parents had lived in New Zealand but returned to England last year. Martha's heart condition was only an issue for short visits. He'd only just found out about the funeral himself and was planning on telling me about it but didn't want to pressure me into going. He thought the funeral would be grim and awkward but it was actually a rather nice service where he got to catch up with old neighbours and even have a drink with Bradley, who was returning to New Zealand now but wanted us to visit, which Tristan appeared to be enthusiastic about. He then took a sip of his pint and nearly choked to death on it.

And, you know, it would have all been totally believable if it hadn't been so blatantly obvious he was LYING THROUGH HIS TEETH.

It took all my self-control not to call him out on it. What good would it have done? He would have denied it and I have no proof that anything he said is either true or not. The bigger question is, of course, why is he lying and what else is he hiding from me? Tristan is a master of cover-ups. Another thing I did not know about my husband.

As we walked home, it started to rain. Lightly at first and then it deluged, flooding the streets in minutes with rivers streaming into the gutters. We ran the short distance home and fell in through the front door, dripping wet. I insisted he have a shower first as I needed to salvage the chicken, if it was indeed salvageable. By the time I trundled upstairs, Tristan was fast asleep in bed, lying on his side, facing the door.

The sky is clear blue again and the air is warm and dry, as though not a drop of rain fell last night. I glance out of the bedroom window and note that the rust bucket looks rather shiny having had the dirt washed off it. I mosey across to the spare room to see what kind of state it's in. It's not as bad as I expected. At least she took all her clothes and belongings with her. The duvet is crooked on the bed and the pillows are flattened, still showing the imprint of Viv's head. The bin is overflowing with pencil shavings and there's a huddle of fluffy dust in the corner under the window. It smells musty and used like a second-hand car. I pull back the duvet to start stripping the bed and find a large piece of folded card. On the front it says: *Him & Her.* I sit down on the bed and open it. Inside are two pencil sketches. The first one is of me. I have a half smile and the corners of my eyes are slightly creased. My hair is wild around my face and shoulders, like I've come in from a raging storm. My expression says I made it, I survived. Pride swells in my chest. If this is how Viv sees me – in charge, unflappable – I'm quite chuffed.

The second sketch is of Tristan and my breath catches in my throat. He is staring out of the picture, intense, handsome, gallant – she made his jawline more defined than it is but it suits him. His hair is thick and wavy, not quite like his actual hair, but it suits him too. But it's his eyes that hold my attention. They are open and alert but at the same time on the verge of filling with tears, of giving in to pain buried inside him, but he's fighting it. He won't let it get the better of him. It is a haunting image and I can't stop looking at it. Is Tristan really in pain? And if he is, how come Viv, practically a stranger, can see it and I can't? It's another of Viv's little games. Flirting with Tristan at the party, taking me skinny-dipping in Shoreham and kissing me, pitting us against each other, and now this harrowing portrait of Tristan to compare to the portrait of me, where I look, well, smug, for want of a better word.

Who the fuck does Viv think she is?

My rigid finger presses against the bell again, not releasing this time. From inside the house I hear the continual pinging of the ringer. I know Viv's in there as she can't exactly go anywhere and I'm not leaving until she opens the door. There's a shuffling noise then the door swings open and Viv stands before me, on her crutches. She is wearing a tight pink vest, jean shorts, frayed from where she cut them off herself, with a pale blue apron loosely tied around her middle. Her hair is scrunched on top of her head, held in place by what looks like an old painting rag, and her grey roots, even more pronounced now, give her a shiny, silver topping like a halo. She's also covered head to foot in smudges of charcoal. From one angle, she looks like an angel. From another, a street urchin from a Dickens novel.

She beams at me as though yesterday never happened. Her son never showed up, she didn't reject him and she didn't walk out of my house, without even a thank you, and leave the front door wide open. Biting my tongue, I force a polite smile.

'Come in, come in,' she sings to me, swinging down the hall, a dab hand on the crutches now, and enters the kitchen. 'Do you want tea?' she calls out.

Her light demeanour throws me a little but the rage is building up, storming inside me, my hands cold as the adrenaline sucks the blood from my extremities.

'Sure,' I reply, shutting the door behind me, hard, to make a point, and follow her into the kitchen. I note that she has at least washed up the dirty glasses. She shuffles around the kitchen, wittering away as she retrieves two cups from different locations.

'I literally woke up this morning, like at 5 a.m., and got straight to work. This idea of how people hold their truth in the lines on their face, even children when they frown or smile,' she says, speaking fast. 'There are so many layers to a human face, as there are to human emotions, and I'm actually seeing through into the depths now, like I have a spyhole into what lies beneath. It's everywhere I look and it's consuming me but I feel so alive.'

'Good for you,' I say, cutting across her, refusing to enter into a joint amnesia pact. I've done enough of that with Tristan. 'What's this about?' I ask, holding the sketches of me and Tristan up for her to see.

'They're a thank-you present,' she replies.

'Flowers would have been fine.' I wave the sketch of Tristan in front of her. 'You see Tristan as a victim?'

'No, I just see him,' she says. 'Like I see you.'

'I'm not interested in your artist bullshit, "I paint what I see" crap.'

'Has something happened, Izzy? Are you okay?' she asks calmly, which only annoys me more. Then the dam breaks and it all comes gushing out.

'Who do you think you are, putting your hands on Tristan's knees, flirting with him, then taking me skinny-dipping and making me your special friend? Trying to force a wedge between us for your own amusement, but I see it now, yes, I see you, this "free spirit" rubbish you go on about, using it as an excuse for being a marriage wrecker and for turning your back on your own son.'

I stop to take a breath. Viv is as still as one of her statues then drops her head, placing her hands on the countertop. I glance down at my own hands, which are shaking, and I notice that the pictures of me and Tristan have fallen on the floor, two pairs of eyes, staring up at me, disapproving of my harsh words.

Viv lifts her head and paints on a bright smile, which is unsettling. Isn't she going to defend herself or at least tell me to get out of her house?

'Now, where were we?' she says. 'Tea, that's right.' She leans her crutches against the breakfast bar and bends to search through one of her mystery shopping bags on the floor. 'I'm afraid I don't have any fresh milk but I have some of those UHT singles. They should still be in date. Or would you rather have it black?' She accidentally bumps one of crutches and it slips away from the counter, taking one of the cups with it, both crashing to the floor, the cup smashed to pieces. Viv, startled, is about to topple over herself but I get to her just in time to hold her up. I pick up her crutches and move her to a sunken chair.

'Thanks,' she says. Being of such a slight frame, her bum sinks quite a way into the chair. She looks squashed in and vulnerable.

The anger inside me gently washes away, caught in an undercurrent, dissipating as it flows down the river, no longer governing my responses. My head throbs with tiredness and my eyelids feel heavy.

'One down, one left,' she says, indicating the broken cup pieces on the floor. 'We'll have to share, if you don't mind.'

I let out a little laugh, Viv does too, but I see her eyes are wet with tears now. She wipes them away, unashamed of her emotions.

'Shit,' I say, feeling terrible for making her cry. 'I didn't mean what I said.'

'It's okay,' she says. 'I know who I am and I'm aware it's not good enough.'

'Don't say that,' I say, desperate for her to feel better about herself. 'I mean, what's "good enough" when it's at home anyway?' I put my arm around her and hug her.

'I don't know how to be any different,' she says. I hug her tighter, feeling her delicate frame fold into my arms.

Viv, the highly anticipated new neighbour that Tristan and I imbued with special gifts and abilities to solve our problems, is just an ordinary woman. She's not a lizard princess or a free spirit or the love of my life or Tristan's, she's simply human, and as messy as the rest of us. Tristan stares up at me from the floor. He doesn't look as pained in the picture now, only wistful and handsome. Maybe I saw the pain before because I've always known it was there and that, like my mother, I'm not emotionally equipped to help him. I'm not what Tristan needs. The lack of communication, the lying, the secrets, the cheating, is all down to the fact that I'm not good enough. And that's okay. I accept my failings and decide it's time to do what's right.

I'll go to Monty's wedding, as I promised Tristan I would, then I'll go away for a while, maybe visit Sophie in France and stay for the rest of the summer. It's a much-needed break and one that could likely be the end of us.

27

Him

I leave the house at 8 a.m. The night before, after the pub, was the most silent Izzy and I have ever been with each other. There was nothing to fill the dead air, nothing to say about the new neighbour anymore. Neither of us feels the same way about Viv as we did when she first arrived, and I'm ashamed now of my overexcitement and enthusiasm. I'm sure Izzy feels at least a little silly too. Who takes in a new neighbour with a broken leg a few days after meeting them? There are no sane answers to this question.

Over the past two weeks, I've been getting in to work at 9 a.m. to assist Deniz with the opening of his new restaurant, Gina's, and to organise Monty's wedding reception, as well as being there to help with all deliveries.

I've been secretly hoping one of the deliveries will be short a few prawns to see if Monty has a meltdown, which might in turn reboot his system, returning him to speaking in three-word sentences, and sulking and shouting his way through the day. Yesterday, I considered hiding the scallops when they arrived in the van just to see how he would handle it. The delivery guy frowned as I gave a disappointed sigh when he said we had everything we ordered. I'm curious to see if this change in Monty is permanent or just a phase. Can people change or is this actually the real Monty?

I left earlier this morning because I had somewhere else to be before work.

The estate agent, a man in his sixties called Lucas, kicks open the graffitied door with his polished shoe, which I'm sure must have hurt, given the loud crack from the steel panel on the door frame as he slammed his foot against it. The torch on his phone beams into the room, revealing a dark and grimy space.

'It's a bit stiff,' he says, referring to the door. 'But you'd be putting on a new shop front anyway.'

The windows to the front of the building are covered with newspaper but the smallest of gaps allow streaks of light to funnel in, cutting through the thick dust in the air. It smells musty and greasy, like someone just turned the chip pan off and walked out.

'Careful of the floor,' says Lucas, as he steps over a loose tile. He makes it to the far wall and flicks on a light switch. A bare bulb hangs precariously from the ceiling, illuminating the dank walls and rusty old kitchen with pots and pans still in situ.

It could be an art installation titled *Hell: No Exit*. It makes me shudder and reminds me of the rotting, soggy boxes of crap in Bradley's garage and the trapped boxes crammed into his shed filled with even more crap.

'As you can see, it was a café in a previous life, so you won't need to apply for change of use. It's 800 square metres, including the loos at the back,' Lucas says with gusto, slapping his hands together to get rid of the settling dust.

I cautiously approach the kitchen area. In the abandoned deep fat fryer, murky brown lumps shimmer on the dense, greasy surface of leftover oil. My stomach churns as the rancid stench shoots up my nostrils.

'Obviously, you'll be gutting the place,' Lucas says.

My eyes travel over the walls and the floor and ceiling. All I see are black stains that seem to be slowly spreading, even as I stand here watching, the damp and rot infiltrating every surface. If you scraped back the plasterboard, I imagine a sap-like substance underneath, creeping over the brickwork, covered in unknown insects feeding off the grime.

Lucas throws his arms out. 'It's all about your vision, isn't it?' he says.

I lie that I have a few other premises to look at and thank him for his time. He shakes my hand, cupping his other hand over mine to communicate he really does like me. I do find him quite genuine.

We step back outside and I wait as Lucas locks the hellhole up again. I'm thankful to be out of it and feel like I could do with a shower.

'Don't leave it too long,' he says with a wink. 'Time catches up with you.'

With that he marches off around the corner, his shoes making a clicking noise on the pavement.

I eye the old café again, with the newspapers stuck to the windows and the steel band running along the base of the door, and try to visualise my own restaurant and what that would be like, but nothing comes to mind.

The viewing was an experiment to see if I would be filled with any sense of excitement or urgency to move ahead and make a success of my life, if not for myself, for Izzy. But all I feel is deflated and lost. I need to face facts. I have no vision, or money. And without a vision I have no hope of getting any money.

I scramble into the back of a taxi, desperate to get away from the grease and stains and my ever-increasing sense of failure.

The taxi driver makes conversation and I manage to be polite and appear engaged. He's worried that the hot summer we're having is due to climate change. I agree. He points out his car is electric. 'Good', I say.

When he pulls up outside Lily's, he tells me it's his wife's favourite restaurant, despite it being a total rip-off. I suggest he book in for Sunday lunch as it's a fixed menu and great value. He says he'll do that. I give him a fifteen per cent tip and get out of the car.

I hang around outside Lily's for a moment, glad to be back, but not ready to enter yet. I want to look at it for a while, appreciate it. After being in the derelict café building, arriving back at

Lily's is like waking from a nightmare and realising you're home and safe.

I've never really belonged anywhere, not after age six anyway. If nothing else comes of today, at least I've realised I belong to Lily's.

Monty comes up to the bar as I arrive. He shows no awareness that I've only just stepped in the door or might have other things to do.

'Look at this,' he says, showing me his phone.

On the screen are two pictures of men in suits. One wears a black tuxedo, the other wears a shiny gold and green snake-print suit with matching tie.

'Which one?' he says. 'I can't decide.'

'For the wedding?' I ask, genuinely thrown.

'Of course, for the wedding,' he says, giving me a funny look.

'What does Flora say?' I ask, trying to be as diplomatic as possible.

'I'm going to surprise her. Either 007 or sexy snake man.'

He stares at me, waiting for a response.

'The tux,' I say.

'Why?' he says, clearly disappointed. 'What's wrong with the snake suit?'

'I think it's a bit risky, if you haven't asked Flora.'

He snatches back his phone and goes downstairs. I'm starting to feel apprehensive for Monty and his wedding day. First the contact lenses then the dramatic change in mood and now possibly a snake-print suit. Just about anything could happen.

I wonder if Flora's going to wear something unusual too. As long as she doesn't wear heels, because she's at least a foot taller than Monty already. I'm planning on wearing a morning suit, to show as much respect for Monty and his nuptials as possible. And Izzy, if she's still coming, will hopefully wear the cape I saw her dancing in. She hasn't worn it since, but I did find it tucked away at the back of her wardrobe.

I admit I went looking for it, my curiosity getting the better of me. I pulled it from the back of the wardrobe and ran it over my hands, gliding it through my fingers.

'Monty wants you,' Maddy says coming up the stairs with three bowls of beef stroganoff, the staff meal today. She puts the food on table two and Spencer comes from behind the bar, inspecting the portion sizes, trying to decide which is the biggest.

'They're all the same size,' Maddy says, a weary tone in her voice. Spencer still takes time to assess them and, when satisfied, selects a bowl and starts tucking in.

I don't have time to worry about the Spencer and Maddy romance. The odds have always been stacked against them, what with Spencer's shallowness and Maddy's pride. And my fear for Spencer treating Maddy badly has now flipped to worry that Maddy might break his heart.

For the first time in the eighteen months I've known Spencer, he seems genuinely committed to a woman. And he thinks because he feels like that, the feeling will automatically be mutual. There's something both arrogant and naive about it.

I trot down the stairs, still at Monty's beck and call, and scoot into the kitchen, breaching the threshold, as I've done every day for the past week. I'm still testing him, to see if he will cave and crack and revert to form.

Monty sings his head off to the Gipsy Kings as he pipes creamy mash potato onto the tops of fish pies.

'Tristan, I have a question for you,' he says.

'Fire away,' I say, taking a step back, suddenly preferring to be safely behind the threshold, not that Monty has noticed.

'Do you think I'm getting married too fast?'

I open my mouth in surprise, but Monty looks at me expectantly, like I'm about to speak and have an answer for him.

We've all been discussing this, of course, behind his back. Maddy thinks it's got something to do with Monty's visa, like an arranged marriage, but Monty's been in England for six years, so it can't be that.

Spencer believes Flora is pregnant, because why else would anyone get married? Bill chuckled when he heard about the wedding but didn't give an opinion, which could have meant anything. Sita said, 'Good for him, he deserves to be happy.' And when she received her invite, she went red in the face and ran outside with her phone.

Deniz thinks there's nothing wrong with a quick wedding. He said he knew within five minutes of meeting Gina he was going to marry her. On matters of love, why wait, is his philosophy.

It was a lightning bolt when I met Izzy, I have to admit. She woke me up from a deep slumber and brought me into the land of the living where I was worth something.

When I made her laugh, or held her attention when telling a story, or made her shudder with pleasure, my heart would soar.

'Say something,' Monty says, holding the piping bag up by his shoulder like he's getting ready to squirt me with it.

The only answer here is no. It cannot be yes or 'I don't know' or 'don't ask me'. Monty isn't looking for an honest answer; he's looking for reassurance.

'No, I don't think it's too fast. You're not getting any younger,' I say, attempting a joke. This would be the first time, in the six years I've worked with him, that I've ever poked fun at him.

Monty looks at me, serious, then his face breaks into a huge beam.

'I'm a lot younger than you, my friend, or at least I look it,' he says.

'Thanks,' I say. 'You ask for my advice and then insult me.'

Monty laughs, banging his free hand on the work surface. We are all still getting used to Monty laughing. All he used to do was grumble and shout, now he opens his mouth as wide as it will go and lets out great guffaws.

There is a possibility, I think, watching his glasses-free, happy face, that he has been replaced by his good twin, the old Monty being the evil one.

'Now, out, out, out,' he shouts, shooing me gently. I hold my hands up to indicate I'm going.

'One other thing,' he says casually. 'Will you be my best man?'

I'm stuck for words. Monty avoids eye contact, piping extra potato over the already topped pies.

'I could ask Deniz or Spencer,' he says. 'But I would like it to be you. We have a connection.'

Close friends and family aren't just thin on the ground, they're obviously non-existent.

'Is your sister coming to the wedding?' I ask, clutching at straws that Monty might be modern enough to have a best woman instead of a man.

'No, my sister is not coming,' he says, deadpan. 'You don't have to make a speech or anything,' he adds quickly, which is a relief. I mean, what would I talk about? How Monty nearly killed me once with a flying saucepan or threatened our veg supplier with a boning knife?

'As long as I'm not stepping on anyone's toes, I'd be delighted,' I say, but I really don't have a choice.

Monty nods and I detect a sense of relief that the awkward question is over. He whacks up the Gipsy Kings, singing his heart out.

As I turn to leave, I almost bump into Spencer, standing outside the kitchen, holding his empty bowl. By the look of utter surprise on his face, he heard every word.

He mouths 'what the fuck?' at me. I shrug like it's no big deal, but I totally agree with Spencer. What the fuck indeed.

28

Her

There's something funereal about the registry office. Every effort has been made to create a bright room with flowers and velvet-covered chairs, but it still feels like it's teetering on the cusp of joy and despair.

Large windows flank two sides of the room and a triptych of printed roses lines another wall. At the front, where Tristan asked me to sit, is a mahogany desk, which casts a heavy presence over the room. In front of the desk are two high-backed chairs for the bride and groom, and another on the other side, all waiting to be filled. It feels serious, like an interview where if you get one question wrong, bang, a lever shoots up, the ground opens and you're tipped from your chair into the underworld, where people who are not fit to be married must walk forever in their wedding outfits.

I try to focus on the positive aspects of the room. There is a cabinet in the corner at the front by the window with a tall white vase on top with pink roses in it. Although I think they might be fake. And everything is cream-coloured, from the walls and ceiling to the chairs and embroidered curtains, which are held open with matching cream-coloured ropes with tassels. That's what I mean by every effort being made, because there really isn't much else they can do. In a room like this, with flowers and chairs in a row, if you turn the mahogany desk longways and put a coffin on it, you're at an entirely different event.

It's a small room, maybe forty chairs, split evenly between both sides. I'm sitting on the right-hand side, the groom's. I'm surprised civil ceremonies still bother with allocating specific sides. When I married Tristan, also in a registry office, I looked up the tradition behind the seating rule to see if we wanted to abide by it. Back in the day, when men were knights and women were fair maidens, the man needed to be on the right to keep his right hand free in case he needed to draw his sword (from his left) to fight any other knights coming to rescue his fair maiden, who had more than likely been kidnapped and forced to marry. I suggested to Tristan that unless he was planning on actually carrying a sword on the day, we should probably ignore it and do what we liked. He agreed, but on the day itself, the registrar requested Tristan be on the right and I on the left. The six guests we had dispersed themselves evenly across both sides.

I shift in my seat, uncrossing and crossing my legs. The tight fabric of my tunic dress cuts into my waist as the light, silky waves of satin from the cape flutter to a standstill around my calves. I'm wearing strappy sandals too. I hadn't decided to wear the cape until the last minute. I bought the cream sleeveless tunic dress to go with it but I still wasn't sure if it would work as an outfit. At first I thought I looked like a giant butterscotch with the wrapper still stuck to it. But as I eyed myself in the mirror, I had never felt stronger or more feminine. When I finally appeared at the top of the stairs, the cape floating elegantly around my body, Tristan looked up from the open front door where he was waiting for me. His expression reminded me of Viv's sketch, only I didn't see pain in his eyes, only need, desire, possibly regret. I reached the bottom of the stairs and Tristan still hadn't said a word. He looked very smart in his morning suit.

'What do you think?' I asked, promising myself I wouldn't change, regardless of how he responds.

'Love the cape,' he said and came over and kissed me on the lips. I kissed him back. It was a regular greeting or farewell kiss between a couple, but as he kissed me, for a fleeting moment my nose nestled into the crook between his nose and his cheek, and I inhaled slightly, smelling his Tristan-ness.

More guests begin to arrive and file into the room. Tristan walks up to the front, followed by Monty who is wearing the most outrageous shiny snake-print suit. They are the oddest groom and best man. Monty has slicked back his hair but it's too dense and straight to stay in place and strands are beginning to defy the gel and fall forward in claggy clumps. He tries to push it back which seems to make the clagging worse.

I'm still the only person sitting on the right-hand side. There are two women sitting in the front row on the other side, both in their sixties, both in two-piece dress suits with matching hats. It must be Flora's mother and possibly her auntie. They see me looking and smile and wave over. They seem nice. Lucky Flora, I think. Lucky Monty, too. Neither Tristan or I can say we have decent in-laws.

Tristan comes up to me, speaking low into my ear. 'What can we do about Monty's hair?' he says.

'Wash the gel out in the men's loo,' I whisper back.

Tristan goes back to Monty, who is smiling inanely at Flora's mum and auntie. Tristan speaks quietly to Monty and Monty quickly exits the room, on his way to the men's room, I assume.

Deniz and Gina arrive and I stand to give them both a hug hello. Gina says she adores my cape. I tell her it was a present. She's squeezed into an expensive-looking white dress covered in sparkling silver sequins. I suggest they sit beside me in the front row, which they gladly do. Deniz says they don't see me enough, as he always does, and I agree, as I always do.

'You're very kind having the reception in Lily's,' I say to them.

'Anything for one of our Lily peeps,' Gina says, as Monty returns with dripping wet hair, but at least it's floppy again and sits properly on his head and around his face.

'Has Monty got wet hair?' says Gina.

'Never mind that,' Deniz says, full of admiration. 'Where did he get that suit?'

Tristan and Monty come up to Deniz and Gina. Deniz leaps up and pulls the guys into a group bear hug. Gina smiles at me and rolls her eyes. Deniz holds Monty at arm's length to get a good look at him.

'I'm proud of you,' he says. 'And you look incredible in that suit.'

I catch Tristan's eye. He gives me a soft smile as he ushers Monty back up to the front, checking his inside pocket again to make sure he hasn't lost the rings in the last two minutes.

Spencer, Maddy and Bill, who I met the day I came into the restaurant, join me, Deniz and Gina. There's more hugging like old friends. I'm hardly ever in Lily's anymore and barely know any of them properly, so it's nice to be included. Spencer has his hand in the small of Maddy's back, protective but also possessive. Two younger people, maybe twenty, rush up to us too. Maddy quickly introduces them to me as Adrian and Nicole who work on weekends. They're in awe of Monty's snake-print suit and have their phones out taking pictures of him. Monty poses for them. I see now what Tristan meant about Monty getting a personality transplant.

Spencer takes Maddy's hand as they all slip into the row behind me. Sita sits further back in a barely-there summer dress with her tattoos on show. I wish I had a tattoo, but I wouldn't know what to get. I thought about getting a mini pineapple once, as I thought it might look cute. But it didn't mean anything. Tattoos are supposed to say something about you, but I don't want to remind myself of the past or think about the future.

Sita sits next to a huge man with a bald head, her husband, I assume. She waves to me. I've only met her a handful of times so it's lovely that she remembers me. Sitting on the other side of Sita is Lucia the cleaner, looking very glamourous in a hat. I remember her because she helped us clean our house when we first moved in. It had definitely been a three-person job. Maddy, Spencer and Bill turn to chat to Sita and Lucia. I turn back to the front. Despite the friendly hugs, I'm still an outsider. This is Tristan's realm and I'm a stranger in it.

Extra guests for the bride now spill over onto the groom's side. It doesn't look like anyone minds, least of all Monty, who is more concerned with smoothing down his snake-print suit, which is starting to grow on me. Maybe I'm wrong about Monty. Maybe he has, as Tristan insists, come out of his shell – or shed his skin, so to speak.

Tristan, as nervous as Monty, checks his pocket for the rings again. He catches my eye and mouths 'okay?' and I nod. He then gives me a kind look that sends a gentle warmth through my body, as if I were immersing myself in a hot bath. If only I could stay there. I look away from Tristan as the panic creeps up my spine. As tempting as it is, I mustn't get drawn into believing Tristan and I are fine again, because we're not. I have not managed to get back on track. Too much has happened and too many lies have been allowed to enter our lives.

I eye the door. There's still time to make a run for it. I could easily be popping to the ladies and then simply not come back. I'll text Tristan and tell him I wasn't feeling well. The thought of sitting at a table in Lily's restaurant, surrounded by Tristan's friends and colleagues, fills me with dread. I can't do it. It's too hard to keep pretending. I grab my bag and go to stand when I feel a hand on my arm. Tristan is beside me.

'Don't go,' he says.

29

Him

Monty totally ignored my advice on the suit and went with the fake leather, green and gold snake-print option with matching tie. If he were driving a Cadillac through the Arizona desert in a pair of shades with a bag of cocaine on the back seat, it might seem like an apt choice.

Anyway, he didn't listen to me and, despite looking cool, now he's sweating, which isn't helping his nerves. He gelled his hair to sweep it back but that didn't work and he had to quickly wash it out per Izzy's advice and now he has wet hair, a sweaty face and shaking hands. He looks like he's been bitten by a snake and requires urgent medical attention.

'How do I look?' he asks me, again.

'Like a rock star,' I reply, again.

He nods, smoothing down his suit. He seems to like this response so I keep saying it.

For someone who has the balls to wear a suit like this to his own wedding, he is surprisingly insecure about his appearance. Monty continues to be a complete enigma.

The registrar joins us. She is wearing bright red lipstick and prison guard shoes and has a single rose in her lapel. She holds a clipboard with papers on it. Monty grins at her, overdoing it, and she looks a little unsettled by him.

Deniz and Gina and the Lily's crew have arrived. They all gave Izzy a warm hello but I can see she doesn't want to be here. Her shoulders are tense like she's cold and her smile is forced.

This morning, waiting for her so we could leave, I almost sank to my knees when she appeared at the top of the stairs dressed in that cape, her hair in wild curls tumbling around her shoulders and down her back. She glided down the stairs, glimmering, and I couldn't get a single word out.

'Do I look alright?' she asked, giving me a funny look. I must have gone quite pale.

'Stunning,' I managed to say and pulled her to me to kiss her. In hindsight, it was probably a masculine power move, wanting to stake my claim and kiss the woman I'm married to because I can. But she kissed me back. It was more than perfunctory and I felt the inner stirrings of hope.

My plan is to get through the wedding then have the talk with Izzy. The conversation has to be had and I will be honest. I will tell her about the crush I had on Viv and why I lied about Martha and Bradley living in New Zealand. I'll tell her about the scrapbook from my past life, and how mean I was to Martha, who's dead now. I also need her to know that I'm probably never going to own my own restaurant and that I only say it to keep up appearances.

I check I still have the rings in my pocket. I catch Izzy's eye and mouth 'alright?' to her. She nods at me, then drops her gaze, rummaging in her bag.

She glances at the door, preparing to stand. She's going to leave, I think.

I quickly move to her side. Deniz and Gina are glued to Gina's phone trying to source a snake-print suit for Deniz. Izzy goes to get to her feet and I gently grab her arm. She looks up, surprised. I give her a pleading look not to go. She seems confused for a moment.

'Let's get through the day,' I say, 'then we can talk.'

'I was just going to the loo,' she says.

'Please,' I say to her.

She nods like 'what's the big deal', and settles back into her chair.

I hurry back to Monty who flashes me the sweat patches under his arms. I tell him to keep his arms down but he's looking more peaky than ever.

A hush descends on the room and everyone turns to the door where the bride has appeared, her father beside her. She is covered from head to foot in a pale pink veil, her statuesque posture commanding silence.

Monty has his mouth open, gaping in wonder. I click my fingers to get his attention and indicate he shut his mouth, which he quickly does.

As they say their vows, I double-check Izzy is still in her seat. She's doing a very good job now of looking interested and pleased to be here. For a fleeting moment, she seems like a stranger. We recognise each other but only because we remind the other of someone we used to know.

Izzy, Maddy, Spencer and I are first to arrive at Lily's for the reception. I asked Nicole, Adrian, Bill and Lucia to hang back at the registry office with Monty as he needs people on his side for the rest of the photographs. Spencer, Maddy and I want to check all is in order after setting up the restaurant the night before.

The fake vine decoration around the entrance looks more realistic in the daylight. The bar is decked out in more fake greenery speckled with small white flowers. The champagne glasses are ready on the bar, and the stand-in barman, Baz, who we borrowed from the Fox and Hounds down the road, is putting champagne bottles into ice buckets – another contribution from Deniz. Baz sees me and salutes, like we're comrades.

Spencer slips in behind the bar, running his trained, possessive eye over everything. Like me, he's going to find it hard to let go of the reins today.

The alcoves are set for lunch with wedding napkins and flowers and decorations. These are the overflow tables in addition to the main table on the upper level, which isn't big enough to seat everyone.

Maddy takes the stairs to the upper level and I follow. The long table spans the length of the room. The chairs are squashed closely together, some of which we had to borrow from one of Deniz's other restaurants to make up the numbers. But it's still going to be tight.

White candles line the middle, some in wedding candelabras that look far more expensive than they actually are, and the same greenery from the bar twists its way down the table, swerving in and out of the candlesticks and wine glasses. To the side is a trestle table, normally stored upstairs in the office, covered in fresh linen with a stack of plates on top ready for the buffet.

Maddy walks up and down making sure nothing is missing or out of place.

'It's pretty fucking amazing,' she says.

'It is,' I say, quite taken myself with how, in the natural light, the decorated table wouldn't look out of place in a castle.

Two servers appear behind me, dressed smartly in black and white. They are twin brothers, Scott and Simon, and from the same school as Adrian and Nicole. I ask them if they're ready for the mayhem. They say they are. Maddy calls them over and asks them to give all the cutlery one last polish.

I take the stairs down to the kitchen to check on the caterers who are in the midst of transferring cold salads into serving dishes. I ask them if everything is in hand and they assure me it is. I head back upstairs, passing the stand-in washer-upper who is leaning against the sink reading a book. I say hi. She says hi back, but doesn't look up from her page.

Up at the bar, Spencer is giving Baz pointers on how to pour the champagne. Then a chill comes over me as I look around.

'Where's Izzy?' I say to Spencer, trying to keep the panic out of my voice.

'She went for a drink across the road,' he says.

I instruct Spencer to make sure the champagne is served the minute guests arrive in case I'm not back in time. Spencer says no worries and turns to Baz, repeating my instructions.

I charge across the street, into the Queen's Head, and there she is sitting up at the bar with a glass of white wine.

There is a numinous quality about her, like she's from another time and place. Her dark hair nearly reaches her waist and with the cape falling over the back of the bar stool, she could be floating.

She is chatting to the barman, who seems quite taken with her, and I don't like it one bit. I want to command that everyone leave the room so I can be alone with my wife. Then I'll walk up to her, gently pushing my body between her legs, running my hands up her thighs and, before I've even touched her, we're both shuddering and gasping.

She sees me standing in the doorway and eyes me with curiosity. I check the status of my bow tie and my jacket buttons. They're all there and in the right place. I walk up to her.

'Can I get you a drink?' she asks.

'There isn't really time. Are you coming back to the restaurant?' I ask, fantasising about putting her over my shoulder and carrying her out myself. I'm starting to get concerned about my Neanderthal thoughts.

'You seemed busy so I got out of your way,' she says.

I don't want her to be out of my way. I want her to be very much in my way.

'I was telling Nick,' she says, indicating the barman, 'about Monty's snake-print suit.'

'Sounds a bit out there, alright,' Nick says.

I don't care what Nick says or thinks.

'Let's go,' I say to Izzy, keen to be at the restaurant when Monty arrives, if he hasn't already. Izzy downs some of her wine and slips off the stool, letting the cape slink behind her. I offer to take her hand. She hesitates for a moment, then takes it.

'See you later,' she says to Nick who gives her a wink.

Fucker, I think.

I lead Izzy out into the sunlight and she lifts her hand to shield her eyes for a moment. The sleek black Mercedes wedding car pulls up outside Lily's, followed by Deniz in his blue metallic

Porsche. Bill, Nicole and Adrian climb out of a taxi, as more cars arrive with wedding guests.

Izzy pulls her hand back, resisting crossing the road. I turn to see she is frowning.

'I don't think I can do it,' she says.

'Celebrate Monty's wedding day with me. After that, we'll talk.'

She gives me a nod, so I take her hand again and we walk across the road to Lily's, just getting in the door before Monty and Flora.

Izzy and I are seated across from each other at the long table. Monty and Flora are at the top of the table, her mum and dad on one side, Maddy and Spencer on the other. Baz, our stand-in barman, might have been a bit pour-happy with the champagne because Flora's mother has dozed off in her chair.

Izzy is sitting beside Sita and appears to be in deep conversation, but I notice she's hardly eaten anything from her plate. The servers are hovering, ready to whip away any dirty plates or take a drinks order. Maddy comes up and squats beside me so we can talk.

'We did well,' she says and high-fives me.

We have a laugh about how Monty will never get through his speech as he'll more than likely start blubbing. Spencer and Bill join us.

'We should do more weddings,' Spencer says. 'We're good at them.'

'Monty's actually not a bad sort after all,' Bill says loudly, trying not to hiccup. Monty squints and looks up, having heard his name. Bill raises his glass to him.

'I think someone's had enough champagne,' Spencer says, jumping to Bill's side.

'You think I'm bad?' says Bill. 'You should see the bride's mother. She's fallen asleep in the coronation chicken salad.'

Maddy and Spencer usher Bill down the steps to the bar, out of harm's way.

I stifle a smile and then catch Izzy watching me. She has finished her conversation with Sita and turned her attention to me. Her eyes are moist, I can't read her. She forces a smile, then picks up her fork and has a tiny mouthful of food, once again listening to Sita.

I wish I knew what she wanted. We've been treading water, biding our time, as the cloud of doom gathers quietly in the background.

Izzy gives her plate to one of the servers, either Scott or Simon, it's impossible to tell, and gets up to go to the toilet, taking her bag with her. I watch her disappear up the staircase to the ladies. I think about following her, unsure at the moment what that would achieve, but Maddy beats me to it and runs up the stairs behind her.

Monty squeezes into the seat beside me and nudges me with his shoulder.

'Thank you,' he says.

'Don't thank me, thank Deniz. It was his idea to give you Lily's for the day.'

Monty puts his arm around my shoulders and pulls me tight. I hear the creaking of his suit.

'This has been the best day of my life,' he says.

'It's supposed to be,' I reply. Monty has not stopped smiling since he said 'I do'. Maybe he's never had a good day before so this is off-the-charts amazing for him.

Maybe Monty has only ever known misery.

He bounds back to the end of the table and takes Flora's hand, gently pushing her hair out of her eyes, completely mesmerised and intoxicated by this special person in his life.

I still feel like that about Izzy. I always have. I just lost it for a while.

30

Her

Tristan wants to arrive at the reception before Monty and Flora. Once we're inside Lily's, he's very distracted, checking over everything, doling out instructions to the barman and fussing around with Spencer and Maddy. This is Tristan's world and I don't belong to it, not anymore anyway. I tell Spencer I'm popping across the road for a drink and bolt out of Lily's straight into the Queen's Head. It's an old pub, with dark timber ceilings and an old fireplace. Unlike the Tiger's Head, they kept their refurbishment as authentic as possible. I can hide here, for a while at least. I'm not sure if I'll even go back to the restaurant.

'White wine, please,' I say to the barman, who's younger than me, but older than Jude. He gives me the once-over, taking in the dress and the cape.

'Either you've just jilted someone at the altar or you're in a play that I definitely need to come and see,' he says, with a cheeky smile.

'Wedding reception deserter,' I say.

He gives me a grin and pours the wine into my glass.

'Will they be sending out a search party?' he says.

'Maybe.'

He goes to serve another customer. I take a sip of the wine. The mildly acidic taste hits the back of my throat then quickly slips into my stomach, warming my chest. I take another sip, no longer acidic as my senses acclimatise. The barman comes back to me, leaning on the bar with both hands. He continues our joke about me being a deserter. I tell him about the groom's snake-print suit and he's impressed. While we chat he tells me his name, Nick, and I tell him mine. He's very charming, just like Jude. Probably trying it on, just like Jude.

I feel his eyes on me before I see him. Tristan is standing at the door. He has a ghostly yet determined expression on his face. He asks if I'm coming back to the restaurant. Nick throws me an amused glance. I quickly introduce Nick and try and lighten the mood by mentioning Monty's snake-print suit. Nick says it sounded awesome but Tristan appears to be ignoring him, which isn't really like him. He always makes an effort with people.

'Let's go,' says Tristan, holding out his hand to take me away. I take it as it would be awkward not to. I say goodbye to Nick who gives me a wink. I'm sure I hear a tiny growl escape from Tristan's throat.

Once outside, it's intensely bright in comparison to the dark pub, and the half a glass of wine I managed to guzzle is making my eyes even more sensitive to the light. Across the road, cars are drawing up and suddenly every cell in my body is yelling for me to run. I can't be a part of Tristan's life for the day only to never be a part of it again. I pull away from him. He keeps a hold of my hand.

'Let's get through this and then we'll talk, properly,' he says.

But once we start talking, where do I start and where do I stop. I nearly had sex with a student who knew I was desperate and thought I'd be easy. I kissed our new neighbour, or I let her kiss me, not that it makes a difference. And I'm still grieving my dog who died when I was nine, which all stems from the fact that my mother's emotionally challenged and I might be too.

'Please,' he says again.

I nod, deciding that I deserve this day with him, as his wife, not estranged, not separated. Not without him.

I'm sitting in the middle of the table across from Tristan. Deniz is sitting further down towards Monty but is closer to Tristan than the top table. In fact, whatever it is about the top table being the centre of attention, Tristan seems to be the person everyone wants to be around. A few of the female guests on Flora's side come up and say hi, congratulating him on the restaurant. He politely corrects them, explaining that Deniz is the owner, he's the manager. I'm seated beside Sita and I've been admiring her tattoos. I tell her about my idea for a pineapple and she says she thinks it's cute and that not every tattoo needs a story. But all the while I'm keeping one eye on Tristan.

Maddy hunkers down beside him, talking quietly. I see them high five. Tristan says something that makes Maddy laugh and she puts her hand on his arm. Spencer joins them, putting both his hands on Tristan's shoulders and squeezing them. Tristan turns and makes Spencer laugh as well, but again I can't hear what he's saying. Then the lovely washer-upper, Bill, who's had far too much to drink, lurches up, his arm around Spencer's shoulders – and even his drunken attention is on Tristan. He says something rather loudly about Monty, and Spencer and Maddy usher him down to the bar. I've had at least two glasses of champagne plus the wine I had at the pub and I'm still feeling sober. And I've been pushing the same piece of salmon around my plate for the last half an hour. My stomach is twisted and knotted. The idea of swallowing food right now seems impossible.

Deniz calls up the table to Tristan and raises his glass to him. Tristan raises his glass in return. And I'm gripped with a sudden sadness: Tristan has a family in Lily's, and while I'm happy for him, he so deserves it, I'm not part of it. Even if he wants to work things out, he'll change his mind once I bare all.

Tristan catches my eye. He knows I've been watching him. I do my best to act natural, passing my plate to one of the servers as they walk by. I turn to Sita to carry on our tattoo conversation. She suggests borrowing a tattoo book she has, to give me some ideas. I say that would be great, but I can't bear sitting at this table any longer. I grab my bag, excuse myself from the conversation with Sita and rush upstairs to the ladies.

I get into one of two cubicles and sit on the toilet lid, my head bent between my knees, which isn't easy to do in my tight dress, but I need to stop the onset of a panic attack.

'Izzy?' Maddy calls out, going into the cubicle beside me.

I can't talk. I don't have the breath.

'Izzy? Are you okay?' Maddy says, sounding worried this time.

'Hey, Maddy,' I say, managing to answer.

'Amazing reception, isn't it? Tristan organised the whole thing. He's brilliant,' she says.

'Yes, it's great,' I say, grabbing a few sheets of toilet roll and dabbing my eyes to stop the tears descending.

'And after his bad news and everything,' she continues.

I hear her flush and exit her cubicle to wash her hands.

I flush the loo and join her at the sink, washing my hands.

'It broke my heart to see him so cut up. Not about his adopted mum dying, but the scrapbook with pictures of his real mum.'

'It was a lot to take in,' I say, my hands suddenly icy cold. *What scrapbook?*

'He seems to be doing alright now,' Maddy says, taking out her phone and absent-mindedly scrolling through it.

'He loves working here with all of you,' I say, getting off the subject quickly.

'He's the reason I stay,' she says, not looking up from her screen. 'Don't tell him, but I moved flat and it's an extra half an hour to get here now, but I don't want to work anywhere else.'

She says this like it's the most normal thing in the world, but it isn't. The staff in Lily's are devoted to him – even Monty adores him. And now there's a scrapbook of pictures of his real mother that he never told me about. Suddenly I'm struck with how unfair it is. How Tristan and I never really stood a chance, both too damaged to ever make this relationship work.

An uncomfortable stirring grips my chest as a surge of adrenaline rises from within, creating a burst of energy and clarity. And now I'm angry. But not normal angry, this is white rage. And I know exactly what I need to do.

31

Him

People finally decide to acknowledge that Flora's mother has passed out and try to wake her. I bring coffee to the table as she comes around, a little wild-eyed. When Flora explains how she fell asleep at the table, she's very embarrassed, her cheeks bright pink.

Maddy returns and plonks herself in Spencer's lap. Izzy still isn't back from the ladies, so I slip away upstairs to find her.

It's quiet in the office. The faint hum of music and chatter from downstairs isn't enough to fill the stark, grey rooms with life. The desk with piles of paper on it, once a retreat for me from my domestic life, has lost its allure. Thoughts of sitting up here when I don't really need to seem ridiculous now.

I move along to the ladies toilet and tap on the door.

'Izzy?'

There's no answer so I push it open. Both cubicle doors are shut. I push one open. It's empty. I try to push the other but it's stuck.

'Izzy?'

I push harder and the door swings to reveal another empty cubicle.

Izzy is gone.

'Speech!' shouts Spencer as I rejoin the table. Monty, waving away the request, gets to his feet and smooths the front of his black shirt. Spencer is now wearing the snake-print jacket although it's far too small for him.

I send Izzy a text asking if she's okay and she replies that she's not well and will see me later, but there's a gnawing doubt in my gut.

I look down at my hands and see I'm shaking. Something is very wrong.

Someone taps a glass, requesting silence. Monty is about to make his speech.

For a man who was sweating like a pig a few hours before, Monty is looking rather marvellous. His hair, now dry and gel-free, is floppy and perfectly straight. He's glassy-eyed from too much champagne and his cheeks are flushed.

He clears his throat and starts by thanking everyone for coming and for making it a perfect day. He says lovely things about Flora and how she changed his life. Then he takes a long pause and lowers his head.

For a moment, I think the evil twin has returned and he's going to revert to his original incarnation and ruin everything. Then he raises his head, a serene look on his face.

'Most of all, I have to thank Lily's. I've never been part of a group before, or felt like I belonged somewhere until I came to work here. I know I didn't always show it and I'm sorry for that. But I love you all and I have always loved you all.'

'Sexy beast,' Spencer shouts. All the Lily's staff whoop and cheer, including me.

'Thank you, Spencer,' Monty says. 'You know you're my favourite.'

'I do, Monty, I do,' Spencer replies.

While the atmosphere is supercharged with happiness and joy, the mist of dread surrounding me is getting thicker and gloomier. Izzy is gone, I tell myself, accusingly. *And it's your fault.*

'Tristan,' Monty says, raising a glass to me, still in speech mode. 'You are the person I am most grateful to. For the last six years you have always been there for me.' Monty gives in to his emotions, getting choked up.

'You're in here,' he says, smacking the left side of his chest.

I raise my glass back to him as the Lily's staff surround me, slapping me on the back. They've all clearly had way too much to drink.

Everyone toasts the bride and groom and congratulates Monty on his speech. And as the Gipsy Kings blare out over the speakers, I slip down the stairs, past Baz at the bar, with his back turned polishing the whiskey bottles, and burst out onto the street where I immediately break into a run, my suit jacket flapping around me and my shoes slapping on the pavement as I sprint past a couple pushing a pram and just about dodge a group of teenagers.

On and on I go, the heat from my body getting trapped under my jacket. I'm sweltering and out of breath, my heart pounding.

I round the corner to our street and stop, sweat pouring from my brow, gasping for air.

Above our house, billowing up into the darkening sky, is a giant plume of black smoke.

32

Her

A hammer's a good place to start. I find one in our scanty tool-box under the kitchen sink. It looks brand new. I weigh it in my hand, getting a sense of the damage I could cause with it. If nothing else, it will get things moving in the right direction. I grab a box of matches from the drawer under the kettle and head for the back door. This overwhelming determination is the same feeling I had the moment before I peed on Clive's rug. Nothing can stop me. Nothing can stand in my way.

With my hand on the back door handle, I pause for a moment. There was a lot of fallout from peeing on Clive's rug. But then the voice of the nine-year-old still living in the shadows of my subconscious yells with glee that she never regretted it, not for a moment, and she'd do it again if she had to. I shove the back door open and march up the garden.

Hammer in hand, I start swinging for the shed, bashing the timber panels holding it together. Splintering and breaking sounds fill my ears, loud and destructive, but after six or seven whacks, I don't seem to be making much of an impact. I aim for the windows instead. The sound of smashing glass gives me great satisfaction. I carry on pummelling the shed, making the timber panels loose, watching it fall apart in front of my eyes. Adrenaline pumping, I drop the hammer and focus on the box of matches in my hand. I slide it open and take out a match. I see the ugly red cushions lying inside the shed. They'll be bone dry in this heat and good kindling to get this party started. I strike the match and it sparks to life, the flame flickering in the calm, still air.

'Wait,' comes a shrill voice. Viv is standing up on her side of the fence, her hands to her head suggesting panic. She is visible from the waist up, but again I wonder how she can be that high on the fence, not holding on to anything, especially as she's just out of her leg cast. She is dressed in a dark green bodice covered in tiny flowers that stops just above her navel. Her mass of blonde hair is wilder than ever, as though she was pulled through a hedge backwards and somehow came out the other side looking perfect, with shrubs and greenery stuck in all the right places.

'If you're going to set fire to it, at least take the lawnmower out first,' Viv says, very matter-of-fact.

'Shit,' I say, blowing out the match as it scorches my fingers. She's right, of course. Without saying a word, I yank the hanging door to the side, pull out the ugly red cushions, push the boxes aside and grab the lawnmower handle, rolling it out and down the garden. Then I pick up the red cushions, throw them back inside, and take another match from the box. I'm aware my hair has fallen into my eyes and I'm still wearing the cape and my summer sandals. I must look deranged.

'Do you want to talk about it?' she asks.

'Nobody wants to talk, Viv, okay?' I say.

'In that case, don't let me stop you,' she says.

I strike the match and hold the flame up to my face. I glance at Viv again. She says something quietly, almost a whisper, I'm not sure what exactly, but it sounds a lot like, 'what are you waiting for?'

And that's the point. I'm not waiting anymore.

I flick my fingers, tossing the match and watching as it lands on the polyester cushions, which instantly catch fire. Viv throws her hands in the air and screams – it's hard to tell if she's celebrating or terrified, as all I can hear is the thumping of my heart in my head. Then whoosh, the fire triples in size as the shed is engulfed in flames, licking the fence between our garden and

Viv's. I stagger back as the heat becomes prickly on my cheeks. A huge plume of smoke gathers above the shed and travels over the house, getting caught in what little breeze there is.

'Izzy!' I hear Tristan call my name from inside the house, but I can't answer. I can't even avert my gaze from the fire. My throat is dry and I can barely stay standing with the heat and exhaustion.

'Izzy!' shouts Tristan again. I look up at Viv, hoping she can answer his calls but she's no longer standing at the fence. I wonder if she was even there to begin with.

Tristan bursts into the garden, his arm up shielding himself from the heat and escaping sparks from the blaze. He pulls me back from the fire, seeing the matches in my hand. In his other hand he holds our fire extinguisher.

'I'm sorry,' I say. And not just for the fire, I want to say, but also for who I am.

'Don't be,' he says. 'You just beat me to it.'

I let out a small laugh but get choked up and end up coughing and crying at the same time. Tristan snaps opens the fire extinguisher and starts to cover the fire in white foam, but it's raging now and spreading to the dry grass.

Extra water comes flying over the fence as Viv appears again, dousing the flames with her garden hose. She's too close to the fire, although she doesn't seem to care or feel the burning heat. Tristan grabs the hose from her and Viv feeds it over into our garden. Tristan yells at her to get back too.

In the distance, sirens ring out, reminding me of the seriousness of what I've done. I should be embarrassed and ashamed, but all I feel is a sense of peace. The shed is gone and that has to be a good thing.

33
Them

Tristan, Izzy and Viv managed to put out the flames before the fire engine arrived. The firemen bought their garbled story about Izzy dropping a lit cigarette, which then ignited a polyester cushion. Before they knew it, they were battling a blaze. One of the firemen gave them a ticking off about lighting cigarettes near flammable materials, especially in this current heat wave.

Now, for the past twenty minutes, all three of them, their hands and faces covered in soot, have been sitting on the ground outside Tristan and Izzy's back door, swigging from a bottle of Bacardi. They pass it up and down the line, almost in a rhythm, eyeing the pile of mulch left by the burnt-down shed. Tristan has his legs crossed and is breathing calmly. Izzy, in the middle, her knees pulled up to her chest, has wrapped the silk cape around her body. The silk cape is also covered in patches of soot. Viv leans against the wall, her legs out in front, smoking a cigarette.

No one has said a word since the firemen left. Izzy gave a big sigh at one point and Tristan and Viv turned to her, expecting her to say something, but she just rested her head on her knees.

Finally, Viv speaks.

'I know a man with a van who'd have taken the shed away for fifty quid,' she says.

Tristan nods, accepting that would have been a better solution all round.

Izzy raises her head. 'Does he take card payments?' she asks.

'Probably cash only,' replies Viv, inhaling deeply on her cigarette.

'Yeah, well, I didn't have any cash on me,' says Izzy.

Viv and Tristan turn to Izzy, frowning.

'Fuck,' Tristan says and starts laughing. Viv begins to giggle too and topples over onto her side, in a foetal position. Izzy starts to laugh too, lightly at first then growing into a big hearty roar.

The hysteria lasts for about thirty seconds then it all calms down again. Tristan returns to breathing deeply and Izzy settles her head back on her knees.

Viv sits up and stubs her cigarette out on the brittle grass, despite the ticking off from the firemen earlier. She stands up.

'Thanks for coming to the rescue,' Tristan says.

'Yeah, thanks,' Izzy murmurs, not raising her head. 'You were amazing.'

Viv says no problem and steps carefully over the white, foamy, charred debris towards the end of the fence, now stained black from the blaze. She swings the loose panel out and crawls through into her garden.

Izzy and Tristan listen to the creak of Viv's back door as it opens and closes.

Izzy takes another big swig of the Bacardi, the bottle almost finished. She passes it to Tristan who drinks the last few drops.

'I don't want this to be it,' he says.

'I don't want it to be either,' she replies. 'But there are things you need to know.'

'There are things I need to tell you too,' he says.

'How about we start at the beginning and see how it goes?' he says.

'Oh God, okay then,' Izzy says, half hiding her face in her hands.

He clears his throat and turns to face her. She turns to face him too.

'Hi, I'm Tristan,' he says, holding out his hand.

She hesitates for a moment, then takes it, feeling his warmth, his pulse.

'Nice to meet you, Tristan. I'm Izzy.'

Epilogue

The clackety sound of the roller door on the truck is enough to wake the sleeping couple. They pad over to the window to peek out onto the driveway next door, staying hidden behind the bunched-up open curtains; him naked, her partly so.

The two removal guys bolt the roller door locked. One climbs into the driver's seat while the other posts house keys though the letterbox before getting into the truck too. The orange Mini Cooper with the red racing stripe down the middle is nowhere to be seen.

The truck pulls away, grumbling and chugging up the road, getting louder as it gains speed, lurching up through the gears then fading into the early morning light.

And that was it.

As quickly as the new neighbour had arrived and altered their lives, so she disappeared. Leaving the house next door vacant once again, its rooms empty, waiting to be filled.

Acknowledgements

A huge thank you to my two amazing editors, Emma Herdman and Charlotte Greig. Your brilliant insights and guidance were invaluable. And to the rest of the wonderful team at Bloomsbury including Charlotte Phillips for the perfect cover design, Francisco Vilhena and Gurdip Ahluwalia. My heartfelt gratitude to my mother, Deike, for her wisdom and knowledge, and the long conversations that made this book possible. Thank you also to the lovely Rachel O'Flanagan for being my very first reader and editor. Also to David O'Shea, Miles Rich-O'Shea, Kirk England and Sophie Russell-Ross for reading early drafts, often more than once, and for all your feedback and continued support. I'd be lost without you. And a very special thank you to Dave and Miles for inspiring me every day.

A Note on the Author

Senta Rich began her career as an advertising copywriter. During this time, she also wrote radio plays and magazine articles, before moving into the world of screenwriting. She now writes regularly for film and TV. She lives in Dublin with her husband and son. *Hotel 21*, her debut novel, was published in 2023 and has been translated into multiple languages, with TV rights pre-empted by MGM. *The Single Neighbour* is her second novel.

A Note on the Type

The text of this book is set in Bembo, which was first used in 1495 by the Venetian printer Aldus Manutius for Cardinal Bembo's *De Aetna*. The original types were cut for Manutius by Francesco Griffo. Bembo was one of the types used by Claude Garamond (1480–1561) as a model for his Romain de l'Université, and so it was a forerunner of what became the standard European type for the following two centuries. Its modern form follows the original types and was designed for Monotype in 1929.